ALSO BY KEVIN P. KEATING

The Natural Order of Things

The Captive Condition

The Captive Condition

Kevin P. Keating

 Pantheon Books   New York

Copyright © 2015 by Kevin P. Keating

Published in the United States by Pantheon Books, a division of Penguin Random House LLC, New York, and distributed in Canada by Random House of Canada, a division of Penguin Random House Ltd., Toronto.

Pantheon Books and colophon are registered trademarks of Penguin Random House LLC.

Keating, Kevin P.
The captive condition : a novel / Kevin P. Keating.
pages cm
ISBN 978-0-8041-6928-8 (hardback). ISBN 978-0-8041-6929-5 (eBook).
1. Drowning victims—Fiction. 2. Murder—Investigation—Fiction. I. Title.
PS3611.E24C37 2015   813'.6—dc23   2014044280

www.pantheonbooks.com
Jacket design by Oliver Munday

Printed in the United States of America
First Edition
2 4 6 8 9 7 5 3 1

For Katie and Rose

I heard all things in the heaven and in the earth. I heard many things in hell. How, then, am I mad? Hearken! and observe how healthily—how calmly I can tell you the whole story.

—EDGAR ALLAN POE, "The Tell-Tale Heart"

Into the Rural Rust Belt Dystopia

During the quiet hours after midnight on New Year's Day, the ghosts of Normandy Falls, manacled like felons to the tomb, temporarily escaped the totalitarian scrutiny of heaven and the moldering prison house of death, and from the forlorn churchyard near the square and the untilled fields in the valley, they assembled under the light of a spectral moon and resolved to haunt those who had denied them love. They rose high in the blustery air, thin sheets of ectoplasm flapping like mainsails in the lashing wind, a vibration of mournful energy that the living, resting uneasily in their homes after the raucous holiday parties had ended, mistook as the leading edge of a storm drafting down unhindered from the polar ice cap. Like a swirling multitude of madhouse muses, the ghosts with their baleful song inspired me to act that fateful night, and through a maze of monster hemlocks that whispered and hissed in the icy wind, they guided me into the valley and then safely back to town.

Just before daybreak, as the horizon began to pale, I emerged from the woods and plodded across a sloping landscape of false contours. Nothing had distance or scale. The light was flat and gray, and the wind-sculpted crusts and cornices of drifting snow quickly transformed the campus quad into an uninhabitable tundra. I felt perfectly alone and anonymous, like a lost Arctic voyager, but even at that early hour, as I battled my way toward the Department of Plant Services, I saw in one of the cracked and filthy windows a yellow light flickering in the darkness and knew the Gonk was waiting for me.

I had been forewarned.

Five years before, on my final day as a student at the Jesuit prep school, I had been summoned to the headmaster's office. Near the imposing set of mahogany double doors, a long line of my fellow freethinkers waited their turn to run the gantlet one more time before donning their caps and gowns and marching in a restless procession to the poorly performed strains of Elgar. Some of us clowned about this penultimate ordeal. It was just a formality, a final gesture, a parting shot, a petty way for some of the more surly Jesuits to denounce our budding apostasy and to express their deep displeasure with our decision to attend colleges and universities with no religious affiliation.

After thirty minutes, when my name was finally called, I entered the office and stood before a desk that looked very presidential and resolute. As every schoolboy knows, the mystery of darkness appeals to old wizards and professional prayer makers, and while my eyes adjusted to the feeble light bleeding through the heavy red drapes, I felt the headmaster's velvety baritone caress my ear and then withdraw into the gloom. A hush fell over the other priests. Seated in a semicircle around his desk, they looked like those chipped and eroded icons in the chapel courtyard, a dozen unsmiling faces set in wet cement, their formal ferraiolos and black cassocks reeking of righteousness, stale cigarette smoke, and musty books of Latin verse. They lacked only a pigeon or two to dance atop their aggressively balding heads.

"Am I to understand, Mr. Campion, that you will be attending Normandy College this fall?"

I tried to sound meek. "Yes, sir, that's correct."

"Like Jonathan Harker to Dracula's castle."

I squinted, and after a moment a pair of unblinking yellow eyes came into sharp focus. Behind the enormous desk, shaking his head in astonishment, sat Father James Rhodes Montague, a man with a steel-trap mind. He detested small talk, and from him you would never get a cheerful hello, how are you, what wonderful weather we're having. With gestures so graceful and so routinely performed they seemed almost balletic, he removed a small tobacco pouch from his coat pocket, carefully packed the bowl of his stubby pipe, tamped it down with his thumb, and then brushed the excess flakes from his knee before lighting a match behind a cupped palm. After sending up three puffs of blue smoke, he waved out the flame, crossed his legs, and swept away a single strand of silver hair that looped over his wrinkled forehead.

"Yes, I confess it's a rather cryptic thing to say, Mr. Campion, but in recent years a few of our more defiant graduates have made the trek to Normandy College, and, becoming helplessly lost in the nearby valley, many of them ended up outside the trailer of a deranged methadone addict or at the creaking iron gates of that infamous farmstead Twisted Willows, where, as some of my colleagues here today can attest, a series of hideous crimes took place more than one hundred years ago. All that remains now of its fallen, baronial splendor is a crumbling stone foundation blackened by a devastating fire."

Father Montague had a peculiar oratory style and a marvelous gift for obfuscation. It probably stemmed from his reading too many nineteenth-century novels written by sexually repressed hysterics and opium eaters. More occultist than scholar, he specialized in and was fanatically dedicated to editing anthologies of obscure tales of terror and the supernatural, stories so predictable that, when read aloud, the florid prose and innumerable clichés sounded almost incantatory: nights were always dark and stormy, wolves were routinely baying under a full moon, and cats were consistently black, plutonic, preternaturally sagacious. In a book edited by J. R. Montague, the world was utterly lacking in proportion, but thanks in part to his meticulous scholarship and prodigious memory, he possessed a rare talent for improvisation, particularly in the presence of a renegade and recalcitrant pupil. Now he wanted badly to tell a new story, something special, and I became the vessel into which he poured another fantastic farrago.

"Father," I said, "I must confess I'm unfamiliar with the events at Twisted Willows."

As if sensing my skepticism, he looked pointedly at me and said with a note of reproof, "Gothic tales feed on the *pleasing* elements of horror and romance, but I assure you, Mr. Campion, that there is nothing pleasing about the town of Normandy Falls or its tragic history. It's a matter of public record. If you haven't done so already, you can visit the college's library and read about it. The newspapermen in those days loved sensationalism just as much as they do today, and their reporting does not lack for detail."

In a final show of my odd, satirical courage I said, "Yes, sir, I'll be sure to delve into the local archives right away."

The headmaster clamped his teeth on his pipe, chewing back and forth on the already masticated stem. "You want specifics, Mr. Campion. Very well." He leaned back in his chair and interlaced his fingers over his ever-expanding paunch. "Twisted Willows was the home of the college's founder, Nathaniel Wakefield, an enduring figure of myth and an accomplished botanist posthumously recognized, along with his near contemporary Gregor Mendel, as a pioneer in the emerging science of genetics. He was a human oddity, a remarkable freak, notorious not only for his nervous tics and his off-putting habit of holding imaginary conversations with the exotic plants in his greenhouse, but also for his more unorthodox practices. There was talk that he'd abandoned a wife in some faraway city and had come to the wilderness for the sole purpose of conducting experiments on the unsuspecting townspeople, demanding that they undergo excruciating procedures that left them hideously maimed and scarred. Silly rumors, really. But it would have been much better for all involved if there *had* been some truth to these garbled and exaggerated accounts. Because you see, Mr. Campion, the things that took place inside that house were far more diabolical than anything the gossipmongers could invent."

Like all-seeing Illuminati, the other priests, either in an attempt to disguise their amusement or express their genuine outrage, cleared their throats, shifted in their seats, and rapped their gnarled ashplants against the polished parquet floor. Some of them, I noticed, drank Belgian beer from frosty snifters and belched softly into palsied fists.

Father Montague continued, "Already steeped in sin, having abandoned the power of scientific inquiry, liberated at last from the irritable necessity of reaching for facts and evidence, Doctor Wakefield fell victim to, shall we say, conjugal mania. To describe his midnight bacchanals as satanic is not an exaggeration, no, not when they involved incest, bestiality, coprophilia. Unwilling to participate any longer in these lascivious *experiments*, the citizens conspired to send strangers passing through town to the doctor's house, tramps and roughneck canal workers mainly, some of whom were never seen or heard from again. Now there were whispers of necrophilia."

Fighting the temptation to roll my eyes and yawn, I listened to the measured ticking of a grandfather clock as it calmly marked off segments of dry, dusty time. "Forgive me, sir," I said, "but I don't think any of this proves the existence of vampires or werewolves—or that they attended orgies. Only that a man of science may have exhibited some unusual behavior."

Father Montague drew in a slow, ragged breath and aimed the pipe stem at my eye. "*Abnormal* behavior, Mr. Campion. And one night a group of men and women gathered in the town square to discuss this *abnormal* behavior. They demanded answers. Who was he, this Wakefield, a man so monstrous, so *human*? Resolving to put a stop to the madness once and for all, they marched into the valley. Hours later, under mysterious circumstances, the doctor's house caught fire aided by a ten-gallon drum of petroleum. The following morning the authorities discovered among the smoldering ruins the unidentifiable remains of a man, a charred, leathery thing no bigger than a dog, its hands clutching its chest. Alas, the doctor had met with a wretched and ignominious end. But there were some who had their doubts and believed the wrong man had died that night, an unsuspecting houseguest, the latest victim of sadomasochistic horrors. The ever-resourceful Wakefield, meanwhile, escaped through an underground passage and fled into the surrounding forest."

The headmaster waved his hand to dispel the smoke that veiled his parchment-white face.

"Now here's the thing. In addition to his dark legacy, Wakefield sired twelve illegitimate and unbaptized children bearing his name, children of sin, children of the laboratory, genetic aberrations. And to this very day their traits live on in the people like a secret blood disease. Godless men cook poison in their cellars, mothers take their own lives, small children vanish without a trace, marriages slowly crumble and fall apart. It's the apotheosis of failure, a shadowland of rootlessness and poverty." He leaned forward in his chair and said with a crafty smile, "You would be wise to keep your curiosity in check, Mr. Campion; otherwise, you may find yourself coarsened and brutalized by that direly indigent town. Worse still, you might discover, possibly to your liking, that Normandy Falls is a most beguiling place, especially for a young man who has lost his way in the world and now belongs nowhere else. An outcast of the universe."

Undeterred by the headmaster's heavy-handed warning, I continued preparing for the big move, thrilled to escape the unremitting turmoil of the city, the busy street corners, the deafening roar of traffic, the strangling exhaust of trucks and buses, the eschatological rants of the homeless, the shootings, the muggings, the mayhem of modernity. No less nerve-racking had been the incessant braying of my ambitious peers who, as worshippers of Mammon, extolled the virtues of a high-dollar education and proudly boasted of prestigious grants and scholarships. What I wanted was the simple life, quiet and free of distractions, and in a place like Normandy Falls, deep in the American hinterland, hundreds of miles from the nearest big city, I would finally be free from those snarky overachievers competing madly for entry-level positions on the college newspaper and literary journal.

The move would be therapeutic in a lot of other ways, too. The countryside would offer an abundance of new experiences, and I would watch the summer go out in grand style. Every morning I would breathe a fragrant bouquet of wildflowers, and at sunset I would paint watercolors in vast meadows of sweet, vernal grass. In the fall I would take long walks down tree-lined lanes, pausing on dew-slick cobblestones to search the dazzling foliage for finches and phoebes and pine siskins. In the spring I would brave the frigid waters of the river that ran dark and straight and long and learn how to fly-fish. And in time, just as soon as I was properly licensed to own a firearm, I would join a gun club, spend weekends at the shooting range, participate in marksmen tournaments.

In short, Normandy Falls would provide a soothing balm for a brain bombarded by big-city anxieties, and I had an irrational and unwavering faith in its creative potential.

On a Friday in early September 2009, during my first morning at the college, I met briefly with my faculty adviser, Martin Kingsley, a young and immodest professor of comparative literature with a newly minted PhD, but the Jesuits had prepared me well to deal with this particular type of stooge. After our meeting, I attended an obligatory freshman orientation program where the beaming provost, reading from an old set of note cards, told us he was eager to help "kick-start this new academic journey," but during the rest of his banal speech he said nothing at all about the town and its bizarre history. Prior to my arrival in Normandy Falls, I took Father Montague's advice and looked into newspaper accounts of the college's founder, but I unearthed no evidence of sinister scientific experiments, no allegations of sexual impropriety, no suggestions that he'd dreamed up novel forms of fornication. This made little sense—the headmaster, though a bit eccentric, wasn't a liar—and at lunchtime, while the other freshmen were getting better acquainted in the dining hall, I decided to leave campus and explore the area on my own.

The town was neatly divided in two by a river named in honor of the doctor. More than a century had passed since his demise (or was it his disappearance?), and yet no one had thought to change the Wakefield back to the Wisakatchekwa, its original Iroquois name. Once teeming with smallmouth bass and rainbow trout, the river was now so polluted that people could no longer see their reflections in it. After decades of runoff from a steel mill upstream, the only species that thrived in its sulfurous-smelling waters and contaminated currents were hog suckers and spotfin shiners. The massive trunks of white ashes and weeping willows cantilevered over the broad sweep of river, their exposed roots gripping the crumbling earth like enormous claws.

On the left bank stood the college, with its perpendicular walkways and neo-Georgian buildings that mimicked Ivy classicism. Across the street, on the other side of Anderson Boulevard, there was a neighbor-hood of Victorian-era homes that had fallen into a state of near decrepi-tude, the pretty flower boxes and decorative dogwoods doing little to disguise the steady and irreversible decay. The wicked winds of a hun-dred winters had bled most of the houses of color, peeling away huge swathes of paint from the polygonal towers, wraparound porches, and intricate latticework. Shattered pieces of slate tile dangled from leak-ing roofs, long planks of warped wood rotted behind hedgerows full of nesting blackbirds, and in backyards sturdy swing sets rusted in a lush jungle of weeds. Though it had fallen on hard times, this neighborhood was still vaguely suburban, thanks in part to a new generation of faculty members on the lookout for rock-bottom real estate prices. No doubt some of them saw themselves as missionaries who could teach "the nat-urals" the benefits of civilization and the necessity of self-reliance. A few had even turned down an opportunity to move into a new housing development three miles away so they could live in this rural dystopia with its many dark doorways and many dark windows.

What Normandy Falls lacked in intellect it made up for in brawn, a town with the pounding of machinery in its soul, the soot of factories and railroad yards in its blood. On the right bank of the river, sur-rounding the village square, stood the remains of a now-defunct cen-ter of industry, ten square blocks of abandoned factories and empty machine shops and blighted warehouses, some dating back to the early twentieth century, giant firetraps of knob-and-tube wiring, exposed-brick walls, galvanized pipes, and ancient ductwork, where a century earlier throngs of hollow-eyed, underfed immigrant children worked fourteen-hour days.

I ambled along these dingy streets and alleys, marveling at the extraordinary human propensity for uprooting trees and grasslands in favor of gravel lots and barbed-wire fences. Occasionally, I stopped to admire the crude graffiti covering the slate sidewalks, the cryptic gang symbols, the obligatory cock and balls, the rare profession of true love. I passed a sleazy cabaret housed in an old movie palace. When it first opened its doors in this ragged corner of the county, the caba-ret attracted groups of college boys and a few traveling salesmen in wrinkled suits and unpolished shoes marked by the soft dust of the open road, but now everyone said the place was fast becoming the regular haunt of men whose lives were so far beyond redemption that even the daft pastor who ran the clapboard church on the square railed against their "septic contagion, their night-spawned and leprous madness!"

From the corner I could see the dented church steeple. It looked like a hypodermic needle pricking the white rump of the sky, its syringe filled with windy hymns and diluted sermons that failed to inoculate the town against a devastating plague of sin. Any alleviation of the symptoms proved temporary at best. In the past few decades, on at least three separate occasions, the steeple had been struck by fiery scraps of space junk tumbling end over end out of the upper atmosphere, and now its spire was dinged and battered, its belfry punched with holes, its stately white tower scarred, blackened, burned. "A sign from God!" proclaimed the pastor, who'd been reduced to a state of shuddering insecurity. To the empty pews he railed, "Instead of lightning and tornadoes, the Lord has updated his signs and wonders so we can recognize that the End Times are fast approaching. Soon we will be free. But free from whom? From our fellow man? Or from God Himself? For the whole of the Bible can be summarized thusly: in the Old Testament God kills man; in the New Testament man kills God. Between these two ill-mannered lunatics, who do you suppose is the more hardhearted?"

Up and down the main drag, a parade of backfiring coupes and pickups interrupted these fevered sermons, poisoning the air with death metal, thrash metal, speed metal, the bass on the stereos cranked to maximum volume. From the tinted windows, rosy-cheeked frat boys and sallow-skinned townies shouted menace and insult at passersby. They disparaged women and children; they would have defamed the pastor, too, had he dared to leave the sanctuary of his church. Every weekend an advancing horde of raving, testosterone-crazed men invaded the strip, prowling the town in packs of three and four, looking for an old-fashioned barroom brawl, an overnight in the clink, a real shitshow to boast about on Monday morning, a story they could embellish each time they told it to doubtful friends. While it was nice to see the social classes mingling, I had a hard time distinguishing one group from another, rich from poor, highborn from hick, their faces ferocious with drugs and alcohol, their features washed away by the pale afternoon light slashing diagonally through a cloud bank.

Rather than connect these two parts of town, the great arch bridge acted as a kind of giant guillotine, separating the brain from the body. Its long deck spanned the high granite walls of a gorge where the roiling river became an impressive waterfall that dropped along several ledges of bedrock and spilled into the valley. There the swift river forged a path through fallow fields and an old-growth forest to the tempestuous Great Lake ten miles to the north. Part of an ancient glacial moraine, the valley was rife with tragedy, past and present, and the bridge, ever since its construction fifty years ago, had been a favorite spot for manic-depressives of every stripe—for professors in tweed blazers and knit ties, for laborers in denim coveralls and steel-toed boots, for heartbroken college students, their uncorrupted souls freshly scarred by sorrow, for the destitute and depressed, the fed up, the inconsolable, the outraged. They scaled the barrier, clung to the rail, and then threw themselves off. How many regretted their decision as they plummeted through the air before hitting the canopy of hardwood trees? The drop was over one hundred feet, and most people ricocheted off the sturdy limbs, snapped their necks on the ashes and oaks, dead before they even hit the smooth bedstraw and creeping buttercups that blanketed the ground. One or two landed in the middle of the river, their bodies floating like driftwood to the lake. In time they either dissolved into fish food or were dredged up by weekend boaters weighing anchor. Those residents blessed with a more sardonic sense of humor joked that the sandbar a half mile offshore had become the town's unofficial cemetery.

Hoping to catch a glimpse of the starveling white-tailed deer that came here to graze on the gray-headed coneflowers and white snakeroot growing from the rocky soil, I leaned over the concrete barrier and listened to the persistent song of falling waters. Soon forest rangers, waiting in camouflaged tree blinds, rifle barrels poking through the leaves, would begin to thin their numbers. I wondered what became of the carcasses. Usually the remains ended up in a rendering plant at the edge of town. Animal fat was a key ingredient in cosmetics. Men shoveled the blubber into steaming kettles, turning it into an oil reduction, all so a woman, with a quick daub of color, could transform her face into a macabre mask. Thinking of the long life ahead of me, I followed a deer path that curled against steep, shale cliffs and immense slabs of bedrock until it reached the valley floor.

For the next hour I traveled along a gravel road that unfurled through great, empty, mist-strangled meadows and skirted pestilential bogs, and for reasons that remain unclear to me I felt like I had assumed a new identity, a new way of life. I was now a nameless wanderer, unknown and unclaimed, and I marveled at the immensity of the poetically weathered terrain. Above the valley walls, wheeling in slow circles across the inverted bowl of the sky, an owl searched for carrion. In the distance, poking through a haze of withered grain, a wrought-iron gate creaked back and forth in a breath of cold wind. Tall and ominous and heavy, it looked like the entrance to oblivion. Someone had smashed the padlock to bits and had cut the heavy chain wrapped around its rusty bars, but as I approached along a carpet of red-brown pine needles, I grew uneasy and hesitated to pass through. The gate was set into a wall made from ragged blocks of stone that disappeared into a copse of lightning-scarred trees, and when I placed my hands on the bars I felt a tingling like sparks.

I peered inside and saw a shallow stream that meandered through an untilled scrap of forsaken acreage fastened to the valley floor, the soil a dark loam on a foundation of white marl and chalk. On the horizon, as the sun shed its sickly white light, I spotted the wooden shell of a barn, a simple A-frame structure that looked like a capsized ark adrift in a sea of undulating yellow waves. That the barn was still standing at all seemed a miracle. Between the rocky walls of the valley and the rolling foothills to the east, there was nothing to protect a rickety structure of significant size. In every direction there stretched a dull patchwork of fields sown with ancient glacial rubble that acted as a conduit for epic storms, feeding the tall, trundling clouds with enough heat and moisture to build into angry black anvils. With alarming regularity the sky unleashed cyclones that corkscrewed down and barreled dumb and pitiless across the county, wreaking havoc on the lives of so many families and burying the dead beneath piles of debris, bowed and jagged and impenetrable.

The gates were ornamented with a fine, tangled ironwork forming the letters *T* and *W* in Gothic script. I knew what the letters meant, and immediately I recalled my meeting with the headmaster. No one could say for certain what Father Montague was thinking—very few people had access to his inner arcanum—but in his eyes I saw an unfamiliar quality of mercy, a look of genuine concern, maybe even pity, as he spoke his parting words to me: "Oh, son, if only you knew what you were getting yourself into."

When certain seeds are planted they almost always grow, and on that September afternoon, as I stood in the moist sod and damp shadows, I felt a deepening sense of exile, a small tremor of self-doubt, and I conjured up an awful image of the mad doctor who ventured to this lonely place to conduct his experiments on the unsuspecting inhabitants of the town. A simplistic explanation, I supposed, for the terrible things that happened here so long ago. In academic circles it had become fashionable to dismiss the universality of human fervor, criticizing one man for clinging to outrageous and murderous doctrines while seeing others as innocent and blameless, but all people at some point get caught up in pure lunacy, and surely the natives of the valley, with their superstitions and totems and exaggerated oral histories, had to contend with their own manias and delusions.

Until the ghosts of Normandy Falls appeared more than five years later and led me through the snowfields, I remained mysteriously free of dangerous ideas, and though I neither expect nor solicit belief, I maintain that the following account is based largely on an honest recollection of the incontrovertible and at times incriminating facts. Since I am an aspiring writer and know a little about the structure of stories, I will describe what I experienced during my final days in that dreary town, but what you must first understand is that, in order to provide this narrative with the proper context it requires, I will need to embellish a detail or two, insert a snippet of conversation, make an educated guess as to what others were thinking. Because every story is an unavoidable mixture of fact and fiction, a limited theme with unlimited variations, and this particular story, the one I will now attempt to tell, is at least in that sense no different from any other. Readers are at liberty to entertain their doubts.

The problem is this: Normandy Falls, in all its gruesome comedy, in all its colorful and agreeable horror, could never properly prepare me for the experiences that awaited me on the other side of those gates. Regrettably, the best I can do is render one version of that unhappy fiasco, and I must rely on my imperfect memory, a thing that, like the Wakefield River, flows with maddening predictability in one direction only, far from its mysterious and secret source.

Emily Ryan Whispers Her Dark Secrets

Friday, August 29–Monday, September 1, 2014

I

"There should be a law," said Professor Martin Kingsley, "a law of nature as well as a law of man, something written into the fabric of the cosmos and hardwired into human consciousness. People should take the wedding vows only after they turn thirty. They need a certain amount of wisdom before committing themselves to marriage, certain kinds of experiences, awful experiences, to harden the soul before a long, brutal winter."

Mrs. Emily Ryan carefully considered the meaning of these words and then repeated them with mild apprehension—or was cruel derision dripping from the tip of her tongue that fine summer day? Kingsley could never be entirely sure.

"A long, brutal winter . . ."

"Yes," he said. "A simple, almost innocuous injunction, don't you think?"

As an associate professor of comparative literature, Kingsley had developed the habit, a boring one, some might argue, of thoroughly analyzing any subject that had even a tangential bearing on his ambitious work in progress, a heavily footnoted, exegetical tome exploring the influences of *Madame Bovary* on contemporary culture, and because he framed every topic of conversation as an argument, he often left Emily wondering if he was joking or being sincere; it had something to do with the pitch and timbre of his voice, the way the final syllable of each enthusiastic syllogism reached a manic falsetto, and he tried to compensate for this "disorder," as he referred to it, by adding with a kind of infantile whine, "But I'm being perfectly *serious*," which served only to confuse Emily all the more.

As if trying to pacify a pouting child, she patted his hand and said, "I suppose you're right. I was only twenty when I married Charlie. Is that what you're getting at?"

Unaccustomed to being challenged, Kingsley crossed his arms and thought for a moment. "Well, would you say things have worked out pretty well between the two of you?"

She took an experimental sip of her drink and turned her face toward the sun. A rare day in late August: scant humidity, temperature in the mid-70s, a soothing northerly breeze stirring the maples and oaks, the leaves sounding like a gently breaking surf, clouds like enormous pink conch shells resting undisturbed at the bottom of a clear blue sea; and for Emily Ryan it was the hour of the Red Death—one cup of pomegranate juice, a heaping tablespoon of sugar, and half a lemon squeezed into a tall jar of hillbilly hooch that she managed to procure from the Gonk.

"At twenty," she said, "most people are still going through the late stages of adolescence, and an adolescent should never make big decisions. But Charlie made those kinds of decisions for me. Back then he seemed so much wiser. He was opposed to cohabitation. Living in sin, he called it. We had to be married first. That's what you don't understand about my husband. He isn't an old-fashioned romantic. And he sure isn't the sentimental sort. No, he's a hard-core traditionalist who wanders around the house humming church hymns." In a small, lilting voice she sang, "Be not afraid, I go before you always . . ."

There was a strong gust, and on the clothesline the white bedsheets came to life, a swarm of angry spirits thrashing at the sky. With eyes that had seen great heights of agitation, Emily regarded those boisterous, billowing spooks like an adept medium determined to interrogate the dearly departed, and when she turned again to Kingsley, she spoke with an intense and humorless smile.

"I haven't told anyone this, but my husband is superstitious. He believes in things, crazy things, in ghosts and goblins and mischievous devils taking possession of people's bodies. To him sin isn't an abstract, philosophical concept. It's a real thing. Part of the natural order. He smells it in the air he breathes, tastes it in the food he eats."

Kingsley laughed uneasily and shifted in his seat. Unlike the other neighborhood women, Emily could lighten the mood with a charming anecdote, an amusing turn of phrase, but lately she revealed things better kept private, and any talk of her husband's delusions made Kingsley, who had yet to set foot in the church near the town square, more than merely uncomfortable; it made him cringe with embarrassment and even a little fear.

Ten years her senior and away from home six months out of twelve, Charlie Ryan seemed more like a phantom than a real man. He was a merchant marine and veteran deckhand who spent half the year on the *Rogue*, a bulk carrier that cruised the Great Lakes from the Port of Cleveland to Mackinac Island to the remote Canadian outposts dotted along Lake Superior. During his time away from home, he expected Emily to raise the children without his help, and the long, lonely months left her depleted, beaten down, slightly hunched, a sad soul with a haunted disposition.

"I need a refill!" she announced and smacked her lips. "How about you, Professor? You ready for one?"

He was genuinely alarmed by the amount of booze she could put away before lunch, but he knew it was unwise to berate her for her excesses. These languid summer afternoons tended to be far more pleasant whenever she imbibed a gentle philter or two. If he hadn't made the blunder of cocking an eyebrow and using the same condescending and self-righteous tone he used when addressing his less ambitious graduate students, he might have convinced her to slow down. She smirked and defiantly added a second splash of moonshine, precious stuff, not something to waste on an ordinary day. But today was no ordinary day.

By law and the will of the people, the county was a dry one, home of the Anti-Saloon League, but the citizens of Normandy Falls, while they had conservative views ("cautious" was the word they preferred) about some social issues, nevertheless insisted on proving that their town could be a lovely oasis of sin in a desert of reactionary politics and morality. The establishment of private clubs was one way to skirt the draconian laws of the religious right and create a safe haven for unrepentant hedonists, but for the privilege of enjoying a bottle of beer at the cabaret or a glass of wine at the bistro, loyal patrons were obliged to pay steep prices. The locals preferred to barter for the grain alcohol brewed in backwoods distilleries, and Emily Ryan, a true townie born and bred, always kept an emergency supply squirreled away in her kitchen cupboards.

"I have to admit," she said, "this stuff tastes a lot better when you're sitting on the beach. Do you know Charlie hasn't treated me to a vacation in years? Not since our sixth wedding anniversary."

Kingsley knew she harbored fantasies about running away from Normandy Falls and seeing the wide world. Her already unbearable isolation was made that much worse by the extraordinarily vicious and largely unpredictable tantrums of her eight-year-old twin girls. She'd become so desperate to hear the voice of another rational human being that she was even willing to tolerate a vapid windbag like Martin Kingsley, a man who believed he had permission to speak for all people in all circumstances.

Although he failed to recognize the degree to which she suffered, Kingsley did have enough compassion to invite her on long walks through campus, a section of town Emily normally avoided. In the summertime, when he was transformed from a promising young professor into a stay-at-home dad, the primary caregiver of his three-year-old son, Christopher, and wanted to escape from his house as much as she wanted to escape from hers, he offered Emily a small reprieve from the grinding routine. They took leisurely strolls along the quiet cobblestone lanes of campus, their children either lagging far behind or running well ahead of them. They passed under green archways of elms that shaded them in arboreal innocence, their voices dampened by the rumble of lawnmowers and the drone of hedge trimmers as a ragtag crew of groundskeepers, frequent guests of the state and federal corrections system, descended on the quad.

To strangers, Kingsley and Emily must have looked like a married couple with three little ones in tow, but in a small college town where there were few strangers and gossip was ubiquitous, discretion was a game everyone was obliged to play. The rules were easy enough to master—never walk too close together, or accidentally brush shoulders, or gaze into each other's eyes—but after several awkward encounters with colleagues and students, Kingsley persuaded Emily that it was a lot less complicated to stay put in her backyard beside the pool where people wouldn't see and secretly cast judgment upon them.

Now they relaxed in a pair of wooden Adirondack chairs and watched the children doggy-paddle around the perimeter of the pool. In this neighborhood of Victorian-era houses, the inground pool was a bit of an anachronism and something of an eyesore—at night it swarmed with amphibious insects and became a pond for the occasional croaking frog—but during the day it served its purpose well. Christopher hitched up his sagging swim shorts and splashed along the edge in a small life preserver. He babbled contentedly to himself while Emily's identical twin girls, Madeline and Sophie, tossed a beach ball back and forth. For once they didn't continually interrupt the conversation like two old-maid chaperones with the demands of the chronically cranky and incontinent: "We're thirsty! We're tired! We want to watch television!"

It was difficult for Kingsley to disguise his feelings for the girls: he found them not merely obnoxious and irritating, which is how he characterized most children, including a few of his students, but abnormally sinister. Though they were only eight years old, they possessed a rugged masculinity and were built like their father—thick, solid, broad shouldered, with eyes so dark and glassy they seemed to be made from perfectly polished pieces of obsidian. Mass murderers of spiders, flies, moths, and the exceptionally brilliant brush-footed butterflies that sailed above the surface of the water, the girls constantly hunted for easy prey. They also proved to be accomplished mimics who delighted in doing impersonations of adults, especially of "Plucky Prolixy Professor King-silly," aping his vocabulary with unnerving precision in a single singsong voice and then squealing with malicious, porcine laughter whenever he shot them a weary and wounded look.

While they certainly enjoyed roughhousing poor, defenseless Christopher, scratching his face, pulling his hair, stomping on his tiny toes, they reserved the brunt of their wickedness for their long-suffering mother, relishing their roles as jailers and persecuting her in ways that only the most heartless of wardens can. Clever, calculating, supremely subversive, they understood intuitively that parenthood was a kind of indefinite prison sentence, one in which beleaguered moms and dads, as a general rule, spent most of their days sequestered from other adults, and from the moment they muscled their way out of the womb, the girls seemed to prattle a maddening refrain: "We condemn you, Mommy, to a decade of solitary confinement."

By this time the girls had already driven Emily quite mad, and Kingsley speculated that the only reason they still lived in the same house with their mother was because a mother's love was unconditional. Ordinary love wouldn't have been enough, not in their case. The love had to be absolute, otherwise they would have found themselves wandering the nighttime streets like a pair of wretched, half-starved urchins out of a folktale, searching through trash cans and dumpsters for rancid scraps of food and seeking shelter in abandoned barns.

Mulling over the infinite possibilities, Kingsley leaned back in his chair and closed his eyes. He envisioned Emily deserting the girls in a Dickensian orphanage, a troll-infested forest, a vast wildlife preserve teeming with ravenous jackals and hyenas. He pictured in exquisite detail smoking electric chairs and old-fashioned firing squads—fusillading, the French called it, which made execution seem almost enlightened. He saw those two chortling brats, handcuffed and blindfolded, cigarettes dangling from the corners of their mouths, standing against a bullet-ridden wall in a prison courtyard; watched the decorated commandant give the signal, the soldiers raise their rifles; and for a split second, in the stillness of the summer day, mistook a backfiring car for the sudden crack of gunshots. Beyond these delightfully gruesome images he would not allow his mind to wander, because, as he liked to remind his students, "An unrestrained imagination poses certain dangers to its owner."

In the dazzling sunshine his daydreams seemed harmless enough, particularly when the breeze died and the ripples on the pool vanished so that its smooth surface rolled back and forth in silver filaments of light, but with the girls lurking nearby it never took long for an idyllic scene to turn sour. Gliding stealthily along the shallow bottom like a couple of perversely smiling moray eels, Madeline and Sophie found Christopher's legs and lavished their pinches upon him. Blue in the face and gasping for air, they rocketed to the surface to shout in their victim's ears, one girl on either side for proper stereophonic effect, "We love you, Christopher, we do, like a brother we do!"

When they grew tired of this game, they ran helter-skelter around the pool, fishing for compliments, doing a late-summer saraband, jack-knifing and cannonballing in the deep end. Then they raced across the yard to the clothesline, where they wrapped themselves in the white sheets and shouted, "Booo!"

Emily jumped from her chair. "You monsters, I just cleaned those!" She tried to coax them back into the water, but Madeline and Sophie let out two horrific shrieks that sent the blackbirds flying in a panic from the treetops.

"Well, that's one thing you definitely forgot to consider," said Emily, slumping into her chair.

"What's that?"

"If people married late in life, there would be far fewer children in this world. The older you get, the less patience you have for them."

"Ah, yes," said Kingsley, "it's an engineering problem. If Nature had the capacity to reason properly, if it weren't so blind, it would have made us eager to reproduce beginning in middle age, not before. Think of all the problems that would solve."

"Are you saying fatherhood doesn't agree with you?"

He pondered this for a moment, and when he finally answered, he tried to sound assertive; for him never an easy thing. "I'm not convinced men, especially young men, are cut out for the job, that's all. You wouldn't trust another man with your children, would you?"

She squeezed his arm and smiled. "I trust *you*, Martin."

From behind the sheets Madeline and Sophie performed an infuriating shadow play, pantomiming the adults, using lewd and obscene gestures, and with awful exuberance they resumed their impersonation of Pontificating Professor King-silly.

"Something to harden the soul," they proclaimed, "something to harden the soul, something to harden the soul before a long, brutal winter!"

Deciding it was time to take shelter from the sun's blistering downward rays, Kingsley and Emily led the children under a patio umbrella and prepared a late lunch of peanut butter and jelly sandwiches. After wiping sticky mouths and fingers, they ordered the children into the family room, where Emily turned on the television. Madeline and Sophie nestled against each other on the sofa, their eyes growing heavy with exhaustion. In the flicker and fog of gray light, the twins looked somewhat less impish, and Christopher, curled up on a recliner, looked positively cherubic. At the first hint of snoring, Kingsley and Emily rushed hand in hand upstairs to the master bedroom. There was always a slim chance that one of the kids might wake up and disturb them, but with any luck they would have an entire hour to make frantic and soulful love in the stifling summertime heat.

To Kingsley's way of thinking, the affair had simply happened just as a rainstorm happens, and surely no one was to blame for a rainstorm, and he refused to believe that he was the sort of sinister character one is likely to encounter in those melodramatic novels he assigned to his students, sprawling nineteenth-century epistolary epics thronging with bourgeois sadists, cruel and vindictive toward their lovers and spouses and thus deserving of some cosmic punishment, condemned by God to mingle among the wanton and lustful souls in Dante's second circle of hell. He was not a savage, he assured himself, a panting maniac yearning to tear off Emily's clothes and gleefully fornicate in filthy public restrooms and the cramped backseat of her minivan—although every now and then these thoughts did cross his mind, or at least that part of his mind still reeling in adolescent fantasies. He wasn't driven by malice or emotional desperation but by pure physical lust, nothing more.

After they satisfied each other's needs, Emily turned to him, sweaty and spent, and her voice, though flat and distant, seemed to fill the hollow room with a vague sense of foreboding. "In a few days Charlie will be coming home. I'll need to wash and dry these sheets again."

"Are you looking forward to seeing him?" Kingsley stretched his arms and legs.

She didn't answer, but her vacant laughter and the pale rigidity of her eyes told him all he needed to know.

"Maybe it will be good having him around," he said. "He'll help you with the girls."

"No, Charlie likes to remind me that he's been working hard and deserves a break. Oh, he'll watch the twins for an hour or two while I make a quick trip to the grocery store. But even that's asking a lot of him. Men can be such selfish bastards. No need to state the obvious, right? But for raising his children, a woman is allowed to make certain demands on a man's life. She deserves more than his respect and loyalty."

Kingsley understood what she meant. Trapped for months in that house, without any close friends or family members to keep her company, Emily had started to "lose her shit," as she frequently put it, and seldom managed to flee her captors. Her situation only worsened when Charlie was home.

In the early evening, while writing in his study, Kingsley sometimes turned to the window and saw a small colony of brown bats coming and going from an air vent at the peak of the Ryans' house, and with growing unease he listened to the shouting and screaming and sudden, portentous silences that issued forth from its dark and dirty rooms. For a long time now he'd suspected Charlie of slapping her, slamming her against doors, shoving her against crumbling sheetrock walls, pinning her face to the floor with his huge, calloused hands, the sort of man who probably slept soundly at night, even with the burden of abuse on his soul.

Once, Kingsley thought he glimpsed a bruise on Emily's left arm, the purple indentation of fingers pressed hard into delicate flesh. She started wearing long-sleeve shirts and jeans in warm weather. It wasn't his business, he told himself, but he did have the right to know what sort of people lived beside him. After all, one's neighbors were a fairly strong indicator of one's own status in this world, and Kingsley worried that he'd slipped a rung on the socioeconomic ladder, that despite his proud middle-class bearing he was just another anonymous wage slave struggling to eke out a modest living in this shabby quarter of town.

He had a more difficult time convincing Marianne. At these idle theories his wife rolled her eyes and scolded him for his snobbery.

"Every man," she said, "no matter his station in life, is capable of ghastly behavior."

He snorted with incredulous laughter. "*Every* man?"

"Affluent husbands beat their affluent wives, too."

"Oh, come on, you have to concede that, statistically speaking, low-income earners are far more likely to resort to physical violence. Young professionals tend to rely on psychological warfare. Our neighbors have limited means, let's be honest. I don't like the looks of that pool anymore. They don't clean it regularly. And any property in advanced stages of decay is a bad omen. Bad for resale values, too."

Even before moving to Normandy Falls five years ago and purchasing their home, he and Marianne had expressed concern about the pool. Despite all of the new child-safety measures—a net over the crib, a microphone on the dresser, a lock on the door—Christopher had become something of a prodigy at escaping from his nursery, and soon the day would come when he decided to scale the chain-link fence and take a fateful midnight dip.

"Have a look at their backyard." Martin guided his wife toward the kitchen window. "Who the hell uses a clothesline these days? I'm surprised the girls haven't decapitated themselves yet."

Marianne smirked. "For god's sake . . ."

"And do you see that? The tiles are falling off the roof."

"All right, so their house could use a makeover. What do you expect? Emily is all alone over there. She can't fix up the place by herself. Charlie will get around to it, eventually." Marianne moved away from the window and planted her hands on her hips. "Our house isn't exactly a palace either. Maybe you should consider taking a few carpentry classes at the college and focus more on home improvement projects this summer. No, you're always working on that damn book. How long have you been at it now, this quest of yours to become the unchallenged doyen of scholarship on Flaubert? Three years? Do you plan to finish it any time soon?"

In actuality, it had been closer to four years, four miserable years of creative constipation, occasional panic attacks, and those all-too-infrequent flashes of inspiration, but he wouldn't admit this to anyone, least of all to Marianne. She wasn't a dedicated maniac as he was. She was a clock watcher, the sort of no-nonsense number cruncher who demanded regular progress reports, spreadsheets, pie charts, colored graphs, accurate word counts. As an adjunct instructor of art history and professional grant writer, she worked regular hours in a small, windowless office, trying to raise the necessary funds to host a swanky New Year's Eve retrospective on the life and work of a local painter and sculptor named Colette Collins, one of the pioneers in the surrealist and psychedelic movements and a cult figure in the world of contemporary art.

Marianne was also an amateur bodybuilder, and every morning she spent an hour in the gym doing shoulder presses, squats, and lunges in front of the floor-to-ceiling mirrors, admiring how the sharply layered and defined muscles cleaved to her bones. She was especially proud of the way her striated deltoids bulged under her taut skin, and she wore her hair pulled back so everyone could admire her broad and sloping shoulders. Her center of gravity wasn't in her impressive upper body, however, but in her muscular thighs, and whenever they made love she squeezed her legs against Kingsley's torso, causing him to cry out in pain. She'd become so adept at this that she could control the tone and rhythm of his yelps and shrieks, and sometimes she referred to him, even around his students, as "my little pipe organ."

She was probably right about his own negligence as a homeowner, but by that point in the conversation Kingsley had grown irritated with her charitable opinions and absolute rectitude. He expected a rhapsodic affirmation of their superiority, a lovely ode to their granite countertops and stainless-steel appliances and the reassuring smell of cleaning solution so pungent it singed the hairs in his nostrils and made his eyes water.

He felt it necessary to be more candid with her and lowered his voice. "Look, I haven't told you this, but I've seen bats, big ones with pointed ears, flying in and out of the attic next door. Once winter comes Charlie won't be able to get rid of those things. They'll hibernate in the walls and die inside the house and decompose if he tries to exterminate them."

"Okay, Martin."

"The entire neighborhood will end up reeking like a slaughterhouse."

"Stop."

"The stench, Marianne, the smell of *death and decay*—"

"I said stop it!" She gave him a look dark with reproach.

Kingsley was taken aback. He'd never seen such loathing in her eyes, and suddenly he worried that she suspected him of misconduct.

"I often wonder, Martin, if there's something wrong with you. I mean something *seriously wrong*." Then she stormed upstairs and slammed the bedroom door with enough force to shake the whole foundation.

Now he scrutinized the ceiling above Emily's bed, counting the cracks, looking for telltale signs of guano, faint patches of gray leaking through loose scabs of plaster, and he listened for the scratch and scuffle of bats nesting in the walls. Only after assuring himself that the place wasn't an unsalvageable wreck did he commence yet another surreptitious appraisal of Emily's body. With the spurious smile of an experienced old lecher, he stroked her soft skin and searched longingly for irrefutable evidence of abuse. Kissing her thighs, her navel, her breasts, her shoulders, he wondered how their respective spouses might react if they chanced to walk in on them in flagrante delicto, a scene so clichéd it was almost comical, but Kingsley could guess what Charlie Ryan might do.

Prior to shipping out on his latest voyage, Charlie wanted to buy a Doberman, a Rottweiler, a Rhodesian Ridgeback, a real monster that would provide Emily with peace of mind while he was away from home, but Emily flatly refused to clean up after it, so Charlie settled on a gun instead, a simple, easy-to-handle .38 revolver, a shiny new weapon that, if the situation presented itself, he would use on another man without a moment's hesitation, emptying all six chambers. About this Kingsley had no doubt whatsoever. There was only a question of whether he would spare Emily's life.

She pushed his head away and reached for her drink on the nightstand. "The kids will wake up soon."

When their affair first began, Kingsley liked the fact that she had a seditious side to her nature, and he tried to guess which revelation would outrage Charlie more—that his wife was screwing the neighbor or that she was in danger of becoming a pill popper and alcoholic—but he worried that her reckless drinking had become a potential hazard not to her long-term health but to his. It was only a matter of time before she put him in serious jeopardy. Despite the risks, he found himself saying, "It's your thirtieth birthday. A milestone. I made reservations for eight o'clock at Belleforest."

"*That* place again?"

"But I thought you liked French food."

"It's always short staffed. One waitress on duty. Plus it's a dump."

Kingsley, who had a habit of being unintentionally funny, shook his head. "No, it isn't. In fact, I'd say it's rather a classy place."

Housed in one of the small converted warehouses on the square, Belleforest inserted a bit of tasteless humor into the drab, uneventful lives of the people who inhabited the town. The new restaurateur believed the old structure had enormous potential to become a charming spot where friends could gather after work to enjoy a glass of Beaujolais. Unfortunately, he refused to make the necessary investments to turn this particular dream into a reality. Not that it mattered. Normandy Falls wasn't a Beaujolais kind of town, and most of its unemployed citizens preferred moonshine and demolition derbies to imported wines and fancy fish stews. For Kingsley the bistro served as an ideal location for an illicit rendezvous. His colleagues avoided those blighted ten square blocks of town with the kind of paranoia that seemed more typical of xenophobic suburbanites than rigidly ideologi-cal intellectuals who never grew tired of extolling their belief in the concept of urban renewal.

"I can't go tonight," said Emily. "Who will watch the girls?"

"Marianne, of course. I'll tell her you'd like to celebrate in style with a few of your friends. She enjoys having the girls over."

"How considerate of her. And how about you, Martin? What's your excuse for leaving the house?"

"The usual—I have to conduct research at the college library."

"Ah, yes, your magnum opus." Her voice had a well-honed edge of contempt. "In order to concentrate on revisions, you need complete silence." She left the bed and walked across the room.

He ignored the remark—she could turn quite suddenly into an angry drunk—and marveled at the silhouette of her body against the white blinds. "So? Is it a date?"

Emily took a contemplative sip of her cocktail and hesitated before speaking. "I read in the paper that the college is screening a David Lean movie. Sounds interesting. It takes place in Ireland during the First World War." Before he could invent a clever excuse she added quickly, "I wouldn't mind a little culture for a change, you know."

"Well, I'm not sure . . ."

"What, aren't those professors worldly and sophisticated? Not eas-ily scandalized by the presence of a colleague's *mistress*?"

She meant for the word to sting, and he found himself pulling the sheet up to his chin. If word got around the department about this affair, it would mean instantaneous and unequivocal ruin for him. It was the main reason he enjoyed heaping maledictions and obscenities upon those chattering academics whose tongues were like knives.

"I don't enjoy socializing with that crowd," he said. "They're a pretty stuffy bunch. Conventional."

"You mean they're normal."

"They're hardly that."

"They have the decency to be shocked. Appalled." From an old dresser lacking three of its glass knobs, she produced a long tangle of turquoise-colored cloth and held it up to her torso. "Don't worry, Martin. I wouldn't even know what to wear around those people. Look at this thing."

"A stunning dress," said Kingsley.

"It's called a sari. Gujarati style. Saris are *comme il faut* this season, that's what all the fashion magazines say."

Kingsley nodded. "Yes, now I see what you mean. I'm sure a few of my colleagues would take umbrage at such an overbearingly vulgar imperialist gesture. Or do I mean postcolonialist? It's hard to keep up with all the changing lingo."

"Charlie bought it during our trip four years ago to Delacroix Cay, a disgusting spit of sand in the middle of the Caribbean. Lots of dead fish floating in the water. At least there were palm trees and stiff drinks, I'll give him credit for that." She shook the sari in her fist. "I guess this was his idea of a souvenir. He insists I wear it whenever he comes home. But it doesn't exactly fit the way it used to. Besides, it's a color for a much younger woman. A happier one."

Kingsley pretended to admire the sari's complicated sequin work, but his eyes drifted to the nightstand, where he saw buried under an untidy pile of pink stationery his paperback copy of *Madame Bovary*, the spine cracked, the pages turning faintly yellow. He'd lent her the book a few months ago when she expressed an interest in learning more about his work, but he doubted she would ever get around to reading it, and he was more concerned that she would forget to return it to him before the semester started.

"You're lovely in whatever you wear," he told her, though what he really wanted to say was that she looked sexy, shamelessly so. After all, it wasn't her erudition that interested him—she admitted to enjoying historical romances about handsome pirates who rescued and fell madly in love with headstrong damsels in distress—but given her sullen mood he thought better of it. "Listen, you deserve an evening of wine and candlelight. It's not like we're doing anything criminal."

She tossed the dress on the bed. "Don't you feel like a lowlife, Martin? Don't you sometimes want to kill yourself? Maybe we should do it together. End it all. Like Romeo and Juliet."

"We're a little old for that sort of thing, aren't we? Romeo and

Juliet were teenagers. And Juliet stabbed herself with Romeo's dagger. Very messy stuff and painful."

"Didn't they take poison? We could take poison."

"A romantic gesture." Kingsley nervously eyed her jar of Red Death and wondered if there was a way he could hide it without her noticing.

"Actually, I thought it sounded logical. Greek. Like Plato. He drank poison, right?"

"Someone like that. You don't have any hemlock in your medicine cabinet, do you?"

"Hemlock? Does it grow in the valley?"

"No, it's not a native species."

Emily yanked up the blinds and squinted at the trembling light on the pool, but before she could finish her thought or accuse him of moral cowardice, she raised a finger to her lips and cocked her head. In the hallway, on the other side of the bedroom door, there came sibilant whispers and the pitter-patter of bare feet as two giggling conspirators raced downstairs. Like sneaks the world over, the twins knew which steps creaked and made sure to avoid them.

Kingsley scrambled out of bed and in a clumsy dance pulled on his polka-dot boxers. He remembered the gun and hoped Emily had sense enough to keep it locked up where the girls couldn't get at it, and for the first time since the start of their affair, he had no regrets that their afternoon together had come to a premature end.

When he first met Emily, Kingsley experienced a *coup de foudre*, as the French say, but now that summer was coming to an end and things were beginning to cool between them, he concluded that their affair was, at least in some sense, a kind of marriage in miniature. If an orgasm is *la petite mort*, then an affair must be *la petite emprisonnement*, because any intimate relationship, whether lawful or not, goes through three distinct stages: the first stage is a lot of fun, too much fun perhaps, like receiving an invitation to a secret party that rages long into the night where everyone is insanely, irresponsibly, obscenely drunk on a spellbinding potion ladled from a ritual basin; the second stage is the obligatory, crushing, shameful hangover, a day of glaring white light that reveals things obscured by the haziness of sweet intoxication, a day of cold sweats, unabated nausea, and bitter sobriety, a day to contemplate with disbelief and horror all of the embarrassing—and possibly unhygienic—things you did the night before and to pledge never again to commit the same terrible mistakes; during the third and final stage you stop deluding yourself and accept the fact that you are unlikely to be invited to another rollicking soirée, and that instead of going it alone it is much wiser to remain faithful to one person, bad breath and all, and try to make the best of it.

Kingsley now suspected that he'd slipped imperceptibly from the first stage into the second; it was as though he had gone through an invisible portal but hadn't realized it until long after the fact and understood much too late that, once crossed, it was virtually impossible to retrace his steps and pass back through to the other side. But by then he believed he had an unspoken agreement with Emily: they weren't committed to each other; they were committed to lying.

All of this became much clearer to him as he waited for her at Belleforest. Although the bistro's exterior was in many ways indistinguishable from an ordinary greasy spoon a traveler might encounter along a lonely stretch of two-lane highway, the interior had a startling carnival-like quality, the colors and music loud as a midway. With its kitschy reprints by Toulouse-Lautrec hanging on every wall and Edith Piaf gargling every *r* of *"Non, je ne regrette rien"* from the tinny speakers, the restaurant would have made for an amusing dining experience in some demented theme park. Certainly the centerpieces, original sculptures created by Colette Collins, contributed to the overall oddness of the atmosphere. Small, misshapen, vaguely amphibious creatures that stood upright on webbed feet, the sculptures threatened to step off their bases and onto the tables to squat with satisfaction over steaming crocks of *tartiflette*. Despite the remarkably bad stagecraft and its reputation for stale baguettes and overcooked hunks of unidentifiable meat drowning in rich sauces, the bistro was bustling with couples, mainly townies who'd scraped together enough cash for a night out, but the longer Kingsley waited near the entrance the more anxious he became that someone might recognize and expose him. After fifteen minutes he stepped outside to the patio, a simple cement slab with cheap wrought-iron tables, folding chairs, and a makeshift bar where he ordered a bottle of Châteauneuf-du-Pape.

At half past eight, after pouring himself a generous glass, Kingsley concealed his face behind a menu and adjusted his chair to avoid making eye contact with a young man who stumbled from the cabaret next door and wandered down the dark alley. In the shadows the drunk could have been an anonymous derelict, a dangerous drifter, a man with a past, or a man with no past at all, but had Kingsley looked more closely, with a Flaubertian flair for conscientiously chronicling the quotidian, he would have recognized him right away and noted how his eye patch made him look less like a brutish buccaneer and more like a James Joyce impersonator, effete, bohemian, doomed to a lifetime of deteriorating health and a dependency on illicit substances.

There were whispers that the chef, aside from being an oversized gourmand, peddled hallucinogens behind the bistro. Evidently, for a small percentage of the profits, the mortician soaked the chef's product du jour—tobacco, marijuana, hashish, a sack of carrots imported from some North African bazaar—in a fifty-gallon drum of formaldehyde that he kept in the basement of the funeral parlor near the boiler room. By adding a dash of PCP to the mix, the chef could then market his wares as mystical substances that transported their habitual users to higher levels of consciousness. Judging from the quality of the fare and the generally bad service, Kingsley believed it would have been difficult for the chef to achieve a living without an additional source of revenue.

Another thirty minutes went by, and he poured a second glass from the bottle, but in the summer heat the wine tasted thick and bitter like medicine. A proper drink was what he really needed, a martini, a bourbon on the rocks, even one of Emily's potent Red Deaths. Alternately checking his watch and gazing profoundly into his wineglass, he'd become the quintessential spurned lover—every restaurant needs one—and his wounded pride shone plainly on his face. Though he didn't know it at the time, his affair with Emily had ended without a single word of warning. He should have trusted her judgment. Women were so much better than men at detecting moral depravity and could more easily throw off the chains of erotic enslavement. Well, what was wild, romantic love without a great renunciation?

At nine o'clock a waitress slunk over to the bar to tell him that his reservation had been invalidated. He grunted and waved her away, and for the next hour, still hoping Emily might show up, he nursed the bottle until it was empty. Finally, he tossed a few bills on the bar and stormed from the bistro, startled by how his emotions had gone from uncontrollable lust to absolute loathing.

Driving recklessly home in the dark, Kingsley forced himself to concentrate on the center line to keep from weaving, and in the rearview mirror he watched for patrol cars. A silver mist rolled with sinister intent from the valley and obscured the bridge, and as he approached his house, he felt an eerie calm descend on the neighborhood. Shafts of ghostly moonlight cut through the blue mottled clouds and illuminated a row of red maples, their heads brutally chopped to make a passage for electric lines. On the back stoop he struggled with the lock, and after angrily shoving open the door, he found Marianne wrapped in a terrycloth robe. She sat at the kitchen table, clutching a box of tissues to her chest, her hair wet, her lips shrunken and trembling, her face inflamed and swollen with sobbing. Even before closing the door, he caught a powerful whiff of chlorine.

He laughed uneasily. "An odd time for a swim, isn't it?"

With caution he entered the house. When it came to picking up on his wife's subtle hints and clues, Kingsley considered himself an expert without rival, but now he worried that, like so many negligent husbands, he was utterly incapable of seeing the most obvious of facts, and it took him a moment to deduce what had happened: Emily, delirious after a long day of hard drinking and reprimanding her untamable brats, had nixed dinner plans in favor of inviting her lover's wife over for a refreshing dip in the pool, and after guzzling a few more jars of moonshine, she'd made a stupid slip of the tongue, hiccupped her confession, slurred a rambling and tearful speech.

From the manic look in Marianne's eyes, Kingsley understood that he would need to pack his things and move out that night. He'd been foolish not to plan for such a contingency, and now he imagined himself living out of a battered suitcase for the next few weeks and sleeping on the couch in his office at the college until he found a studio apartment in town. He recalled seeing a sign in one of those frightening row houses at the river's edge: ROOMS FOR RENT. Eventually, he would need to solicit the services of a slick attorney who worked for reasonable fees and then wait for the disgraceful day when he had to appear before a judge. Worst of all he pictured the confused and desperate expression on Christopher's face when Daddy had to explain the concepts of separation and divorce.

"I phoned the library," said Marianne, "but they weren't able to find you."

"Okay, listen to me . . ."

His wife choked. "It's so senseless."

"Here, let me get you some water."

But Marianne's hands shook so badly that she couldn't hold the glass without spilling it.

"I think you're in shock," he said. "Try to stay calm. We'll get through this thing."

Marianne regarded him with astonishment. "Who cares if *we'll* get through it? What about the twins? What are *they* going to do? Those girls, they're just babies. They need their mother. And what about Charlie? He'll be lost without her."

Although it dawned on him that he was missing a crucial piece of information, Kingsley didn't possess the imagination to fathom anything more terrible than an act of infidelity to upset his wife in such a dramatic way. He sat beside her and with escalating horror listened as she told him in the iciest of whispers the terrible facts.

At eight o'clock she put Christopher to bed and asked the girls to play quietly in the guest room. Then she went downstairs to work on her speech for the retrospective and must have nodded off on the sofa because when she opened her eyes the girls were standing beside her, gently swaying and smiling sweetly. "Mommy is in the pool," they told her with strange indifference. Marianne didn't know what to make of these words. Somewhat dazed, still groggy with sleep, she put her notepad aside and went to the kitchen window. In the twilight she saw the vacillating and indistinct outline of a dark figure floating in the water.

"There wasn't anything I could do, Martin. I made the girls stay put and then ran next door. But she'd been in the pool for too long. I thought the paramedics would be able to revive her, but they wouldn't let me near the ambulance while they worked on her. Even when I tried to explain the situation to them, even when I told them that I was watching the girls because their mother was supposed to be out for the night." By this point in her story, Marianne was crushing his hands, twisting his fingers. "The police found a mason jar of alcohol and a vial of pills near one of the Adirondack chairs. But when I asked what it all meant, they just stared at the tips of their shoes and scratched their heads like idiots. Then one of them said to me, 'We need to speak to the next of kin.'"

From where he stood in the kitchen, Kingsley could see a glassy shimmer of moonlight on the surface of the pool. The water seemed to heave weirdly back and forth like mercury. He wanted suddenly to take his wife by the shoulders, to shake her violently, to shout, "What the hell are you talking about! Start making sense!" But the wine bubbled in the cauldron of his stomach, and he found he was incapable of saying anything at all. The room started to spin. He closed his eyes, began to pant. He contrived to make his way to the bathroom before the worst could happen, but Marianne wrapped her arms around his shoulders and pressed her face against his chest.

She sniffed, and with tears streaming down her cheeks she jerked away from him and said, "My God, Martin, have you been *drinking*?"

2

When the delirium of love dies and the asphyxiating cloud of romantic ruin finally dissipates, the bruised and battered survivors will often find lurking among the rubble and ashes of the human heart an insidious beast who yearns to wreak more havoc. Since he could think of no one else to blame for his wretched fate, Kingsley would later convince himself that I was the beast, and to a certain extent I suppose he was right, but my involvement in the events of that tragic night could be traced back to the demise of my own long-term relationship. The breakup wasn't something I took lightly. I'd given the matter serious thought and concluded I had little choice. My reasoning was sound, my philosophy admirable: no sane man, if he wishes to remain sane for long, can live with a woman foolish enough to pin all of her hopes for the future on him.

Morgan Fey, who came from desperately poor circumstances and who suffered big dreams, believed I would not only finish my master's degree in comparative literature but also go on to earn a PhD and then, with her encouragement and wise counsel, become a tenured professor at a prestigious university, a noted essayist, a prizewinning novelist, a public intellectual, a sophisticated and debonair cosmopolite strolling in tweeds and bow tie through the bustling streets of some famous and glittering big city, and she would make sure my inquisitive admirers knew that, as my sole muse and confidante, she deserved half the credit for my extraordinary achievements.

I had ambitions to be a writer and had already seen a few of my shamelessly autobiographical stories of teen angst published in middling literary journals associated with third-rate university writing programs, though one journal was based in Spokane and edited by Charles Pierce Flitcraft, a reclusive curmudgeon who'd garnered moderate fame for his hard-boiled detective stories that, as they progressed, became devious little exercises in metafiction and intertextuality. This wasn't a total defeat. Intellectual anonymity was, for a budding writer, an important and nurturing thing, and from out of the black marshes and muddy bottoms of small-town experience, I was determined to wrest a book, an enigmatic, ruthlessly apocalyptic, elegantly filthy dirigible of a novel that, in order to make its points all the more salient and startling, was unafraid to suffer under the weight of its own showiness and pretense, and for a little while I believed I might actually succeed.

After earning our undergraduate degrees from Normandy College, Morgan and I rented an apartment in a row house of soot-covered brick and calcified limestone that teetered at the river's edge. A single bay window offered an unobstructed view of the flotsam that accumulated and swirled in the powerful eddies—plastic bags, cardboard boxes, wooden crates—before it continued downstream and plummeted over the falls into the valley. In front of our building, atop a muddy knoll, there was a sandlot where serious children played their serious games. Every night someone draped a flannel shirt on the rusty bars of the jungle gym, and as it flapped in the wind, the shirt looked like the cruciform figure of a headless man, arms reaching out in a lunatic embrace, another body ripe for the river, unloved and casually discarded.

With its beige carpets and dirty plaster walls covered in a machine-gun fire of nail holes, the one-bedroom apartment was a dun-colored shell that seemed intentionally designed to expunge from the minds of its broke and directionless tenants any traces of hope or dreams for the future, but Morgan worked diligently at transforming the place into a personal refuge, a sanctuary for the quiet contemplation of complex ideas. She spent nights and weekends patching and painting the cracked walls, choosing the best spots to display her small "art collection," framed reprints of masterpieces by Cézanne, Pissarro, Rousseau, Gauguin, Degas, Cassatt, Doré. Though she endeavored to turn the place into a cozy gallery, she succeeded only in making it look like a consignment shop or the waiting room of a dentist's office, minus the algae-filled aquarium.

For the most part the other tenants—overworked and sleep-deprived machinists, gas station attendants, fast-food workers—seemed friendly enough, and whenever they passed us on the street with their brood of wailing toddlers strapped into unwieldy, puke-splattered, secondhand strollers, they stopped to ask, "So when are you two love-birds gonna bite the bullet, tie the knot, have a couple of kids?" They smiled, but I never failed to notice how they looked imploringly at me as if begging for rescue from some forced-labor camp and warning me away from the nascent hell of domesticity.

In Normandy Falls people too often resigned themselves to a pre-dictable pattern of unintended pregnancy, reluctant cohabitation, long stretches of unemployment, substance abuse, battery, incarceration. Some days parents sent their children to school, other days they did not. Men and women partied all night and slept all day. It made little difference to them financially and professionally, and it certainly cost them nothing socially because in Normandy Falls there were no rou-tines, and the only real constant was the mayhem that lurked at the periphery of this forlorn place.

Morgan and I had no immediate plans for marriage, and we agreed not to have kids for a long, *long* time. Things continued just as before until one day, after sitting through a three-hour graduate seminar, I returned to the apartment to discover—whether by accident or design, I was never entirely sure—that she had stopped taking the pill. At the bottom of the bathroom trash can, clumsily concealed under a sheet of tissue paper, I found her unopened prescription. More mystified than alarmed, I fished the container out of the trash and confronted her.

She had just finished her afternoon shift at the bistro, and as always the work had taken its terrible toll. By then I worried that my notion of Morgan as the unrefined but industrious native had been incorrect all along. Unable to afford the cost of graduate school and unwilling to sign for another student loan, she decided to wait tables at Belleforest, earning just enough money to make her half of the rent. I rarely went into town anymore, but on occasion I would eat lunch at the bistro, the only time of day I could afford anything on the menu. Sitting alone in a corner booth, enjoying a *quiche poireaux* and glass of tap water, I removed my moleskin notebook and fountain pen from my leather satchel, and then in front of everyone, including my mortified *serveuse*, I began to tinker with my novel, a bloated behemoth of self-indulgent excess, while the other patrons paused from their impassioned debates about the incompetence of government to shake their heads and quietly condemn me for pursuing such foolish dreams.

Now, after adjusting Van Gogh's bright yellow and summer-swollen sunflowers, Morgan kicked off her shoes and slumped onto the futon. Her clothes smelled of grease fires and her hair was so tangled and oily it may have been combustible—one spark from a lighter and the whole block would have detonated like a bomb, turning the neighborhood into a raging inferno of poverty and madness. In a gruff voice she castigated herself, her coarseness on full display. "What the *fuck* was I thinking? Why the hell did I major in art history? Why did I focus on heists, stolen paintings, Modigliani's *Woman with a Fan*?"

I shrugged, wondering the same thing myself. Some women were meant for the wide world, but Normandy Falls seemed to suit Morgan Fey just fine. At twenty-two she already looked too washed away to be playing the part of a chain-smoking, alienated, bohemian waitress at a bistro that billed itself as "the finest upscale dining for a hundred miles around." Not that my field of study offered a clear path to success. In the eyes of the world, a degree in comparative literature was equally worthless, and we both seemed to be in real danger of sliding toward premature middle age and a kind of permanent plainness.

Even though I no longer possessed the patience for drawn-out negotiations, I realized that in a delicate situation like this one I needed to be diplomatic, take my time, pay Morgan a compliment or two, it was a matter of common courtesy, but I'd grown so accustomed to the simple lines of communication offered by a serious relationship—a few key phrases churlishly spoken, a couple of impatient grunts, exasperated sighs—that I no longer knew the appropriate things to say or do. Also, a small part of me actually looked forward to ending the relationship. I'd been on the receiving end of breakups plenty of times and had always wondered how it might feel to see that stunned and puzzled expression on another's face. But when the big moment arrived, I was unable to look her directly in the eye.

Trying hard not to sound wheedling or appeasing, I asked her to vacate the premises. "The lease is in my name, after all, not yours." With a mixture of curiosity and dread, I waited for her to thrust a knife, or at the very least a hatpin, deep into my small, dark heart. I expected a stormy exchange of words, and when she didn't respond I said, "Listen, Morgan, a fresh start might be a good thing for us both. You're miserable and I'm clearly incapable of making you happy. And I certainly don't think a child is the answer to your problems."

Morgan laughed scornfully. If I could tear her down with a few choice words she could certainly do the same to me, and I shrank from the awful spectrum of her excessively sharp and narrow teeth.

"Are you suggesting this breakup is mutual? Because there is no such thing, Edmund." She gave me a withering look and then, sinking into a serene lethargy, walked slowly toward the window, where she gestured to the river slithering darkly through the forsaken town of her birth. "I've often wondered," she said in a quiet, measured way, "what kind of person voluntarily comes to a hellmouth like Normandy Falls. Now I know the answer. Welcome home, Edmund."

For the first time in many months, I experienced the alien sensation of freedom. It made me feel oddly weightless, invisible, insignificant, and soon I developed a number of curious new habits. Before rising from the futon every morning and facing the day, I spread my arms in the wide and solitary waste of an empty bed and then sparked a big bowl of the really fine sinsemilla I purchased once a week from Xavier D'Avignon, the gnomic *chef de cuisine* who sold his homegrown bud in the alley behind the bistro ("Marijuana and sunshine go together like milk and cookies, don't they, son?"). I wanted badly to see my new life as an adventure, and in the afternoons I often paged through *The Odyssey*, the one book on which I relied to navigate life's unexpected twists and turns, committing to memory Homer's unrivaled descriptions of human striving and caprice. In time, I assured myself, I would meet a bewitching Circe, an insatiable Calypso. In the evenings my mood darkened sharply, and with the blinds pulled down and the volume on the TV turned way up, I watched black-and-white films directed by famously acidulous auteurs of the French New Wave until I nodded off to the ironic laughter of self-important Parisians.

Although I no longer suffered so acutely from the Catholic guilt that, as a child, I'd been encouraged to cultivate and keep close to my craven soul, I found that my Sunday-morning ritual, which used to consist of a quick lay followed by a bland breakfast of milk and cereal, now included a visit to that strange church near the square, refuge of heresiarchs and proselytizing cranks. I wasn't religious in any conventional sense of the word, but from the back pew I sang hymns with great enthusiasm as if beseeching heaven for a miracle, the transubstantiation of the bread and wine not into the Body and Blood but into a potent aphrodisiac that would resurrect my sex life, and this made me wonder if the church had a patron saint of concupiscence, of orgasms, of libidinous games and freaky fetishes.

At night I fantasized about inviting a bevy of pretty coeds back to my bachelor pad. I'd be like a wild animal released from its enclosure at the zoo, a tiger, a panther, a mountain lion, but then I felt idiotic for having thought of myself as a noble hunter instead of a more suitable creature like a ferret or a frog or a lice-infested vulture. The absence of physical love, I believed, was to blame for this terrible funk, and after a few months without the familiar cushion of Morgan's warm rump and the comfort of her firm tits, I worried that my own plans for a happy future might never come to fruition.

I fought the urge to call her and beg forgiveness, but one sleepless night, while staring into the whistling void of my threadbare apartment and listening to the dripping faucets, I suffered a sudden panic attack. I looked at the pages of my neglected thesis scattered on the coffee table and raced to the bathroom. In the mirror I saw an unshaven beast, stooped and haggard, with tartar-caked teeth and unspeakable impulses incubating in the back of its reptilian brain. Only then did it occur to me that sex was not the problem. The real reason so many people remained in unhealthy relationships was because they were incapable of caring for themselves, and as I shivered in the dark, appalled by the distorted, fun-house reflection staring back at me, I now understood that I belonged to their shameful number.

By the spring my grades began to suffer, and after weeks of procrastination and unproductive research on my thesis about the more sordid stories of the syphilitic genius Guy de Maupassant, I was placed on academic probation and summoned to my adviser's office. He answered my knock and showed me into the room. Small-featured, meticulously groomed, dressed in a herringbone blazer and a cornflower-blue button-down shirt, Professor Kingsley could have passed for a petite male model. With the certitude of academic privilege and the condescending air of a louche languid soul luxuriating in the warmth of his own intelligence, he leaned far back in his chair, held his hands up to the light, and frowned at his manicured fingernails. At least he didn't put his feet up on the desk—a small show of deference for which I was grateful—but he did tell me, rather glibly, I thought, that the provost had revoked my teaching assistantship for the following semester.

"I would also urge you, Mr. Campion, to abandon your thesis in favor of a new one. The simple fact of the matter is that in order to be taken seriously as a candidate for a master's degree, you must show your scholarly chops by reading something more substantial than de Maupassant, something more penetrating and insightful. Starting now I want you to focus on Flaubert. I think so, yes. We can credit Flaubert for having changed the direction of literary fiction as we know it today. You have aspirations to be a man of *belles-lettres*, *oui*? And *Madame Bovary* can offer practical instruction if not outright inspiration. After all, you can't be a *flaneur* your entire life, can you?"

I rolled my eyes at his slavish imitation of a French Canadian accent, full of Quebecois allophones and affrications. Despite his WASPy name, he insisted that his family came from old French stock—"My people helped settle Montreal with the Jesuit missionaries"—and claimed that his grandparents hailed from an abandoned logging town somewhere in the Quebec wilderness. "Fierce separatists," he boldly lied, "cunning saboteurs on the lam for their terrorist activities."

As our brief meeting came to an end, Kingsley must have sensed my profound disappointment. I was drawn to tales of the grotesque and fantastic, not to those obscure and tumescent tomes about the influence of naturalism on modern literature that evangelizing professors so revered. I told him so, and before escorting me to the door he offered a small compromise by graciously granting me an incomplete for the semester.

"Provided," he said with a sharp, impatient mouth, "you submit a draft of your new thesis on the first day of the fall term. The *first* day, Mr. Campion, and no later."

In addition to my abysmal grades, I was now nearly broke. Without a roommate to split the expenses, I watched with mounting panic as the funds in my bank account didn't merely dwindle little by little but vanished into a bottomless black hole of bills. I worried that I might even have to sell the car I'd recently purchased, an unreliable clunker with a dirty carburetor and a clean title. My prospects for the immediate future looked bleak. I needed to find a job without delay, and in desperation I applied for a summer position at the Department of Plant Operations, known on campus as the Bloated Tick.

Every semester, in long and detailed letters to the editor of the college newspaper, the professors complained bitterly about the Bloated Tick's employees, who, according to the college handbook, were responsible for "providing students, faculty, and visitors with an aesthetically pleasing and well-maintained environment." Because they feared upsetting "the ticks," the professors never signed their names to these letters and always delivered them to the newspaper office under cover of darkness. Disgruntled ticks were known to seek revenge in ways only service employees can. They could, for instance, start a lawnmower in front of a classroom window just as an important lecture or exam was about to get under way, and if especially "ticked off" they might smear a foul mixture of dog feces and grass clippings on the door handles and windshields of targeted cars in the faculty parking lot.

After their shift ended, the men often lingered outside the garage doors and scoped out the desolate sections of campus, patrolling the streets, peeking in car windows, sniffing out misery and heartbreak. With unsettling intensity they stared at the neo-Georgian buildings that lined the quad, but they never entered the buildings, nor did they speak to the lovely young women or comment on their long legs and ample breasts. In particular they liked the formal dances held in the opulent Town & Gown Ballroom and gawked at the twinkle lights strung across the entrance that formed a dazzling fractal of endlessly repeating arcs and loops. From the wide bed of their pickup truck, they listened to the steady thump and drone of music and observed the fashionable couples sneaking outside to share a cigarette, to take a quick swig from a flask, to steal a breathless moment beneath the elms. The thick and swampy air was a marvel of fabricated sin, and the men laughed at the couples as they lost themselves in the irrationality of love, how their fingers unclasped hooks and fumbled with buttons and zippers. The men waited until the right moment, the supreme moment, and then flew out of the gloom. On those rare occasions when they hadn't drunk themselves blind, the ticks said, "Beg your pardon. Didn't mean to interrupt. Continue what you were doing." But if they were drunk—and usually they were plenty drunk—they invited the startled couples to take a ride down to the river, where the ticks yearned to stuff them headfirst into a tire swing and violate their "sweet virgin asses." With caution the couples stepped away, as if from a pack of snarling coyotes, and hurried back inside.

Worse than their improprieties on campus, the ticks were occasionally accused of stealing prescription medication from the local pharmacy; of crushing pills into a fine powder and snorting long lines on the dashboards of stolen cars; of fighting in the bistro, in the cabaret, in the town square, in emergency rooms where they sought treatment for their broken noses, busted jaws, chipped incisors; of hallucinating on a fierce cocktail of moonshine and formaldehyde; of running wild through the streets and cornering victims, men and women both, in lonely alleyways and pinning them against urine-splattered walls, pawing at their pants, giggling as their victims pleaded for mercy.

Where they went at night—to a government-subsidized apartment complex, a trailer park, a campground, a highway underpass, an abandoned warehouse on the square—the men did not say, but there were whispers around town that they lived on a sailboat illegally tied to a set of crooked pylons below the falls where the wide sweep of river was deep and calm. As darkness shot across the sky they drove their pickup to the valley and took turns ferrying each other out to the vessel on a rowboat. This story struck some townspeople as odd since the ticks, by their own admission, were not men of the water, of the lakes and rivers and streams, but keepers of livestock and reapers of grain, the wayward children of subsistence farmers with only a tangential connection to the modern age, a fatalistic people who would have adopted Stoicism as their one true faith had someone preached it to them from the pulpit. Indigent and unwanted, driven by hunger and poverty from misty knobs and swampy hollows, the men regularly traversed the rutted roads looking for employment, listening for the sound of growling tractors, following the long, strangling coils of yellow dust that unfurled high above the empty plains.

When they arrived in Normandy Falls, they found the sailboat in an abandoned barn in the valley. Concealed under a blue tarpaulin on a trailer, the thirty-foot sloop seemed to be waiting there for them. The boat was in a sorry state, its small, sinister galley and four narrow berths infested with spiders and termites. In the evenings, after snaring a wild turkey near the fens, the men clambered aboard to clean and breast the bird and prepare their meal. The warped and dry-rotted planks of the deck groaned under their feet and threatened to split in two, and all through that summer they tried to restore the boat to its former glory, painting it an exotic crimson color, a festive shade of tropical fruit, pomegranate maybe or red jaina that had been crushed into a paste and slapped unevenly on the boards. Across the transom, in big black script, they stenciled the name *Be Knot Afraid* next to a crude drawing of a mooring rope tied in a bowline; they cut and beveled new boards to replace the ones ripped violently from the gunwale and cockpit; they swapped the old ropes in the snake pit for new cables scavenged from junkyards; they patched the torn jib and mainsail; they worked with such industry and purpose that they started to resemble biblical patriarchs, hunched and bearded and slightly daft, as if trying to stave off an insidious, dictatorial voice that boomed and echoed in their brains.

Life had treated the men unfairly, but now in the lunchroom at the Bloated Tick they began to formulate a plan. Like fugitives who against all conceivable odds have found a way to elude their pursuers, they turned to their supervisor and said, "We'll cruise down the river and out to the lake. We'll sit on the bow, catch walleye and yellow perch and smallmouth bass for supper, gut and clean the fish, toss the fillets in a batter of stale breadcrumbs, grill them over open flames and eat them with a side of sweet corn picked from the fields—wild onions, radishes, carrots. And then we'll wash down this feast with jars of moonshine. Sure, and if we work fast enough we can have her seaworthy for her maiden voyage before the blizzards barricade us indoors this winter. Imagine it. Drifting out there on the open water, why, she'll look just like a ghost ship."

At this inspired piece of nonsense, the Gonk's red-rimmed eyes suddenly widened in disbelief. As the longtime director of the Department of Plant Operations, he'd listened to hundreds of plots and schemes over the years, each one more outrageous than the last, and now at his nefarious crew of drunken maniacs he laughed and said, "I have this theory that you are all brothers bound not by blood but by the same malevolent, nameless spirit. I think you men came into the world all at once, not like a litter of adorable pups, no, more like a twenty-four-armed, twenty-four-legged roving centipede, a thing blind with rage and hunger, eager for the sustenance of a mother's teat. But I know women, pride myself on my knowledge of them, and I contend that any sane mother, after she laid eyes on you twelve, would have put an end to your lives, pinched your noses, clamped a hand over your squalling mouths."

"Well, that ain't such a nice thing to say," the men complained.

"Nope, it isn't nice," agreed the Gonk, "but neither are you. Not very nice at all."

. . .

The ticks were used to tangling with their fellow thieves, stalkers, addicts, anarchists, arsonists, but of all the unsavory characters they'd encountered during their travels it was the Gonk whom they feared and respected most. A clever and forthright man who harbored deep suspicions of colleges large and small, the Gonk despised the professors, with their adherence to social hierarchies and their pathological compulsion for strict, administrative procedures, prompting him to describe the entire system of higher education as an unwieldy Sodom of bureaucracy.

"One big mind fuck," as he succinctly put it.

A native of the valley and its dark forest, the Gonk was the last known descendant of a proud and ancient bloodline destined for extinction. He was also among the last of that great American generation of serious bone breakers—humble laborers who once toiled in the now shuttered mills and factories upriver, bruised and broken-boned brawlers knocking back beers in smoky saloons, slouched and slow-witted reapers of rotten luck staring blankly at the insubstantial specters on their flickering television screens. Now that he'd reached his fifty-first year, with its accompanying phantom pains, creaking knees, inflamed joints, and obligatory backaches, he felt like a brain trapped inside an antiquated machine that was in serious danger of being hauled away and melted down for scrap, and now he feared, because he had no progeny, that his storied family name would drift into obscurity and soon be expunged from the town's collective memory.

On a rainy morning in late May, I met with him in the lunchroom of a low brick building at the edge of campus. The entire interview lasted less than five minutes. I sat in a folding chair at a table that looked like it hadn't been cleaned in weeks, the surface crusted with mustard and ketchup and dusted with cigarette ashes. The Gonk stood in the doorway, a broad-shouldered, swag-bellied figure in denim with welding goggles strapped to his creased forehead. He lit a cigarette and turned his hard gray eyes on me.

"What's that?" He pointed to the book I'd brought along.

Like a grinning idiot, I answered, "You never know when you'll have a little downtime."

The fluorescent light cast a harsh shadow across his face, accentuating the deep and permanent lines of exasperation on his forehead. Without asking permission he snatched *The Odyssey* from my hands and opened it to a dog-eared page. He held it close to his pitted nose and read the words in the same plodding monotone as Professor Kingsley.

"'Cyclops, you ask my honorable name? Remember the gift you promised me, and I shall tell you. My name is Nobody: mother, father, and friends, everyone calls me Nobody.'" The Gonk lifted his leg and farted with impunity. He scratched his leathery neck and tossed the book on the lunchroom table. "Christ almighty, kid, what are they teaching you at this college? Don't they have any practical courses? Accounting? Nursing? Hairdressing? Culinary school?" With his tattooed arms crossed and one foot drumming the floor, he looked me up and down and said, "Okay, Nobody, you're hired. But better not let me catch you reading that shit on the job, or else Nobody is my meat, got it? Consider this your probationary period. I'll be watching you. Watching you real good."

3

The Bloated Tick turned out to be a hideous hive of hourly humiliations and daily indignities, an indestructible organism that sucked the lifeblood from its employees and drained them of energy and ambition, mainly because the men had to attend to those menial but unavoidable tasks that fell upon all plant operations workers at every college and university across the country. Each morning we straggled through the garage doors with our lunch boxes, thermoses, and cigarettes, and for the next eight hours we cleaned and treated the Olympic-sized swimming pool at the recreation center, mowed hundreds of acres of grass, bundled and burned fallen tree limbs and branches, repaired overflowing toilets and examined the dizzying labyrinth of sewers beneath the campus for possible blockages. Eager for a cheap thrill, my coworkers pried open manhole covers and pushed me down rickety ladders. "Always fun to send our new tunnel rat into the pit!" Like everyone else in this world, I'd taken a lot of shit over the years from a lot of different people, but now for the first time in my life I had to decide, in a literal rather than figurative sense, how far into the sewer I was willing to crawl. For these labors I was paid a couple of dollars over the minimum, ditchdiggers' wages, dirt money.

In the summer, as I toiled in the dizzy blaze of heat, trimming shrubs and bushes, pulling weeds, spreading mulch in flowerbeds, planting flats of celosia and marigolds around the stately bell tower, I spied Professor Kingsley walking through campus with Emily Ryan. I didn't know who she was at the time—I would find all of that out soon enough—but I certainly knew Kingsley, knew his sheepish grin, recognized his nervous, shifting eyes, cringed at the sound of his pompous voice, and I could tell even from a distance that he was embarrassed to be seen with Mrs. Ryan. Once, as a kind of academic exercise and as part of the research for my unfinished thesis, I followed them into the art gallery. After all, it's not every day that a student sees his former adviser strolling the quad with an attractive woman. Pretending to search for the nearest drinking fountain, feeling like a part-time student and full-time troll, I stepped inside the lobby and slipped behind a cluster of phony ficus trees, where I observed the professor and Mrs. Ryan wandering through the galleries where there was an exhibition of famous stolen paintings.

"Vermeer. Van Gogh. Picasso. Monet. Gauguin."

Emily struggled to read each placard next to the poorly executed copies of original masterworks, and Kingsley tried to suppress a smug smile of superiority. As an educated man, and one married to an art enthusiast, he knew the power of proper pronunciation, especially in a cultural backwater like Normandy Falls, where a nasally drawl and a healthy dose of double negatives had become status symbols, the means by which someone like Emily could broadcast that she possessed knowledge of a kind for which there were no degrees. To his credit Kingsley knew all about the disruptive effects of an improperly placed editorial intrusion and wisely kept his trap shut.

"*The Storm on the Sea of Galilee* by Rembrandt van Rijn," Emily said with a frown. "This looks so familiar—"

She took a step forward to scrutinize a small fishing boat buffeted by gale-force winds, the bow lifted by a massive swell toward parting black clouds. The panicked crew appealed to a serene passenger and begged him for calm seas and a safe harbor.

One of the girls screamed—it was only a matter of time before Madeline and Sophie began to test their voices for an echo in the open space—and the startled curator politely asked them to leave the gallery. I dashed out the door before Kingsley could spot me, but those crafty ticks had prepared an ambush, and as I galloped down the steps I heard their high-pitched cackles of derision. "Stop ogling the professor's wench!" they shouted. "Yeah, don't play dumb. You know what we're talking about. We've seen you watching her, drooling, fantasizing. Don't deny it."

Giraffeneck, Cockburn, Mudflap, Jittery, Frosty, Monkey, Leper, Sliver—they all crowded around and laughed in my face, dousing me in spittle. At the Department of Plant Services every employee had a nickname, typically an allusion to some calamity that had left its owner physically and psychologically scarred, and though I wasn't entirely certain about the legitimacy of some—Peter, Skip, Ralph, Randy—I could guess the truth about most, and in a vaguely masochistic way I hoped to earn my own nickname, one that like Molière, Voltaire, Twain, Orwell could serve as a clever and timeless nom de plume if I ever managed to finish my novel.

"Can't have a nickname till he initiates you. Has he initiated you yet?" Whenever the men asked this question, as they often did, they slapped their hands on the lunchroom table and convulsed with mad laughter. A few laughed so hard they nearly fell out of their chairs. "No? Well, he's just waiting for the right opportunity, that's all. I wouldn't worry about it. You'll get your new name, sure as shit. You must become one of us, you understand. Because the Gonk doesn't tolerate interlopers in this town."

The Gonk's name alone remained a total mystery to me, and the men, unwilling to give up the secret just yet, were circumspect with their answers when I questioned them.

"Oh, he probably got that name when he was born. The doctor took one look at that face and called him the Gonk."

Some said the name had its roots in sound, in music, in an accidental drumbeat, a stick clattering against an empty can; it reminded the men of the oddball stuff I played on the radio, dissonant, cacophonous, atonal symphonies and string quartets, Bartók, Schönberg, Penderecki, composers who saw the world as a series of bleak, sonic landscapes. Others claimed it wasn't a name at all but a verb, as when, for instance, the men, who were continually running out of cigarettes, gonked a smoke from one another. A few of the ticks wished to gonk the ladies who frequented the bowling alley and demolition derby. Indeed, a number of them *had* gonked these women, sometimes on a regular basis and to no good end, fiery strumpets of Welsh and Irish extraction in late middle age with hard faces, underslung jaws, and huge, dangling breasts. At the Department of Plant Operations the rates of venereal disease had reached epidemic proportions, and it made me wonder why my colleagues bothered with women at all.

"Oh, we're not particular. We like them in all shapes and sizes, but for the Gonk there is one favorite girl. But of course favorites have to fall." They hooted and barked and stomped their boots against the floor. "Moonshine and women, son. One of them is a vice. But it seems the Gonk hasn't figured out which one it is. Most men, when they reach a certain age, buy themselves a dog for companionship. Not the Gonk. Oh, no. Fifty years old and he's still chasing after the pussycats."

They loved this bit of phony folk wisdom and played the redneck card to the hilt, stretching out the word "dog" until it sounded like *daaaawwwg*, landing the *g* with a hard glottal stop.

For weeks they tantalized me with their riddle. Some said the name came from the Gonk's imbecilic mispronunciation of the word "Glock." While a Luddite in most respects, the Gonk was an avid gun enthusiast who owned, in addition to a Civil War musket he proudly displayed on the wall of his new backwoods cottage, a first-generation Glock 17 and a brand-new Glock 36. He had guns for shooting empty beer cans off the crooked fence posts around his property, guns for picking off the rabbits and chipmunks that invaded his yard at night, guns for hunting the twelve-point bucks rutting in the valley, guns for firing into the starry sky at the stroke of midnight on New Year's Eve, guns for a hundred secret purposes. He owned night-vision goggles and exploding bullets and glimmering bayonets. He was a veritable one-man arsenal well prepared for the long overdue revolution and the apocalypse that would follow soon after.

Besides firearms, the Gonk had taken a keen interest in the solitary pleasures of studying genealogies and reading histories of the town, and though he disliked the idea of disclosing personal information, he applied for a library card at the college and ordered stacks of books. Sometimes he requested mystery novels and studied their plots, which like the streets of town were straight, perpendicular, Euclidean in their logic and predictability, cobbled together with prefabricated blocks of prose, a black-and-white world that was precisely structured, carefully framed, and inhabited by characters as flat as the surrounding country-side. In those stories death was a farce, an amusing way to pass the time, but the Gonk, who was building something grandiose and dangerous in his mind, read these novels the same way he might read books on carpentry and electrical wiring—with a craftsman's keen eye for detail and with the implicit understanding that he was bound to run into unexpected problems somewhere down the road.

He persisted with this enterprise because he understood the meaning and consequences of failure and because he didn't want the whole town to think him entirely strange or crazy or just plain stupid, though in truth they thought all of those things and things far worse. The professors, whenever they saw him browsing the shelves in the college library, secured their wallets and purses, worried that his conniving coworkers might be lurking nearby. They needn't have worried. The men of the Bloated Tick had no use for books. Many of them were functionally illiterate and signed their names with pentacles and hexagrams and occult crosses meant to signify their belief in the world's end.

"One thing's for sure," they told me. "The Gonk bought that cottage in the woods for a reason. And he reads them books for a reason, too."

But what this reason may have been the men did not know and would not hazard to guess, nor did they attempt to interpret the strange things he mumbled as he drew up his plans. They simply accepted the fact that they would never know anything more than what the Gonk wanted them to know.

During that interminable summer the ticks butchered and burned the grass, cutting it too short and spilling big bags of fertilizer on the quad so the campus resembled a barren wasteland with an occasional oasis of dogwoods and sycamores instead of cactuses and tumbleweeds. The Gonk did not always pardon their brainless behavior, but in his more generous moods, whenever he had the rare desire for camaraderie, he invited the men back to the cottage to play poker at a makeshift table of particleboard and sawhorses and to sample the moonshine he made in the antiquated still that hissed and rumbled in the stone cellar.

The still came with the cottage, part of the deal when he purchased the place from Colette Collins. In his estimation the old woman was an indisputable genius and the still her bona fide masterpiece. Sequestered for decades in that vaulted cave, scrupulously avoiding contact with humanity, never seeking recognition, waiting for the black hour of death to arrive, Colette Collins built the enormous still from durable pieces of fine copper and pliable tin. Using only a clawhammer and tongs and her prescient inner eye, she moved nimbly around the still and crafted a series of well-wrought scenes on the boiler walls. Below the vapor cone, circling the uppermost portion of the still like an elaborate garland, she fashioned a deep shaded valley, a powerful girdling river, a vast churning lake, a lonesome village and its unruly multitude. There was a funeral and an epic conflagration and a sailboat tossed asunder by heavy seas. On one side of the boiler a young woman hid in the hayloft of an abandoned barn; on another an immense ship awaited rescue, its mighty hull trapped in a frozen lake under a sky crowded with constellations.

"The boneyard comes with the cottage, too," said the old woman.

It was a warm day in early June when she handed over the keys, the sky an intense and burning blue, and she gazed wistfully at the crumbling monuments in the adjacent cemetery. Despite the decayed grandeur of her exterior, Colette Collins seemed as old-school tough as the Gonk.

"There isn't much in the way of maintenance, if that worries you," she said. "Mow the grass before it gets completely out of hand and spray the weeds. Put the headstones back in place whenever a storm blows through the valley or if a pack of those frat boys comes loping down the road late at night. They always scatter after I fire a warning shot from my Winchester, but I find I can't keep up with their nonsense anymore."

Between small sips of grain alcohol from a mason jar and two quick drags on a cigarette already reduced to a wobbling pillar of ash, she assured the Gonk he had no obligation to provide guided tours should anyone show up unannounced, not that he would have to worry too much about unexpected visitors since the covered bridge spanning the river had been washed away in a flash flood in spring so now there was no direct connection with the main highway except the narrow road that snaked through woods and fields until it reached the cottage of unmortared stone sitting atop a low hill silent and inviolable like an ancient oracle awaiting a wizened seer to read the signs and make grim pronouncements.

"In the fall," she said, her voice occasionally cracking from infrequent use, "a few graduate students may come along and try to decipher the engravings on the headstones. I like to think they feel obligated to check on the eccentric octogenarian living alone in the woods, what with all the squalid meth labs dotting these hills and the desperate junkies willing to murder you for a dollar, but mainly I think they come to purchase my shine and hear a few of my crazy stories." She tapped the jar with a crooked index finger and winked. "Ah, looks like you could stand for another taste of the creature yourself."

The Gonk, who had a fondness for homemade potions, accepted her offer; it made him weak in the knees, hot and sinewy and cathartic beyond all reason, like sex after many months of celibacy, something he knew a bit about, especially after his wife left him for his nemesis at the bistro and didn't bother to send him the terms of the divorce until several weeks later, only after she made certain the uninhibited sucking and fucking had a real shot at long-term success. In the months that followed, he conditioned himself through rigorous practice and discipline to abstain from any activity that might compromise his goal, but now he allowed himself a celebratory drink or two.

Dismissing the whole notion of abstinence with a knowing smile and a wave of her hand, the old woman proclaimed, "Sobriety is a myth. We all live at various levels of intoxication." From a glass pitcher she kept close by, she poured him a tall drink, and they clinked their jars together like two old friends. "I learned it's easier to give up a mate than it is to give up the bottle. For nearly forty years I lived in this valley, sometimes with a husband, more often not. I lured them here, you might say, to the undertaker's old cottage because the asylum seemed too romantic. I'd reached my breaking point in the city, you see. Everyone has a breaking point, I believe that, but I reached mine sooner than most. Unfortunately, my ex-husbands didn't take to the valley."

The Gonk looked at the wrinkled flesh of her small, animated hands and the long spirals of gray hair protruding from under her straw hat, and suddenly he wished this whispery husk of a woman, with her flair for psychotropic pedagogics, taught a class or two at the college. On those rare occasions when loneliness got the better of her and she didn't have the heart to putter around the headstones, she visited the college to deliver guest lectures to undergraduates. Unused to her odd way of speaking in grammatically correct sentences, the students grew restless and fidgeted at their desks. She hardly noticed. While standing at the podium, she sipped her moonshine and smoked her cigarettes, a bent and shriveled elf from a forest that had forfeited its sundry enchantments for the false promises of progress—a country road that served no purpose other than to bury the vegetation under miles of crushed gravel; a hideous tangle of power lines that cut through the canopy of hardwood trees—and with eyes sharpened by decades of living hand to mouth, she told her unenthusiastic audience, "I used to get drunk on art, you understand, but over the years I built up a tolerance to it. These days I find that I need something a wee bit stronger."

Instead of fleeing to New York or Paris, what she called "the centers of cultural confinement," Colette Collins chose to remain in Normandy Falls, where for most of her career she lived in the humble cottage. She chose the cottage not for its seclusion and scenic beauty but for its proximity to the ancient cemetery. Every morning, before the sun funneled into the valley, she rose from her bed and stood at her window, where, as if searching for a way to alleviate the burden of her genius, she surveyed the headstones and contemplated the ephemeral nature of existence. In this way her home became a kind of memento mori, an around-the-clock meditation and constant reminder that fame and fortune were as fleeting as the phantoms that, for a few brief hours in the night, floated freely among the monuments. For this reason a few excoriating critics dared to assert that she bore an uncanny resemblance to a medium at a séance, summoning spirits from the ether, a two-bit charlatan exploiting her gifts at some silly spook session for a bunch of gullible fools holding hands around a table.

Completely at ease among the gravestone slabs, she rested an elbow against the porch railing and said to the Gonk, "One of those instructors at the college, oh, what's her name? I'm having another senior moment." Her arms were like winter branches, and the wind snatched the cigarette from her fingers. "Marianne Kingsley! She's planning a retrospective of my work on New Year's Eve, a modest exhibition for a nearly forgotten sculptor who spent more than four decades hiding in a tiny tinderbox in the woods. People ask why I no longer pursue fellowships and awards, and I tell them I don't want my tombstone to read: 'She was always scrounging for money.' But deep down I'm as venally vain as the next sculptor or painter or pornographer, and this retrospective will serve as the epitaph to my career. I'll never enjoy another exhibition at a prestigious gallery. No, a farcical French bistro on the square in Normandy Falls, that's my last stand before my work is destined for the cultural trash heap. Takes courage to admit that." She shrugged. "I'm told you have artistic ambitions. Even taking a couple of classes at the college."

He shook his head. "I'm an amateur. Art is just a hobby. I do a little carpentry, too, but mostly I work with steel. Helps take my mind off things."

Her smile became a disapproving frown. "My good man, art isn't a pastime, it's an ordeal, and it's apt to make your suffering a whole lot worse, intolerable even. Watch yourself. The human heart is an inexhaustible fountain of creativity, and those who drink from it have been known to develop a very dangerous addiction, one that all too often proves to be incurable, irreversible, and final."

Not even noon, and already she was making a rambling speech, slurring her words, disguising her gaseous eruptions with a hacking cough, but the Gonk was in neither the habit nor the position of judging someone as accomplished and highly lauded as the great Colette Collins, a sculptor long retired from the world of art and now living in obscurity. In her prime she had been the recipient of several prestigious grants and high-profile commissions, the town's first hippie before anyone even knew what hippies were, but with the steady decline of her health, and some might argue her creative capacities, she made fewer public appearances and preferred to spend her days, what days were left to her, in almost total seclusion, drinking herself toward the sweet oblivion of a midafternoon nap.

"I'm not holding my breath, but I hope the college will hire a preservationist to fix up these headstones and do a little excavating. That's the sort of thing that excites them, fixing up graveyards. They wouldn't have an interest in this house, of course. It's petty and hypocritical, I realize, to think the college might raise a few dollars to put a small plaque beside the door, but I ask you, sir"—with difficulty she raised her bamboo cane and indicated an immense sandstone obelisk, cracked and jigsawed together, near a row of gargantuan white oaks—"what purpose does *that* hideous thing serve? I never dishonored the memory of my three husbands with anything so ostentatious. You can hardly make out the infamous name carved on that appalling edifice. I'll wager you're the only man in town who knows the poor fellow planted beneath that rock pile, am I right? The only descendant to return to this human wilderness, this moronic inferno to pay his respects?"

She swallowed the dregs from her mason jar, this time gasping at its searing heat, and all at once the thin film of intoxication that clouded her eyes seemed to vanish. The pale blue irises flashed with spinster eccentricity and artistic torment. As if reading his thoughts, she smiled and said, "Experience has taught me that God is quick to forgive crimes and slow to punish them. And sometimes He forgets to punish crimes at all. Oh, yes, I do believe the moonshine still will come in handy one day. One day very soon . . ."

The valley was even more isolated than the Gonk had anticipated, and for days at a time he saw not a soul. With no shopping plazas, no restaurants, no movie theaters, no friendly neighbors to happen down the dusty road curious to find out why he'd been banished to this lonely corner of creation, he learned, or at least forced himself to endure, the troublesome solitude of the place. To make everything official in his own mind, he painted his last name in bold Gothic script above the solid brass mail slot.

On the weekends he routinely worked in the dank cellar, building an unusually wide box made from the wood of a birch tree he felled in the forest, and in the hot summer afternoons he went to the cemetery, where he mowed the grass in a precise diagonal pattern, giving it the manicured look of a professional baseball diamond. Around the wrought-iron fence, he planted hostas and azaleas and decorative rosebushes and spent an inordinate amount of time pulling weeds. By leafing through the brittle pages of a book Colette Collins left on a shelf, he was able to identify several species of crabgrass, nut sedge, and common ragweed, the scientific name for which was *Ambrosia artemisiifolia*, a notion he might have found laughable if only he'd read Homer. Who could imagine the gods deserting the battlefield outside the walls of Troy to loll in the soft comforts of Olympus and enjoy the ambrosia that grew in a place like this, a remote valley where, for two centuries, disturbed men and women voluntarily exiled themselves for fear of what they might do back in the towns and cities?

The oldest graves dated from the early 1800s, though now there wasn't enough bone meal to appease the voracious appetites of the immortals. Even the white oaks looked famished, judging from their stunted and contorted trunks. With infinite patience and single-minded purpose, the roots searched the graveyard for nourishment, exploring every crypt and casket, coiling around every calcified femur and skull. In many places the roots were so dense that the Gonk had trouble digging the new hole, and he wondered how the homesteaders managed to clear away the heavy timber with their simple saws and felling axes. According to the headstones, some of the men buried here fought in the War of 1812 and then, with wives and children in tow, made the dangerous and grueling journey into the wilderness to conquer the land and its primitive inhabitants.

Insects scuttled over the upturned soil and burrowed into the earth, and all at once the Gonk understood that every living creature, no matter how insignificant, interacted in ways that could only be described as harmonious, so much so that to think of them as separate organisms was an illusion; they were all one and the same, a single entity, a family, indissoluble and complete, each with its own unique function, but all working together toward a fate unknown and irreversible.

Had it not been for the saving grace of old routines, the Gonk by that summer's end might have turned into a foul and filthy hermit, doomed to fitful fantasies and drunken rumination, but he was tough-minded, disciplined, and had little respect for those who daydreamed and harbored superstitions. Each weekday morning, bright and early, he arrived at the Bloated Tick and in a strong, clear voice rattled off a long list of commands from a clipboard stuffed with work orders. He then proceeded to scoff at the men for beatifying the storms and other natural prodigies, for always reaching into their pockets and clinging to cheap amulets purchased from self-proclaimed witches and necromancers. Evidently, there was something about Normandy Falls that troubled them. Worried that their crystals and coins and silver-mounted rabbit's feet held insufficient power to drive away evil spirits and bad luck, they started to build makeshift altars around the garage.

At first I made the mistake of dismissing the ticks as run-of-the-mill religious crackpots and ideologues, uneducated men whose convictions consisted of a patchwork of inconsistent creeds, a riotous Babel of disparate and ultimately irreconcilable Christian doctrines—Baptist, Pentecostal, Branch Davidian—and I envisioned them sitting on fold-out chairs in the unbearably humid evenings, eating fresh bell peppers and beefsteak tomatoes scavenged from gardens and listening to the hypnotic cadences of televangelists who preached fiery sermons about the abominations of modernity, buggery, godless city slickers, and the sinister teachings of radical college professors who relished the opportunity to indoctrinate classrooms crowded with credulous communists in training. But it soon became clear to me that these men believed in the illimitable forces of Nature and the dominion of eternal darkness to hold sway over all things. Their personal savior, if they had one, was a nameless, faceless power that could only be appeased through ritual blood sacrifice, a notion that made little sense to a wayward Catholic schoolboy whose idea of a messiah was a gentle soul who would lead me safely to the healing waters of self-acceptance and there allow me to drink my fill.

I often bore witness to their peculiar form of worship. After an especially powerful storm ripped through the county, the men awaited the return not of sunshine and blue skies but of a deluge of apocalyptic proportions, the river rising above its shifting banks and sweeping them all away to the lake, and they felt an urgent need to appease their jealous and temperamental god, who kept a wary eye on them and who yearned to drown them one by one, slowly and with pleasure, for daring to transgress his innumerable and wickedly contradictory laws, pages and pages of arcane rules and regulations that proved impossible to memorize.

Inside the garage, high in the rafters, there lived an avatar of their redoubtable god, a white-breasted barn owl that hunted for prey in silent flight. At lunchtime and during their breaks, the men stomped across the cement floor and captured field mice, maiming and placing them inside the makeshift altar of a shoebox and offering them to the owl. They believed these humble propitiations, like a burnt offering from pagan days, would mollify this capricious deity, who might spare them from some future cataclysm. The mice, failing to understand the importance of their role in this scheme, tried to evade capture, squealing with fear and seeking out dark corners, but the men shook their heads and laughed as they twisted each tiny leg. Unlike human beings, mice had yet to learn that it was sometimes best to resign oneself to one's fate.

4

I met with my own disastrous fate on a Friday in late August when out of pure desperation I dared to trespass upon the Gonk's phantasmagorically peculiar lair. During the afternoon, when he should have been sorting through stacks of paperwork or managing his crew of incompetent groundskeepers, the Gonk stood behind an orange tarp in the back of the building where he wasted many productive hours perfecting a perfectly useless craft. For him this was serious business, and the men took it as a bad sign if he had cause to leave his workstation.

I'd been searching for a secluded spot where for one hour I could read *The Odyssey* in peace, and though I tried my best to tune out the laryngitic coughs and tympanic farts of my fellow ticks, I found it impossible to concentrate for very long on Homer's epic verse in the sweltering, fly-infested lunchroom. Sitting beside them at the table, I felt like I was chained in the cargo hold of a prison ship bound for a remote penal colony, an icy, windswept gulag where the use of one's brain was punishable by flogging and maiming. It seemed only a matter of time before one of the men pointed a knife at me and shouted, "Out with his eyes!" This was a thought that played over and over again like an evil memory, and I was convinced that in the end I would die in Normandy Falls, not from an act of random violence but from sheer boredom. Maybe that's why the men used so many illegal substances— to hasten the process of death and thus unburden themselves of another day's dull work.

All of this was distracting enough, but now the ticks crowded around a small transistor radio, and after fiddling with the dials and making several small adjustments to the antenna, they listened with unusual interest to a local talk show in which contestants phoned in to answer trivia. They silenced me when I asked them to turn down the volume, but when an ad came on they could hardly contain their excitement.

"Every year one lucky caller wins an all-expenses-paid trip to the Caribbean. The islanders speak French and say a man can find a *maison close* on the beach where he can pay a *fille de joie* to do the things he's too ashamed to ask a normal woman to do. Yeah, the women on Delacroix Cay are martyrs for love and will gladly service your lust, nothing at all like those prima donnas who dance at Little Morty's joint. It's true. We sent away for the brochures and read about it. We'll never win the contest, but one day we'll sail to Delacroix Cay on our boat." There was a general murmur of excitement, and then the men said, "Hey, kid, you've got some learning. Maybe you should try your luck. You gotta stop jerking it eventually and find yourself a new woman. Hey, where you going? The show's about to come back on. What, the thought of the professor's wench driving you bananas? Gotta go beat your meat again?"

With my heavily underscored copy of *The Odyssey* stuffed in my pocket, I stormed from the lunchroom and hurried into the shadows at the back of the building, but the moment I saw the Gonk I forgot about those dullards and their juvenile insults. Surrounded by long shafts of summer sunlight that filtered through a blue checkerboard of steel windows, the Gonk stood before a workbench, looking for all the world like a deranged holy man about to make some vast pronouncement. He ignited a blowtorch with a striker, he smoked cigarettes under his welding hood, he adjusted his balls with a chipping hammer, he uttered strange and blasphemous oaths under his breath, and the things he summoned forth from his disordered imagination beggared description.

With great concentration he slowly cut elaborate fish from long sheets of scrap metal—rainbow trout, smallmouth bass, yellow perch, and monstrous sea lampreys rumored to inhabit the foaming brown waters of the river and lake. After cutting three or four new fish, he brushed away a small pyramid of metal shavings and then clamped them one by one to several vices, where he prepared to chip away the slag and smooth the rough edges with a grinder.

Dozens of these miniature masterpieces already dangled from the ceiling by long wires, and when a current of warm air came through the open window, the fish began to spin and clatter against each other like wind chimes, their meticulously painted fins and scales transforming the colorless room into a riveting kaleidoscope of pink and purple light. There were small and startlingly realistic ones, large and curiously stylized ones, but there were other, less familiar specimens as well, cruelly shaped things that may have washed up in the fecal mire and interstitial wastes along the river, web-footed, membranous monsters of inconceivable ugliness. They were not vampire fish or anglerfish or blobfish or snakeheads or crooked-toothed goblin sharks, and as they floated freely and without consequence in the smoky air, they gonged weirdly and gave off a gangrenous and chlorotic glare.

In an era when so many part-time artists continually jockeyed with one another for gallery space to showcase their insipid, politically correct, paint-by-numbers artwork, shamelessly arguing for its profound cultural and social significance, I knew without question that the Gonk possessed serious talent. I wanted to applaud his vitality of style, and since the devil can cite scripture for his purpose I said, "I see the fishes but where are the loaves?"

No sooner had I spoken these imprudent words than an explosion of pain ripped through my skull, and though I cannot say for certain what happened next, I do remember how the metal head of the blowtorch, still blazing with blue jets of fire, hurtled through the air like a viper. In a bright flash and brutal burst of color, I tumbled into the hot slag and red embers, clutching my face and screaming, "I'm blind! I'm *blind*!"

The Gonk flung his goggles to the floor and through barred teeth said, "Christ almighty. Can't swing a dead cat in this place without hitting an asshole." He dragged me to the first-aid station and flushed my eye with cold water and saline solution. "Aw, quit your bellyaching, would you? You're okay. Calm your ass down. Didn't they teach you etiquette at school? You don't creep up on a man that way."

"Injury report . . . ," I said between inconsolable whimpers.

With the firmness of a pair of channel locks, the Gonk squeezed my head in his hands. "You wouldn't do that, would you? File a report?"

"Well, I'm not sure. Maybe I should—"

"A scratched cornea is all. Here, wear this for twenty-four hours and you'll be good as new. Hell, with a shiner like that you're practically a full-fledged member of the gang. Might as well finish your initiation, right?"

I didn't like his elusive, mocking smile or the sound of his harsh and broken voice. I just wanted to return to the row house, collapse on my futon, and forget that this accident had ever happened, that I'd ever worked for this wild man.

"You've been here all summer," he said, "and I haven't invited you to the cottage for a drink. That means you haven't been properly initiated. Seems like a terrible oversight, doesn't it? Unconscionable. I think that's the word."

Because I couldn't bear the idea of the other men ridiculing me, I nodded and against my better judgment followed the Gonk into the furnace light of a late August afternoon. He hoisted me into the wide bed of his truck and handed me my copy of *The Odyssey*, and even though I was beginning to doubt the great books could save me, or anyone else, from a world so full of menace and peril, I clutched it to my chest like a talisman.

"Where are we going?" I asked. The words echoed strangely inside my skull.

"Aw, just for a little ride, is all." He started buttoning the mud-encrusted tarp over my head, and just before everything went totally black, he said, "Hey, kid, I just thought of a new name for you . . ."

A lance of burning sunlight punctured hundreds of tiny holes in the vinyl tarp under which, in the textured haze and stifling heat, I lay trapped and struggling to breathe. Abducted by alien gods who yearned to see me suffer, I moaned with the self-pity that so often comes to those whose blind faith has been smashed to pieces by reality, and I found it impossible to focus on anything other than my own survival. Desperate to see where we were going, I adjusted my new eye patch, and by pressing my face close to the tarp I could make out an impressionistic blur of woods so deep and dark that, even on this bright afternoon, the light looked green and tarnished.

The Gonk's pickup jounced downhill and abruptly fishtailed, and like a blue-collar version of Dorothy wishing for a safe return to Kansas, I slid along the eight-foot bed toward the rattling tailgate, the heels of my steel-toed boots clicking together three times. Above the revving engine and the din of gravel churning beneath the heavy-duty tires, I heard grunts of approval from the Gonk. He stomped on the accelerator, jerked the wheel hard to the left, and for one breathless moment the truck was airborne. As if under the spell of a sinister sorcerer, I levitated briefly above the bed and then, just as suddenly, came crashing down with a loud thud.

Something stabbed the small of my back, and in a panic I searched for the offending object. A jagged piece of steel, fashioned to look like the dorsal fin of a freakishly large freshwater fish, had sliced through my flannel shirt, drawing blood. When my eye adjusted to the darkness, I realized to my horror that the truck was littered with dozens of these ferocious, sharp-toothed piranhas. They clattered against the stamped-metal bed like a demented Friday-night fish fry in reverse, where the entrée was eager to leap from the platter and feast on the flabby flesh of the gluttonous diners. It then occurred to me that I was trapped not in the back of an ordinary pickup but in a surreal country bumpkin art gallery and that the fish were in fact the Gonk's lunatic contribution to the world of high culture.

To a certain degree every work of art had a claustrophobic effect on me. The most accomplished artists possessed an uncanny ability to lock me in their own personal prisons and torture chambers, and some works of art, if they were very good indeed, never relinquished their hold on me, not entirely, and as I tumbled across the bed, I believed the Gonk had taken the art of claustrophobia to the next level.

Now here they came, a whole school of metallic mackerel swimming through swift currents of open highway and darting along silent streams of lonely, gravel road. As the pickup slowed and trundled up a long driveway, I rubbed my good eye and through the small holes in the tarp saw the peak of a mossy roof and the crumbling stone chimney of an ancient cottage partly concealed from the road by a grove of white oaks, their knobby trunks infested with burrowing bugs. The windows of the cottage were cracked, the lopsided wooden shutters stripped of paint and starting to warp. Piled high next to the front door were plastic bags bursting with garbage that attracted a shimmering cloud of fierce flies, and surrounding the porch were dead yellow shrubs that served as a communal toilet. From under the tarp I caught the sulfurous stench of piss.

The truck came to an abrupt stop.

"Just sit tight," he said, "and nurse your wounds while I grab a little contraband. Be out in a flash."

I massaged the back of my head, and when I felt sure the Gonk had disappeared inside the cottage, I decided it was time to make my escape. For leverage I pressed my back against the wheel well and thrust both legs against the tailgate, kicking and stomping until my face turned bright red, but the thing wouldn't budge. I rested a moment, panting from exhaustion, then thought of a better idea. Using one of the steel fish, I began to saw at the tarp, but before I could make significant progress I heard heavy footsteps plodding toward me.

Through the small slit I'd made, I saw a mosquito land on a sun-freckled forearm and suck greedily at angry scar tissue. In one swift motion the Gonk flattened the bug and wiped the dark blood imprinted on his palm across the back of his jeans. A wad of tobacco exploded from his ruddy cheeks, and the juice dribbled darkly down his scruffy chin and through the thick stubble on his neck like a diseased river meandering through a forest of tree stumps. When he spoke, his words were slow and soft, a voice that seemed to ooze under the tarp and trickle like warm mud into my ear.

"Around these parts the bugs can sometimes get as big as sparrows. Damn annoying, too. Know anything about that, Cyclops? About pests? Parasites?" Stepping away from the bed, he twisted open a jar and swallowed the contents, and I saw the alarming way his Neolithic brow ridge contorted and how his close-set eyes came suddenly to life and glimmered like a pair of bayonets. "God*damn* is that fine. Might be the best batch all summer. Now listen up, Cyclops. You better settle down or I'll have to give you one hell of an ass whooping. Save your energy. Gotta be pretty hot under there. But try not to worry yourself about it too much. Your initiation will come to an end. Of course, I can't say for certain when that will be. Haven't given it a whole lot of thought, not exactly. All depends on how well you behave."

"Excuse me, sir," I rasped, "but I'm not sure I understand the purpose of this . . . initiation."

"Everybody who works for me must be initiated. And remember, if you don't cause any more trouble you can be my guest tonight at the Normandy Cabaret. Haven't been there yet, have you? Sure as hell beats the adventures you've been reading about in that book of yours. Damn if there ain't a catfish there that can swallow a baby's leg."

This remark brought on a bout of laughter, and the laughter turned into an inevitable coughing fit so loud and wet that the truck seemed to rattle with phlegm. "A monster fish with a powerful bite," the Gonk managed to say with a loud gasp. "Her blood is pure, like my own, but I'm worried she doesn't have a taste for rednecks. Well, let's see what happens when I test her matronly instincts. I'll use you as bait, try to lure her outside. I suspect she'll have some sympathy for a cute college boy. Oh, you're gonna like her, too, Cyclops. You won't believe your eyes. I mean, your *eye*." Another explosion of wet laughter, another coughing fit, and then the Gonk swung his enormous frame into the cab, stones flying from his long and leaping shadow.

An expert at rolling dozens of plant species, tobacco, cannabis, *Zornia latifolia*, he had a fresh cigarette ready in no time, funky smelling, exceptionally slow burning, and for the rest of the afternoon he raced up and down a dirt road that twisted through the valley, the molten sunlight softened by swirling pillars of saffron-colored dust. He listened to the hiss and static of a ball game on the radio, nursed his jar of moonshine, and when nature called he pulled over to sprinkle the wilting goldenrod that grew in a ditch.

Feeling like a despised child unable to escape the wrath of his abusive parents, I tucked my legs beneath my chin and fought back tears. By clamping shut my right eye, I could at least pretend that the peals of drunken laughter and the clangor of steel fish would not hurt me. I could also console myself with the dim hope that this awful initiation was almost over, and soon I, too, would be an official member of the Bloated Tick.

Hours later, just before nightfall, I felt the steady thump of distant jungle drums dancing up and down my aching spine, a delirious tropical rhythm, a cannibal chant summoning me back to the land of the living, and though I wanted badly to vanish again into the sweet oblivion of unconsciousness, I forced myself to crack open my good eye and investigate the music's source. Above me, just out of reach, enormous fireflies floated through the purple twilight like corkscrewing constellations, and I tried unsuccessfully to decipher in their ever-changing patterns a hidden meaning and purpose. With some effort I managed to sit up, and it took me a few minutes to realize that the tarp had been rolled away from the bed and that I was now bathed in the sultry evening air. I must have been out cold, though for how long I could not say.

Mad with thirst, desperate for even a single drop of water, I half climbed, half fell out of the bed. My knees buckled as I hit the ground, and I almost collapsed. Clinging to the side of the truck, I gathered what was left of my strength and took a few tentative steps toward the cab, willing my boots to move one at a time. When I finally dared to lift my head, I was startled to find that I was standing not in front of the Gonk's stone cottage but in the middle of a gravel lot. Dozens of cars and pickups were parked behind a tall barbed wire fence—freshly waxed foreign sedans and muddy 4x4s and rusty station wagons long overdue for the demolition derby, their cracked windshields reflecting the garish pink light of a marquee above the town's main drag.

After adjusting my eye patch, I searched the cab for the keys, determined to tear out of there and teach the Gonk a lesson of my own. Instead, I found a few empty mason jars on the seat and dozens of rolling papers scattered on the floor. Not far from the truck stood the old movie palace, a squat two-story structure of soot-covered bricks that might have been a showplace in the days when two-reel, silent comedies were all the rage. Though the building was a mere fifty yards away, to me it might as well have been a mile, and I wasn't sure if I would make it to the entrance without falling down and dry heaving.

At the door of the cabaret, a man in a wine-colored sport coat and black bow tie greeted me with amusement and concern. He pawed at his shaved head with a giant hand weighed down by a half-dozen gold rings. "Good evening, sir. Is everything all right?"

I nodded and reached for the door handle.

"Beg your pardon, sir. Just a moment. This is a private club. If you plan to see tonight's entertainment you must purchase a one-day guest pass. Unless you're a college student. Are you a college student?"

The man belonged inside the gates of a steel mill, crawling inside a boiler tank, not working the door of a small-town cabaret and trying to pass himself off as a sophisticated British butler. He bounced from one foot to the other, drummed his fingers against his legs, scratched his ass. His clothes made the charade all the more obvious and absurd. His cheap dinner jacket was too tight in the shoulders and too short in the arms, his wrinkled black trousers were too long in the legs, his shoes were scuffed and unlaced and sprinkled with mud. At five feet six, he was small of stature but solidly built, a fireplug of a man without a discernible neck, just a head like a granite block resting atop an equally square and thickly muscled torso, a rough-hewn pillar, an immovable, prehistoric monument, a miniature Stonehenge of stability and toughness. His shaved head revealed the jagged scars of his pugnacious past. No doubt the scars worked to his advantage at a place like this.

"Sir, may I make a bold suggestion? For fifty dollars you can purchase a G.O.N.C. card. It's good for a full year."

"A what?"

He pointed to the marquee. He must have thought I was crazy or dimwitted or both, and at that moment maybe my sanity *had* slipped just a bit, my mind inching closer to the precipice. As I wobbled on my heels outside the door, with that deep bass thrumming in my ears and the neon light dousing me in the hues of a smutty inferno, I repeated with wonderment and dread that peculiar word on the marquee like some salacious epithet, as if by doing so I could turn a blind eye to the terrible fact that a great mystery had been solved only to be replaced by the aggravating mundanity of existence.

G.O.N.C.

Gentlemen of Normandy College
For just $50 you can enjoy all the privileges of preferred membership
Ask for details at the door

I showed the man my expired college ID and absently handed him cash. "Gonc," I whispered, "Gonc, Gonc . . ."

Through a tragedy of chipped and tarnished teeth, the doorman said, "Sir, are you sure you're okay? What the hell happened to your eye? Someone skull-fuck you? Oh, the crime rate in this damned town. Listen, if you need any assistance just ask for me, Little Morty."

Taking long and reckless strides down a dimly lit corridor, I careened into a red velvet curtain that opened to a vast, smoke-filled room where a dozen aging G.O.N.C.s concentrated on a mirrored catwalk that jutted like a magnificent, crystal harpoon into the center of the club. The locker-room stench of perspiring men and the boudoir odors of painted and powered harlots slithered through the room, and somewhere in the shadows the Gonk sat at his regular table, enjoying a legal drink and waiting for the show to begin.

Running my tongue over leathery lips, I lowered my head and hurried to the bar at the back of the cabaret, where I ordered a tall glass of ice water, but before I could take that gratifying first sip the music stopped and the room went suddenly dark. From out of the toxic cloud of sweaty flesh, I heard a hushed murmur, a whistle, a familiar cackle. Caught in the collective grip of sexual hysteria, suffering from the contagion of lust, the men leaned forward in their chairs, a strange tableau of sinister faces, their mouths twisted with a freakish fantasy, a dangerous desire, their anticipation bordering on torment. In every direction

I turned, I saw a sick genetic stew of unknown origin about to burst its dam and inundate the world, and within seconds the shouts and screams had reached a maddening crescendo. The place had become a tinderbox full of misdemeanors, and all it would take to light the fuse and turn it into a pandemonium of fistfights and squad cars was one soused and stinking working-class stiff stupid enough to storm the stage and slobber over a dancer. I considered searching for an emergency exit but was startled by a voice that spoke to us from the loudspeakers.

"Gentlemen, please turn your attention to the main stage and give a warm welcome to tonight's featured performer—the Lorelei!"

Enthusiastic applause, whistles, anguished howls of longing. A beam of indigo light penetrated a cloud of dry ice rising like a mist from the floor and found in the middle of the catwalk the svelte figure of a young woman, by far the most curvaceous of the cabaret's underequipped dancers, an unusually nubile nymph uprooted from some ethnic slum and one that added much-needed novelty to this menagerie of rather commonplace, workaday girls. The music started up again, a low-down dirty blues, and the woman, naked except for a G-string, a garter on her left thigh, and a pair of black stilettos strapped to her feet, began her routine. With her sinewy limbs wrapped tightly around a pole, she did not dance or swing but seemed rather to float on the rippling waves of light, graceful as the fish tattooed to her wrists and arms and shoulders. The intricate creatures, both vivid and dreamlike, appeared to pass right through the woman's body as though she were an apparition, a puff of smoke, a mirage. This was no ordinary woman. By her caustic smile I could tell this was a *bad* woman, a sensationally *wicked* woman, positively villainous, a filthy phantasm, and the longer I sat and watched her, the more I became convinced that she wasn't an erotic dancer at all but an evil magician, and I hoped she wouldn't pause in her act to call on me—"I need a volunteer from the audience to assist me with my next trick"—because at that point no magician in the world had the power to make that irksome and capricious magic wand between my legs vanish into thin air.

For thirty minutes I gazed into the violet light of this erotic aquarium and watched with almost scientific interest as Lorelei's fish swam around the shining brass pole, swift as a school of mackerel in the deepest sea, slow as whiskered catfish in a lazy river. Some of the men bounded toward the stage, drawn to her gratuitous beauty, the extravagance of her bare flesh, and they competed with one another to stuff crisp dollar bills into her swelling garter only to be beaten back by the doorman. The woman made no effort to disguise her cupidity. Even her eyes were a greedy green, the color of cold, hard cash.

After taking in this sad spectacle, I motioned to the bartender. Although I much preferred hallucinogens to alcohol, I decided, like any good working stiff, to order multiple mugs of flat beer until I approached that state of bliss commonly known as the blackout, my way of coming to terms with my decision to quit college once and for all and embrace my new identity. Instead of another obnoxious, mollycoddled college kid who came looking for a summer job, I saw myself working indefinitely at the Bloated Tick, gradually turning into a middle-aged grunt with creaking knees and thinning hair. I often wondered how my coworkers coped with the prospect of having to do hard physical labor for the rest of their lives, but they didn't seem to worry much about the future or about the consequences of their actions. They behaved as though they'd never known punishment or guilt or abject poverty, and I saw great power in this.

I gulped my beer and with each new round belched in exultation, but after the fifth foamy mug, when my vision started to blur and my chin sank lower and lower until it rested comfortably against the polished wood of the bar, I began to ponder a matter of great importance. Was it worth shelling out an entire fifty dollars to become a member of this club? Like an endless loop of hard-core smut playing in my head, I tried to memorize every clinical close-up, every theatrical gasp, every lubricious pose and acrobatic contortion, and even though it may have been another illusion conjured up by the lovely and beguiling Lorelei, I understood that in some odd way I'd been a member of this club all along.

. . .

I badly needed Morgan Fey that night, and as I stumbled in a drunken stupor from the cabaret and through the ashen twilight of the alley, I hoped she might see me and rush to my aid. An ardent smoker, Morgan sometimes appeared behind the bistro during her irregular cigarette breaks. Instead, I saw perched on the stoop outside the kitchen door a black muskrat licking its long claws. It regarded me with brazen indifference and then, dragging its belly through a debris field of broken beer bottles and cigarette butts, waddled lazily toward the patio, where Professor Martin Kingsley, a victim of ignorance, waited for a woman to share a meal with him followed by a bit of kissing and cuddling in his car before the drive home. Out of shame and embarrassment I hurried away before he could see me, and I veered along the sidewalk in a direction I hoped would lead me back to my apartment. Thoughts of college made me miserable, but I was made more miserable still by the thought of returning to the empty row house that seemed with each passing day to sink deeper and deeper into the mudflats.

Having walked the streets of Normandy Falls many times before, I felt confident I knew the way back home—all I had to do was keep going east, or maybe it was south, definitely not back to the square—but now my good eye was giving me trouble. The world looked faceted, fragmented, sharp cornered like one of Morgan's Cubist paintings, *Drunk Descending a Staircase*, and while I jerked and careened along monochromatic lanes painted by Duchamp and stomped through masses of wet newspaper that soaked up the rural defilement, I didn't realize until it was too late that I'd crossed the arch bridge and was now on the wrong side of the river.

In the neighborhood of Victorian-era homes, I kicked piles of plastic toys out of my path and pushed my way between rows of thick shrubs; I dragged my feet through flowerbeds, crushing freshly planted chrysanthemums, thrilling at the mindless destruction, the hilarious havoc. Taking pride in my own marginal coordination, I managed to scale a chain-link fence and crept across a quadrupled landscape until I hit a clothesline and fell flat on my back. Dazed by the blow, my brains cudgeled by a flagon of flat beer, I struggled to my feet and rubbed my neck to make sure my head hadn't been severed from my torso and was now rolling around like—I squinted in the dark—like a *beach ball*? An odd thing to see in this working-class neighborhood where few people had been to an ocean or had the pleasure of walking along a sweeping breadth of white sand beach. I gave the ball a gentle tap with my foot and watched with childish delight as it sailed through the air and landed with a soft plop in a swimming pool. Another surprise. A couple more steps and I would have fallen into the water, split my skull open against the concrete ledge, drowned.

In the stillness of the night I sensed a presence and worried it might be a young couple concealed in the brush, making love. No, an afternoon picnic under the noonday sun, that was the proper hour for a romantic tryst. Of course, moonlight had an allure all its own. Blood-swollen mosquitoes and the curious stares of raccoons weren't always enough to deter the truly horny from quick consummation. Unattractive people more often than not, overweight and over the hill. Fleshy buttocks sinking slowly into the stiff grass. In desperation they tried to recapture the enchantments of youth. Disappointment awaited those who yearned to fulfill even the most humble of fantasies.

With caution I approached the pool and watched the rings widening across the surface. When I finally noticed the figure floating facedown, legs spread wide, a turquoise gown billowing below the surface, I paused and muttered an embarrassed "Pardon me," a force of habit from my days at that despotic Jesuit school, and then, because I wasn't entirely convinced by what I was seeing, I dropped to my knees and looked more closely. I picked up a stick and gave the body a sharp jab. The woman rolled like a log and drifted counterclockwise, faceup, toward the center of the pool, her nose breaking the surface like a dorsal fin, arms floating above her head in a gesture of surrender.

That she was dead and freshly dead, too, I had no doubt, and I thought it senseless to check for a pulse, call 911, massage her heart, perform mouth-to-mouth resuscitation, the kiss of life. I stared at her face for a moment, a corpse's face, already turning faintly blue like a wax effigy. Her lips, drawn back from her teeth in a grimace of terror, pain, metaphysical angst, seemed to move with ghoulish loquacity, and her eyes wept an oil slick of mascara down her pale cheeks. Water boatmen and backswimmers skimmed along the surface and nested in her tawny hair, an incompetent mermaid robbed by death of any beauty she may have once possessed, and it took me a moment to recognize her as the young woman who strolled through campus with Professor Kingsley. How old was she? Twenty-five? Thirty? Maybe she'd left her bed in the night, a somnambulist haunted by bad dreams. But then why was she wearing such an unusual dress?

I decided to wait until she floated a bit closer before trying again to snag her and fish her out. Then I remembered from having watched so many movies that a witness was never supposed to tamper with a crime scene, if indeed this was a crime. Maybe it was suicide, someone too depressed to walk to the bridge and take the leap. Some people in this town treated suicide as a serious offense. Harshly sentenced, too. Unflattering write-ups in the newspaper, denial of proper Christian burial, contemptuous whispers from friends and neighbors, a hundred indignations. To the religiously inclined she would no longer be a real person but a sloughed husk, no better than a slimy skin left behind by a water snake. "Suicide," said my Jesuit teachers, "always gives Satan special pleasure." I remembered, too, the old custom of burying suicides at crossroads, and how at night a traveler could sometimes hear eerie sounds under the trampled clay.

I slumped into one of the Adirondack chairs, thinking it a terrible pity that the owners didn't own a dog to warn away strangers. On a table beside the chair, I found a copy of *Madame Bovary*, its spine cracked, the glue barely holding the pages together. An unusual choice for a summer read. The story of Emma Bovary and her callous lovers always made my eyes flutter with boredom, but now I wondered if the professor had been right all along. Maybe Flaubert really did have something important to teach. Funny, I thought, that life should imitate art and not the other way around.

While making a mental note to refer to Kingsley's scandalous rendez-vous in my thesis, I opened the cover, and into my lap fell several pieces of pink stationery. By the dim light of the quarter moon I managed to make out a few words, and it didn't take me long to realize that this was a message from beyond the grave, its small letters precise in their severity and single-minded purpose. In the quiet night I heard the woman's voice calling to me, a faint whisper soured by death, her cold breath washing over me and making my flesh tingle. I tried to decipher the full meaning of her bleak and bitter maxims, but my eyes grew heavy, and I placed the pages in my shirt pocket, fully intending to finish reading the letter after I rested.

If a light hadn't gone on next door, I would have nodded off and slept until dawn. In a panic I jumped from the chair, deeply disoriented, groggy with drink, unsure of where I was or how I had gotten there. At the neighbor's window I saw two young girls looking directly at me. Their cheerless eyes seemed to lack any childlike quality whatsoever, and I shuddered at the pale vampiric coloring of their faces. In general small children frightened me. They were ruthless and unprincipled. If given an opportunity they squealed on their elders. And what would the police say if they found me like this, an intoxicated stranger lounging on the patio of a reputable taxpayer's home as a body puttered back and forth across the pool as though death had equipped it with an outboard motor? They always thought the worst of people, these small-town cops with their truncheons and pepper spray and itchy trigger fingers. I decided to make a run for it before they could gun me down like a rabid dog.

I sprinted across the yard, but this time when I tried to scale the fence I lost my footing and smashed my balls against one of the exposed knuckles. Certain I'd been castrated, I toppled to the other side and immediately curled into a fetal position, clutching my torn pants and gasping for air. The police would apprehend me now, a stewed eunuch squealing a neutered nocturne. After mocking me ("Look on the bright side, kid, it's not like you was ever gonna use dem things again"), they would level the most serious charges against me—public intoxication, trespassing, *murder*—but if they had any compassion at all, they would first take me to the ER and let the doctors suture my shredded sack.

Five minutes passed, and though I was unable to summon the willpower to rise to my feet, I did manage to inch my way on hands and knees under a box hedge and through a pile of crab apples heaped beneath the limbs of a scrub tree. Behind me, somewhere in the vicinity of the swimming pool, a woman started to scream. Her animalistic skirls and screaks were so primal they had a curative effect on me, and I found I had the strength to run.

With the invincible laughter of a drunkard, I limped into a cool summer mist that curled over the dark rim of the valley, concealing me from view and making everything look like a blank page, no one around to fill it with words, a world not yet created, and I felt euphoric and very much alive.

5

Some people were tormented by the past; others, like Emily Ryan, were tormented by the future. On Saturday morning I was tormented by a debilitating hangover. At daybreak, when the awful specter of sobriety sidled into my room and slipped uninvited into my bed, I knew only one thing: that in order to survive the next twenty-four hours it was essential that I keep the apartment in total darkness, black and silent as a tomb. Failure to do so would lead to the awful prospect of waking early to empty cupboards and an empty stomach, not even a single slice of stale bread to help soak up whatever beer remained in my belly, but now, with the windows wide open and the blinds up, the room was flooded with punishing summer sunlight so hot and unbearably bright it seemed to melt the paint on the walls and make it drip from the ceiling like warm glue. I buried my face beneath a pile of pillows and wished to be dead, but for some reason the idea of death didn't sit well with me. I tried to think why this might be so, tried to piece together the events of last night, but it hurt too much. My throbbing brain conjured up an image of a floating dragon whispering its dark secrets and spreading its glittering snakefolds under the face of the sea.

On the windowsill a bird sounded an alarm, a single sharp note repeated over and over, and then went suddenly silent. I heard footsteps outside the apartment. Worried that a loud knock would come at any moment, I remained perfectly still and tried not to breathe. Awful things awaited me on the other side of the door, I was certain of it, and I had an uneasy feeling that it wasn't Death but Life that was about to come knocking, like a truculent salesman determined to pressure me into buying something I didn't want and couldn't afford—no returns, no exchanges, thank you for your business, enjoy the rest of your day. I waited for five minutes, ten, fifteen, and when no knock came, I decided to investigate. Terrified I might find gray matter seeping from the socket of my injured left eye and smeared against the white sheets, I struggled to lift the pillows from my skull, and then slunk toward the window.

"What the hell . . . ," I whispered.

For the next thirty minutes, with almost vertiginous incomprehension, I watched Morgan Fey carry her prized paintings from the back of a rental truck into the vacant row house next door. This wasn't playing nice, not at all, but I now realized that Morgan, like any cruel competitor, was fully prepared to bend the rules and resort to using dirty tricks in order to triumph over her opponent. After months of sofa surfing in the apartments of friends and family members, after countless hours of dreaming up dark and diabolical schemes, she now made her first strategic move.

I opened the window. The warm air vibrated with the hum of cicadas and the distant wails of a newborn baby. I gestured to the poster she was holding.

"Haven't seen that one," I said. "Poor lady looks like she needs some snorkeling gear."

Morgan halted on the front step, her lips forming the stiff scowl of an anxious curator of a doomed art gallery. "What happened to your eye?"

I gently touched the black patch and said casually, "Work-related injury."

"Your face is swollen. Did you have a doctor check it out?"

"Oh, sure, just as soon as I qualify for medical insurance. So what's that painting called?"

"It's not a painting," she corrected me, "it's a lithograph by Eugène Delacroix. *The Death of Ophelia*. What everyone fails to understand is that Normandy Falls isn't a town but a hamlet, and every hamlet needs its Ophelia, a green girl mad in grief. In *Hamlet* Shakespeare mentions Lethe, the mythological river of forgetfulness. You understand the meaning behind it, don't you, Edmund? It's not enough that your sins are forgiven. They must be washed from your memory, too. I suppose that's what it means to be born again. To suddenly come down with a serious case of amnesia. To willfully deny your past. To take no responsibility for the sins you've committed." She sighed. "I guess for a lot of people it's the only way they can live with themselves. But how about the people who can't forget? What do they do?"

"They go back to bed," I said, and slammed the window shut.

There were untold numbers of lonely little towns along the river that the world had forgotten or shunned or ridiculed from a comfortable distance, and I was mystified that Morgan had decided to remain in Normandy Falls. And for what purpose? To spite me? To continue working in that ghastly bistro and attending to the needs of her own barbarous tribe? No, she was up to something, had a plan in mind, and was just biding her time, waiting for the right moment to strike.

I collapsed onto the futon and only then did I see the pieces of pink stationery on the coffee table, left there like a bill of sale. At first, the letter was just a jumble of words, no different from an abandoned game of Scrabble, but after several slow and careful readings, I vaguely recalled the events of last night, and soon the meaning of the letter became increasingly clear. It left me with much to consider, but I knew that from now on the outside world would never cease to encroach upon my simple and humdrum existence.

Dear Marianne Kingsley,

By writing this letter I know I'm putting into jeopardy our good friendship. But I think it's important to face unhappy facts and I have to do what I think is best for everyone. This will come as painful news to you but I had no intention of letting matters get so out of hand. All summer long while you were at work your husband invited himself over to my house, used my pool, and visited my bed. At the beginning I was drawn to Martin because I thought his insights were wise, but I suppose professors say lots of things that sound intelligent to an uneducated woman like me. But then as the weeks went by he started saying things that frightened me. After he left my house I jotted down his words. Maybe you can make some sense of them:

— *College is an intellectual garbage dump.*
— *Students are free spirits, a term that best describes the dispirited, the enslaved, the unenlightened.*
— *Enlightenment is a religious euphemism for death.*
— *Death is a consistent and universal truth, the afterlife only a speculation.*
— *God is a mask used by weak individuals to disguise their own insignificant egos.*
— *The ego is a hallucination with no clear foundation, no ultimate reality.*

All of this was weird enough, but then he kept repeating that marriage was "a long, brutal winter." Again and again he would tell me this—a long, brutal winter—even while we sat under the warm sun and watched the kids swim. Happy men don't say such things, do they Mrs. Kingsley? Now I'm worried he's infatuated with me.

I know you have every reason to despise me, but now I'm asking for your help before your husband does something rash. Martin is a man possessed by many demons, I believe this. I think he's capable of harming himself and others. I'm concerned not only for my own personal safety but for the safety of my children. He fantasizes about injuring my little girls. I can see it in his eyes. One minute he's kind, the next cruel, and lately he has taken great pleasure in humiliating me.

You probably wonder why I tolerate that kind of behavior from a man. It's a fair question, and I'm not sure I have a good answer other than to say I now fear him. If he knew we were in communication he would try to harm me. I just hope there is still time for us to solve this situation peacefully. Please contact me. But I beg of you, be discreet. All men are potential cheats and killers.

Sincerely,
Emily Ryan

What surprised me most about this letter was that, aside from the occasional loops and fancy flourishes, her penmanship was not unlike my own—a firm masculine hand, bold block letters, a compression of words upon the page. I folded the note neatly and placed it back on the coffee table. In my mind I began to devise a top-secret mission, but I dared not embark on my dangerous quest until the afternoon when I could replenish my stock of locally grown bud. "Normandy Waterfall," Xavier D'Avignon called it. "Primo shit, my good man, nature's medicine."

For now I desperately needed sleep and closed my eyes to the sounds of Morgan lugging that awful lithograph into the apartment next door, a black-and-white rendering of a distressed swimmer with long hair and flowing robes as she struggled to keep her head above the water of a swift-moving river.

In the alley between the bistro and the cabaret, anxiously marching in and out of the shadows, trying to invent plausible alibis to give to suspicious wives and girlfriends, nodding to each other in grim solidarity and nervously eyeing the patrol cars that rolled intermittently through the flat afternoon light, a dozen men waited for the chef to emerge from Belleforest, "the factory," as they called it, where he cooked his product and then sold it at exorbitant rates. In recent months the stoop had become Xavier D'Avignon's personal pulpit, where he ministered to and collected cash from the low-caste deviants who congregated there in anticipation of their thirty minutes of bliss. Sometimes, while they waited for him to appear at the back door, the men grumbled about the rank smell of raw sewage wafting from the river, but after taking a few sips from a quart of his treasured *jazar* juice, they sincerely believed they were standing along the banks of an island stream in the steamy tropics, surrounded by fragrant fauna and flora. A few of the men realized they had a sickness, were painfully aware of their hacking coughs and high blood pressure, their knotted and quivering intestines, their violent, bloody excretions, and they worried that before the year was out they would find themselves spread-eagled on the coroner's metal table.

Morgan Fey had little sympathy for them. Resigned to a slow death at the hands of her own addiction, she stood on the concrete stoop and took a contemplative drag on her cigarette. Lately, she avoided venturing out here to take her break for fear of being mistaken for Xavier's business partner, but curiosity had gotten the better of her, and she wanted to see if she could spot any familiar faces among this pathetic crew loitering in the alley—professors, students, her ex-boyfriend. Mine was the unfortunate and slightly grotesque face of a man who yearned for either a kick in the teeth or the services of a talented cosmetic surgeon, and right away Morgan saw me among that chemically dependent horde, a sepulchral figure, sunken eyed, hollow cheeked, and she knew perfectly well why I was there. Under the right circumstances, if I were the only customer waiting in line, she would grab me by the back of my neck, push me toward the river's edge, and then give me a forceful shove into the boiling rapids. A weakling like me wouldn't last five minutes, and from my puny lungs would burst a wholly unnatural sound, like the sustained wails of a sickly infant abandoned on a piece of driftwood by its murderous mother.

Things were beginning to fall apart here, Morgan understood this, and the day was fast approaching when the local authorities, silent, secretive, supremely patient, uncommonly corrupt, would raid the bistro and plunder the safe upstairs. In ten minutes flat the cops would drill into the door and manipulate the dial to disengage the bolt. From having written several term papers about famous art heists around the globe, Morgan was familiar with the techniques of safecracking and knew what tools were needed to get the job done. Her hands began to tremble, and she crushed out her cigarette, last one in the pack.

Before going back inside the bistro, she looked over this awful infestation of shifty-eyed miscreants, lifted her middle finger, and waved it high in the air.

Having lived with her for so many months, I knew Morgan's habits, her routines, her litany of complaints, and I could guess what was on her mind. She expected an average day of glutting the dogs with flesh and fat, but by the time she arrived for her shift at Belleforest, she could see quite plainly that the Saturday-afternoon freak show was already in full swing. Typically, it was full dark before the crazies crawled out of their claustrophobic hovels and fetid firetraps—the cluttered studio apartments, the wind-battered trailers, the dens, dungeons, dirty cabins in the woods—but now Morgan saw a deeper pattern and was beginning to suspect that it didn't matter what time of day or night it happened to be, the crazies were everywhere, a never-ending parade of demoted demons coughed up from a sad, smoldering suburb of hell and sent on a mission to redeem themselves by methodically tormenting her.

Saturdays were somehow the worst. On Saturdays she was guaranteed to witness things so startling and difficult to forget that, in order to retain what little sanity she had left, she had to close her eyes and for five minutes focus her mind on the transitory nature of existence. Meditation, while an imperfect science, helped her to understand that life wasn't an artifact but a process, and sooner or later all processes ground to a halt. Armed with this knowledge, she could endure whatever terrible reality awaited her inside the double doors.

To a continuous clatter of dishes and a chorus of angry voices calling for service, Morgan raced from table to table, the only waitress to show up on time. The bistro had become a haven for otherwise unemployable misfits, the drifters and derelicts and parolees who worked as part-time busboys and dishwashers and short-order cooks. Many of them, after collecting their pay in the morning, went to the nearest check-cashing shop and then, without bothering to tell the boss they were calling it quits, fled town.

Consequently, Morgan was forced to do double duty, and now, like a psychoanalyst preparing to write a detailed report on a problem case, she reached for her notepad and approached a booth of grumbling, slack-thewed, knock-kneed geezers who asked about the *confit de canard*. With an ingratiating smile, she told them that the chef had truly outdone himself today. "May I also recommend the *foie gras*. We use only locally raised ducks and geese, as I'm sure you're aware." Scribbling orders in a crabbed hand, her frantic fingertips sliding through the black sludge that gushed from her pen, she left loops, whorls, arches, and unsightly smears of black ink on the paper and across the front of her white apron. She apologized, returned to the kitchen, scrubbed her hands with scalding water and industrial cleaner, searched for a sharpened pencil, a fresh notepad, a functioning clock to check the time.

After months of waiting tables, she knew that the key to success was to concentrate on her work and to ignore the peevishness and stupidity of her fellow townies, their belligerent comments, their nasty insinuations. Irascible by nature, eager to unleash their pent-up vitriol, the ornery customers made her job a constant challenge—the entrées were too rich, too salty, too bland, too hot, too cold, too clumpy and metallic-tasting like dog food scraped from the bottom of a rusty can. Strangely, this never deterred them from shoveling every last morsel of the repulsive grub down their greedy gullets. They belched, coughed, picked their teeth. They dabbed their lips with napkins dipped in the water glasses, and with great reluctance they reached into their wallets and change purses to produce a couple of crumpled bills and a handful of coins that they ceremoniously dumped on the table.

Most terrible of all, however, were those rowdy assholes from fraternity row. Drawn to the bright beacon of the bistro's blue neon light, the boys stopped in before going to the demolition derby at the edge of town. Evidently, Xavier had been hard at work advertising his wares on campus. Crammed into a corner booth, they looked like dissolute prep school boys who'd been cast away on an uninhabited malarial island and, after a long monsoon season, had turned into a tribe of howling, bottle-tossing, fist-swinging, spear-wielding savages.

"Hey, baby," they said to her, "how about a little pie?"

Morgan tolerated their obnoxious banter and suppressed the anger building deep at the center of her soul because if she delivered a spot-on performance, batting her eyes and offering the customers her most obsequious smile, she might make a few extra bucks. She also had a natural gift for coquettish conversation, an infuriating way of laughing too loudly and too lustily at every dirty joke that popped into the minds of those drooling brutes yearning to nuzzle her perfumed throat. She stroked and squeezed and slapped their arms in such a way as to suggest that, if they played their cards right, they might enjoy more intimate physical contact later in the evening. With a salacious smile she swept aside her hair to reveal those delectable earlobes and continued to tease and tantalize until those fumbling jackrabbit boys emptied their pockets.

On a good day she could bring home a hundred dollars, but of late that nice round number had started to dwindle, and she suspected her employer of garnishing her tips. A part of her believed Xavier D'Avignon, the chef and proprietor of Belleforest, was determined to keep her financially shackled to the bistro as his indentured servant, but the real reason he took some of her tips was because, several days ago, she'd dared to swipe a bottle of Châteauneuf-du-Pape from the wine rack and smuggled it home in her purse. He'd also caught her giving away free coffee and dessert to one of the dancers who, between acts, hurried from the cabaret for a quick bite to eat, an *éclair*, an espresso, anything so long as it had plenty of sugar and caffeine. Today was no different. After dancing for the carousing G.O.N.C.s, Lorelei, to conceal her tattoos and thus her identity, donned a black cloak with a hood and took a seat in a far corner, where she glanced at a menu and waited for the waitress to take her order.

Morgan battled her way through the heat and havoc of the kitchen, feeling the grease and oil seep into her pores, through her hair, between her teeth, under her bra. She prepared a fresh pot of coffee and tried to avoid the chef's accusatory gaze.

Without looking up from a sizzling skillet, Xavier said, "Thick as thieves, you two. A couple of working-class girls looking out for each other, huh?"

From beneath his soiled apron he produced a half-empty bottle of wine. Slowly stroking the neck and grinding his groin into the shallow punt, he let out a groan of gastronomic pleasure and then splashed the skillet, incinerating the unidentifiable hunks of butchered fowl in flames.

"Were you perhaps looking for this? Forgive me, *mademoiselle*. It seems I've uncorked the last bottle to marinate my medley of mushrooms and succulent *coq au vin*. Ah, but perhaps together, if you cared to join me upstairs in my quarters, we can hunt for an unopened crate."

Morgan sniffed. She had trouble believing that he could fit through the narrow stairwell and successfully climb the steps to the dark warren of rooms without tripping over his own swollen feet and tumbling to the ground floor, snapping his neck, rupturing his spleen. In the last year he'd put on an enormous amount of weight, and she marveled at his size, the bulk of him, the heft, the way his bones buckled and bent under his rippling rolls of fat, a positively gelatinous creature, wide and waddling, every inch of him jiggling in a different direction. Now, despite his monstrous girth, he managed to do a nimble pirouette behind the burners and looked through the window of the swinging door.

"My future sister-in-law is back again, I see. A real beauty, that one. A temptress. I think she might be a witch. Dabbles in the black arts, sorcery, that sort of thing. Maybe that's why she's draped from head to toe in a cloak. She's trying to disguise something more than those tattoos." He sidled closer to Morgan. "Did you hear the news? Sadie kicked her out of the house a few weeks ago."

"Really?" Morgan grabbed a handful of napkins. "Because Lorelei told me she left on her own. Ran away."

Xavier stared at her with the glazed look of a man approaching sleep. "Sadie refuses to tell me the reason for Lorelei's overhasty departure, but there is certainly something *fishy* about that girl, if I may be permitted a *bon mot*. Maybe you can find out what happened. And where she's staying these days. After all, you seem to be friendly with her. Very friendly."

Though it took a great deal of willpower, Morgan managed to suppress a sneer, turning it into a smile that too many men mistook to be not merely politeness or professional courtesy but flirtatiousness and, more and more often, a thinly veiled proposition. While it was certainly true that most men, on average, were emotional cripples who couldn't understand the difference between a kind gesture and a come-on, Xavier's innuendos went beyond bad taste.

A true connoisseur of turpitude, he pinched the ends of his preposterous waxed mustache and then, using a dripping spatula, tapped out a competent bossa nova beat against his ever-present glass of carrot juice. He spiked the juice with a combination of chemicals that smelled like gasoline, and he drank so much of the stuff that a deep flush of orange suffused his cheeks. Of course, people who worked in kitchens the world over, in big cities and small towns alike, were notorious drunkards and dope fiends, but Xavier was more self-medicated than most. He often whispered to himself and stared into the distance. Spaced out, that was the best way to describe him. Drugged, numb, unstrung. Whatever combination of pills he'd already popped that day, whatever illicit substances he regularly smoked, huffed, snorted, or mainlined had evidently robbed him of the capacity to reason properly, leaving him with a malfunctioning hemisphere of gray matter that rendered him incapable of communicating with anyone other than the denizens of some fourth dimension—gods, ghouls, goblins, who knows what, just so long as reality remained concealed behind the curtain of an impaired mind.

Again and again he'd proven himself to be an utterly inept restaurateur who depended absolutely on Morgan, a serious woman who anticipated and prepared for daily catastrophes. Need to order more napkins, straws, paper towels, toilet paper, lightbulbs? Have Morgan take care of it. Need to have the tablecloths laundered? Tell Morgan. She knew the business better than anyone else, and as senior staff member she'd become the de facto manager of Belleforest.

"I'm considering enrolling in a few business classes at the college," he told her. "Management and accounting. Always a good idea to have a backup plan."

Morgan laughed. "Before you finish a single class, you'll poison everyone in this town with your awful cooking. Or with that junk you peddle in the alley. Lucky for you the county health inspector hasn't shut the place down. Or the cops."

"You're an alarmist, my dear. And speaking of school, have you registered for classes yet? I'm sure there's time to enroll. The fall semester starts Monday."

"I'm still saving up."

With another birthday looming on the horizon, Morgan had to accept the fact that school was definitely out for good and that she was in danger of growing old in this unsanitary dump, slowly and inexorably turning into an emblem of modern spinsterdom—the sexually irrelevant, waddling, wide-hipped, wisecracking, worn-out waitress everyone pitied and secretly scorned, the loneliest person in town, with no family at all to speak of: no children, no husband, no mother, no father, no siblings, no prospects. It troubled her that in so short a time she'd gone from being a high-minded idealist to a low-class cynic, and like some underpaid village soothsayer she could see her future just as clearly as she could see her past.

"It's tough times for everyone, Morgan. Especially around here." Xavier slid beside her and touched her shoulder. "I know we've had this conversation before, but I've always thought you were an intelligent woman, plus you have your shit together, which is more than I can say about the other servers. You'd like to continue your education, I understand that, but we both know there's no future in art history, just like we both know I'll never become a highly regarded chef in a reputable four-star restaurant. I'm presenting you with an opportunity to earn some serious cash. I'm talking an extra two hundred dollars a week. Maybe even three hundred. There are a dozen suckers waiting in the alley to part with their paychecks. Why not use the situation to your advantage?"

Morgan smirked. "Is that why you've been walking off with my tips?"

"Listen, when the time comes, I don't intend to leave you high and dry. I still have a plan in the works to build a beach bungalow on Delacroix Cay. I'm even brushing up on my French, *ma petite putain*, to better interact with the natives." He produced one of the faded brochures that he kept handy in his apron pocket. "See, a beautiful island in the West Indies where the sea and sky are always blue and—"

"I've heard this speech a hundred times."

"—and where the sun always shines on the smiling faces of its friendly people. You can stay there with me for as long as you like. We can start a little beachside restaurant."

Morgan laughed. "But you're engaged to the Gonk's ex-wife."

Xavier poured himself another tall glass of carrot juice. "Ah, yes, Sadie is a sweet woman, but she's better at spending my money than managing it. Besides, you do realize, *mademoiselle*, how intolerably hot it gets behind the grill?" He moistened his lips with a tongue that resembled a piece of marbled meat, fatty and purple and just a little translucent, and, judging from the way he smiled, he seemed to delight in the taste of his own corporeality. "It's a veritable inferno back here, positively scorching, and I've developed a serious thirst, one that's difficult to quench."

Morgan gestured to his pitcher of carrot juice. "One of these days you're going to set fire to this place. You're starting to look like a pumpkin, do you know that? And if the Gonk doesn't carve you up like a jack-o'-lantern, I will. A single deep incision, that's all it would take, and an orange ocean will spill out of you."

At these remarks his eyes danced. "If I'm a pumpkin then you're Cinderella, both of us *sans* fairy godmother, and until you receive an invitation to the ball, my dear, you better learn a little humility. Sometimes a princess has to get down in the dirt and sweep up the ashes. *À votre santé!*" He raised his glass and drained it in one, long swallow. Returning to his pots and pans he said, "Oh, don't forget the *crème brûlée* for Lorelei! And please tell my future sister-in-law it's on the house."

When it came to the preparation and presentation of haute cuisine, Xavier D'Avignon felt an intellectual, spiritual, even sexual empowerment that far surpassed anything he'd ever experienced, and he often boasted that his perfectly executed recipes were not only manna from heaven but also potent aphrodisiacs raining down from the sky like Cupid's arrows, and while his cooking didn't always conform to the precepts of contemporary nutritional wisdom, it did offer alternative forms of wisdom, as that feebleminded minx was about to discover. Though she was young and beautiful and would soon be blood, Lorelei was not entitled to free meals and needed to be taught an invaluable lesson. From the container of goodies he kept beneath the counter, Xavier added a dangerous dose of *jazar* extract to the sweet vanilla and smooth, concupiscent curds of a *crème brûlée*.

Lorelei was a lost cause, but he still held out hope that Morgan might share his growing fascination with "mind manifestation" and help him sell his *jazar* juice. Sooner or later moralists like Morgan had to accept the fact that drugs were no different from the genetically modified soybeans the farmers grew in their fields on the outskirts of town, basic commodities that would always be controlled by market forces, and he couldn't understand why anyone would begrudge him for temporarily alleviating the spiritual torments of so many people. Doctors had a diagnosis for these symptoms and could treat them with expensive pills and injections, but the medicines Xavier concocted in his kitchen, though a bit crude, proved nearly as effective. If only Morgan could find a similar form of release from her troubles. A soupçon of carrots might weaken her inhibitions, but so far she had only scoffed at his weird obsession, calling him a madman and worse, but Xavier firmly believed the greatest accomplishments—the composition of grand operas and sonnet cycles, the sudden, rapturous seizure of mystical insights and scientific breakthroughs—were symptomatic of madness. After all, who else but a lunatic and reigning god of gastronomy would devote his life, year after year, to the preparation of carrot juice, heavy on the ginger, light on the orange peel?

"Those of us who like to take a pinch of psychedelic, that's who," he said to himself, replenishing his glass and taking another slug.

He savored the sharp flavor, relishing the way it abraded his throat and how its vapor stung his eyes. While some people ended up having severe psychotic episodes from the juice, Xavier found the effects wonderfully serene. The stuff fired his imagination, made the rusty wheels turn, and it pleased him to know that in the ether there existed a real thing called "perfection" and that it presented itself each day, as if by magic, in the form of a tangy glass of juice.

By some estimates there were eighty varieties of carrot, each with an evocative name, the Tip Top, Oxheart, Bolero, Crusader, Swamp King. There were carrots of different shapes and sizes, colors and textures, roots and cores. Some were rough and some smooth, some had a sweet and mellow flavor, others a complex and earthy one, and a discerning chef was always at pains to decide whether to use those robust carrots grown in the warmer climes of Louisiana or heartier ones grown in the tough soils of Saskatchewan. After months of experimentation, Xavier now preferred the *jazar* carrot, a diminutive reddish variety reputedly found only in North Africa and one with strong hallucinogenic properties. Its flowers resembled those of the deadly hemlock and its taproot was more crisp and woody textured than other varieties. Unfortunately, given the constant political unrest and shifting alliances in that part of the world, the *jazar* was exceedingly difficult to come by, and Xavier was now the only man in Normandy Falls from whom the precious carrot could be procured. He fashioned himself the *jazar*'s unofficial ambassador and proud herald and charged his clients accordingly.

Curious to learn more about his favorite root vegetable, he read books and magazines about the international drug trade. According to his sources, Tangier was a famous smuggling center, and every small firearm, sex-trade worker, and sack of *jazar* passed through its shady underworld. During his sojourn in the city, the author Paul Bowles cultivated the carrot, and when no kif could be found in the mean alleys of the old town, he served it to certain houseguests who'd overstayed their welcome, the most famous being the master addict William Burroughs, whose ensuing visions and ecstasies produced some of his most startling work. "That skinny, little fruit served up the carrots raw," wrote Burroughs, "a naked lunch, a frozen moment when everyone sees what is on the end of every fork."

The carrot had become so prized for its reputed medicinal and mind-altering effects that half-starved refugees making their way across the Mediterranean to the shores of France brought bunches of them in their rafts. They were the finest source of foreign exchange, easily converted into euros. In the narrow streets of sunny Nice the police raided flats and seized entire crates of the stuff. Inevitably, because the carrots were used in a variety of *apéritifs* the same way wormwood was used in absinthe, some corrupt, low-ranking official, a sergeant or lieutenant, sold them to various *brasseries* in the fashionable Marais neighborhood of Paris where dignitaries dining along the rue Sainte-Croix-de-la-Bretonnerie discussed the plight of the poor and powerless North Africans, all the while knowing full well how the delectable carrots had been obtained. None of this seemed to trouble members of the ruling class, who tended to regard irony of this sort as *très chic*.

Xavier yearned to explain these things, but Morgan had no patience for his long-winded lectures about produce, and as the day dragged on, she ignored him altogether. For a while things were actually quiet, almost tranquil, but in Normandy Falls anything approximating tranquillity was short lived, and Xavier sensed trouble well before he heard the terrible commotion coming from the dining room, the sound of shattering glass, a sharp cry for help. At first he presumed it was another feuding couple trying to bludgeon each other with the ugly centerpieces designed by Colette Collins. Full-scale domestic disputes were not out of the ordinary, especially when the weather was hot and muggy and the bistro became the domain of unhappy couples whose commitment to each other had devolved into something tenuous and strained. In silence these sullen husbands and wives slurped their drinks and ate their *pot au feu* and tried, but often failed, to camouflage their looks of disdain and outright hostility by pretending to be interested in what the other was saying. The soft glow of candlelight was meant to disguise more than the wrinkles and blemishes they'd accumulated over the course of their shared lives. A kind word poorly delivered could set them off, and like bad actors in a low-budget movie performing their own stunts, they leaped out of their chairs and lunged at each other across the tables; they pushed, shoved, slapped, strangled; they hacked, hawked, gagged, bellowed. In the end someone always stormed out of the restaurant in a rage.

But this was different, the racket far more intense, fierce, manic. Remembering how the Gonk had promised to pay him a visit one fine day, Xavier grabbed his trusty "master of cooking" knife from the counter and hurried to the dining room, but he was so stunned by the macabre scene unfolding before him that he thought he was having another bad episode from the *jazar*.

Gathered in a semicircle, chattering in an incomprehensible Iron Age dialect, three college boys clapped and whistled at Lorelei as she danced on top of the bar, her hips gyrating, her head bobbing in time to a secret turbo tempo blasting inside her skull. Like a demented dervish on high-octane smack, she twirled round and round lost in an ecstatic trance, drawing her extended arms closer to her torso until her body revolved at impossible speeds so that, for an instant, she appeared to float a few inches in the air. The black cloak rose above her ankles and calves, billowing higher and higher until it exposed the tender flesh of her pale thighs, but it wasn't until she unclasped the hook and let the cloak fly to the floor that she managed to draw a round of applause from the trio of hyperactively horny frat boys.

"Dude, this joint is better than the cabaret!"

"A kick-ass private show."

"Fucking sick, man, *sick*."

Morgan, who failed to coax Lorelei down from the bar, shot Xavier an accusatory look. "Drugged," she spat.

As the other diners scampered from the bistro without paying their tabs, Xavier wrapped his arms around Lorelei's legs and lowered her from the bar, but when he attempted to lead her through the kitchen door, he met with resistance. A discernible change had come over her, like someone who'd been rudely awakened from a marvelous dream. Her eyes spun like pinwheels and sparkled not from the concentrated sugar and powerful drugs but with a clear and unambiguous animosity. The thousand miseries and insults she'd endured at the hands of a thousand different men were compressed into an unblinking gaze of animal hatred directed squarely at Xavier. She became a vindictive, execrating hellcat with splintering fingernails that she used like the whirling blades of a high-speed blender to disfigure his fat face.

"Out the back door!" he commanded.

But the college boys wanted the show to go on.

"Hey, dude, let her finish the performance."

"Yeah, man, leave her alone."

"Here's a dollar, honey!"

Xavier reached into his back pocket and flashed the knife at the college boys. "I think it's time you children ran along."

"Whoa, dude, you a fucking psycho or something?"

"You gonna try to cut us with that thing?"

"Yeah, let's see your skills!"

Before Xavier could react, the boys grabbed Lorelei's black cloak from the floor and raced around the bistro, pulling it away from Xavier each time he made a clumsy attempt to grab it, fingers just out of reach. He huffed and shook and panted; he stomped his feet and charged like an exhausted old bull. The boys were quick to capitalize on his lumbering passes, and right before delivering the *coup de grâce*, they yanked Xavier's apron from his jiggling waist and kicked it into a corner.

"I don't need this shit right now!" Morgan shouted. "I'm moving into a new apartment this weekend." She reached for the phone on the wall. "I'm calling the police."

"No!" Xavier cried.

In a steady, thundering beat the boys belted out the college fight song and stomped in single file out the door.

Gasping for air, listening in alarm to his own choked and clotted breathing, Xavier collapsed into a booth and thumped his chest a half-dozen times, hoping to correct his irregular heartbeat and somehow slacken the steady pounding in his temples.

"Morgan," he rasped, "I want you to know that I had absolutely nothing to do with this. I swear, I have no idea who is responsible."

Morgan scowled. "You're fucking disgusting." She gathered the cloak from the floor, draped it over Lorelei's shoulders, and led her outside.

In the past there had been plenty of disruptions on Saturday afternoon, but this was on a whole different order of trouble. Every time a group of swinging dicks in blue uniforms paid him a visit and ordered their usual coffee and pastries, Xavier gritted his teeth and prepared to get fucked in the ass by the United States government. One dick he could handle, but not a whole army of them. Those law-and-order men knew at a glance when something was wrong and no doubt were looking forward to the day when Xavier finally screwed up. From having read dozens of books and articles on the subject, he knew it was safer to deal out of a private residence, but he felt the alley was far less conspicuous. As long as he played it cool and didn't get too greedy, he could hold on to this side operation for another year before the feds raided it. The trick, of course, was knowing when to get out before some irate moral crusader finally blew the whistle.

With the slow and deliberate footsteps of a much older man nearly crippled by gout, Xavier grabbed a broom and dustpan from the corner and swept up the shattered glass on the floor. After he finished tidying up, he went to the kitchen and climbed the back stairs to his quarters above the bistro. Dyspeptic and paranoid to the point of exhaustion, he cracked open one of the blinds, and like a schizophrenic sentry who tensed up whenever a patrol car drove by, he watched the alley.

To reassure himself that he was still the wily, small-town factotum and culinary craftsman, always one step ahead of the law, he went to the wall and removed a faded poster of black-stockinged cancan dancers doing the Infernal Galop. Hidden in a shallow recess, the new combination safe contained close to fifty thousand dollars, big bricks of glorious greenbacks, many in small denominations held together with colorful straps—yellow, violet, brown, mustard. He stroked and caressed the cash, lifted the bills close to his nose, smelled the ink and cotton fibers. As far as financial improprieties went, Xavier, by his own estimation, had used poor judgment only once, bringing a duffel bag of money to the bank to be changed into hundred-dollar bills. Benjamins took up less space in the safe and were much easier to account for, but even the tellers knew that the bistro hadn't enjoyed that kind of success, and he'd stopped the practice shortly after the drug money started rolling in.

He set aside the cash and flipped through the brochures of Delacroix Cay that he'd collected over the years, full-colored pamphlets advertising new condominiums and rental properties. He studied the pictures of copper-colored nymphs in string bikinis sunbathing under swaying palm trees and swimming beside large schools of damselfish gathered around a cathedral of purple pipe organ coral. The bright, tropical flowers looked like idealized human genitalia and gave him a definite sense of hope and purpose, but sometimes he wondered if it was foolhardy to sock away so much money in order to purchase a scrap of land in the hurricane-prone tropics on a desperately poor island with an unstable government.

He sat on the corner of his bed and pared his dirty nails with the tip of his enormous knife, and from these pictures he gleaned a single, invaluable lesson: that a life of decadence and unspeakable depravity was permissible provided a man had incredible luck and no remorse, and he now feared he was in dangerously short supply of both.

Before any of this madness transpired, I was able to make my purchase from Xavier. Still standing in the alley, I took that first restorative hit of the day and wrinkled my nose at the pall of purple smoke circling my head, a strange mixture of turpentine and savory seasonings—tarragon, fennel, sage. I counted the seconds until the cannabis steadied my nerves and eased the symptoms of my stubborn hangover. Its effects were sublime and helped me to forget every ridiculous trifle, every neurotic crisis, every delusion, not that I was delusional, no, but sooner or later life does have an irritating way of making us believe in things that may not exist or that we do not fully understand.

I left the alley and traipsed across the square but stopped to watch in amazement as the killer came walking down the street. Evidently, he dressed for a Saturday afternoon the same way he dressed for the classroom—a stylish blazer, a freshly pressed collared shirt, a pair of brown shoes polished to a high gloss—but now he seemed decidedly less confident in his powers of intellectual bamboozlement, almost contrite for having subjected his students to so many inconsequential abstractions, someone weighed down by the awful burden of unpleasant realities. For a man who must have been wondering when the homicide detectives would come to put the cuffs on and bring him down to headquarters for a grueling interrogation, he seemed calm enough, but even the most innocent and well meaning of men couldn't live for long without packing away a few sins, secrets, serious missteps, deeds too terrible to admit especially to oneself, and his expression hinted at things subterranean, twisted, evil. Like most professors and other venerable frauds the world over, he had about him an air of entitlement and invincibility, but of course crimes of passion were the easiest of all to solve, and in this day and age of high-tech forensics no one, not even the brightest instructor of comparative literature, could get away with drowning his mistress in a swimming pool. "But she was *depressed*, I swear!" How many times had the cops heard that one?

Martin Kingsley looked at the menu taped to one of the bistro's windows. He seemed undecided, unsure of what to do next, and as I lingered on the square I wondered what it might be like to have dinner with a woman like Emily Ryan, to reach across the table and hold her hand and watch as she became charmingly drunk on a bottle of wine, knowing as we enjoyed each sumptuous course that she would come home with me for a night of love, that she was mine whenever I wanted her, a scenario for which the poets had invented many names: bliss, heaven, nirvana. Unlike Kinglsey, who enjoyed a steady and reliable income and knew a big fat pension waited for him at the end of the rainbow, I was on a tight budget, and I understood how comical it would be to finish a candlelit dinner and then expect someone as ravishing as Emily to walk back to the row house on the edge of the river. Few women in this world were willing to have a romantic tryst with an impoverished graduate student, and the first rule for a night on the town was to have a clean and cheerful apartment with a proper bed instead of a sagging futon.

Like a spurned lover burning with sexual jealousy, I envied Kingsley's status, his money, his petty power, his inexplicable ability to woo a married woman, and I wished for one small taste of his former happiness. It didn't seem fair to me. I was a writer of *belles lettres*, as was Emily, and like her I had suffered at the hands of that narcissistic egghead. But what frustrated me most of all was that I was living the appallingly familiar cliché of unrequited love. Alive or dead, Emily Ryan was permanently unattainable, and the best I could ever do was settle for a kind of platonic necrophilia.

Before these thoughts could drive me completely mad, I looked on as Kingsley, to my disbelief, ducked into the alley beside the bistro and made a hasty purchase from Xavier. He glanced over his shoulder, as if he sensed someone watching him, and for the first time I saw real terror in his eyes. Quickly, I pressed my back against the gazebo and made small adjustments to my eye patch, pretending to read the faded and peeling posters of missing teens and toddlers slapped on nearly every lamppost. Bound to become famous for its runaways, abductions, and unsolved cases, Normandy Falls was said to have adopted Moloch as its patron saint, chewer of children's corpses.

Confined within the prison of his own warped logic, trying to act as normal as possible, nothing out of the ordinary here, no blood on his hands, Kingsley gave Xavier some cash and then slid a small bottle of *jazar* into his coat pocket. After leaving the alley, he strolled through town, aimlessly it seemed, pretending to admire the tumbledown walls of long-abandoned warehouses and factories until he crossed the bridge and headed toward the college campus. With obscene confidence, foolishly believing he was beyond suspicion, he walked along the quadrangle, passing the neo-Georgian redbrick buildings, and then entered the small art gallery, where he contemplated the spectacular number of nudes on display, immense canvases depicting libertine gods, wood nymphs, lecherous satyrs frolicking in enchanted dales and beside green tidal pools. For a full thirty minutes he meditated deeply on the images in the gallery, studying lush landscapes and pretty women reading books in flower gardens. The artwork seemed to have a calming effect on him, somehow indicating, like tea leaves to a superstitious crackpot, that what he had done was perfectly aligned with the natural order.

Having achieved the requisite sense of serenity, he exited the gallery and walked across Anderson Boulevard to the neighborhood of Victorian houses. With one hand thrust deep in his coat pocket, his fingers no doubt fondling the contraband stowed safely there, he went up the walkway to his house and stood on the porch, where he stared at the ground like a squirrel hunting for acorns before the big winter freeze, trying to horde nuggets of ingenious thought. He had about him a sense of fatigue, resignation, a reluctant acceptance of Emily's wretched fate.

With bated breath I scurried behind the trunk of a pin oak and picked absently at the bark. Never a fan of detective novels, I made for a clumsy and incompetent gumshoe. Like any well-established culture, the pursuit of a killer was a fine art, one that took years to master, and my biggest mistake, other than getting high, was to wear the eye patch. A good investigator must appear nondescript and draw as little attention to himself as possible, but I wanted my eye to heal properly and was now worried that it was seriously infected. I also believed the patch made for a clever disguise, instantaneously transforming me from an aimless college dropout into a talented sleuth.

It would be a simple matter for me to call the police and present them with the evidence, but I wanted to let this game play out just a little while longer. Murderers may have been justifiably famous for their fancy prose style, but extortionists were equally renowned for their gift of recitation. I could quote Emily's note from memory and was prepared to do so in the unlikely event that Kingsley saw me snooping and decided to confront me.

In the treetops blackbirds whistled and sang, but when a passing pickup backfired they fluttered away in a dark cloud of cowardice. Clearly irritated by the noise, the murderer stepped inside and wandered distractedly through the spacious rooms of his house.

The professor wasn't a flight risk, I decided, and he certainly wasn't a homicidal maniac, at least not in the usual sense of that term. The logistics alone made it impossible. A swimming pool wasn't a very private place for a murder, and the sounds of a woman thrashing in the water and trying to fight off her assailant would have attracted far too much attention. The real mystery of this story wasn't how Emily died but how a cream puff like Kingsley had managed to seduce her. In fact, the man seemed competent at only one thing: critiquing the hastily written essays of his idle students. Still, I continued to wonder: Was his the last face Emily saw before she died? And as she resigned herself to her fate, did she decide that the only way she could retaliate was to haunt this self-obsessed man for the rest of his life?

6

On Monday morning, the first day of the fall semester and the dead-
line for my thesis on Flaubert, I punched in at the Bloated Tick, fully
prepared to withstand a barrage of insults from those pernicious bul-
lies from the bottom bins. Over the course of the summer some of the
ticks had put on so much weight that they'd metamorphosed into a
nest of mindless, roaming esophagi, searching with rheumy eyes for
boxes of jelly doughnuts and generous slices of meat pie. Others, from
a steady diet of pills and liquor, had shed so many pounds that they
resembled scarecrows, their ill-fitting clothes hanging from their emaciated frames.

When they saw me enter the building the men cheered, they
applauded, they marched around the lunchroom table and chanted,
"The Cyclops! The Cyclops! Love the eye patch! It suits you! Bestowed
upon you by the gods as punishment for your crimes. Yes, punishment
from the gods for your crimes!"

"What crimes?" I said, maybe more defensively than I'd intended.

"The Gonk already gave us the scoop, told us how he took you up
to the titty bar on Friday night. Now, why in the hell would you throw
away your hard-earned cash in a sinful place like the cabaret? That's not
what we had in mind when we told you to find a woman. Plenty of fish
in the sea, you know?"

Yes, I knew, and I was tempted to tell them that I *had* found a
woman, the *right* woman, and that she was a heaven-sent muse, an
unpretentious poet, a small-town sage, a mystic whose words tran-

scended time and space, but of course I could never adequately explain to that obstreperous crew of unwashed scamps that she was also, to use their own words, "the professor's wench." If any consolation was to be found, it was in Emily's carefully composed note, which I carried in my shirt pocket like pages torn from a hymnal, and for the rest of the day, as I stroked the folded sheets and endured the predictably child-ish taunts of the men, I wondered why matters pertaining to love and lust had to be so strangely conspiratorial and why old-fashioned letters, written with black ink on pink stationery, became repositories for unut-terable thoughts, the nuclear waste of the human heart.

Ordinarily, at five o'clock, shortly after the jackhammer of practical concerns finished chipping away at my brain, reducing my mind to rubble, my thoughts to an impenetrable cloud of neural dust, I hur-ried from the Bloated Tick and returned to my apartment, but now things had changed. First I stopped at the corner store to purchase a newspaper, a shameful extravagance, and consulted the obituaries to find visiting hours. I'd never made a practice of seeking sorrow, but now, with a renewed sense of purpose, I showered and shaved and doused myself in cheap cologne. Donning an ill-fitting, cream-colored, department-store suit, the only one I owned, and a paisley tie that was so wide and loud it looked like I'd stolen it from an old steam trunk in a circus clown's dressing room, I walked to the funeral home five blocks from the bistro. At the last minute, before entering the lobby, I debated whether I should wear the eye patch or take it off and use it as a pocket square. In the past twenty-four hours my eye had become red with infection, the eyelid pink and swollen, and since I didn't want to cause the mourners any undo alarm, I decided to wear it. Besides, it seemed like the kind of thing a merchant marine might appreciate.

Inside, I was greeted not by some obsequiously smiling funeral director but by the cloying perfume of flowers, hundreds of white lil-ies that had been strategically arranged around the air vents in order to disguise the faint whiff of formaldehyde drifting up from the base-ment. The otherwise clean and cornered rooms seemed to amplify the muffled sobs of the mourners as they filed by the open casket, and while I waited to view the body and offer my improbable condolences to Emily's husband and their mischievous twin daughters, I contemplated the macabre pageant of grief and the gruesome ritual of interment. I also kept a keen eye out for Professor Kingsley.

Emily's husband stood at the other end of the casket, his neck and cheeks clawed from hasty shaving, his eyes bloodshot and bleary from what appeared to be a crippling hangover. Thickly muscled, rawboned, square jawed, casually racist, unmistakably American, Charlie Ryan might have been in an earlier epoch a pioneer, or a notorious outlaw who by the dusty light of a prairie moon went on cattle raids, or the first mate of a Nantucket whaling ship, an old salt inclined to signs and portents, his face as weathered as the tattered sails flapping from the foremast after an epic ocean crossing. In his present incarnation he played an abrasive merchant marine who seemed impervious to both pain and pleasure. He stared into the middle distance and remained strangely impassive, but it has always been my understanding that a distraught widower, when faced with an unexpected loss, becomes so emotionally exhausted that he is unable to shed even one more tear, and perhaps this was the case with Charlie Ryan.

His little girls, rather than standing in an attitude of respectful attention, grudgingly accepted the tearful embraces of aunts and uncles and then laughed like a pair of bleating goats.

Now, fighting hard to keep my paranoia in check (I had taken a few quick tokes from the old bong before leaving the row house), I inched ever closer to the casket, and though I promised myself I wouldn't do it, I let my burning eye drift toward the bloodless figure supine in the cheap wooden box, the folded hands stiff and artificial as those of a porcelain doll's, the waxen face painted with a half-dozen coats of makeup. A small, strangling sound escaped my lips. Experience had taught me that a woman's presence always brightened the dreariest of rooms, but not this time, not now. Emily looked carved, molded, a gruesome marionette cut free of its strings, a poorly built dummy lampooning a posture of repose. Could this really have been the same woman who walked along the campus quad with Martin Kingsley?

I kneeled and bowed my head, and as I mumbled a prayer just like the one uttered by the mourners before me, I worried that Emily could perceive my voice and that, with some effort, she could force open her eyes and give me an imploring look. *"Please, help me . . ."* It wasn't totally impossible. I read somewhere that neuroscientists had new research indicating that the synapses in the neocortex continued firing for twenty-four hours or more after the heart stopped beating and the other vital organs had started the process of decomposition. The idea made me shudder. Bad enough to be imprisoned in a perfectly healthy body, but to be trapped in a dead and inert one, a hardening shell of embalmed membranes, well, that seemed the most nightmarish fate of all. Although ensnared forevermore in that inert flesh, Emily, through her words, had transcended death, and I wondered if, at least in some strange scientific sense, she was *aware* of what was happening to her, outraged by the indignation and powerlessness of death. If I leaned in close, pressed my ear to her lips, would I hear her teeth clicking together like tiny castanets, all of her darkest secrets revealed in a kind of Morse code?

"Emily, can you hear me?" I prayed. "Emily, are you *in there?*"

I was so distracted by these thoughts that I didn't immediately notice how Professor Kingsley and his wife, electing to bypass this little ceremony at the casket, had jumped ahead of me in line. Rather than object I kept my head bowed and listened carefully to what they had to say.

"If there is anything we can do for you and the girls," Mrs. Kingsley sniffled, "anything at all, Charlie, please let us know. Emily was such a lovely woman, so warm and friendly. It just isn't fair."

"I was quite fond of your wife," Kingsley chimed in. "Yes, very fond of her. A wonderful woman, long-forbearing and abundant in faithfulness. I would have done anything for her, provided her with any kind of help she needed."

I was puzzled by the professor's initial composure. No doubt prior to the wake he had rehearsed a few inane and platitudinous lines. I expected the man to howl, to weep, to fall on his knees, to tear his shirt and pound his chest with clenched fists. A moment like this called for a theatrical display of grief, particularly when an adulterer was in the presence of his dead lover's unsuspecting spouse, but someone as arrogant as Kingsley probably planned to deliver an impromptu eulogy, hoping to console the bereaved with his linguistic effluvium and esoteric tautologies.

"I suppose," he continued, "the question we're all asking is Why? Why did this happen? The main thing is that we not dwell on it. With a little practice a man can learn to control his thoughts and emotions and in time even his breathing and heart rate. It's a kind of subconscious athleticism. Almost like being a swimmer . . ."

At the regrettable choice of the word "swimmer," Kingsley began to stammer, and it was then that I knew he'd been drinking some of Xavier's magic potion prior to the wake.

Fortunately for him Charlie didn't seem to be listening. "I can't thank you enough," he muttered. "I know how hard it must have been for you to call me."

"Oh, it was nothing at all," said Kingsley, though in truth he wanted to eradicate from his memory every detail of that terrible night. "It was my duty to call you. My duty as a good neighbor."

The scene on Friday evening wasn't a difficult one for me to imagine, and I clasped my hands more tightly and prayed with greater fervor.

While the twins slept soundly in the guest room, Kingsley went to his study and brooded over serious matters. Madeline and Sophie seemed unable to comprehend what had happened that night, the police, the paramedics, the sirens and flashing lights, but he found their innocence wholly unconvincing. The girls were eight, after all, not three, not Christopher's age, and yet Kingsley trusted his son to have enough common sense to seek help the moment he saw anyone, especially his mother, floating in a swimming pool. Maybe Marianne had fabricated the story for reasons of her own. Maybe she knew about the affair and had taken extreme measures, disposing of her husband's hillbilly whore out of sheer jealousy. This theory made even less sense to him, and he decided no one was to blame. It was just an unfortunate accident, that's all. But were there such things as accidents?

For one full hour he sat alone in his well-furnished study, gazing into the future and his own ungraspable destiny. He thumbed through his unruly manuscript on *Madame Bovary* and looked hopelessly at his glass-fronted bookcases crammed with leather-bound volumes. Ever since he was a boy, he'd regarded the great books of Western civilization as oracles. He need only flip to a random page and read a paragraph of cogent prose or a verse of poetry to find wisdom and solace. A stanza by Aeschylus, Sophocles, or Euripides offered simple solutions to some of life's most vexing problems and impenetrable mysteries, but Kingsley, much like the Greek tragedians, preferred that all deaths take place offstage. Forced to confront every scholar's worst nightmare—the prospect of actually experiencing firsthand all of the dreadful things he'd spent his entire professional life only reading about—he discovered that the books he so cherished, just when he needed them most, refused to provide him with easy answers, and he worried they might never have anything of value to say to him again.

Out of habit he scanned a collection of stories by Flaubert but knew he was torturing himself by delaying the inevitable. Under a rock in the flowerbed near the pool, Emily kept a spare key. Kingsley entered the house through the back door, half expecting to see a massive oil portrait of Emily hanging on the wall, her unrefined beauty smoldering down at him, a tear dripping from the corner of one eye. Inside, the air seemed stale and contaminated, and he found the kitchen in total disarray, the countertops piled high with dirty dishes. He spotted a recipe written in Emily's hand on an index card pinned to the center of a bulletin board cluttered with unpaid bills.

The Red Death

> *3 oz. pomegranate juice*
> *1 tbsp. sugar*
> *½ lemon squeezed*
> *1½ oz. 3 oz. grain alcohol (see the Gonk)*

He almost tossed the recipe to the floor but chanced to see another index card tacked to a corkboard with a phone number and the words

"In Case of Emergency." The *Rogue* might have been eighty miles away or eight hundred; it might have been cruising by the sandbar near the mouth of the Wakefield River or it might have been loading iron ore into its enormous holds at a port along the north coast of Lake Superior.

Before he picked up the phone, Kingsley slumped against the counter, and in a quiet place where his wife wouldn't see him and begin to wonder, he bawled like a child, a wretched, inconsolable wail that didn't stop until he heard, faintly at first and then with increasing persistence and volume, the noises coming from within the walls of that shunned and deserted house. Kingsley wiped away his tears and listened. Bats, dozens of them, hundreds maybe, with their diseased teeth and talons, scratched and clawed their way through the insulation and plaster. Females formed maternity colonies in the summer and fed their blind and pale pups at night before hunting for moths and mayflies. He recoiled from the wall and wondered which news to break first—the infestation of bats or Emily's drowning.

Now, standing face-to-face with Charlie in the funeral parlor, he found he was too petrified to say anything more.

Charlie turned to Mrs. Kingsley, and his voice when he finally spoke was thin and raw, the sound of a man who'd been drinking nonstop for days and chain-smoking for years. "There's just one thing I don't understand," he said. "On the night she died, Emily was wearing the turquoise sari I bought for her on our sixth anniversary. She wore it whenever I came home after a long journey. Special occasions only. I'm not sure what to think of it."

"Emily made plans with her friends," Marianne explained. "Sometimes a woman just wants to look nice. It's not that peculiar."

"Her friends? I suppose she was pretty lonely," he said, more to himself than to anyone else. "She never even left me a note. But I guess she didn't need to. No, I already knew what was wrong."

There was a moment of awkward silence before Marianne said, "Don't hesitate to stop by the house. We'd love to see you and the girls."

Kingsley took his wife by the hand and led her away. To him the casket had started to resemble a confessional box where he could bury all of his evil deeds. But as he and Marianne retreated to a far corner of the crowded funeral parlor, he noticed how the twins occasionally looked in his direction, their eyes small and hard and filled with a larval hatred, two conquering graveworms eager to feed on their mother's foul secrets and to spread her corruption.

Now it was my turn to speak to Emily's husband. Odd that I didn't feel any jealousy toward him, none at all, but then it was hard to be jealous of a cuckold. Bereft of his wife, the poor fellow appeared lost in a fog so thick he didn't realize, or perhaps didn't care, that he'd never met the stranger now offering his sympathies. Charlie Ryan didn't ask my name or how I knew Emily. For the hundredth time that day, he mechanically spoke the words, "Thank you so much for coming," and I mechanically replied, "I'm sorry for your loss." We shook hands, a pair of impotent Prince Charmings unable to liberate Sleeping Beauty from the powerful spell of eternal darkness. The entire exchange lasted no more than thirty seconds.

I stepped aside, afraid to linger and appear ghoulish, and walked casually around the perimeter of the room, overwhelmed by the nauseating bouquet of carnations and gladioli and the ostentatious serenity wreaths hanging from lopsided tripods. Pretending to read the cards and admire the flower arrangements, I considered approaching Kingsley and giving him Emily's note, but then I decided that the best thing to do, the most *devious* thing, would be to wait for the right opportunity to deliver the note to the person for whom it was originally intended.

I made my way to the exit, but as I was leaving I noticed how the two little girls smiled queerly at me. Like two trolls skipping along moonlit stones in a dark wood, they vanished behind their father's massive trunk and tugged on his sleeves. With a small shudder, I hurried from the funeral parlor, and somewhere behind me I heard them say, "That's him, Daddy, that's the pirate. The *pirate*, Daddy."

That night, plagued by troubled dreams and unable to sleep, I removed the pink stationery from the pocket of my suit coat, laid the pieces side by side on the Formica countertop in the kitchenette, and for the next hour transcribed Emily's words onto sheets of crisp white paper. I intended to deliver the note to Mrs. Kingsley in the morning and wanted a copy as a keepsake for myself. It was a slow and methodical process that became a kind of meditation, and soon my mind entered the dominions of monastic thought. Strangers walking by my window might have mistaken my threadbare apartment for the scriptorium of a medieval monastery, and they might have mistaken the hunched and solitary figure perched near the lamp as a pensive and diligent Trappist trying to cleanse his tortured mind of dark visions by transcribing lines of deathless verse. For an hour I focused intently on this work until my concentration was broken by the sounds of a terrible struggle next door and a series of frightful screams.

I was more or less accustomed to loud and sudden disruptions in this part of town. After the civilized world had turned out the lights in preparation for another working day, the squalid row houses came to life, and because the walls were so thin, my apartment often reverberated with a madhouse chorus of the damned and downtrodden—the snarls of a Rottweiler, the impossibly high-pitched and inconsolable cries of a small child, the lusty laughter of a drunk couple. The place was rife with dangers of all kinds. After sundown the addicts, thieves, and squatters broke into abandoned buildings to share needles and build fires. Maybe they thought the apartment next door was still unoccupied and had entered through a back window. The police typically put a stop to the anarchy, but never at night and never right away.

Convinced that Morgan was in serious danger, my irritation turned to genuine concern, and I was about to leap to her rescue when I stopped and listened more closely. Taking care not to let the floorboards creak, I tiptoed across the room, crouched low to the ground, and pressed my ear against the register. To describe Morgan's cries as bloodcurdling would not be too great an exaggeration, but gradually her squeals and shrieks transformed into those familiar whimpers of pleasure I still longed for, and soon the terrible struggle on the other side of the wall became the repulsive and rhythmic squeaking of bedsprings.

As I listened to her gasps and moans and hearty bellows of pleasure, I imagined an assortment of low-class Lotharios in her bed, trailer trash, rednecks, hayseeds, their dirty coveralls pulled down to their hairy knees. Some of the scenes I envisioned were, even by the depraved standards of the modern age, appallingly vivid, pornographically obscene: a former high school running back with small, murderous eyes pressing his pulsating, foreskinned scepter against my darling's flushed face; an affluent college kid wearing brand-name clothes and a smug smile, ripping open her blouse and snorting a fat line of blow between her fabulously tight tits; an emaciated, inbred bumpkin with greasy black hair and bad skin, asking her, with the nervous laughter universal to all sexual deviants, to massage his prostate with a rigid index finger.

The horror show went on and on, and to block out the constant drumming of devils in my head, the cancer spreading in my brain, I clamped my hands over my ears and vowed to match Morgan, lay for lay. A lofty goal, no doubt, and one not without its challenges. I had never been particularly skillful when it came to talking attractive, young ladies into the sack. What's more, our breakup put our mutual friends in an uncomfortable position, and because they wanted to postpone for as long as possible the awful business of choosing sides, they no longer extended invitations to the kinds of parties where I might actually meet an available woman.

After an hour, as I was starting to nod off beside the window, I heard Morgan's door creak open. I squinted, my good eye serving as a spyglass.

Flickering votive candles cast wildly shifting shadows across the threshold, turning her apartment into an uninviting cavern covered in prehistoric cave paintings that pulsated with a terrible inner energy. I glimpsed a glossy reprint of a pair of morose-looking, strung-out absinthe drinkers. From a distance they seemed to come alive and turn their pitted faces toward me, their lips parted as if to serenade me with a mournful and maniacal song.

A tall silhouette appeared in the doorway. Draped from head to toe in a black cloak, her face concealed under a hood, the woman could have passed for the mad governess in a Victorian ghost story or the high priestess in some bizarre backwoods cult that allowed women to preside over high ceremonies, perhaps the ritualistic slaughter of the innocent, but there was something so unmistakably beguiling and Circean about the way she carried herself that, despite her entreating eyes and the grim severity of her wraithlike disguise, she made for a striking and alluring figure.

Morgan appeared beside her in an unknotted robe, and from her sweaty flesh I thought I caught the odor of sweet fulfillment. She touched Lorelei's shoulder and said, "Please stay."

Lorelei shook her head. "I really need to go."

"But I have plenty of room. You can stay as long as you'd like."

"No, it wouldn't be right."

Morgan pressed an empty bottle of Châteauneuf-du-Pape into Lorelei's arms. "Here, take this, then. A memento."

Emboldened by the wine and using the chilly night air as a pretense, they embraced and exchanged a long, lingering kiss in the guttering candlelight. With bottle in hand, Lorelei climbed on a bicycle that looked as though some demented sculptor, using a blowtorch and a welder, had assembled the frame from dozens of spare parts. She pedaled away, her mouth hanging open to gobble up the black and gritty winds of midnight, her cloak trailing behind her like the spectacular rags of a witch.

In shock I stumbled away from the window, and all at once I felt entangled in a hundred dark and twisting arms, thousands of fingers pressing down on my throat. The accusing mirror in the corner only seemed to confirm just how worn down I looked, not prematurely old exactly but grotesquely boyish. My infected left eye now wept a viscous yellow discharge, and the first faint wrinkles on my forehead had noticeably deepened and spread into forking tributaries of misery and self-loathing.

I sank into a chair at the counter, wondering if I would ever again experience an evening of passion, and when I looked once more at the note I'd transcribed earlier that night, I saw several new lines that did not appear in the original and that I could not recall jotting down—an extraordinary instance of automatic writing! With trembling fingers I picked up the page and read aloud the cryptic words that the restless spirit of Emily Ryan, trying to communicate through my humble pen, must have written while I was in a trancelike state.

> *I know about the terrible longing that exists in the hearts of loveless*
> *men, and I can lead you to a love that is unconditional. This favor*
> *I will do for you if you will first do a small favor for me. Now*
> *listen . . .*

In Fascination
We Gravitate to the Irrational

Saturday, October 25–Monday, October 27, 2014

7

On a Saturday afternoon in late October, Madeline and Sophie Ryan marched in step through the high grass of a fallow field while listening to the piercing notes of a police siren. The sustained wails shot sharply across the soughing treetops and disappeared with mechanical precision through a window near the peak of a lichen-spotted barn that sat on a rise in the distance. One shard of glass dangled from the sill like the rotten tooth of a jack-o'-lantern and glimmered in the brilliant light of this unusually warm October afternoon, momentarily blinding the girls whenever they looked in that direction. Moribund, sun scorched, dead silent in its wild seclusion, the old post-and-beam horse barn seemed to lean forward as if to eavesdrop on the precocious pair stomping determinedly through the brush like emissaries from an enemy army's camp.

Madeline, the older of the twins by fifteen minutes and therefore the more perceptive of the two, smiled with satisfaction. "They're finally coming to take her away," she said. "See, I told you so."

Sophie, the younger but wiser one, gave her sister an apprehensive look. "No, they're not. They're after somebody else. The siren is far away now. Listen."

Madeline, swinging a hot-pink plastic pail in wide arcs, stopped to inspect the bottom for holes and cracks. "I bet she heard the squad car and ran as fast as she could."

Sophie's expression turned stony. "She'll still be there waiting for us, just like she said she would. You'll see."

"The barn was only temporary. That's what she told us. It isn't safe.

The floor is about to collapse. Probably she found a better hideout."
She glanced over her shoulder and said, "Besides, there's werewolves
in this valley."

"Coyotes," Sophie corrected her.

"Werewolves," Madeline insisted.

"How do you know?"

"Everybody knows. Neighbors won't let their dogs out at night
anymore. Werewolves eat everything. Dogs, cats, rats, people. Maybe
they already ate Lorelei. Betcha we find a big pile of her bones and
clumps of red hair."

Sophie shook her head. "Lorelei can protect herself."

"Yeah, thanks to us." Madeline pointed her right index finger at her
sister and pretended to cock her thumb. "I bet she's a good shot, too.
Bang bang! You're dead."

"She wouldn't leave without telling us first."

Madeline snorted with derision. "You think she'll marry Daddy,
don't you?"

"I do not."

"You think she'll come live with us and be our new mommy."

"You're stupid."

Madeline laughed and sprinted ahead. She pushed open the iron
gates looming large at the edge of a wasted field and ran along a stone
wall that marked the property line of an ancient farmstead. Using a
long stick that swoosh-swooshed through the air, one wide arc after
another, she cleared a path through a dense patch of purple coneflowers
and yellow fox sedge, a last glimpse of nature's ephemeral beauty before
the lacerating winter winds trapped them for the next five months in
the domestic desolation of a motherless home.

Sophie followed at a safe distance, shooing away a cloud of sluggish
greenbottle flies, her knees and shins crisscrossed with angry scratches
crusted with blood, her fingers stained with dark juices from having
ventured into the bushes where she'd picked wild berries, a dozen varieties, and placed them gingerly in mason jars that clinked together in
a satchel slung over her shoulder. She already had three jars filled with
red, purple, and white fruit. Pausing beside a thicket of jewelweed,

Sophie dabbed at the blood with a handful of orange petals and wished badly for someone to hug her and make the stinging go away. What she required was nothing less than a mother's solicitude, but the job of comforter and protector had fallen to their father.

At a rocky creek that twisted through the field, the sisters stopped to scan the surface for signs of life. With pail in hand Madeline slid down the clay slope and jumped into the stagnant green water. She giggled as her new sneakers sank slowly in the thick silt, her ankles pinned in the cool ooze, and when she tried to scoop up a school of scattering minnows with her pail, she swayed dangerously back and forth and nearly fell into the bubbling, burping film of algae. After regaining her balance and catching her breath, she announced, "Must be a thousand of 'em!"

"Minnows don't live in dirty water," said Sophie with revulsion. Taking care not to soil her own shoes, she skipped across a crooked causeway of slick rocks, and when she reached the other side, she looked back and made a prediction: "Daddy's gonna kill you."

Madeline scrambled up the embankment and peeled away a moldering brown sash of cattails from her legs. "Oh, he won't care. He went to Metal Mayhem. Won't be home till late. Besides, it's worth it."

"Why?"

She set the pail of minnows down and said, "Because Lorelei will like me more than she likes you. Minnows are better than those poisoned berries you picked. She can fry them up in a skillet. Or use them as bait to catch bigger fish in the river." She reached into the pail and threw a handful of minnows high into the air. A flock of blackbirds exploded from the swaying broomsedge and circled overhead. "Look! Bats!"

Sophie kept her distance, taking one tottering step back. "Crows, dummy."

"No, they're vampire bats. Just like the ones that live in our attic." She lobbed another minnow, and this one slapped against her sister's neck and slid down the front of her shirt.

"Stop!"

"Oh, no! They're coming to get you! They're coming to suck your blood!"

Shrieking with outrage and fear, trying to keep the mason jars from shattering, Sophie dashed through the nettles and ragweed and headed for the shell of the abandoned barn. The birds descended. Stumbling through the open doors, Sophie shook her T-shirt, desperate to wipe away the slimy residue, and she reeled in disgust when the minnow flopped on the floorboards. Beyond the threshold the birds gathered in a semicircle and regarded her with eyes filled with cunning. They sang and danced as though participating in a pagan ritual, a dozen black-clad supplicants daring to mock the god to whom they pled for sustenance. Cowering in the gloom, Sophie tossed the minnow outside and cringed as they fought over it in a frenzy of feathers.

Afraid the birds might find this scant offering unsatisfying and raid the barn to pick at her body until another fish fell magically from her shirt, Sophie waved her arms wildly back and forth and shouted, "Shoo! Go on! Get away from here!"

Sensing that the fun was over, the birds scratched at the dust and made strange rattling sounds deep in their throats, and then with cries of protest and a vigorous flapping of wings they took to the sky, eclipsing the sun before vanishing like a passing storm. From the field there came the unceasing drone of crickets and grasshoppers, and the wooden doors of the barn squeaked on rusty hinges.

Sophie tried to assure herself that nothing scary had happened. After catching her breath, she set the satchel off to the side and walked into the shadows.

"Hello!" she called. "Lorelei?"

Her sister's voice echoed, "Hello! Lorelei! Lorelei! Oh, help me, Lorelei! The bats are trying to suck my blood!"

Like an agitated insect, Madeline buzzed into the barn, flitting through the hazy beams of light, before crashing against a small corncrib and dropping the pail to the ground. The remaining minnows jumped in the dirt, dying a grim, waterless death.

"Dummy!" Sophie jeered.

Madeline ignored her, picking pieces of straw from her knees. "She isn't here, is she? See, I told you!"

Aggrieved and sullen, Sophie turned away. "She'll be back."

"Sure she will." Madeline went to a ladder near the center of the barn, its rungs dusted with chaff, and peered into the darkness above. "I'm going up."

"We're not supposed to."

Sophie attempted to stop her, but Madeline had already climbed the first few rungs and knocked her sister in the chin with the heel of a muddy shoe before disappearing through the opening.

Sophie rubbed her bruised face. Lorelei was sure to be back any minute now, and if she caught the girls in the loft she wouldn't let them visit her again. Lorelei didn't trust them, thought they might give away her secret, but Sophie would never tell, she was not like the other kids in the neighborhood, not like Madeline at least, she could keep her mouth shut, and so she waited, but the longer she stood there, listening to the creaking crossbeams and the shotgun crack of planks above her head, the more frightened she became. Those conniving blackbirds might erupt from a swale to feast on her flesh. She refused to budge, but when she heard a sudden rustle of grass, she slung the satchel over her shoulder and climbed to the top of the ladder with astonishing speed.

Like everyone else in town, Lorelei knew about their mother, and during those sunny autumn afternoons, whenever the twins came to visit her, she tried to impress upon them the many dangers of the valley, a place where ancient cultivators lay like steel traps and where the broken blades of enormous combines and rusted tractors waited, *just waited*, for the unfortunate day when careless children tripped and impaled themselves on the jagged tines. "A land so dangerous," she warned them, "that boys will not build tree forts here and grown men will not hunt for pheasant and farmers will not plant crops in its tainted soil. Nothing grows but briars and thistles and diseased plants that bear poisonous fruit."

When she failed to dissuade them from coming, Lorelei took the girls on long hikes to gather pawpaws and wild grapes and tried to teach them how to identify different types of berries—deadly, edible, therapeutic. "Ah, but this," she said, bending the stalk of a tall plant to eye level, "this one might have the most medicinal properties of all." With great care she harvested its brown and green buds and then crushed them up and spread them onto rolling papers. Lounging in the tall grass, she attempted to explain the peculiar behavior of adults, using big words like "addiction," "dependency," "clinical depression," and once, after taking a drag of her "hippie lettuce," as she called it, she used the puzzling phrase "death with dignity."

"You girls need to understand something. It's not weakness but the unraveling of the lies people tell themselves. After all their means of coping have disappeared, and they're faced with the certainty that their dreams will never come true, some people decide that a quick death is preferable to one more agonizing day of bitterness and resentment."

A passage quoted from one of her books, no doubt, and far too mysterious for the twins to fully grasp, but these observations sounded somehow right. Books were a cabinet of wonders that contained secret wisdom and magic formulae that could alleviate suffering, at least temporarily, and in the coming days and weeks, whenever they needed quick answers to a life that seemed increasingly confusing and chaotic, the girls returned to the barn to consult Lorelei and ask that she recite a paragraph or two that might help them make better sense of their troubles at home. She sat near the window, listening to spiders mend their damaged webs, and if the twins looked particularly morose she offered them a rueful grin. "Now, now," she said, "no need for tears. Everything will be fine, you'll see. I'm always here if you need me. And if you ever feel sad or lonely, or if you need anything at all, you can always close your eyes and call my name. Just imagine you're sailing through the air and across the valley to the barn. Let's see you try it now. Close your eyes, close your eyes . . ."

Lorelei had always been kind to them, and this was why Sophie, now poking her head above the trapdoor, was aghast to find Madeline running wild through the hayloft. It took a few seconds for her eyes to adjust to the diffused sunlight in the loft, but then, like the darkened auditorium at school with its red curtain rising above the stage, Sophie gradually saw beyond the swirling dust motes and found her sister, with her impressive aptitude for mindless destruction, rummaging through the objects of Lorelei's private world—an empty bottle of wine, a shattered mirror that divided her image into a dozen dazzling specters, a menagerie of stuffed animals, a coffee can filled with matches and candles, a small Styrofoam cooler packed with the good things the girls had pilfered from the refrigerator and pantry back home, thick slices of salami, a jar of kosher pickles, a bag of carrots. Madeline overturned Lorelei's cherished collection of paperbacks carefully arranged against the far wall, old books with faded covers, some stolen from the college library, others scavenged from yard sales. Lorelei had a passion for tales of the macabre and supernatural, and sometimes, when the sky was overcast and the wind was up, she read to the girls from an omnibus of ghost stories compiled by an eccentric old sorcerer named J. R. Montague.

Madeline lifted a corner of the mattress from the floor, and Sophie wrinkled her nose. Stained with mysterious brown and yellow patches, the mattress emitted a high, sour odor, and the girls wondered if Lorelei actually slept there. Didn't she worry about field mice burrowing into the stuffing in the middle of the night or rat snakes slithering under the sheets? Didn't she cringe at the thought of slimy salamanders creeping across her body and stinging centipedes covering her legs and arms with angry red welts? Didn't she dread the possibility of those ravenous birds rocketing through the window, tugging at her hair and pecking at her eyelids?

Most frightening of all were the strange wind chimes hanging from wires above the mattress, small creatures cut from scrap metal and painted cobalt blue, maroon, indigo. They reminded Sophie of the diseased fish that fed on dead things at the bottom of the river, brindled madtoms and frog-faced mottled sculpins. Here they were, snagged by hooks, tamed to dance fantastically to the discordant tune of their own incessant clanging.

Madeline was drenched in sweat. The morning had been cool, but by late afternoon, when the sun broke through the clouds and beat down on the barn, the rumbling heat and pressure inside the loft seemed capable of crushing a person, and the twins wondered how Lorelei tolerated it. The cluster of pale yellow leaves hanging heavy and limp from the enormous branches of white oaks offered little shade, and the earth around the barn looked parched and broken. Finding only dirt beneath the mattress and the dried wings of moths and the shattered shells of field crickets, Madeline let out a protracted sigh. In her most convincing imitation of a matronly voice she said, "Okay, where is it?" She crossed her arms and tapped one foot on the floor. "I asked you a question. Where did she put it?"

"We shouldn't be up here."

"I'll ask you just one more time."

Sophie's own voice wavered, and she made the mistake of letting her eyes drift to a loose plank on the floor. "She hid it someplace safe—"

Madeline raced to the spot, lifted the plank, and reached a hand inside.

"—so you wouldn't fool with it again." Sophie moaned. "But Lorelei said—"

"Lorelei, Lorelei, Lorelei!" Like a practiced gunslinger, Madeline twirled the .38 on an outstretched finger and then pointed the revolver at her sister. "I want you to confess. It was *your* idea to give her this gun, wasn't it?"

"People have been killed that way!"

Though terrified by her sister's unpredictable behavior, Sophie stood her ground, refusing to admit guilt. They were both responsible, and Madeline knew it. They never planned to steal the gun and didn't even know of its existence until one night last month when their dad went outside to gaze at his haggard reflection in the black water of the pool and, like so many small-town people bereft of hope, to nip at a jar of grain alcohol until he fell fast asleep in one of the Adirondack chairs. The girls slunk into the master bedroom to take regular inventory of their mother's belongings—the costume jewelry, the curious creams and powders, the combs, brushes, hair clips, and the wrinkled and musty turquoise sari now sealed in a plastic bag. After assessing the items in the dresser drawers, they explored the dark recesses of the closet, and there, behind an untidy pile of their dad's dirty magazines, they discovered the small mahogany case containing the gun and a full box of cartridges. They opened the lid, carefully removed the revolver from its dusty sarcophagus, and counted the bullets. "They're silver," said Madeline, holding one up to the light. "Daddy musta bought these special. To kill the werewolves. Do you think maybe we should give the gun to Lorelei?"

At the time Sophie thought it was a good idea, but now, as she backed slowly toward the ladder, she regretted having been an accomplice. "Please, Madeline, put the gun away."

"No, I'm bringing it back home. Before Daddy finds out it's gone."

"But what if Lorelei needs it? You even said there are werewolves, remember?"

Madeline shook her head. "I finally figured it out. I think Lorelei turns into a werewolf. And tonight there's supposed to be a full moon. We need to get out of here. It's not safe."

Sophie intuitively understood the seriousness of their transgression and knew from hard experience that adults, women in particular, had an innate ability to detect mischief and could, if they so wished, materialize out of thin air whenever things got out of control. And so it came as no surprise, at least to Sophie, when a tall figure rose phantomlike from the hole and screeched, "What the hell is wrong with you two!"

Sophie lowered her head in shame but raised her eyes just enough to see Lorelei stomping toward them, her long hair still dripping from her afternoon swim in the river, her T-shirt clinging to her belly. As always, Sophie marveled at the array of fish tattooed to her arms, from her wrists up to her shoulders. "My sleeves," Lorelei called them. "The morning I turned eighteen I went to see Colette Collins. She sat me down in a chair and went to work. Took her a whole month to finish them, but then she's a true artist and takes her sweet time. She's gifted as hell, that old lady. She can do almost anything—paint, sculpt, tattoo, distill moonshine. Calls herself a Renaissance woman."

But tattoos were a sign of trouble, that's what their mother always said, even though their dad had a few on his arms and legs.

"You have to be quiet in this barn," Lorelei now lectured them, her face pinched with chronic fear and worry, her eyes dark and hooded from so many sleepless nights. "How many times do I have to tell you? What a racket you two make. You sound like a couple of hyenas. I don't want any more unexpected visits, okay?"

Madeline tried to conceal the gun behind her back and looked at her sister. "Well, it's all *her* fault."

"Yeah, I bet." Lorelei snatched the .38 and slid it into the back pocket of her jeans. "You're both old enough to be held accountable for your crimes. Because in real life it's always a matter of accountability."

"So what are you accountable for?" Madeline asked brightly. "Are you going to tell us more of your secrets?"

"Like what?" Lorelei scowled and began organizing her books, Hawthorne, Poe, Lovecraft, King, placing them in proper order on the makeshift shelf she'd constructed from old milk crates and pieces of plywood.

"Who did you kill?" Madeline wanted to know.

"I never killed anyone. At least not yet."

"I bet you murdered someone. That's why you're hiding here. You're on the run from the law, aren't you? I can see it in your eyes. You've got the eyes of a killer."

Lorelei smirked. "Nobody has the eyes of a killer. You can't tell a killer from a regular person. No one can. That's why we have judges and juries in this country. People have to hear the whole story and think things over."

"Well, you musta done *something* bad."

Lorelei seemed to consider this for a moment, and her eyes fixed on the bottle of wine beside the mattress. "I sort of did something bad once. With another girl. But only once."

Sophie, who'd remained silent during this exchange, now stepped forward and presented her with the satchel. "Look what I brought you!"

Lorelei held one of the mason jars up to the light. She shook her head. "Some of these come from pokeweeds. And these are baneberries, I think. Very poisonous. I'm not sure about the white ones. Mulberries? Ah, but here"—she plunged her fingers into another jar—"we can eat these." She popped a handful of blueberries into her mouth. She didn't even bother to chew; she just swallowed them whole.

"How do you know all this stuff?" Madeline demanded.

Lorelei's eyes flashed with confidence and fiery aspiration. "The wilderness is the best schoolroom, a place for sojourners seeking enlightenment on the road of life."

"Is that poetry or something?"

"Kind of."

"We're already in second grade!" Sophie boasted.

Lorelei set the jars down and flipped through the pages of a hard-cover, examining them for damage. "Well, just wait until you get to college. Sometimes I think my professor doesn't care about anything except collecting a paycheck. No different from a high school teacher, I suppose. That's the one practical lesson I learned. School is just a way for adults to make ends meet because they aren't clever enough to earn a living any other way. You'd think at least one of those pointy-heads would have the guts to say to his students, 'Let's face facts, folks. I'm here because I have bills to pay. Don't expect much from me and I won't expect much from you.' That's essentially what it boils down to. It's just no one ever tells the truth about it."

"If you're so smart," asked Madeline, "why'd you run away?"

"I *told* you." She scrutinized the dust jacket and tried to rub out a small nick with her thumb. "After my mom died I went to live with my sister but she was married to a predator. Only a sick man would make eyes at his wife's kid sister. Anyway, I saved some money from a summer job. Good tips. Too bad I had to quit. I almost had enough for the first and last month's rent on an apartment."

"The boss fired you, huh?" said Madeline matter-of-factly.

"I had to take a leave of absence, you might say. Personal reasons."

"Cold weather'll be here soon." Sophie wiggled her fingers between the planks of wood. "A freak snowstorm is on the way. That's what the weatherman says."

"Yeah, you'll end up freezing in this barn." Madeline seemed delighted by the thought. "It must get awfully cold at night."

Lorelei adjusted the mattress and a lumpy pillow. "Oh, it'll be warm for a while longer yet. Besides, I have a pile of blankets and a heavy black cloak with a hood. I also have a bag of flour and a little sugar. And over there, in the cooler, I have a stick of butter and a couple of eggs. I even have a little cinnamon and nutmeg." She pointed to a wooden crate where she kept the small treasures of her lonely existence—salt and pepper shakers, a box of baking soda, a tin filled with lard, a stainless-steel bowl, a wooden spoon, a rubber spatula, a dozen plastic jugs of spring water. "Hey, do you wanna help me bake a pie?"

The twins smiled and clapped their hands. "Yes!"

And now all three of them, as they hastily gathered up the utensils and ingredients, seemed to be genuinely happy for the first time in many days.

In the field near the barn, keeping an eye out for those deranged birds, Sophie collected a bundle of dried sticks and placed it inside a kiln, a vaguely geometric jumble of chipped and broken limestone blocks that over time had turned white and chalky. The kiln reminded her of the photographs in one of Lorelei's books—the ruins of an ancient city, its excavated streets and avenues littered with what looked like the plaster casts of bodies, a dog curled against its master, a man and woman locked in a final embrace, a mother clutching her two wailing children—and she remembered what Lorelei had told her: "They suffocated under thirty feet of hot, volcanic ash . . ."

Madeline helped knead and roll the dough and then stirred the berries and sugar together in a wooden bowl. Lorelei then placed the dough in a dish, carefully tore away the overhanging edges, and after pouring the heady mixture from the bowl, draped a lumpy sheet of dough on top and then pinched the crust closed with thumb and forefinger. They listened to the hiss and crackle of the fire, and when the pie was done baking, the three returned to the loft, where Lorelei struck a match and lit the scented candle she'd been saving for a special occasion that never seemed to come. The malformed concoction, with dark juices oozing from its cratered center, roughly resembled a pie, but these imperfections didn't deter the girls from gorging themselves on slice after slice.

"It's just like a party!" Sophie said, sitting cross-legged at a cardboard box that served as a table.

On the horizon a band of clouds stained with the soft lavender hues of sunset floated toward the barn. From the shattered window near the peak, they could also make out a cluster of houses crowded along the rim of the valley—"a working-class penal colony," Lorelei called it—including their own house with its peeling paint, its disintegrating chimney, its dark and empty windows.

"See how pretty it can be from high up here?" said Lorelei, embracing her knees. "It's like a giant smashed a handful of berries and smeared it across the roof of the world. Too bad the world isn't so sweet. I suppose there has to be one person stuck with the burnt piece. Forced every day to eat charcoal. You never get used to that taste either. Starts to make you sick after a while."

Madeline and Sophie nodded their heads. They knew exactly what Lorelei meant. The pie was beginning to make them a bit queasy, and they rubbed their grumbling tummies.

"People want too much of a good thing, that's how the addicted mind works. They're never satisfied with what life has given them so they try to take what's yours. Did you ever learn about the food chain in school? People need to feed constantly, sometimes on one another. The people of this town, they feed on me, too. I'm the feral creature that feeds their fears, the monster that lives beneath the surface, the unspeakable thing from the dreaded depths that no one wants to see and will not admit exists."

Soon an inky twilight seeped into the loft, and a gust of cold air made the scarf of orange flame flicker, a gentle reminder that in the weeks to come Lorelei would be shivering under her black cloak, fighting against killing blizzards, icy tempests, the interminable winter squalls that savaged the loose planks of wood and sent restless fingers of snow searching deep inside the heart of the barn to squash any hint of warmth and life. Above the treetops the hunter's moon gazed at them red and unblinking like an inflamed, omniscient eye before it slipped behind the thin gauze of a vapor trail.

Sophie smacked her lips. "That was really good, Lorelei, but I think it's time for us to go home."

"You're probably right." Lorelei slid between the girls and stroked their backs. "Listen to the crickets. At this time of year it gets dark so quickly. What if you lose your way in the woods? I've seen coyotes prowling around lately. I think it's best if you stay here with me. I don't mind."

Sophie shifted uncomfortably and ran one finger through the remnants inside the pie dish. "Well, we'd have to go home first and ask our dad."

"Your dad? I thought you said he drinks himself into a stupor every night."

Madeline seemed doubtful. "But we'll get into trouble."

"You don't have to go back home anymore. Whether you girls know it or not, you've been living on your own for a long time now. Even before your mom died."

Sophie knew there was only one thing that might make Lorelei happy, but even she sensed the absurdity of the idea, the childishness of it, knew it for what it was, a supreme cliché, something she'd heard on TV, but she went ahead and said it anyway. "You could come live with us. We have lots of extra room at our house."

"Our daddy would want you to come live with us," Madeline agreed. "We'll go home and ask right now."

Lorelei shook her head. "I would never live with your dad."

"Why not?"

"Think. Think real hard." She wiped her lips on the pillowcase, leaving a streak of color like fresh blood.

The girls listened to the moan of warped joists and trusses and the pop of rusted nails freeing themselves from the barn's heavy timbers. Above the mattress, spinning faster and faster, the grotesque wind chimes created a dissonant clank and clatter that mimicked the rattle of ghostly chains.

"A gift from the Gonk," said Lorelei. "A reminder that he wants certain favors."

"The Gonk?"

"Yes, he was greedy with lust. Probably no different from your father."

"Our dad isn't like that at all!" Sophie snapped.

Lorelei smirked. "What do you two know? You're just a couple of dumb kids."

"Maybe *you're* the dumb one," said Madeline. "You're fat. Getting fatter by the day. Maybe we should stop feeding you. Or maybe you've been hunting on your own." She turned to her sister. "See, she *is* a werewolf. Didn't I tell you? She has the evil eye."

"You girls watch too much TV," Lorelei said.

"Evil eye! Evil eye!"

"If I was your father, I'd swat you for watching so much TV."

"What's wrong with TV?"

"It turns people into dummies," Lorelei answered. "Fills their heads with silly ideas. Makes them think and say stupid things. Me, I never watch TV."

"Yeah, because you don't have one," Sophie jeered. "You don't have anything. You don't have a mommy or a daddy."

"That's enough," Lorelei mumbled.

"See, she's just like us," said Madeline. "She wants a mommy, too!"

"That's enough, I said."

"Aw, look, she's tongue-tied," Madeline continued. "She's trauma-tized. She's got issues. We learned all those fancy words from TV. We learn lots of good stuff from TV. You're troubled. Emotionally dis-turbed. You need counseling, medication, around-the-clock psychiatric care."

Lorelei leveled her eyes at Madeline and slapped her with enough force to knock her to the floor. "Why don't you go home, you brat?" she said with a scowl. "Go home to your daddy. Go on, both of you."

Sophie shrank from a face that seemed so suddenly unfamiliar to her, a nightmare mask distorted by uncontrollable rage. She should have known better than to be taken in by Lorelei's counterfeit affection. "You can't hit my sister!" she cried. With surprising agility she lunged across the mattress and managed to snatch the gun from Lorelei's back pocket.

Lorelei screamed. "Don't point that thing at anyone!"

Sophie ignored her and lifted the barrel so it lined up nicely with Lorelei's heart, where all of the nastiness could be found. Hearts were known to explode from gunshot wounds, and there would be much blood, foul and black and bitter splashed against the faded wood.

A single tear ran slow and heavy down Lorelei's stricken face. "I know you're upset with me. But please put the gun down. I'm asking nicely."

Sophie now aimed at the bottle of Châteauneuf-du-Pape beside the mattress. "You shouldn't drink wine," she said coldly. "Alcohol is a very bad thing. You oughta see what it's done to our daddy."

Unable to cope with this new nightmare, Lorelei buried her head under a pile of pillows and seemed to dissolve bit by bit into the shadows so that all that remained of her body was a round, heaving mass at the center of the mattress.

Sophie squeezed the trigger, and before the force of the blast sent her flying backward and the bottle exploded in a thousand pieces, she saw a single silver bullet suspended magically in the air. She threw the gun to the floor, faint smoke curling whitely from the hot barrel. Careful to avoid the jagged shards of glass, she scampered across the loft and hurried down the ladder, Madeline following close behind her.

Racing home through the twilight fields, plowing through trussed cornstalks and withered goldenrod, giggling like a pair of madhouse sisters, Sophie and Madeline suddenly wanted Lorelei to suffer in new and unimaginable ways, wanted her to die if such a thing could be arranged, and they prayed for the sinister flapping of wings, a storm of vampire bats unleashing a torrent of deafening squeals and drowning out Lorelei's cries of terror. Deep in the woods the gamesome girls, their hearts untouched by sin, heard the unsettling song of coyotes and wished for a famished pack to invade the barn, to pounce on Lorelei, to tear at her tender flesh, a dozen beasts competing madly to be the first to crouch on her belly and feast on her guts all stuffed with that tantalizing wild fruit.

8

Wrecked lives, wrecked marriages, wrecked college careers, wrecked cars. In Normandy Falls the boundaries between these things could never be clearly delineated. Desperate to break free from the confinement of his house, hoping to put an end to his maddening thoughts, Charlie Ryan donned a baseball cap and jacket and went to Metal Mayhem, held every Saturday night at the edge of town. "Any car! Any year! Station wagon, limo, or hearse!" He sat near the top row of the bleachers and for hours watched teams of wild-eyed men ("pree-cision car crushers," as they billed themselves) careen their three-thousand-pound steel skeletons into one another at terrific speeds. Like everyone else in attendance, Charlie applauded the spectacular head-on collision of two Corsairs that came plunging through moonlit breakers of black exhaust. Unrecognizable hunks of cast iron whirled like shrapnel through the stadium lights. The destruction was utterly inane, the cheers wonderfully mindless, and the evening air reeked of a witch's brew of gasoline and hot oil.

Unprepared for the ferocity with which it wormed its warm way into his brain, Charlie took surreptitious sips of moonshine from a jar that his wife had stashed away in one of the kitchen cupboards, and then let out a satisfying belch, the proud and uninhibited roar of a mountain man. All around him the boozed townies slapped their knees and laughed. I laughed, too, appreciated their good humor, their easygoing manner. Back home the people I knew would have scowled with disapproval at such low-class antics, and they would have flinched at my horrifically swollen face, but not the good citizens of this town, and certainly not here, not at Metal Mayhem, because in Normandy Falls ugliness reigned supreme, and beauty, if it could be found at all, existed only in the degree of ugliness, the ferocity of it. Ugliness, if ugly enough, could sometimes be sublime.

The men seated beside Charlie said, "We've missed you, fella. Haven't seen you at the derby all fall. Where've you been?"

In order to hear his response above the terrible grind of twisting metal, I leaned forward and cocked my head. Charlie sat one row below me and looked just as terrible tonight as he had on that late summer afternoon at the funeral home.

"Haven't been anywhere," he said. "Just trying to manage Madeline and Sophie."

"And how are the girls doing?"

"The best they can, I suppose," he answered. "We all are."

"Bet they keep you plenty occupied."

He drummed his fingers on his knees. "Oh, they're rambunctious all right. It's a full-time job keeping track of those two. Their mother could barely handle them. Probably drove the poor woman batty." Startled by his own words, he quickly added, "I mean, they've reached the age when children become very willful. It must have happened while I was sailing the lakes. Six months ago I waved farewell to two sweet little girls. But when I came home I found a pair of hellions. I actually thought about calling the pastor and asking him to perform an exorcism. Maybe he'd be willing to give me a deal. A two-for-one discount or something."

Charlie cracked a weak and wavering smile but stopped short of telling them that he'd left the house while the girls were off exploring the valley. He was convinced the twins possessed unholy powers—telepathy, clairvoyance, a tyrannical taste for retribution. On those rare occasions when he was sober enough to formulate a coherent sentence, he often accused them of trying to publicly shame him by disclosing some awful impropriety. He had betrayed their mother, and somehow they knew about it. From his subtlest gestures and the slightest shift of his eyes, the girls could divine what he was thinking, or so he believed, and for this reason he tried his best to avoid them, leaving them to fend for themselves.

Ultimately, his apparent lack of concern turned out to be a blessing. Children tend to derive comfort from the familiar, but such was not the case with Madeline and Sophie. They eagerly sought out new and secret worlds, far from a father who fostered hopelessness and misery, miles from a home seething with insurmountable problems, a place with no past and no future, only a terrible present. Restless by nature, the girls often hurried home from school and then disappeared down the dark tunnel of trees that led to the valley floor. Charlie didn't seem to care. If anything, he was grateful the girls weren't around to torment him with their tall tales. "But we swear it, Daddy. We saw a *pirate* sleeping by the pool on the night Mommy drowned!"

He promised himself he would be gone for a couple of hours, three at most. The girls could survive on their own until he returned. He just needed a break, needed to see something other than those two bereaved and wretched faces floating in the dark like disembodied Venetian masks, watching him with constant worry and wondering if Daddy, just like Mommy, would ever come home again. Dirty, hungry, slightly terrified, they looked more like penned-up animals wallowing in their own filth than darling little girls. If only there were some way he could help them. Late at night, while lying alone in bed, he was forced to press a pillow over his head in order to silence the sounds of the girls crying themselves to sleep. He felt guilty about this, but he felt guilty about a lot of things. He hadn't cleaned the house or cooked a meal or washed a load of laundry in weeks. He hadn't answered the phone or spoken to the neighbors or paid a single bill. In the mailbox angry notices from collections agencies were piling up. All of the down-to-earth duties of running a household had been left to Emily, and Charlie didn't quite know where to begin.

Now, since he had no one in his life to whom he could unburden his heart, he turned to the other spectators and said, "Yeah, I came back to a house swarming with devils. But that's not the worst of it, no, not even close." He shook his head like a man mildly astonished by a streak of bad luck. "Whenever I returned from a long voyage, I made my wife wear a turquoise sari. Every time, every single time. Forcing Emily to wear the sari, that was the worst thing I ever did, the very worst thing."

The spectators had no idea what he was talking about and hoped they weren't about to witness a public breakdown. The poor man, twenty years on the high seas had given him intimate knowledge of tempests so terrific that storms must have raged day and night in the back of his brain. But I knew all about the sari. Emily had revealed everything to me, left nothing out. On my kitchen countertop I now had several notepads covered in her careful handwriting, long and detailed descriptions of their very own South Seas adventure, and I knew the sari was a grim reminder of that fateful moment in Emily's life when she discovered how her husband no longer loved and respected her.

Before leaving Metal Mayhem that night, Charlie waited in line at the concession stand behind a group of whining children who demanded waffle cones, cotton candy, chocolate-covered potato chips. He ordered a hard cider to cut whatever moonshine remained in his jar and then shoved his way through the crowd. As I followed a few paces behind him in the gravel lot, I heard an echo of familiar laughter and saw my fellow ticks loafing outside the gates of the derby.

"Hey, Cyclops!" they called. "We have a question for you. Do you think it's possible to capture an owl and keep it as a pet? Do people do such things in these parts?"

"Lunatics," I muttered, and strode toward my car.

"What's the hurry, Cyclops? Listen, we have some important news for you. We're launching the sailboat tomorrow morning. We intend to pass through the fifteen locks and five canals of the Saint Lawrence Seaway. A distance of more than two thousand miles! And then we'll follow the great, beetling headlands of the East Coast. She gave us all the information we need and told us to set sail for the South Seas."

I stopped. "*Who* told you this?"

"The goddess. For years we thought a god was speaking to us. But we were mistaken." The men looked around as though she might be listening. "We heard her voice in the night. Like the song of the dove when it returned to Noah. Like the song of the rainbow after the deluge. A siren song. And her voice has the power to inspire, to incite, to inflame."

"To render insane," I said, opening my car door.

"You're learning the ways of the world, Cyclops, and now it's time you stop with all of your fiction writing and your Greek poets with their fondness for buggery and enchanted islands. Instead of those candy-ass professors, maybe you oughta listen to us fanatics for a change. Them teachers spend too much time trying to figure out reasons why a god don't exist instead of reasons why a god *does* exist. Maybe they should start studying the world as it is, the world as god, *any* god, made it. What if they're wrong, huh? At least if they believed in a power greater than themselves, they wouldn't suffer from so many questions, their brains wouldn't burn with so much fire. Either there is a supernatural order or there is not. You must place your bet. You have no alternative."

Listening to them express their philosophical views was like listening to them discuss their sex lives. It was mildly disgusting and incredibly dull; it was also easy to see through their certainty, their bullshit, their braggadocio. Brainless beyond description, they had fallen completely under the sway of some pitiless paranormal power and now lived in constant fear of it. I climbed into my car and turned the ignition. The wind was beginning to pick up now, shifting direction out of the northwest, and on the radio the announcer warned of a freak snowstorm, the first of the season, with sub-zero temperatures and significant lake-effect snow. Donner Party kind of stuff, judging from the irrepressible excitement in the man's voice.

"Gentlemen," I said, rolling down my window, "you've inadvertently stumbled upon an argument of sheer genius."

"Huh?"

"You know. Pascal's wager."

They continued to shake their heads. With soot-covered fingers they probed the waxy canals of their great, flopping ears and massaged the bloody gums of their crooked, yellow teeth. "Huh? *Huh?*"

"Pascal's wager," I repeated. "Pascal's *wager!*"

"So you got yourself a little learning. And that's supposed to make you better than the rest of us, right?"

"Oh, do I give you that impression? That I'm somehow better than you?" I flashed a superior smile of straight white teeth. I'd started brushing regularly again, three times a day. The advantages of having clean teeth and healthy gums were not to be underestimated. One could always tell the difference between the townies and the college students from the condition of their choppers.

"Naw, we know you're not better, Cyclops. We said *you* think you're better. You think a whole lot of things. That's your problem. You think too much. You don't stop thinking. But it's all in your head. None of it's real."

"What you're saying is I'm neurotic."

"Well, if that's what 'neurotic' means, then yes, you're neurotic as they come. Your mind spins round and round like a hamster running on one of them wheels. The hamster thinks he's pretty clever, too, going absolutely nowhere."

I put the car in drive. "I'd say I'm more like the ball in a roulette wheel."

"You see! Pure crazy. But we know the truth. We're here for a purpose, and soon, very soon, we'll know what that purpose is."

Finding this whole conversation a terrific bore, I pulled away and tailed Charlie Ryan, but I could not ignore their final words to me, and from the rearview mirror I glared at them, my eye glowing like a burning brand.

"Remember, Cyclops! You're one of us now! And on Sunday at dawn we sail south! Did you hear, Cyclops? Tomorrow at dawn!"

Charlie Ryan hadn't thought about his own South Seas adventure in quite a long time, wouldn't permit himself to think of it, tried to blot it from his memory, but instead of a black ribbon of road cutting through the barren countryside, he found himself gazing again at the methylene-blue waters of Delacroix Cay, a holograph whose diaphanous image seemed to solidify in the autumn air. For a moment he was in two places at once, hovering somewhere between the reality of the open road and his suppressed memories of fishing boats moored to the pontoon docks along the shore, a thatched-roof palapa bar surrounded by palmettos, and in a distant sweep of green fields the small shipwrecked shanty that for seven days and nights he and Emily shared.

On the afternoon he told her the exciting news, Charlie noticed how his wife's expression became faintly clouded by suspicion. Emily wanted to know why a merchant marine who worked six months out of twelve on the Great Lakes thought they should spend their anniversary on a remote island in the middle of the Caribbean. Wouldn't he prefer to see the Smoky Mountains, the Rockies, the Grand Canyon, Yosemite, Joshua Tree, any incalculably vast land mass or rock pile or dusty desert? Charlie forced a smile, trying to disguise the shameful fact that he'd forgotten it was their anniversary. When a man sails the lakes in winter, he told her, when for a six-month stretch he has to stare at endless miles of gray ice floes, he gets desperate to see a fair sky, a blue and cloudless horizon.

"The holy trinity of sun, sand, and serenity," he said.

There was some truth to this, and on his better days, when his mind wasn't muddled by lust, Charlie envisioned a pristine bay teeming with schools of tropical fish instead of heaps of sheepshead and walleye moldering on stony beaches, the screeching gulls picking madly at tough scales and bones. What he failed to tell his wife was that he'd won the trip by answering trivia on a radio talk show. He'd phoned the station on multiple occasions, but every time his calls got through, he suddenly lost his nerve and hung up. He shook, he trembled, he gasped for air, fighting desperately for every breath. With the receiver still in his hand, he fell to his knees and called upon heaven for guidance, but his flesh was weak, and no matter how intensely he prayed he could not rid his mind of the tormenting images he'd seen in those brochures.

In the end he convinced Emily to make the journey with him. Known for its ecotourism, Delacroix Cay catered to scuba divers from around the globe eager to explore the virgin coral reef, but of late the island had garnered a reputation as an international destination for big-bellied, married American men who came for weekend getaways to take full advantage of those notorious beachside "fish markets" found nowhere else in the Caribbean. The government was tolerant of even the most shameful of professions.

On the island there were no big resorts or casinos or chain restaurants, and during the shuttle ride from the airport through the eerily quiet streets of an old port town, Charlie and Emily glimpsed packs of starved dogs trotting through evil-smelling alleyways. Groups of tense young men dressed in military fatigues stood on every corner, submachine guns at the ready. The soldiers waved the shuttle through a series of roadblocks, and in the whole of that dreary shantytown Charlie didn't see a single white face.

After crossing its mountainous spine, they came to the leeward side of the island, where large trees darkened the dirt road, their dead leaves falling to the ground and crackling like fire under the tires. Here there were very few enchanting details of landscape, and upon reaching a village near the beach, the stone-faced driver, who only spoke a patois of French and Carib, pointed to a small, whitewashed cottage with a pyramidal roof of corrugated iron lit by the afternoon sun. He gave the American couple an odd look as they collected their luggage and disembarked.

"Missionaries?" he asked.

Charlie shook his head. The driver closed the door and sped away.

Emily stood in the middle of the road and watched hummingbirds of iridescent green darting through tall clusters of trumpet flowers. Charlie took her suitcase and walked doubtfully down a muddy path bordered by palm trees and bougainvillea and past a rusty cistern on stilts entangled in creeping vines hungry for sunlight. Through a fire-red door glazed with rain they entered the cottage, and inside they found three concrete rooms, including one with a toilet and a shower. Except for a few pieces of wicker furniture and a bed draped with a stiff mosquito net, the rooms were bare.

Charlie had expected the accommodations to be a bit rough, a condo in need of updating, a fresh coat of paint, new appliances, modern decor, but the condition of the cottage shocked him; it was little more than a crude hut with running water, and he felt an urgent need to apologize to his wife. He waited for a sharp rebuke, or at least some show of disappointment, but Emily threw open one of the frosted windows in the kitchenette and looked out at the ocean. The air smelled vaguely of the bright masses of rhododendrons and hibiscus surrounding the property, and in the tidal winds the cottage began to creak.

With tears in her eyes, she turned to him and said, "Oh, thank you for this, Charlie. Thank you. It's lovely."

He smiled with a sense of accomplishment, and it took him a moment to register the subtle note of sarcasm in her voice.

They spent most of the week in bed, violently ill from eating fried fish, burned plantains, and cold rice and from swimming in the polluted bay after the rain-swollen streams came pouring down the mountainside. A plague cast down from heaven, Charlie was sure of it, but during their last day on the island, determined to enjoy himself, he threw off the soiled sheets from their sickbed and left Emily to convalesce on her own. He staggered over the dunes toward the ocean, and like a haggard beachcomber on some forgotten atoll, he searched the shore for souvenirs, for whelks and rayed shells and creamy pink stones polished smooth by the ocean. Every time the gentle waves foamed around his ankles and the warm sand enveloped his toes, he caught a whiff of raw sewage, a powerful and persistent reminder of the disease and crushing poverty that bedeviled this small island nation. By then the sun was already sinking toward the horizon, and a strong wind kicked up whitecaps on the lagoon. Dry coconuts and mango flowers and bright pomanders tumbled in the hissing surf.

Aside from an ugly, colonial-era church of faded yellow brick, the palapa bar at the end of the beach was the tallest structure in that sorry village, where tourists could, for ruinous prices, buy key chains, bottle openers, small figurines carved from the wood of the native nutmeg trees, and, according to the guidebook, "certain attractions that leave very little to the imagination."

Surrounded by a dozen or so palm-leaf huts, the palapa looked deserted, cleaned out, the shelves empty of liquor bottles, cocktail umbrellas, and fancy garnishes. Charlie panicked. Without alcohol to ease his nerves, he would never be able to summon the necessary courage to fulfill his fantasy. The bar smelled of sandalwood paste and sea air. Several coats of varnish had made a thick, uneven skin on the wood. From hidden speakers the steel drums of the ever-present calypso music produced a plump, round sound. The proprietor, a painfully thin man of Indian descent who carried himself with the regal bearing of a Brahmin, adjusted the brim of his close-fitting cork hat, which was damp with sweat, and rested his wrinkled elbows on the bar.

"Refreshment, sir?"

Charlie nodded and said hopefully, "What do you recommend?"

The man reached beneath the bar and produced several bottles hidden in a cabinet. "The Red Death. It's the unofficial drink of Delacroix Cay. An old recipe named for the legendary corsair that three hundred years ago struck the shoals on the windward side of the island during a storm and sank with all hands." Using an old rag he polished an enormous glass goblet and served his sole customer that day a slightly frothy mixture, so syrupy and foul tasting that it made Charlie wince. "As you probably know, sir, we are not a cay at all but an island. The pirates who named Delacroix thought they could confuse the French. The colonial powers might bypass the island if they thought it to be an unprotected pile of sand without a cove or sheltering bay. Eventually, of course, the French prevailed and turned Delacroix into a penal colony for unreformed buccaneers, an overcrowded, equatorial Alcatraz crawling with sea dogs suffering from scurvy and rickets, all of them trying either to sodomize or strangle one another."

Charlie pushed his empty glass across the bar. "Interesting."

"I'm pleased you enjoy the drink, sir." The man searched his pockets and handed Charlie a small yellow card. "For my honored American guests—the recipe for the Red Death. I think the pomegranate juice strikes just the right note, but the key ingredient, and the one that gives it such complexity, is the grain alcohol produced in the remote hilltop villages." He laughed and told Charlie the lore of the hills and the ways of the people. "Local legends persist, and some of the older men and women, a few, not many these days, still practice strange and primitive rites. Whenever they become ill, they ask loved ones to behead a chicken and perform a ritual dance."

Charlie snapped his fingers. "That's what I should have done. Killed a couple of chickens." He chewed loudly on the crushed ice from the bottom of his glass. "I'm an old pirate myself and know all about unusual superstitions." After only one drink he was beginning to speak with a pronounced slur. He hadn't eaten in days and was wary of ordering anything from the menu at a place like this. "My wife has been pretty sick and it's our last day on the island. I want to find a conch shell to bring back to her. The guidebook says the reef is littered with them. A 'conch graveyard,' the writer called it."

"Oh, no, no," said the proprietor, "you mustn't remove anything from the reef." Using a large wooden spoon that had turned black and green, he stirred another batch of the Red Death. "Our prime minister was quite cavalier about the condition of the coral, even after it showed unmistakable signs of damage and bleaching from the influx of tourists. A distressed reef means a distressed economy, and the business community demanded strict enforcement of all laws pertaining to the reef. Of course we never fathomed that the military would take action and depose our prime minister. I avoid politics, but trust me, friend, you do not want to provoke the new junta. If the authorities discover a shell in your luggage as you pass through security, they may detain you. These days tourists must be vigilant. For Lord Shiva has many arms with which to ensnare his prey." The proprietor spoke in the relaxed fashion of a man used to living in a state of gentle anarchy. He topped off Charlie's glass and lowered his voice. "But perhaps, sir, I can interest you in a souvenir of another kind?" He clapped his hands and shouted, *"Maharani!"*

The air moved a little faster now, becoming a steady breeze. Purple clouds piled on the horizon and billowed above the banana trees of stormy green. From one of the creaking railings, a solitary chameleon stared at Charlie and then scuttled across the bar top, vanishing beneath a pile of napkins. A moment later a young woman with big sloping shoulders and runny eyeshadow emerged from a nearby hut and lumbered into the palapa bar. She wore a turquoise-colored sari. With its silver beads and its precise sequins and stonework, the sari fairly sparkled like tropical moonlight on the water. The proprietor touched the soft fabric. Then his fingers crawled up the woman's arm, over her neck, across her lips, through her unruly mop of black hair.

"How do you like it, sir? Exquisite workmanship, don't you think? Gujarati style. Regarded by many as the epitome of high Indian culture. Worn correctly it—how shall I put this—highlights a woman's figure in all the right places. Truly a timeless piece."

The girl smiled, revealing a mouthful of gold teeth.

Charlie scratched his chin. A few of his shipmates—divorcées, philanderers, incorrigible sea dogs—had a lot more practice with this kind of thing, but he was new to the game and proceeded with caution.

"And who is this?" he asked.

"Forgive me, sir," said the proprietor. "May I have the pleasure of introducing you to my niece, Sita. A very open-minded and, I must say, accommodating girl. If this sari is not to your liking, she would be most happy to take you to her hut and model a number of others for you. But first, if it isn't too much of an imposition, we can come to terms that would be agreeable to both parties? For your convenience, we accept both cash and traveler's checks."

Charlie blinked in amazement, but he reached into his back pocket for his wallet, and his skeptical frown gradually formed into a wide and libidinous smile.

The walk back to the cottage was a long one, and he kept looking over his shoulder for signs of the teenage soldiers who regularly patrolled the beach at night. He spit a sugary glob of the Red Death into the surf, and the air instantly swarmed with biting sand fleas. The wind buffed and curried the shifting dunes littered with sick banana leaves. In the distance an old trawler steamed along the coast. The sky, thronging with the freakish pterodactyl shapes of cormorants, was enfolded in a blanket of tropical clouds. Behind him, in the gray-blue sweep of sugarcane fields, he could see two small figures slashing at the sharp, fibrous stalks with their long knives and heard them singing a simple work song, their voices rising in fractious harmony above the wind that played in the scorched palms. They waved their knives above the crumbling walls that partitioned the land and then resumed their work.

The wind changed direction, rolling off the land, and Charlie nearly retched at the stench of rotten bagasse that came wafting from the field. With his heavy, splayfooted walk and his arms swinging at his sides, he approached the cottage and spotted his wife waiting for him by the sea. Waves tumbled over the reef and into the lagoon where they spread along the shore and splashed against the black, volcanic rocks. Emily gazed into a tidal pool where cuttlefish and crabs hid in the shadows and fat sea cucumbers inched their way along the sandy bottom. She sat on the rocks and plunged a hand into the renewal of the warm water, unafraid of the sharp sting of sea urchins and poisonous tiger fish.

He called to her, told her it was dangerous.

"But they're such bizarre creatures, Charlie."

Her exaggerated slouch suggested boredom, disdain, a quiet agitation building toward epic anger. How much did she know about the palapa bar, about this playground of the debauched, the perverted, the morally bankrupt? How much could she intuit from the guilty look on his face? His experience inside the hut hadn't been nearly as fulfilling as the guidebook promised him it would be, though he did learn a few new kinky tricks. Initially, the proprietor's "niece" seemed almost diffident, speaking to him in a timorous and tongue-tied language that he couldn't understand, but after a few minutes she took charge and pushed him toward a small bed. Nervous, fumbling, stubbornly limp, Charlie had to be coached, coaxed, constantly reassured, excessively stroked and fondled. The woman was patient and forgave his clumsi-

ness and uncertainty. For her professionalism Charlie tipped her gener-
ously, but when he left the hut he saw open hatred stamped on her eyes,
a look that was sharp, piercing, extraordinarily clear in its loathing for
him. The same look he now saw in Emily's eyes.

He was a great dispenser of bad luck and bad feelings, and he had
to remind himself never to underestimate just how miserable he could
make his wife feel. Obscenely drunk, clutching the sari in his fist, he
stumbled toward Emily and said in a small, strangled voice, "Look, I
bought this beautiful dress for you."

Again, he watched for soldiers, and when he turned around to face
his wife he saw with upending, smothering astonishment a small yellow
card in her hand.

"What's that?" he asked, and could actually feel a stupid expression
coming down over his ruddy face.

"A souvenir," she answered, and flung herself into the bay.

He rushed to the water's edge. "Come back!"

Emily blinked at the brine. "Do you want me to come back, Charlie? Do you *really*?"

Fighting the urge to scream, he bent over, picked up the card, and
crumpled it in his fist without bothering to look at the recipe for the
Red Death. He waited for her under a palm tree and stared at an iguana
climbing through a heap of coconut shells. He hesitated from plunging in after her because he knew that if he dared to jump into that
loathsome water he might never return to the shore. Emily would keep
swimming farther and farther out to sea, and then she would clasp her
arms around his waist and try to pull him under. In a way it was a damn
shame. The reef would have been such a beautiful place to die together.

Back at his house, slumped sideways in an Adirondack chair by the
swimming pool, an empty jar of the Red Death wedged precariously
between his legs, five or six cigarette butts scattered around his boots
and one burning between his limp fingers, Charlie stared into the night
sky and waited for Madeline and Sophie to return from the valley.

Unlike his wife, who knew all about the stars and from their precise arrangement in the heavens could interpret many meanings, Charlie never sat with the girls and pointed out the mythic creatures lurking among those first constellations cresting the horizon, here the pincers of a crab, there a stinging scorpion, its ponderous tail bulbed with poison. He never told them about Auster, whose south winds brought heavy cloud cover and impenetrable mists, or about Boreas, who sent sleet and snow tearing across the planet from his icy lair way up north. He didn't teach them these things because he had no interest in learning them himself. Mainly he stared at the black spaces between the stars, the widening chasm of infinite space. Sometimes, too, he stared at a crack in the pavement, a stone, a beetle, a red clover mite as it scuttled across the back of his hand. For hours he stared and stared, his eyes blank and glassy, and he never uttered a word, not even to the twins when they stood on either side of his chair and whimpered for him.

As he started to nod off, he began to imagine things, crazy things, the summer skies spinning with fortunes good and bad, meteors plummeting from some remote sector of the solar system, ill omens falling across water so still it might have been a magic mirror polished smooth by the wind, and he worried that he would be swept away by the momentum of the whole reeling cosmos, propelled into the void among the terrors of space. He dreamed his daughters had come home and were standing in the center of the swimming pool, the water frozen solid and gleaming like a midnight anvil. With mischievous twitters the girls asked their father to follow them. "Mommy would like a word with you," they told him, and despite Charlie's stern commands to stop, the twins jumped up and down until the ice started to crack. "She's under here, Daddy! She's *under here*!"

Now, after their adventure in the barn, Madeline and Sophie burst through the gate only to find their father whining and thrashing like a sleeping dog. He waved his arms and drummed his fists against his knees. He moaned and cursed and whimpered. They usually discovered him this way. Easily agitated, half-witted, insensibly drunk, prone to violent outbursts, Charlie often passed out in the chair. If the weather was especially cold, he managed to crawl on all fours back into the house. Sometimes he made it to his bed, sometimes not. Typically, the girls found him the next morning on the kitchen floor, a big pile of disorder sprawled halfway under the table.

They approached him now with caution. Madeline pelted him with small stones; Sophie poked him with a stick. His eyes briefly fluttered but did not open all the way. The glass jar in his lap toppled to the ground and rolled toward the edge of the pool, where it fell with a quiet plop into the shock of bilious green water. The sound roused him, and he lifted his head.

"I was dreaming again about your mother," he said foggily. "I forgot she was dead. Ghosts can do that, you know. Visit you while you sleep."

They smiled. "Yes, we know."

He stood up, his legs a bit unsteady, and rubbed his eyes. Slowly the world became more clear, and the air grew heavy with the smell of distant wood fire and the delicate bouquet of unwashed little girls. He gazed into the murky depths, and with a groan he fished the mason jar from the pool and placed it on the patio table.

"An absolute disgrace," he said, shaking his head, grunting, assessing. He reached into the linty pocket of his flannel shirt and searched for a cigarette. "You two haven't seen anything out here, have you? Anything *weird*, I mean?"

The twins nodded. "We almost killed a werewolf tonight, Daddy!"

"A werewolf, huh?" Charlie crossed his arms and gave his daughters a disapproving look. "I want you to listen to me carefully. We have to roll the tarp over this pool right now. Because there's a monster living under the water, understand? A monster with a hundred arms that will clamp onto you and drag you under if you ever get too close."

The girls peered over the edge, indifferent to the danger.

"Promise me you'll never go near the pool. Can you promise me that? You have to promise."

They promised.

"Well, okay then. I guess we've waited long enough to do this." He clapped his hard, powdery palms together and cleared his throat harshly, tried to muster the autocratic tone he'd perfected over the years, but his voice no longer rang with the confidence it possessed before he shipped off on his last voyage. It wheezed and creaked; it sounded thin and scratchy and morose, the voice of a man dying of thirst in the desert, and he rubbed his scruffy neck and winced as each syllable clawed its painful way from his burning larynx. "The three of us should have this pool cleaned up in no time. What's done is done, right? Life goes on, doesn't it?"

The girls seemed to consider this for a moment.

"You're afraid of Mommy, aren't you?" said Madeline.

"You shut your mouth," he warned.

"You're afraid she'll come back and try to drown you," said Sophie.

Charlie loosened his belt. "I'll smarten you up, all right!"

The girls skittered away to the opposite end of the pool before he could swat them. Their bodies already bore the hallmarks of hard experience, of paddles and leather straps and brooms that went whooshing through the air and cracked sharply against their bare flesh, leaving unsightly bruises.

"Get inside the house!" he snapped, but they just stood there and giggled. "Go on! I'll close up the pool on my own. Gotta be something on TV."

They ran inside, still laughing, and Charlie berated himself for having waited until the last possible minute to put the tarp on the pool; for having waited until the surface of the water resembled an alien organism, eyeless, mossy, kaleidoscopically oily, an amorphous creature that yearned to swallow him whole and slowly digest his flesh and bones beneath the rotting leaves that glinted under the October moon; for having waited until Madeline and Sophie, now back in the safe and familiar tranquillity of their bedroom, could no longer quell their curiosity and looked out the window to observe their father as they might observe an alarming silhouette inside their closet, wondering just what sort of bloodthirsty beast lurked in the shadows and then, when he caught them staring, quickly cowered behind the blinds, pretending to play with their dolls.

"Crazy, both of you," he muttered. "Like your mother."

Madeline and Sophie were strong swimmers, Charlie knew this for a fact, and they were perfectly capable of pulling Emily from the water. So why had they not plunged into the pool and saved her life? Why had they not screamed for help? Why had they taken the time to walk calmly downstairs and hover like a couple of ghouls before the couch where Marianne Kingsley slept? Were they relieved by their mother's death, overjoyed? Charlie recoiled at the thought. He wouldn't allow himself to contemplate such a terrible thing.

He flicked his cigarette into the water, and the glowing ember hissed for a second before going dark. Though the pool was in a sorry state, he had managed to turn the backyard into a kind of grotto, a white-trash Lourdes with a statue of Mother Mary looking over the swampy water, the radio playing vespers of the Blessed Virgin, all of it a testament to his unspeakable misery, but sometimes it was unclear to him if he'd erected the icon to summon the spirit of his wife or to cast it out. Because even though all the evidence was against it, Charlie still believed in ghosts, in restless spirits determined to air the dirty laundry of the dead.

Attending Sunday services at the white clapboard church on the square used to be part of his normal routine, but nothing about his life was normal anymore, all routines had been disrupted and indefinitely postponed, and the pool was now his sole place of worship, the temple where he prayed most every night. During the funeral service, the organist played the chorus of a forgettable hymn, and Charlie, convulsed with grief, developed the maddening habit of singing the refrain whenever he approached the pool—"Be not afraid, I go before you always . . ."—as if waiting for Emily to emerge from the murky water and through gibbering blue lips assure him that he need not blame himself for the terrible thing she'd done. On that dark day of disgrace, the pastor, who had a fondness for spouting quasi-biblical clichés, took him aside and said, "We're all made of the same clay, you know. And we all burn in the furnace of God's love, ordeal by fire, while a whole host of His angels takes bets on which of us will harden and crack first. But you're not going to crack, are you?" Words meant to provide comfort. But after the funeral Charlie never returned to the church.

These days he found nothing more comforting than the sensation of darkness, and he sat once more in the Adirondack chair, hands folded across his chest, and in the silence, as his eyes grew heavy again with sleep, he thought he heard his wife's gravelly voice.

"Listen, Charlie, listen now if you dare. No matter what the scriptures tell you, there are certain things for which a man cannot be forgiven. It's easy to forgive people when you're unaware of the sins they've committed. But I *do* know, Charlie. I know your sins, and I know the sins you're destined to commit. For what you did to me, I can forgive you. But should any harm come to the girls, to our daughters, to *our babies* . . ."

9

Like Charlie Ryan, I had no one willing to listen to my troubles, and on Saturday night after Metal Mayhem, as I drove aimlessly through town, I contemplated stopping by the bistro to squander the last of my cash on an appetizer. I knew such a visit would be pointless, and I could already hear Morgan Fey's mocking voice as I proposed a truce: "Oh, what a bunch of melodramatic, self-pitying crybabies you boys are. You're all the same." From the day she moved into the row house next door, my encounters with Morgan, while infrequent, became increasingly hostile. In the mornings and on the weekends we would sometimes run into each other—how could we not?—and while I tried to be civil, smiled, waved hello, commented on the weather, Morgan hurried away without speaking a word. In a note she slipped under my door one night, she accused me, among other things, of being a stalker and threatened to obtain a protective order if I ever acted aggressively toward her. *I carry a bottle of pepper spray and I'm not afraid to use it.* Fortunately, she never made good on these threats, never served me with papers or blinded my one good eye as I tried to collect the mail jammed into my door slot.

Even though I knew such a visit was pointless, I entered the bistro and ordered a beer at the bar, but as luck would have it, Morgan was not working that night. At a table in a far corner of the dining room, a comfortable distance from the stifling heat of the kitchen, a representative couple of middle-aged loonies from the college practiced their elocution, pursing their lips and rolling their *r*'s. Loud and messy masticators, they indiscriminately mixed their salads with their buttered bread and jabbered away without bothering to savor or swallow. Having already killed one bottle of red wine before their entrées arrived and showing no signs of slaking their epic thirst, the associate professor and his wife continued speaking just as before, their clipped and precise consonants starting to slur ever so slightly, the overall thrust of their words acrimonious as ever.

Martin Kingsley was now a loyal customer in the bistro's alley, paying nearly double the going rate for large quantities of *jazar*. And no doubt Mrs. Kingsley was here tonight to find out how the plans were coming along for the party on New Year's Eve. Irritated perhaps by the tacky Norman-inspired decor of the bistro, the sham beams, the lights on the walls done up as candlesticks, they both looked like they were about to launch into choric howls of complaint. It was always these preening, posturing cognoscenti, worrying themselves sick about cultural debasement, who looked down their noses at the residuum, the underclass, the impure and unrefined proles who peopled this pitiful town.

"You still haven't explained to me," I overheard Kingsley say to his wife, "why you insist on conducting business with this chef." He fidgeted with the napkin on his lap. He seemed agitated, nervous, paranoid, and I guessed he'd been drinking more than just red wine tonight. "I think it's a mistake having the party here."

"Too late to change venues, dear. I've already mailed out the invitations." Mrs. Kingsley's hair was pulled back so tightly from her face that instead of a smile her lips formed a ferocious sneer. "This establishment seems to enjoy repeat business. Always a good sign. It means the penny-pinching geezers haven't found feathers in their *duck à l'orange* or fur in their rabbit stew." Unsightly squares of diced kale clung to her teeth, giving her a decidedly rustic look. "It's also a cozy spot. Almost romantic, you know. In a pathetic sort of way." She ran a finger around the rim of her empty wineglass. "Is something wrong, Martin? You look ill."

Kingsley pretended not to see me sitting alone at the bar. Maybe he didn't recognize me, didn't associate me in any way with the college, a sad possibility that served to reinforce my suspicion that I'd become an expendable extra in the tragicomedy of this town, insignificant and utterly forgettable. These patronizing professors liked to tell their students that they could choose any path in life they liked, but I knew I would never enjoy Kingsley's kind of success and happiness. For most people—for people like me—paths didn't open at all, and when they did open they were just as likely to be bad ones as good. But Emily Ryan had presented me with another kind of path. While it wasn't a noble path, it was a realistic one, and only a damn fool waited around all his life, hoping for the right one to materialize, the one he wanted, the one he felt he deserved. Like Xavier D'Avignon, a man with an absurd sense of entitlement.

Through the round window of the kitchen door, I could see the chef standing behind the six-burner gas range, juggling three copper saucepans and a hot skillet. On Saturday nights, when the bistro was at its busiest, Xavier had to contend with the voices of dissatisfied customers whose constant complaints sounded more and more like the snarls of coyotes tracking the sickly scent of social failure. Somehow he managed to inoculate himself against clinical depression and at the same time keep properly hydrated by nursing a pitcher of carrot juice.

Although he was an impoverished chef toiling away in the claustrophobic kitchen of a failing restaurant and could only dream of attaining a high level of culinary virtuosity, he was an autodidact with an insatiable appetite for information of all kinds, especially knowledge about the bewildering history of food preparation. Had Normandy College offered a degree in food history instead of culinary arts, he might have pursued a much different path in life. Maybe he would have studied the ecological history of root vegetables, but the administration at Normandy College failed to see the profound message concealed in the time capsule of a carrot carved thick and coarse like sheets of parchment, a practice that for millennia had gone virtually unchanged. Evidence suggested that in Mesopotamia the dour priests of the Sumerian mystery cults sliced carrots atop their menacing ziggurats, and in the beautifully argued pages of medieval midrash, one could find innumerable passages suggesting that Father Abraham, before binding Isaac on Mount Moriah, served his son a sumptuous meal of chickpeas and finely chopped carrots drizzled with olive oil. That the cutting of carrots might be as old as Genesis and *The Epic of Gilgamesh* filled Xavier with a sense of awe that left him trembling and close to tears, but these reflections were short-lived as always. He stormed across the steamy kitchen and glanced out the window of the swinging door to spy on the professor and his wife.

"*Mon Dieu!* Who are these fools to make such demands on a great artist?"

A small part of Xavier looked forward to the *soirée*. Here at long last was an opportunity to escape, however briefly, from the onerous working-class world to which he'd become accustomed, his big chance to give in to new temptations, if one had to think of such things as being so unabashedly sinful, so improper, so lascivious and corrupt as to call them temptations, a glorious night hobnobbing with the town's power brokers and intelligentsia, an escapade into the rarefied realm of elitism, snobbery, exclusivity. He was growing tired of how disappointing life always turned out to be, and as he put the finishing touches on a *choux à la crème* drenched in dark chocolate for some diabetic slob in the dining room, he envisioned an elegant evening serving dignitaries and philanthropists, conversing at length with men and women who, despite their extensive travels, had yet to come across cooking so unique and revolutionary in its ability to seamlessly blend elements of the old world and the new. Lifting the lid on a silver platter, he would announce to the charmed guests, "*Mesdames et messieurs*, may I present tonight's main course. Turkey vulture *confit*, a special recipe of my own." The provost would vigorously shake his hand, congratulate him on a job well done, and inquire about his plans for the future. "Mr. D'Avignon, do you intend to write a cookbook? Might you have an interest in guest lecturing at the college? Have you given serious consideration to teaching professionally? As you may know, I'm searching for a *chef de cuisine*." But Xavier was no fool. Beneath the sedate surface of respectable society, there existed a kind of spiritual squalor that rivaled the worst poverty of the town. These men and women weren't as genteel as they pretended to be, and some of them, an unscrupulous few, tried to hide their checkered pasts behind empty words and forged references.

Now, with some hesitation, Xavier stepped into the dining room, fully prepared to have his humble fantasies shattered, and he noticed right off that the carrots on Mrs. Kingsley's plate had gone untouched.

"Ah, Mr. D'Avignon!" She produced an embossed business card from her purse and thrust it at him like a straight razor. When he reached for it, Xavier managed to sustain a nasty paper cut and sucked on the tip of his injured finger. "Did you lose my phone number, sir? I'm beginning to worry about our partnership. I searched high and low for a suitable location to host the party on New Year's Eve, not to mention a responsible chef capable of providing an eclectic menu for our guests, but so far you've given me very little information. From now on I expect regular updates about your arrangements for the retrospective on Colette Collins."

She gestured to the unnerving centerpiece looming over their basket of sliced baguette. A humanoid clay figure with thin limbs that tapered into menacing crustacean claws, the thing seemed more prehistoric than modern, a grotesque totem unearthed by archeologists at the sight of an ancient pit for human sacrifices. He knew nothing at all about these small sculptures; it was Morgan who'd purchased the pieces for the bistro, but like any competent businessman, Xavier had an instinct for equivocation and evasive answers and pretended to be an enthusiastic collector of Colette Collins's work.

Equipped with a fine sense of attack, more or less accustomed to bullying her social inferiors, Mrs. Kingsley said, "Now, then, how many dishes will you be serving, *monsieur*? And how soon can you present me with a menu?"

Xavier gawped at her. He could feel her extracting information from him the way a powerful magnet might forcibly extract the metal fillings from his chronically aching and worn-down teeth. Judging from her staid demeanor and the intensity of her unwavering stare, he suspected she would be far more comfortable in a courtroom setting, asking pointed questions of sociopaths atop rickety scaffolds, their necks festooned with the hangman's noose. To a hard-nosed, uncompromising, autocratic ballbuster like Mrs. Kingsley, a man could say anything he liked and never run the risk of offending her. Nothing was beyond her. She'd heard every filthy slander, every vile admission of guilt, every conceivable description of perversion and evil. The only thing she wouldn't tolerate was a lie, but for Xavier D'Avignon lying was more or less a way of life. He was a cheat, a chiseler, and he found it difficult to camouflage his dishonesty.

"The menu is set," he assured her. "I'll be serving *moules à la crème Normande, matelote,* and for dessert a marvelous *terrinné.* Not to worry. The party will come off without a hitch—"

"Christopher!" she interjected. "I almost forgot. I need to arrange for a babysitter. And I still have to order place cards and rent audio equipment for my speech. And, oh, yes, we must install a large clay sculpture over there in the corner. And I have no idea what I'm going to wear. Something tasteful and original. But not too flashy. Understated, sartorial restraint. Now, as to the terms of our agreement. I've never believed in written contracts, complicated clauses, fine print. I'm not running a corporation, not even limited liability. But when I entered into a verbal agreement with you last month, I expected good service at a reasonable price."

"You won't be disappointed," he said.

"I'm glad to hear it. And perhaps you can recommend a competent bartender?"

Xavier rested his fingers against his greasy chin. "Oh, yes," he said, "I believe I know just the person . . ."

With nowhere else to go, I returned to my empty apartment and salved my loneliness by taking dictation from the ghost of Emily Ryan, but as I sat at the kitchen counter and furiously filled a fresh notepad with another badly worded dream, I felt an unmistakable presence scratching at the brick walls outside the building. Since I believed there were more ghosts in Normandy Falls than there were people, I crept to the window, cracked the blinds, and discovered wandering through the shadows a shuddering figure whose hideous, hollow breathing so fouled the air that I feared the time had finally come to flee from this forsaken town.

Morgan must have sensed it as well. For reasons she could not explain, she'd taken the night off work and waited at home for something unusual to happen. Maybe Emily Ryan had certain secrets to share with her, too. As if heeding the call of a solemn and mysterious voice, she threw open the door and stepped outside. The light spilling from her apartment touched Lorelei's oval face, illuminating a shock of red hair and protuberant eyes that betrayed a kind of murky mindlessness, green and depthless as a scummy pond. Wrapped in her black cloak, Lorelei looked not like a dancer at the Normandy Cabaret but like a ragged mendicant and the last surviving member of a medieval village stricken with the plague.

Morgan crossed her arms and approached her as she might an unfamiliar dog. "Haven't seen you in, what, almost eight weeks now? What do you want?"

Lorelei's face retreated beneath the hood. "I didn't come to pick a fight."

Morgan rolled her eyes and laughed cruelly. "Oh, yes, you did. You wouldn't be here otherwise."

An expert at disguising her own vulnerabilities, Lorelei tried to smile, but it was obvious that something terrible had happened.

Morgan struck a match and with the fitful flash of fire lit a cigarette. "Look, I'd like to enjoy a quick smoke and then go to bed, okay? Do you need to use the phone or something? Call your sister? Are you in trouble?"

"The barn," Lorelei breathed.

"The barn?"

"In the valley."

Morgan frowned. "A barn in the valley?"

"They threatened me."

"Who threatened you? What are you saying?"

"The twins . . ."

Lorelei cringed as though anticipating a blow. In a place like Nor-

mandy Falls, where trust was a hard thing to come by and people seldom risked their feelings by revealing too much of themselves, Lorelei
knew to brace herself for rejection and began to tell the whole story,
slowly and with many false starts.

After listening to the tale, Morgan asked, "Do you still have the
gun?"

"No, I left it in the hayloft." Lorelei was silent for a moment and
then said, "There is one other thing I haven't told you. Haven't told
anyone. But I can't disguise it anymore. It happened last summer.
Before I ran away."

Beneath her cloak Lorelei's belly was beginning to resemble a giant
egg, hugely spherical, something an ostrich might lay, the taut skin
around the navel pitted and cratered and turning faintly blue. Morgan
was stunned. Someone her size wasn't carrying one child but a litter. It
was true that by the end of summer Lorelei had gained a little weight,
some noticeable swelling around the middle, and while Morgan may
have had suspicions, it never seriously occurred to her that Lorelei
might be in the family way. Maybe the degenerates who came to watch
her dance at the cabaret suspected as much, too. Those sexually frustrated, henpecked, closet fetishists, how they must have enjoyed ogling
the trashy, gravid girl as she straddled the stripper pole, swinging her
sturdy, child-bearing hips round and round.

Morgan lit another cigarette. "Who . . ."

"The Gonk," Lorelei said. "He was on the lookout for a good, reliable womb."

"How do you feel?"

"Physically or mentally? I have different answers for each."

"What do you plan to do?"

"I plan to get rid of it."

"You mean adoption?"

"I mean get rid of it."

Morgan wasn't opposed in any philosophical sense to abortion, but
even she had a few principles and knew she had a moral obligation to
set things straight, to make certain something positive came from this
bleak situation. Moved by profound pity and feeling less like an over-

worked waitress and more like a harried keeper holding the mortification chains of some drooling idiot on display at the annual county fair, she took a final drag on her cigarette, flicked the butt onto the pavement, and then led Lorelei inside.

I stepped away from the window and crawled on hands and knees across the floor. Pressing my ear against the dusty vent and trying to suppress my cynical laughter, I envisioned the touching scene next door. Only then did it occur to me that I wasn't even sure if Lorelei was this woman's real name or her stage name.

"In the beginning," said Lorelei, "when I still lived with Sadie, I didn't mind it when he came to my room. I thought it was funny how the Gonk seemed to want me more than my sister. For a while I actually thought he was a little in love with me. But he is incapable of love. And he isn't an adulterer, either. Not in the usual sense of the word. He didn't seduce me because he thought I was easy or convenient. We possess a very special kind of pedigree, you know. We're like royalty in this town. The Gonk and I share some of the same blood and can trace our family trees back to the founder of the college, the last of an ancient line of Wakefields. But when he found out Sadie couldn't provide him with an heir, he decided a surrogate was in order. Just before I fell asleep, he would knock on my bedroom door. I couldn't move, couldn't breathe. It was like a dark power had me tied to the bed. He made me feel like I was fulfilling some kind of sacred obligation. 'We must put forth an enduring branch,' he would whisper. But after a while I couldn't stand the sight of him, the smell of cigarettes on his fingertips. Turned my stomach, if you want to know the truth. Probably had something to do with my mother. She was a chain smoker. Esophageal cancer finally got her in the end. That's how I came to live with Sadie in the first place."

I pictured the horrified expression on Morgan's face. At the start and the end of each day, she tried to remember her practice, how one should always focus on something positive and peaceful, and as she took this all in she began to meditate on an image of Delacroix Cay. Aside from Xavier's brochures, she'd never seen photographs of the island, had never read any books or articles about its people and culture; in fact, she didn't know if the place actually existed; for all she knew it could have been just another of Xavier's sick jokes, one more way for him to manipulate her; but it was late and she was tired and she chose to believe there was such a place and that it was the most beautiful island in all the world and that one day very soon she would go there and spend many glorious hours swimming in the blue sea, far from the biting cold and the demoniac doings of the dumb, greedy men of this wretched town. But most of all she thought about the tidy stacks of cash that Xavier kept in the safe hidden behind a Toulouse-Lautrec poster in that oppressive sty above the bistro.

"Poor Mom," Lorelei continued in a dreamy voice, "she didn't live long enough to escape from this town. She could barely scrape together enough money for a weekend getaway. In the summertime she rented a cabin on the lake. The place smelled musty and closed up. The beach didn't smell much better. It was littered with dead fish and big clumps of algae. And you couldn't build sandcastles, not on a stony beach like that. When the waves broke against the strand they left a brown and frothy residue. The county posted signs warning people not to swim in the lake because of the high bacteria count. In the afternoons I'd sit under an umbrella and watch the bulk carriers crossing the horizon, some of them a thousand feet long, and I started to wonder what life was like for the crew. I imagined a working-class Sinbad sailing the Seven Seas. What kinds of places did he see? What kinds of people did he meet?"

Morgan thought for a moment, troubled by the arrangement she was about to propose, but now she understood that the family unit, like everything else in this world, was constantly evolving into something that, at least initially, may have struck some people as strange, weird, unnatural, but it only proved that, over time, human beings were capable of adaptation. The important thing was that couples found a way to cope with unforeseen circumstances and learned to endure.

"A few of those ships," said Morgan, "actually take on passengers. From what I hear the cabins are pretty basic, but it's an affordable way to travel. They go all over the world, too. Even the Caribbean. I know about an island in the French Antilles where we can rent a grass shack on a hilltop overlooking the ocean. Why don't we buy tickets and sail away on one of those ships? We'll find jobs serving drinks or selling trinkets to tourists, and every night we'll eat fresh lobster tail. A perfect place to forget about the squalor of small-town America. We're survivors, Lorelei. Maybe we can learn to live as one big, happy family."

Lorelei shook her head. "I thought you were a hard-bitten realist, not a dreamer."

"This idea isn't as crazy as it sounds. Listen, I know where we can get a little startup money. Are you game?"

Lorelei said flatly, "Be serious. I'm already taking a class at the college this semester. Remedial English. I'm going to earn a degree in nursing or something."

"But you *can't* take classes there."

"Why not?"

"Because the Gonk runs the Department of Plant Operations. Sooner or later he'll see you on campus. And if the Gonk doesn't see you, then one of his spies will. Those men must know who you are, must have watched you dancing at the cabaret."

"I can take care of myself."

"But I'd like to take care of you." Morgan kissed Lorelei on the forehead. "Will you let me? I have plenty of room here."

Lorelei shrugged and answered rather demurely, "It's still too early to tell."

That same night, as an uneasy gloom settled over the town, I fell asleep on my futon and dreamed that the men of the Bloated Tick, possessed by some criminal, anarchic force, discovered that it wasn't just possible but a rather simple thing to capture and cage an owl. The twelve marched across the campus and removed a screen from one of the windows at the Department of Plant Operations. In the dark they trooped into the lunchroom with all their swagger and waited for the owl to accept their humble offering and provide them with wise counsel; for animals, as is well known, briefly gain the power of speech during certain enchanted times of year, and for the past several days the owl had been communicating secretly with them, hooting and screeching an alluring promise of a grand life in a faraway South Seas paradise.

After thirty minutes, the bird swooped down from the rafters to devour the mouse. Fascinated by the ferocity of nature, they watched as the tail of the mouse thrashed wildly in its powerful beak. They studied the owl and the owl studied them, the fearsome goddess of the Bloated Tick, its large black eyes brimming with concentrated fury and frightful accusation. On one talon it hopped along the floor and then in two swift jerks of its head gobbled down its crippled quarry.

Taking this as their cue, the men acted quickly. One of the ticks, wearing a pair of leather welding gloves, swatted the owl over the head with the screen, momentarily stunning it, and managed to snag the warm and trembling creature by its silky wings. He smoothed back its gray-tinged feathers and placed it inside a small chicken coop.

With their goddess safely enthroned inside her majestic new temple of plywood and chicken wire, the men returned to the river, where they made final preparations for the sailboat's maiden voyage. In the biting cold, one hour before daybreak on Sunday morning, they checked the rigging, fastened the sails, and then untied the lines from the pylon. They puttered ten miles downriver, and at dawn they reached the harbor, by which time powerful gusts whipped the waves on the lake into a cauldron of whitecaps that crashed violently against long jetties of jumbled granite blocks. In the marina few boats remained in their slips: *Disco Volante, Busted Flush, Orca, Nellie, Discovery One, Bounty, Argo.* Taking note of these well-worn names, the men smashed a jar of moonshine against the green barnacled bow of their vessel and proclaimed, "We christen thee *Be Knot Afraid*!" But the men were very afraid.

Below deck, huddled on bowed cross benches, they studied distant clouds that portended disaster and debated the wisdom of listening to the goddess and sailing in such wicked weather. They carried no compass or charts and had never piloted a ship in their lives. Had they noted the absence of the Pleiades, they would have known, like any competent navigator, that the seafaring season had come to an end. But now the owl peered into the hold of the vessel freighted with its insane cargo of unclean men and shouted terse commands: "The full brunt of the storm won't hit for hours. Look alive, ye hearties! This ain't some pleasure cruise! I'll not be cheated of my life by a company of idle drunkards!"

Transfixed by the owl's huge, immobile eyes, the men bowed humbly, sprang to orders, and with braided halyards hoisted the white sails high and wide. A bracing following wind hit full, the canvas bellied out, and through the polluted harbor the boat dragged its poisonous brown wake. Beyond the breakwater the lake turned filthy and horrible, each wave like a piece of warped sheet metal rippling with dim sunlight. Unlike the river where each ripple seemed significant and charged with meaning, out here in the immensity of open water, a single ripple was soon lost in a thousand others, one overlapping and blending with the next so that there was never any clear distinction between them. The chaos, or perhaps the order of it, failed to mesmerize, and the men turned their attention instead to the clouds ramming together and building high on the horizon. They quaked at the sight of the black tendrils unleashing their spinning helixes of snow that, like massive augers, bored holes deep into the leaping waves. The sloop made wild progress toward the immense wall of clouds, and darkness swept over the earth.

The voice boomed, "There's no time to waste, you deck apes! A perfect day for a maiden voyage. The winds are north-northwest. Watch those lines! Batten down those hatches!"

The prow plunged low in the water, goring the heaving swells. White foam flew over the bulwarks, spraying the small deckhouse and blinding the men. With a terrible roar the gale winds struck full force, driving the boat yawingly across rolling seas. The cables frayed and snapped, and the wind ripped the patched mainsail from the mast, sending it flying like a ghost through the nightmare sky. For a while the men drifted, the wheel wrenched free of their grasp, and the white, curling crests rocked the boat violently back and forth, spinning it round and round. From afar the vessel must have looked like the last surviving ship of a doomed armada escaped from unknown cannibal lands, a skeleton crew of raving maniacs trying to keep her afloat.

The hull didn't begin taking on water until the snow started falling and the sea and sky became uniformly gray and the coast was little more than a hopeful smudge of soft shale cliffs, the craggy headlands thrashed by shrieking gusts. The men did not break into a buoyant sea shanty or dance a spirited jig. Their piety had limits, and a few blasphemers dared to mutiny, their wills shaken by the tempest. They abandoned the helm and with quick sidelong strides made their way across the creaking deck.

"As leaky as an unstaunched wench!" they cried and retched over the side, clinging to ropes and rails and to distant, happy memories they knew would be their last. There were no life jackets aboard and no radio to make a distress call—these provisions, the goddess had assured them, were unnecessary—and in great haste the men used the rigging to lash themselves to the mast.

"Only cowards wish to die a dry death," said the voice, "and now this leviathan is going to swallow you and drag you down into the abyss. Ah, but maybe the sea will reject you, spit you out. The lake might miraculously freeze, and you'll be able to walk across a kingdom of ice to safety. If not, hell might cast you out, decide that the world is a more suitable place for your kind of evil. But I doubt it. Because you've done things, unnatural things, things the universe will not tolerate."

Another blast of wind snapped the rotting timbers at the prow, and as the boat listed perilously to its side, the men were thrown clear of the deck and into the churning water, littering the lake with long tentacles of terror. The heavy flakes of snow looked like a furious swarm of albino locusts hurtling in a suicide pact toward the hull. They splattered against the wood until one by one their unique patterns dissolved and vanished forever into the void.

Trapped inside the coop, the owl, now unsure of its sovereignty, flapped its wings at the furious gale and in a voice heavily laden with grief said, "We split! We split! I believe you did assist the storm!"

Cleaving their way through the riotous waves, the men struggled to the surface, their jeans and boots and flannel shirts pulling them under, and they fought hard to hang on to the cracked planks scattered across the surface. Strange forms darted below their thrashing legs, a crazed circling school of fabled sea monsters, and the men, choking on the yellow spume and oily spectra, pounded on the water with their fists. By then the boat was almost entirely submerged. Those who could swim fought hard to tread water, but in the frigid lake they found it exhausting work. Only the chicken coop managed to stay afloat, as if the world cared more about the owl than it did the crew. No doubt the goddess would find a way to escape, resourceful as she was, and this filled the men with great hope.

Minutes passed, their legs became heavy and numb, and as they flailed desperately in the tempestuous lake, they looked like helpless babes taken mewling and puking from the incubator of a satanic hatchery. Before they disappeared one by one beneath the murderous waves and their lives were blotted out, they glimpsed a thin band of pink light struggling to brighten the horizon, and among a fantastic squadron of white gulls, they saw the owl circling the heavens for carrion, its song a restless and ancient lamentation.

10

In an effort to shore up its waning commitment to cultural diversity and social justice, the administration of Normandy College started admitting, on a probationary basis, more of the local high school graduates, and each semester the chair of the Department of English and Comparative Literature selected at random one professor to teach a section of remedial composition to help prepare these "at risk" students for college-level work, a state of affairs that put Martin Kingsley, this semester's lucky winner, in the foulest of moods. These days the big word in academic circles was "inclusion," but many professors, Kingsley among them, believed in *exclusion*. After all, how could someone feel a sense of superiority if he couldn't give his perceived social inferiors the proverbial boot? No matter how dedicated or well intentioned they may have been, the locals would inevitably drag standards down and turn the college into a third-rate intellectual backwater. Higher education had succumbed long ago to the pressures of the marketplace, and its unscrupulous administrators, like carnival barkers standing outside the circus tent of the college, harangued innocent passersby and persuaded them to empty their pockets and step through the tent flap in order to witness an inauthentic and fabricated spectacle. Now it was Kingsley's turn to put on a good show.

On Monday afternoon, behind the closed door of his office, he topped off his coffee mug with *jazar* juice and took a long and sloppy swig. He was drinking far too much of the stuff these days, and he could feel the terrible strains of paranoia and hypocrisy brought on by the powerful juice. When he chose teaching as his vocation, Kingsley wanted badly to believe in an enduring cause, a fixed creed, an ineradicable philosophy, but experience had taught him that everything in the world was more or less fraudulent and everyone was a fraud, including himself. To believe in something—in the institution of higher learning that engaged his services, in his colleagues, in his ignorant and slothful students with their dull chimpanzee eyes—meant to be content with self-delusion, and he had now reached a point in his life where it was difficult for him to believe wholeheartedly in anything at all.

He weaved his way through the halls, and as he stumbled into the classroom, he said in a blustering manner, "Okay, folks, listen up! I'd like to begin today's class by discussing your next writing assignment."

The students emitted a collective groan and slouched lower in their seats. Kingsley wanted to groan, too, wanted to weep, wanted to run back to his office and drink more of the *jazar*. Their essays infuriated him, the slovenliness of their arguments, the violence of their horrifically twisted and mangled prose, but if he couldn't teach them how to write grammatically correct sentences, he could at least try to inoculate them against the virulent strain of the small-town ethos and the crawling chaos of anti-intellectualism that threatened to destroy their lives. Maybe by preventing them from becoming the next Emily Ryan, he could redeem himself in some small way, he could atone.

Kingsley walked up and down the crowded rows, distributing a handout. For one week each semester he prepared and delivered a series of lectures on the topic of love in all of its multitudinous forms, and today's talk was supposed to focus specifically on Eros, but he couldn't bring himself to discuss such a thing, not directly at least. To his relief the *jazar* had inspired a last-minute solution to the problem.

"Your task," he said with a hiccup, "is to compose a letter to the editor of the college newspaper, expressing your opinion about the presence of a gentlemen's club in this town. When it first opened its doors, the Normandy Cabaret introduced an element of vice into this otherwise bucolic setting. You've seen the menacing characters that drive into town from all corners of the county, and this may explain the sharp increase in crime in our area. And I probably don't need to tell you how the management exploits dozens of destitute young women desperate to make a dollar." When he saw his students losing interest, Kingsley rapped his knuckles sharply on the lectern. "So! Do some of you have any thoughts on this matter?"

One of the commuters raised her hand.

Kingsley pointed. "Yes, Lorelei?"

"Um, what does this assignment have to do with composition?"

"It's what we call 'experiential learning.' Over the centuries many people have recognized how the pen can facilitate social progress more readily than brute force. Today's reading assignment discusses this principle in detail. Did anyone bother to do the reading? No? Well, the essay points out how it is essential for students to actively engage in some form of social protest. By doing so you will feel empowered. More importantly, you will learn the consequences of speaking your mind. Because there are always consequences. Nothing irritates the opposition more than free expression."

Lorelei raised her hand again. "But what if we don't want to protest the Normandy Cabaret? Aren't we just saying what's on your mind? I mean, has the Normandy Cabaret been on your mind lately?"

His patience wearing thin, Kingsley replied, "It's an immoral establishment. Fully tax abated, too. You'll see. We'll go there one day and picket outside the door and wave signs."

"How long should this letter be?"

"There is no mandatory length. Simply develop each of your ideas and make your points clear and direct. But the important thing is that you base your argument on sound reasoning and research. The editor is more likely to take you seriously if you do."

Lorelei frowned. "How much research should we do? What if one of us decided to get a job at the Normandy Cabaret and make some money?"

"I beg your pardon?"

"That's called primary research, right? Seriously, what if I worked there? And what if I enjoyed the job and I was making decent cash. What gives you, or anyone else in this classroom, the right to judge what I do for a living?"

Kingsley wiped his feverish forehead with the back of his hand, and in his eyes there was nothing left of the intellectual's solemn manner. "Oh, Lorelei, do cooperate. It's just a simple exercise."

"A kind of hypothetical situation, right?"

"Yes, very good! Hypothetical."

"Okay. Sorry, one more question."

Lorelei gave him an unwholesome grin and chewed her gum loudly, deliberately, making sure it cracked and popped in her mouth, maximizing its full potential to drive her teacher bananas, and Kingsley now understood that he'd been wrong about this young woman that he once believed to be so slow of wit and swift of tongue. She was a talented actress treating him to a stellar performance as a scatterbrained sorority sister.

"Should it be, like, a business letter? Do we have to, like, include all of that junk at the top? A header and all of that? The date and stuff? Oh, and does the dictionary count as research?"

"No, no, no," Kingsley sputtered. He could feel his face turning dangerously dark red and took a deep breath. "We'll discuss legitimate resources during our next class. Today, I would like to focus on general practices. Step one, writing an introduction . . ."

There was only one authority—the authority of a student to think for herself—and by bravely expressing an opinion that must have struck her fellow townies as counterintuitive, Lorelei had taken an important first step toward independent, critical thinking. For this Kingsley, a brilliant hater, had tried to belittle her. As I swabbed the floors in the hallway outside the classroom, I listened to the professor's tedious bunk, and from the tone of his voice I could tell he was drunk. Using an old teacher's trick, he stood behind the lectern, opened the textbook to a random page, and blabbered on and on about a topic barely relevant to the discussion at hand, each garbled word weighed down and dragged under by his leaden delivery. Within minutes he managed to lull his students into passivity, their eyes growing heavy with boredom, but Kingsley looked perceptively weakened. Desperate for another quick fix, he soon dismissed his class and returned to his office, where he could apply himself to the bottle and focus on his own selfish pursuits.

I knew all about the *jazar*'s effects and decided to have a little fun. With mop and bucket in hand I hurried back to Plant Operations. I intended to commit a small act of academic treason, even though, technically speaking, I was no longer a student since I'd failed to enroll in classes that semester. Smiling in anticipation, I made my way along the corridor and went to the phone on the wall outside the empty lunchroom. My fellow ticks had not come to work today, and the assumption, at least on the part of the Gonk, was that they were either dead or in jail. I lifted the receiver, wondering if my dream had actually been a premonition, and asked the campus operator to connect me with the correct office. After several rings the professor picked up on the other end.

"Kingsley speaking."

I could practically smell the booze on his breath. Lowering my voice an octave, I gruffly said, "Kingsley, Little Morty here."

"I'm sorry, who?"

"Cut the shit, pal. You know who I am."

"No, actually—"

"I'm the lowlife who runs the Normandy Cabaret."

"Ah, I see. Well, thank you for calling—"

"Do you have any idea how long it takes to put together a business deal?"

"No, I'm afraid I—"

"Years, Kingsley, years. I could have opened my club in any town I damn well pleased. In Camden, Clyde, Elyria, Winesburg. But I convinced the mayor and town trustees to let me open it right here. I'm only giving the people what they asked for—tits and ass and an occasional drink. Is that so terrible?"

"But, sir, that isn't the point."

"Put a lid on it, chump. I don't think you understand what's at stake here. Men travel great distances to visit our town and spend their money in my club. This small enterprise might start a wave of economic redevelopment and help some of our citizens climb out of poverty. I'm talking *jobs*, Kingsley, real jobs, not a college writing exercise. People can't feed their families by bellyaching about the philosophical shortcomings of capitalism and the sinfulness of seeing a bit of trim now and then. Maybe that's what you need, eh, Professor? A little trimming?"

"Sir, there's no need for vulgarity. As I see it, you have no intention of hiring full-time employees and giving them medical and dental—"

"As *you* see it?"

"I've looked into your business practices and—"

"Oh, right, right, you have more business savvy than I do, or the mayor does. Okay, so it isn't an automobile assembly line or an oil refinery, but the citizens don't have a choice in these matters, do they? A big corporation isn't going to set up shop here. The good old days of heavy industry and manufacturing are over. Sometimes you have to take whatever comes your way—"

"Sir, if I might have a word," he interrupted, his voice full of indignation. "Yes, perhaps it's generous of you to open your business here, fine, but it would be more generous if the Normandy Cabaret paid a fair and equitable tax rate, thereby contributing to the public school system. Isn't it more important to have an educated populace? Without a proper education, the common people can never flourish in a free and democratic society. Thomas Jefferson believed—"

"Thomas Jefferson! Are you fucking kidding me? That immoral fool, drinking his booze and knocking up his slave women. If he were around today, Jefferson would be a loyal, card-carrying member of the cabaret. We aren't one nation under God; we're one nation united under the guiding force of despicable human nature. Jefferson understood that principle all too well. And he also knew the best way to keep our nasty little urges from turning into big ugly problems was to legalize a couple of harmless vices."

"I really don't want to get into an argument with you."

"No argument from me, Kingsley. I already know who's going to win this round."

"I'm not sure I understand—"

"I don't want any letters sent to that idiotic college rag. Those little shits in your class don't know any better. And you better lay off my girls."

"Your girls?"

"Don't get cute with me, Kingsley. You know exactly what I mean."

"No, I'm afraid I don't."

"Beware, Kingsley. Do not fuck with my ladies, or you'll have to worry about the entire town rising up against you. Trust me on this. We know your terrible secret."

I heard the sharp squeak of a chair as Kingsley leaned forward and strained to comprehend the meaning of my words. I could picture his bloodshot eyes, and in the sudden stillness of his office I could detect his labored breathing, the wild pounding of his heart, the terrible avalanche of his thoughts.

"Better watch your step, Professor, or you may get an unexpected message from beyond the grave." I paused for a moment. At some point the student must challenge the master for supremacy. By what other method does one become autonomous and free? One cannot go on being an acolyte forever. Unable now to disguise the small tremor in my own voice, I held the receiver close to my lips and whispered, "Emily Ryan sends her love, Kingsley."

Then I hung up the phone.

More determined than ever to master any new technique that might help him improve his curious craft, the Gonk that fall audited another evening class at the college, Introduction to Studio Art, and during a lecture on Monday afternoon, as he sat at a desk surrounded by apathetic freshman, he gripped his pencil like grim death and pressed the sharpened tip deep into his sketch pad. No one spoke to him. No one dared. Into the classroom the instructor wheeled a large, bronze figure of a six-armed god dancing with perfect impassivity through a circle of fire, one hand clicking a drum, another holding a small flame, his left foot stomping on the back of a demonic dwarf, his right foot lifted in a dance that seemed acrobatic in its contortions. Hoping to inspire her students and impart some kind of meaning to the sorrows of everyday life, Marianne Kingsley recited a verse in Sanskrit while on the stereo a virtuoso sitarist played a delirious raga. She could speak for hours, and often did, her voice becoming increasingly shrill as the class dragged on.

"I'm sure everyone is wondering to what great excesses of mental torture I'm going to subject you. Never fear. Today, I'll refrain from using academic jargon or delivering a long-winded lecture. But I would like to talk about the supernatural because I do believe quite strongly that there is a supernatural element at play in the process of creating a work of art. First, you'll forgive me if I profane a sacred symbol, but I am of the opinion that this sculpture of Shiva is a rather simple mnemonic device to aid the common people. It helps them grasp the awesome and incomprehensible power that revels in the total annihilation of a universe that has grown weary of its own folly. But the philosophers tell us that to plunge joyfully into the abyss, to celebrate and embrace the dance of death, is to act in accordance with one's true nature. *Tat tvam asi.*"

Religious icons, she argued, were too conventional, too *collective* in their character to properly convey a sense of the supernatural, the transcendental, that which was beyond all categories of thought. Only individual artistic genius could accomplish such a task, someone with the singular vision of, say, Caravaggio with his fondness, or perhaps fetish, for severed heads—John the Baptist, Holofernes, Medusa, Goliath— and as the hour drew to a close, Marianne Kingsley showed her students a series of gruesome paintings. The Gonk found the image of Goliath, with his gaping mouth and mop of wild black hair, not only intriguing but unnervingly familiar, almost like gazing into a mirror. The great Philistine warrior stared into the void beyond the frame, a pale specter whose malevolent eyes drifted in different directions, his expression one of insanity, confusion, unutterable misery.

At the goriness of these images, Mrs. Kingsley sighed as though in the throes of an ecstatic trance. "Caravaggio created canvases of star-

tling originality," she said, "each one a chronicle of private mytholo-
gies and collective anxieties. He always insisted that the greatest human
potential was not in the giving of oneself to another, but in one's will-
ingness to participate fully in the game of life right up until the bitter,
terrible, despicable end, the moment when one was forced to confront
death and stare it directly in the eye, a strong and unfailing commitment, even at the final hour, to fully engage in this mysterious experience we call existence. And certainly Caravaggio met this challenge
head-on, as it were."

The Gonk, making frenzied sketches in his notebook, tried to tune
out her bad puns and soporific droning, but Marianne Kingsley had a
foolish tendency to creep up behind her students and whisper in their
ears.

"Such sublime beauty, such irony," she said to him, breathing
warmly on his neck. "I've been quite impressed with your work for this
class. Those steel fish you make, they're so—oh, how should I describe
them?— so wonderfully, so scintillatingly *repulsive*." She reached into
her blouse and presented him with a card. "Here's something that may
interest you. On New Year's Eve at Belleforest I'm hosting a retrospective on Colette Collins."

The Gonk shoved the invitation into his pocket and fought the
urge to bat her away like a fly. "I have plans that night," he said, his face
remaining imperturbable as a waxen mask. "Important plans that can't
be changed."

"I see. Well, in the unlikely event that your plans *do* change, please
feel free to stop by the bistro for a cocktail. I think you would appreciate the artistic sensibilities of someone like Ms. Collins."

The Gonk cracked his knuckles. "Maybe so."

She touched his arm and moved on to the next student.

The Gonk chuckled quietly to himself. If only she knew what he
had in mind for New Year's Eve, Marianne Kingsley would have revoked
the invitation and recoiled in horror. He found this ironic since, strictly
speaking, his vision was just as deeply religious as those depicted in the
chiaroscuro light of Caravaggio's canvases, religious because of its epic

violence and moral necessity and because it bestowed upon the true believer a sense of vindication.

Later that evening, as the cold winds picked up and the static clouds blanketed the autumn sky, the Gonk sat alone on his cottage porch. After finishing a second jar of moonshine, he gathered up his tools, and with a kerosene lamp swinging from his fingertips he descended the steps. He had to get cracking before winter arrived and the ground became iron hard.

In the field just beyond the cemetery, a pack of coyotes pushed through the broomstraw and peered through a curtain of grass blades, but they dared not venture any closer, maybe because they sensed something peculiar about the new caretaker, who, grappling with his unwieldy array of shovels and spades and hoes, looked not unlike that six-armed sculpture of Shiva with its ancient outlook on the rhythmic cycle of creation and destruction. The Gonk saluted them, and the coyotes pricked up their ears and bounded away. From the safety of the woods they observed him as he began to dig deep into the earth, and they howled their awful cadenzas of approval as he kicked away a few loose clods of dirt and endeavored to make the hole perfect in its proportions for what would prove to be the cemetery's most magnificent interment in more than a century.

The nights were much cooler now, the late October sky hardening into an impenetrable slab of steel, and as I walked to my car after working overtime, I lowered my head into a wicked wind that numbed my nose and cheeks. Around the empty parking lot the bare branches of the weather-whitened trees rattled together and cast idiot shadows across the dented hood of my silver sedan. Miserable with the knowledge that it would not survive a harsh winter and that soon I would need to find alternative forms of transportation, I climbed inside the car and went through my usual ritual: I whispered a prayer, pumped the accelerator three times, the magic number, and then with my eyes closed turned the key in the ignition. The battery cranked, the dying carburetor gurgled and wheezed. After two or three tries the engine rumbled loudly to life, but before I could put the car in drive and pull away, I heard a high-pitched squeaking sound. Worried the fan belt was slipping, I began calculating repair costs, but then in the rearview mirror I saw a bicycle flying under the malfunctioning gas lamps that flickered and blinked. The bike's rusty chain screamed against the gears, and the glimmering spokes ground up the brown leaves, scattering them in the rider's wide wake. I eased my foot down on the gas, and the sedan lurched forward.

I often observed Lorelei cruising around campus on that rattling whirligig with two wobbly wheels, and every time I saw her in the golden sunlight of an autumn day or under the long rags of purple clouds, I momentarily lost myself in an egregiously shameful fantasy. A lot of college girls were pretty, but Lorelei was a raving beauty, exquisitely designed, precisely built, and it was easy for me to understand why Morgan was so drawn to her. Instead of an ordinary townie, her body ruined by a steady diet of sugary soda and fast food, Lorelei was a daring succubus brought low by indigence and unyielding despair. Judging from the expression on her face, it wasn't difficult for me to imagine how she'd been mistreated over the years by friends and family alike and how in the years to come she expected to be mistreated by countless others, the betrayals, the broken promises, the abandonments she would later use to convince herself that she deserved such deplorable treatment. Ah, yes, Little Morty, he sure knew what he was doing when he hired her. Always on the lookout for young talent, he scoped out the campus for new inventory, a fresh batch of truly impressive specimens, freaks of nature really, gorgeous mutants with bodies for which men were willing to pay good money.

Imbued with the undying spirit of hope, I pulled alongside Lorelei and rolled down my window. "Excuse me, miss. Would you like a ride?"

Never taking her eyes from the street, she answered, "Thanks, I can manage."

"Really, it's no trouble. I can fit your bike in the trunk."

She peered through the window and regarded me with deep suspicion. "What the hell happened to your eye?"

The black patch and the gathering dusk did little to conceal my squashed and purple face. "Work-related injury," I said.

"I thought I saw you mopping floors tonight. You have a job on campus, don't you?"

"That's right. I work at the Bloated, er, at the Department of Plant Operations."

"Then you know him."

"Know who?"

"The Gonk."

I waved my hand and smiled. "Aw, sure, everyone knows the Gonk! Helluva guy, too. Do anything for you." When I saw the alarm in her eyes, I quickly added, "But I used to be a student at the college. Actually, Professor Kingsley was my faculty adviser."

Lorelei didn't seem to believe me and began to pedal faster.

I said, "Do you think someone in your condition should be riding a bicycle?" I thrust a hand outside the window and tried to grab her arm.

"Don't you touch me," she said in a grating voice, her mouth drawn down in a rictus of anger. "Yeah, now I know who you are."

I felt my stomach tighten.

"Morgan told you about me, didn't she?" I said. "Showed you some pictures, I bet. She still talks about me all the time, right? Well, I suppose that's only normal. She can be a little obsessive. But you're probably tired of hearing her stories."

"Morgan?" Lorelei's laughter was cold and sunless. "I saw you at the cabaret. Another sexually repressed loser. A lonely little deviant, living all by yourself. I bet you want to screw every girl you see on campus, don't you? I bet you fantasize about it every night. You fantasize about me, about sticking it in my ass." She cut across a pedestrian walkway, vanishing behind a cluster of buildings.

I gripped the steering wheel with both hands. I wasn't about to take that kind of shit, not from some hick, no way, no how. I smashed the gas pedal flat against the floor. The needle of the speedometer jumped wildly, the tires kicked up loose dirt and stone, but the car wheezed pitiably and jerked forward, dark and empty as a hearse. From the open window, with the wind roughly slapping my face, I shouted, "Come back! Do you hear me?"

For almost thirty minutes, I patrolled the campus. When I found no sign of her, I raced across the bridge and headed toward the square. With all of the potholes and large pools of standing water, the streets of the town had become a veritable obstacle course, and my car jounced and complained as I circled the dilapidated gazebo. From the marquee outside the cabaret, a thousand tons of neon light came crashing down like a rose-colored comet, and on the corner an army of restless, undead Don Juans shambled blind with drink on a quest to see a naked girl straddling the brass pole before last call, the cock's crow, when the law commanded them back to the crypt of their dismal trailers, studio apartments, dormitories.

Anderson Boulevard took me past the row houses, and still I did not see her. I drove beyond the town limits, and soon the scattered lights of the square blinked out one by one. Infuriated and disheartened, lost under the unfathomable logic of cold constellations that would never offer me any satisfactory answers to the impenetrable mysteries of the female heart, I turned down a dirt road that dipped and pitched and rose again past the low hills before it switchbacked along the forested ridge overlooking the wide rip of the valley. The clouds parted and a full moon crested the treetops, burning a huge hole in the sky and giving the needles of the swaying pines a dangerous and metallic glister. In the moonlight I searched for a lone bicyclist, but when the car took a plunge into the yawning darkness, I had to focus entirely on the road. After negotiating a series of sickening sharp turns, I was able to straighten out the wheel, and saw the reflection of nocturnal eyes glowing in a thicket of nettles. I drove another mile before I finally caught sight of Lorelei hovering above a perfectly smooth ground fog that came up to her knees and swallowed the tires of her bicycle. When she heard the belching engine and saw the high beams cutting through the mist, she glared at me and hissed like a teakettle. She no longer looked like a college student but an old woman with inscrutable eyes, dead and dusty as marbles. In the tall weeds near a creek, she ditched her bike and then melted away into the gloom.

"What the hell is this place?" I said, but when I saw those two iron gates I knew precisely where I was, and against my better judgment I stopped the car, killed the engine, and opened the door.

At night the sounds of the forest changed, and I noted how the pleasant daytime chirping of migratory warblers had been replaced by the distressed cries of a baby bird calling to its mother. A forked tongue of drifting mist, dull and slate gray, curled gently around my throat, and for the first time since coming to Normandy Falls I passed through those ominous gates and into a land that looked like a monument to death, a place of dark and draggling horrors thick with spirits, each with its own secret and malicious intentions.

Short grass, stiff with frost, crackled underfoot and then turned into a grasping autumn ooze. My boots, slathered with mud, broke through a thin scum of ice, and I hopped from one cracked paving stone to the next. Just ahead, no more than one hundred yards away, I could see the silhouette of what I remembered to be an abandoned barn. In the window near the peak a dark figure looked down at me.

I cupped my hands around my mouth and called into the night, "You should never have come back here, Lorelei! You should have taken Morgan up on her offer!"

As I waited for her response, for her *surrender*, I listened to the wind rumble through the long, narrow trench of the valley. And then I heard a loud explosion like the boom of a cannon. My days on the mean streets around the Jesuit school had given me some experience with the sounds of distant gunfire and of the bloody carnage that often followed, and in a panic I tried to turn around, but my rundown boot heels were fastened to the earth as though trapped in quicksand. I stumbled over a broad hummock and fell into the wet grass. There was another sharp crack, only this time I felt something go whistling by my ear. The thought of death wasn't an entirely unpleasant one, and maybe with luck a bullet to the brain would end a pathetic life characterized by disaffection, longing, and boredom. It would also silence forever the alluring voice that spoke to me whenever I was alone.

All around me the underbrush rattled with the sounds of startled skunks and possums. An animal arrowed suddenly out of the cattails and stopped to snarl at the foolish trespasser before skittering away. Bugs crawled across my back and shoulders. Unsure if they were furry wolf spiders or a writhing cluster of mating earwigs, I scrambled to my feet, my mouth opened in a racked and silent scream.

The night took me in unknown directions, and soon I found myself wandering into a ring of mighty ironwoods, their massive limbs armored in silver leaves, the calloused bark transformed into a gallery of leering faces, some with horns and protruding jaws, tricksters of misdirection that led me down an ever-dimming course of counterclockwise circles. Eventually, the labyrinth emptied into a sizable clearing where shafts of moonlight pierced the dense canopy and revealed among midden heaps the ruins of a modest country estate.

In fascination we gravitate toward the irrational, and despite my spiraling fear and instinctual urge to flee, I felt that I was under the protection of some uncanny power. No one, not even somebody as bat-shit crazy as Lorelei, would follow me here. I slowed my pace, tried to breathe more easily, and in the eerie silence examined the remains of a dwelling slowly destroyed by the avenging hand of time. Only the bleached and eroded stones of the foundation remained, and around the crumbling structure there were few items of interest—an empty gas can, a pair of wire-rim spectacles with cracked lenses, a book whose leather cover had turned green with mildew, the pages crawling with wood lice and wireworms.

Not far from the foundation I came upon a rusted shell of an automobile propped on cinder blocks, an immense Jazz Age touring car with running boards and spare tires mounted on the side, a Duesenberg, a Cunningham, something out of a silent movie, a one-reel black-and-white comedy accompanied by music from a tinny player piano. I wandered through the clearing until I discovered buried beneath a thin layer of dirt and leaves a small steel door. Curious to know the secrets of this place, greedy to unearth its ancient artifacts, I crouched down and though I strained my back in the process managed to pry open the door.

With only a butane lighter to guide my way, fully prepared to reap the consequences of my own lunacy, straining to meet my fate bravely, gallantly, competently, I descended a winding staircase, its stone steps slippery with mold and the excreta of mice. Here the darkness was absolute, like a cavern. Translucent bugs scuttled blindly across dripping limestone walls fringed with moss and plugged with lichens. In the flickering light the cellar seemed to dance and spin, and with outstretched hands I groped the deteriorating masonry until my feet touched the floor and sank slowly into treacherous slime. Before me an enormous passage gradually sloped down into unknown regions, and I realized I wasn't in a cellar at all but in a raw, scoured pipe deep in the earth whose marvels were strange and terrific, a slippery black tube of immense dimensions shaped by the slow, steady trickle of calcite-rich water, the earthen ceiling interlaced with sturdy roots covered in a thin film of oozing clay, its stalactites hanging like petrified icicles and crawling with millipedes and albino troglobites.

Along one of the walls I found a row of storage shelves, and lining those shelves from floor to ceiling were hundreds of glass jars, some the size of growlers, their contents sealed tight with zinc canning lids. Heedful of the dying light, I approached the jars and studied the small, fetal, fish-eyed things floating inside, bloated masses of flesh incubating outside their mother's womb, insensate creatures neither terrestrial nor aquatic caught in the collective grip of a curious dream, their eyes twitching, their forked and tufted tails swaying in a cloudy fluid that glowed goblin green.

The earth, blind to the needs of the people who inhabited it, incubated curious and horrible things in its womb, and I understood now that Normandy Falls contained a secret, a colossal creeping sentient madness hibernating beneath the fulgurite-pitted earth. For the better part of a century, the hereditary horrors of the Wakefield clan had been anticipating the arrival of a weary traveler who would set them free so they might lurk among the roadless reaches of swamp and forest and swim once again in the river. Because given enough time something always manages to escape from the laboratory and foul the water.

I felt like I was sleepwalking, that this entire episode was an extravagant horror show from some dimly remembered dream, but before I could scurry up the steps and slam shut the door, I thought I heard the faintest whisper, a mysterious cantillation. Like a squirming horde of mutant djinns desperate to explode from their magic lamps, the creatures, eager to bestow upon their liberator three wishes, turned their white eyes on me, and in the roaring silence of the cellar they asked me three questions.

"What is it that you seek? What is it that you need? What is it that you intend to do?"

Before the Long, Brutal Winter

Tuesday, December 23, 2014–Thursday, January 1, 2015

II

After the fall semester ended and the winter settled in, Martin Kingsley rarely left his home. Every night, after eating dinner with his family and then helping Marianne put Christopher to bed, he marched dutifully downstairs to the stifling pit of his study. There, with the resignation of a galley slave, he labored late into the night, bleeding more words onto the page, consulting his voluminous notes on Flaubert, trying mightily to decipher the illegible marginalia he'd scribbled in his books over the years. It was depressing work and hard going, but the sorrowful circumstances surrounding Emily's death made everything in his life seem like an existential crisis and gave him the impetus to leave a modest legacy for his son, a small scrap of evidence proving that he'd been a productive member of society.

This didn't necessarily make the writing process any easier. His desk was in danger of becoming an altar of self-worship, and every night as he sat with pen in hand and pages spread all around him, he found it increasingly difficult to focus on the interminable revisions he needed to make. In some sense he felt trapped by a book he might never complete to his satisfaction, and even if he did manage to finish and publish it, he worried that his colleagues might revile him as an arriviste, a pretentious litterateur warped by black-hearted ambition. Worse, they might guess that he'd started the slow and irreversible descent into deviance and debauchery. Like a deep and brutal scar, his treachery shone plainly on his face, and by now it must have been clear to everyone in the department that he lacked the moral fortitude to extract himself from the treacly mire of his foul and wicked ways. Confronted for the first time with the grim possibility of professional extinction, he furiously revised sentences, deleted entire paragraphs, and because it was necessary for the preservation of his mental health, he pressed his hands over his ears whenever he heard from next door the faint cry of rusty hinges and the sound of heavy footsteps circling the swimming pool.

"Persistence!" he said with savage hope and a look of messianic determination.

As a kind of penance, he forced himself to work past midnight, lost for hours in his own loose and rambling thoughts, listening to the wind howl around the eaves, the branches rattling against the thin panes of glass. To aid him in his efforts, hoping it might provide him with much-needed inspiration, he drank mug after mug of the orange slurry he purchased from Xavier and then waited for the visions to begin. Despite its unpleasant oily texture and terrible aftertaste, he relished the toxicity of its dense vapors. The delightfully complex combination of food and drink made him feel, at least for a little while, oddly euphoric, almost invincible, but as the night wore on his mood darkened sharply and his stomach began to rumble.

Sometimes he fell into the fitful sleep of the insomniac, assailed by dreams of murderous solidity. In one recurring dream he sat on the patio outside Belleforest, waiting for Emily to arrive. As he sipped his wine, he watched a dozen townspeople gathering along the muddy embankment of the river to gawk at a limp and broken body bobbing in the turbulent waters. Trapped under a tessellated boulder balancing midstream, her tumid flesh stripped and peeled by the jagged rocks, her stomach bloated with corpse gas, Emily gazed blankly into the sky like an evil putto in some freak-show fountain. The wind picked up, the crowd gave a little cry, and all at once the powerful current freed her. With a silent scream Emily lifted her head and in a lifeless voice beseeched her lover to rescue her.

A whirlpool of brown foam pulled her under, and for a moment Martin thought she'd been swept toward the bridge and over the falls into the valley, but then he saw her rising slowly to the surface near the riverbank, her limbs weighted down by the turquoise sari. She struggled up the embankment and sidled through the muck, her hoary toenails scraping like talons against the rocks and stones. In her wake she dragged a stench as terrible as the raw sewage churned up by the eddies. She had changed, about that there was no question. The light in her eyes had been extinguished forever, replaced by a mocking expression that was cold and unforgiving, and her once lovely features had melted like candle wax, her nose gone altogether, eaten away by decay. Kingsley whimpered and turned from the hollow cavity at the center of her bloodless face.

"You did this to me," she said.

He shook his head. "No, Emily, you made a mistake. A terrible mistake."

"But you are not innocent, Martin."

"Neither of us is innocent," he said. "Now you must leave me alone. *Will* you leave me alone?"

Ignoring his strangled pleas for mercy, she brushed her gelatinous lips against his ear and in a voice that gurgled with festering water whispered, "First you must kiss me, Martin. Kiss me goodbye."

Kingsley woke suddenly to a sky glowing pink with morning sunlight, and into his heart crept a profound feeling of isolation and bitterness. In the terrible silence of dawn, his home seemed nested with domestic dangers of all kinds. This was unfair. He wanted to move on with his life, wanted to enjoy the holidays in peace with his family, but now he sensed an unmistakable presence behind him.

"You must have fallen asleep down here again."

His wife loomed over his desk, the sleeves of her thermal shirt rolled above her elbows. Kingsley found it difficult to meet her censorious gaze and hastily picked up the coffee mug he'd knocked over during his dream. Even before Emily's death there had been small fissures in his relationship with Marianne that now threatened to become deep crevasses. There were serious disputes and long stretches of icy silence that sometimes lasted for days. Things were now at their most fragile, and he worried that his marriage was on the verge of total collapse.

"Evidently your ghosts were misbehaving, Martin. You were dreaming of Emily Ryan, weren't you?" She jerked open the blinds, and when the light touched his face she said, "Oh, yes, I can still see her in your eyes."

Two days before Christmas, Kingsley returned to his desk, which he now believed to be haunted, and resumed the awful business of putting his book into some semblance of order, but as he riffled through his manuscript with all of its clumsy typographical errors, its biases, distortions, its intellectually slothful misattributions, he heard a knock at the back door, a loud rapping, a testing, a clawing. When he saw Charlie Ryan standing on the stoop, he let out a small gasp and jumped from his chair. So the great abuser of booze and women had come at long last to collect his due.

Charlie wore his workman's clothes, the Carhartt jacket, flannel shirt, faded jeans, steel-toed boots. Behind him lurked the twins, their knotted and greasy hair tied in pigtails, their pudgy faces dulled by grime, their chapped lips frozen into insolent smirks. Kingsley hadn't seen the girls since the wake, and he'd wondered if they had crawled inside the coffin and been interred with their mother in the churchyard. He remembered reading an essay about those horrid practices in India known as *sati*, whereby the bereaved were voluntarily buried with loved ones.

Marianne, when she heard the knock, came racing from the kitchen. She opened the door and knelt to take the girls in her arms. "We're so happy to see you. Aren't we, Martin?" She nudged him. "Are you hungry, girls? You look hungry. We were about to sit down to a late dinner." She waved them all into the house. "Please, come in out of the cold."

Charlie stepped back and tested out a sober smile. His mouth moved with inarticulate anxiety and then twisted into an expression that roughly resembled a grin, a flash of yellow incisors, a prolonged bulge of bloodshot eyes, a flare of hairy nostrils, but he was so out of practice with the simple mechanics of smiling, of making the upward turn of his lips appear natural and spontaneous, that he succeeded only in looking deranged, like a man who'd seen a ghost or was waiting for one to arrive and rattle off a long list of his sins and to describe in excruciating detail the unspeakably shameful contents of his conscience. Disheveled, unshaven, underfed, he might have been an ulcerated inmate just released from solitary confinement and trying without much success to reintegrate back into society, but it was becoming abundantly clear to Kingsley that what the man really needed was to be institutionalized indefinitely and closely monitored each day, his meals brought to a padded cell and fed to him, intravenously if necessary, by a pair of strapping male nurses.

"I'm sure," Charlie said, "Madeline and Sophie would appreciate a home-cooked meal for a change." He gave the twins a gentle shove, a man unaccustomed to coddling his children. "You girls go ahead without me. I think I'm gonna stay outside and have a smoke with Professor Marty. I have a few things I'd like to discuss with him."

Kingsley cleared his throat. "Oh, I don't smoke. I wouldn't dare. I have an addictive personality. I'd get hooked on them, I know I would. Books, reading, those are my only vices."

"Is that so?" Charlie laughed gently. "Well, join me anyway."

Having skimmed several articles about body language in his wife's fashion magazines, Kingsley recognized Charlie's posture as one of unease rather than a bold display of aggression. Nevertheless, in order to buy himself more time, Kingsley acted the part of absent-minded professor and claimed to have misplaced his winter coat. He looked at his neighbor, searching for signs of violent and erratic behavior, the rolling white eyes of a man half mad with grief and jealousy, and every time Charlie reached a hand inside his jacket Kingsley imagined he saw the glimmer of a black barrel.

When he could no longer delay the inevitable, he put on his shoes and donned his winter coat. Fulminating against his miserable fate, nearly incapacitated by fear, he followed Charlie outside. They walked across the patio, through the gate to the Ryans' yard, and over to the Adirondack chairs beside the pool.

"I wanted to speak to you in private," Charlie said. "Here, take a seat."

Kingsley brushed away the snow and prepared himself for that long-overdue, inexpiable exchange of words, wondering how pathetic he would look as he pleaded for his life. It was a scene he'd rehearsed over and over again in his mind.

"Haven't seen any pirates, have you?" Charlie asked.

Kingsley shook his head. Maybe the man had cracked, after all. "You're the only pirate I've seen, Mr. Ryan."

Charlie grunted. He searched the pocket of his flannel shirt for a cigarette and scowled when he found an empty pack. Through the clamped teeth of an agitated addict, he said, "Started smoking when I was twelve, if you can believe that. What a world, huh?" His voice was low, slightly emphysemic. "Anyway, I wanted to tell you that I'm shipping out after Christmas. I need to get back to work. In this day and age, when half the people in this town are out of a job, an able-bodied man can't simply walk away from a steady gig with a good salary and excellent benefits."

"You're absolutely correct."

"How am I supposed to earn a living in a place like this? Wash dishes, tend bar, wait tables at Belleforest?"

"That would be crazy."

"I think it'll help me get my head straight, too, returning to the ship. Oh, I know it's not what you'd call an ideal situation, but hell, you have to consider the predicament I'm in. It's been nearly four months since I've worked, and I'm running low on cash. Confidentially, just between the two of us, I'm flat broke. So you see, I have no choice in the matter, do I?"

Kingsley nodded vigorously. "I think you're making the right decision."

"The girls may not understand any of this now, but one day they will. I think."

"Of course they will."

"I'm certainly glad you see things my way, Professor. Because I don't want to send the girls away to live with my sister. I'd rather have them stay here in school with their friends. Things have been hard enough, you know, and a move in the middle of the school year would be another trauma. I haven't been much good to them, I admit that. For

a while I was on one helluva bender. But I'm better now. Much better."
He shrugged. "Well, what family doesn't have its little problems?"

Kingsley dug his fingernails into his palms. He thought he heard a
faint scratching, and then he remembered the bats in the walls. To keep
from visibly shaking, he lowered his head and focused on the brittle
leaves swirling near the base of an oak.

Charlie leaned toward him and now spoke with unsettling calm and
clarity. "I don't know how to ask you this so I'll just come right out with
it. Would you and Marianne be willing to take the girls in? You're such
good people and the girls love you. They especially love Christopher.
Like a brother. I'm not asking you to support my children financially,
understand? Money isn't the issue here. I'll transfer cash into your
account every month."

Kingsley squirmed. Gastronomic juices swirled and gurgled in his
empty stomach. "Well, uh, you see, the thing is my wife is throwing this
big party . . ."

"Would you at least think about it for a day or two? Talk it over
with her? The girls know they're safe here. It's like a second home to
them." Charlie seemed to ponder his dereliction and cocked his head
as if trying to decipher some kind of message, however oblique, in the
winter wind. He stood up slowly, sweeping snowflakes from his knees.
"Oh, yeah, I almost forgot." He reached a hand inside his coat, but
instead of the .38 he produced a worn paperback. "I think this belongs
to you."

Martin didn't look at the cover. He knew perfectly well which book
it was.

Charlie stomped through snowdrifts shining like the white marble of eroded headstones, but before going inside his house he looked
back and said, "No man really knows his wife, Kingsley. Women keep
secrets. Even from the people they love most."

A mass of swirling Arctic air had descended on the town, and a thin layer
of snow sparkled red and green from the lights draped across the houses
on the street. Above the swaying treetops, the gray hammer of cold air

pounded the clouds into dust, the twilight into fine purple particles that drifted in the unrelenting wind. For almost thirty minutes Kingsley sat alone and stared at Charlie's trail of footprints, but the longer he sat there the more convinced he became that he saw another set of prints beside them. He marveled at the high arches and tiny toes that led to the edge of the pool. Though he wasn't a religious man and could never bring himself to believe in an afterlife, he thought he sensed Emily's presence and suspected she'd been standing there all along, listening to her husband speak, even making him say the words, her hands planted on her hips, her eyes blazing with hellfire, but if Emily had been watching them and monitoring their conversation, she had already vanished under the tarp and deep into the obdurate heart of the water.

It occurred to him that he might never succeed in exorcising Emily's ghost from his memory. Kingsley had treated her cruelly, had opened vistas of hope where before there had been none, and for this she would never forgive him. He shivered in the cold night and waited for a limb from the old oak to come crashing down on his head and put an end to his vile existence. When nothing happened he stood up, and with *Madame Bovary* tucked under his arm, he plodded toward his house.

Guilty of the life within him, he surveyed the pool and backyard, a onetime oasis and carefully manicured Eden that had been swallowed up by a blinding sandstorm of grief, harsh and barren as the Sinai. Like some haggard, middle-aged American Moses, he gazed hopefully at the light inside his study as though it were a burning bush capable of providing a dose of divine revelation. He need only step through the door, remove his shoes, and announce, "Here I am!" But when he entered the house, he heard the voices of those two little fiends repeating their perverse and familiar refrain.

"Something to harden the soul, something to harden the soul, something to harden the soul before a long, brutal winter!"

12

If the girls found their new living arrangements comfortable, they also found them intimidating and, to a certain extent, rather unsettling. For one thing, the Kingsleys' house, though it was an old Victorian with dimensions roughly the same as their own, had been renovated from top to bottom and gave the impression of being far more spacious and filled with sunlight even on the dreariest of days when there was no sunlight at all and springtime seemed a hundred years off. For another, every room was kept neat and tidy. The hardwood floors gleamed with a fresh coat of polyurethane, the glass tabletops sparkled from harsh chemical solutions and obsessive dustings, and the books lining the walls of Professor Kingsley's study, systematically shelved by subject and carefully arranged so their spines were flush, emitted a kind of forbidden aura, the tiny print and incomprehensible prose accessible to those neophytes who'd been ritualistically cleansed of their offensive ignorance after long years of intense study. The girls were also baffled by the bizarre collection of original sculptures proudly displayed on the fireplace mantel. To them the house resembled a museum and the Kingsleys grouchy curators who were aghast to find themselves surrounded by so many unruly children, but rather than guide Madeline and Sophie from room to room, explaining the meaning of each book and painting and sculpture, the Kingsleys, who had a great sense of possession, repeatedly enjoined them to keep their hands off *everything*.

For the most part their days were quiet and uneventful, and the girls were treated to regular meals, usually steaming piles of colorless tofu cooked down to a pasty sweetness and an assortment of steamed vegetables seasoned with a touch of salt. Hot showers were mandatory each evening and bedsheets were changed first thing on Saturday morning. At night the girls were treated to elaborate bedtime stories that Mrs. Kingsley didn't so much read as perform with a dozen different voices from an illustrated book of wonderfully gruesome fairy tales in which wicked stepsisters lopped off their own heels and toes and then stuffed their bloody stumps into glass slippers. It was Marianne Kingsley's company the girls most enjoyed, or at least tolerated, and from her they learned to say "please" and "thank you" and to carry their dirty dishes to the kitchen sink after they were finished eating. Unlike their mother, Mrs. Kingsley rarely raised her voice or rushed off to the medicine cabinet to take a handful of pills whenever she grew tired of listening to her husband's "tedious bloviating" and "secular piety."

The peevish professor, when he launched into another self-righteous sermon, had an irritating habit of raising his chin and lowering his eyelids, and he used perplexing words and phrases that the girls enjoyed repeating with the same silly bluster—"gentrification" and "upward mobility" and "empowering the working classes." Aside from his extensive vocabulary, he sounded a lot like their father. Neither man seemed to have any idea what he was talking about. There were, of course, a number of key differences between them. Instead of jeans and flannel shirts, Martin Kingsley wore striped ties and sweater vests and khaki trousers that he had professionally laundered and pressed, and instead of cigarettes he kept a half-dozen ballpoint pens in his shirt pocket. He was also a big believer in "structured playtime" and "maintaining strict schedules," which precluded the girls from going outside and dragging snow into the house. But what irritated the girls most about these antiseptic surroundings was the presence of the Kingsleys' three-year-old son, Christopher.

Golden-haired, blue-eyed, developmentally challenged Christopher, long drunk on his mother's breast milk, stumbled in mad fits around the house, drooling over his shirt and wiping snot on the walls. Like some horror-movie toddler possessed by a legion of devils, he soiled his pants with absolute impunity and puked up the solid food he ate—scraps from beneath the dinner table, insects he'd found crawling in dark corners, buttons, marbles, bobby pins. He smashed, snapped, bent, scraped, and chewed all of his toys, and when he finished with this dastardly work, he hunted down and then viciously savaged the porcelain dolls Madeline and Sophie tried so hard to hide from him. The porcelain dolls had imperturbable faces, unbruised and free of blemishes, and shiny red ringlets of hair that fell into their penetrating green eyes. Their mother told them the dolls had been fired in a giant kiln long ago by an eccentric old woman who once lived in a lonely cottage in the valley, and the twins found in them some small measure of solace and comfort.

Whenever he saw the dolls, Christopher howled his head off with desire. He escaped from his playpen and with determined grunts and growls seized the dolls by their hair, twisted their arms, lifted their skirts, and searched longingly for orifices to violate with his sticky fingers. For these heinous crimes he was never punished. The girls were not pleased. After witnessing yet another molestation, Madeline and Sophie decided the entire family should pay the price, and in the quiet hours of the night, when everyone else in the house had fallen fast asleep, the twins sat in bed and began to plot their revenge.

The New Year's Eve party was a grand undertaking and the talk of the town; the college newspaper said so. As Marianne Kingsley, a shameless self-promoter, hyperbolically put it, "By eight o'clock the bistro will be bustling with *tout le monde.*" But on the night of the big event there was a quarrel that sent Madeline and Sophie scampering for the safety of blankets and pillows in the guest bedroom. Like a pair of stowaways, they huddled together on the canopied bed, their backs pressed against the cold plaster wall, their bodies warmed by an itchy wool quilt pulled up to their chins, their battered dolls cradled safely in the crux of their arms. From behind closed doors they listened to the heated exchange.

"Absolutely outrageous!" said the professor.

"Keep your voice down," said Mrs. Kingsley.

"But she's known about this event for weeks."

"Nothing we can do about it now, I'm afraid. I'm already late, Martin. You'll need to stay home and watch the children. I can think of no other solution to our predicament."

"You seem almost happy about it, like you've been planning this all along."

"Planning what? The babysitter canceling at the last minute?"

"Precisely. Now you can go to the party without me. And please tell me you're not wearing that dress."

"Certainly I am." Mrs. Kingsley's voice had a lurking scratch of mordant sarcasm. "Oh, I suppose you think it's in poor taste for me to wear something that looks so much like the sari my rival wore. Uncanny, isn't it? It's almost like wearing a burial shroud."

"Your rival?"

She grabbed a scarf off the hook in the foyer and then added tartly, "I'm sure you remember how Mrs. Ryan wore a turquoise sari on the night she took her own life. Or was she murdered? Investigators never made a definite ruling on the case."

Studiously ignoring her insinuating tones, Kingsley said, "That is by far the most outlandish thing you've ever said to me. Who put such a crazy idea into your head?" He followed her to the front door. "It was those two hellions upstairs, wasn't it? Didn't I warn you, Marianne? Didn't I tell you they were trouble, not to be trusted? They come from a world where vulgarity is considered a virtue, intellectual ambition ridiculed. Their dumb daddy should have sent them to an orphanage, a psychiatric ward, an animal shelter, a laboratory. They were born in captivity, and that's where they should have stayed."

Mrs. Kingsley silenced him with a fluttering gesture, a diamond ring flashing on her finger. She glanced at herself in the mirror beside the door and arranged her hair a final time. "The girls are perfectly innocent, Martin. And I do wish you would stop drinking. I'm not stupid, you know. I can smell the alcohol on your breath. You reek like an oil refinery." Her words had a cool edge to them. "I'll be home after midnight. Don't bother waiting up for me."

"You can't leave me alone. Not with those girls. Marianne, wait!"

She slammed the door behind her.

Engulfed in the dread silence of the house, Madeline and Sophie could feel the seconds crawling by, the minutes, the hours, and as midnight approached they heard footsteps, muffled and indistinct, outside the guest room. Coming from a troubled home made the girls natural watchers, and in the contained darkness they followed Professor Kingsley's portentous shadow as it floated in the hallway through a pool of dirty yellow light. Above the prolonged gusts that battered the gabled roof and made the slate tiles clatter like a heap of restless bones inside a crypt, they heard his raspy voice. The man muttered, he snarled. A rolling fog of hatred clouded his brain, obscured his thoughts. His words turned into a low, stifled laughter, his lips puckering with a seething distaste for his houseguests. Like a riddle or a difficult math problem at school, the exact meaning of his slurred and bitter ramblings perplexed the twins, but they both knew it was only a matter of time before he burst into their room to provide the solution.

Clutching their dolls more tightly, they moved closer together and held hands under sheets that smelled of harsh detergent. As the glass knob began to wiggle and turn, they thought how awful it was to have such an embittered and wayward man as their guardian. Little by little, oh, so gently, careful not to let the hinges squeak, the professor opened the bedroom door. The twins remained stock-still, like two animals frozen against the background, and clamped their eyes shut against a thin ray of light that cut through the darkness and fell across their faces. Slowly, very slowly, the professor moved his head through the narrow opening, and in the terrible gloom the girls caught a familiar whiff of formaldehyde that reminded them of the funeral parlor.

"Are you awake? Ha! Of course you are. Watching me with those vulture eyes. You're so clever, the two of you." In his voice the girls could hear the crushing self-pity and staggering incompetence that had led him to this moment of reckoning, and with one corner of his mouth turned up in a piratical leer he whispered, "You've said discreditable things about me, haven't you? Told my wife about our pool parties over the summer. Yes, I think so. I think I have two moles in the house. Moles that perpetually burrow beneath the ramparts of my happiness. Marianne thinks I'm paranoid. But I'm not paranoid. Not in the least."

In a gesture of self-defense, he gave a tug at his collar and brushed away a forelock of pomaded hair with his scrubbed, red hands. "What do I have to fear? It's your word against mine, isn't it? And I'm tired of you making a mockery of my marriage. But just to be safe, I'm going to speak to my wife at the bistro. I won't be gone long. And then tomorrow morning we'll all sit down and discuss what should be done with you. Because something must be done."

When they were certain he'd left the house, the girls hopped out of bed, put on their winter coats, pulled on their boots, and packed up their dolls. Having already given the matter a great deal of thought, they decided it was now time to move forward with their plan. They went from room to room, systematically unscrewing every lightbulb and unplugging every electronic device; they opened the toy chest and scattered Christopher's trucks and rubber reptiles all around the house; they poured salt into the sugar bowl; they tossed greasy banana peels beneath the couch where no one would find them until after the living room began to reek; they snapped the heads off the sculptures on the mantel. These tasks completed, they entered the professor's private study.

Working quickly, keeping an eye on the clock in the corner, they pulled his precious books from the shelves and arranged them according to the color of their dust jackets. They had just finished reshelving the red covers and were about to start on the black when they could no longer resist the lure of the professor's cherished manuscript on *Madame Bovary*. Like some flimsy tower, the thing sat atop his desk in a precise stack sorted by chapter, the pages held in place by small brass paperweights shaped like coffins—a gift that Christmas from Mrs. Kingsley. The girls looked at each other and squealed. Joyfully, they set upon his work in progress and took a particular, giant-killing glee in ripping the pages into tiny pieces. First, they trampled on them and kicked them across the room like confetti, then they collected the tattered fragments and stapled them to the walls. It became a kind of art project, and as they created ever more elaborate patterns, the girls called back and forth to each other.

"What are *you* making?"

"I'm making a *fish*!"

"I'm making a *bird*!"

In fact, the study now resembled nothing so much as a library in the aftermath of an explosion.

When they ran out of staples they barged into Christopher's room and screamed in his ears. They pounced on him, pulled his hair, rejoiced at his shrieks of terror and confusion, and when his tears finally subsided, they led him downstairs and into the forbidden outdoors—the one place children were never supposed to go. There, beside the holly bushes, they pushed him into a snowdrift. Not unexpectedly he took to it like a rutting sow and with eager hands heaped hard clumps of yellow snow on his head until he looked like a strange geological formation come to life, a giant calcium deposit from the depths of a salt mine. They brought him back inside and planted him on the couch in front of the television, but instead of letting him watch mallet-wielding cartoon cats and dogs with eyes hanging from their sockets on enormous springs, they flipped through the channels until they found a program about serial killers, war criminals, deposed dictators, scratchy black-and-white footage of unrepentant men being led to electric chairs and the gallows. Christopher applauded with each jolt of electricity, each snap of the neck and strangulation of the hangman's noose.

Satisfied with their handiwork, Madeline and Sophie slipped out the back door and hurried over to their own yard, where they unearthed the spare key beneath a rock in the flowerbed, but the tiny ruin of a house held no warm memories for them. It looked just as abandoned and empty as the barn in the valley and just as likely to be infested with hibernating creatures from out of bad dreams. Making sure to avoid the clothesline, they went inside through the patio door. A gentle snow quickly covered their tracks, and by disappearing without a trace, the girls knew the Kingsleys would have to call their father. The captain of the *Rogue* would set a new course for the nearest port, and within a day or two their dad would be back home.

13

After months of preparation, the Gonk decided it was finally time to put his own plan into motion. In the end it wasn't some phony New Year's resolution that convinced his ex-wife to accept the terms of a meeting but a simple business deal that would clear the Gonk of all financial obligations to her and at the same time help Xavier achieve his goal of taking an early retirement on Delacroix Cay. Why she believed such a preposterous story he didn't know and didn't particularly care, but for someone like Sadie, the daughter of an indigent and alcoholic pig farmer, the prospect of making lots of money was always a motivating factor.

That morning the Gonk called her with the details of what he claimed to be "a potentially life-changing opportunity."

Sadie laughed. "But it's New Year's Eve."

"Well, you know me. I don't fuck around. I want this thing out of the cellar. Today if possible. Starting tomorrow I'm turning over a new leaf."

"And I'm supposed to believe that bullshit, huh?"

Sadie knew how his mind worked. To her way of thinking he was an unapologetic cheat, an angry drunk with a short fuse, a common laborer earning a modest wage at the Department of Plant Services, a lowlife who'd abandoned his dreams while he was still young and whose sole ambition was to go fishing on the river and pay an occasional visit to the titty bar. But the worst of his shortcomings by far was his sick and unnatural desire for her kid sister Lorelei, a nasty piece of business that had precipitated an ugly divorce and a year of unseemly legal battles.

"I don't much care what you believe," said the Gonk. "If you're not interested, I know a dozen other takers."

"How much you asking for it?"

The Gonk chuckled. "You're a smart woman, Sadie. You know it's never a good idea to talk business over the phone."

Now there was nothing for him to do but sit on the porch and hope she would take the bait. There was a shiver in the north wind, and at ten o'clock that night, much later than he'd expected, he heard a pickup thundering down the driveway. In the red taillights he saw a set of flesh-colored truck nuts dangling obscenely from the trailer hitch.

Sadie pulled closer to the cottage and from the open window said, "I forgot what a true wilderness this place is." She killed the engine, hopped down from the cab, brushed snow from the cuffs of her jeans, and breathed the clean, country air. "With all of the wide open spaces in this valley, you'd think someone would raise horses. It would be nice, wouldn't it, to see a pretty girl astride a sorrel with flaxen mane and tail?"

The Gonk walked over to greet her. "Wait, I thought Xavier was coming with you."

"Busy, baby, busy. He's catering a big bash at the bistro. Some kind of art show for Colette Collins. Said he'll stop down later tonight. I'm just here to appraise the merchandise. See if this deal is legit."

The Gonk tried to control his rage. This wasn't part of the original plan. "Xavier claims to be the expert."

"We're business partners now, him and me. We split everything down the middle, fifty-fifty. A man has to love a woman to give up half of his assets, don't you think?"

"Love or hate," he fumed. "You took half of what I owned."

"No, you forfeited it. That was the price for diddling my kid sister. A real bargain, too." She winked.

"Let's not start up with that, okay?"

"Whatever you say, sweetheart." She sauntered to the back of the pickup.

"So where is Lorelei these days?"

"Still smitten, aren't you?" Sadie gave a little impatient shrug of her shoulders. "Well, let's see, I can't say for certain where she is now. I sent the little slut packing months ago. Last I heard she was dancing at the Normandy Cabaret. Probably trying to earn a quick buck giving deviants like you hand jobs in the back room. But she wasn't likely to last very long there."

The Gonk tapped the truck nuts with the toe of one shoe. "I see you're driving Xavier's pickup."

"Ain't his anymore. It's mine. He gave it to me. An engagement gift."

"Engagement?"

She lit a cigarette, picked a fleck of tobacco from her lower lip, and then spit into the snow. "That's right, darling."

"Sure is a classy thing to give a lady."

Sadie sat on the back bumper so the nuts seemed to hang between her legs. With one hand she gently massaged them, scratching them lightly with her long nails. "Oh, I dunno. I sort of like having a pair. Helps me understand why you boys take so much pride in them." She bounced on the bumper, and the nuts swung massively back and forth.

The Gonk grunted. Even a scene of great tragedy had elements of the comic and absurd. Weighing in his mind the course he must chart, he started walking toward the cottage. "So what's Xavier up to these days? Still getting innocent couples hopped up on that lust-inducing hellbroth?"

"His secret formula never worked on you, did it?" Sadie followed behind him. "Well, if hubby can't take care of business then it's the woman's prerogative to bring in a stunt cock, am I right?"

"That sonofabitch tried to poison me with the shit he peddles."

"If it's poison he sells, honey, then why are his customers so loyal? Repeat business is the name of the game. Xavier is an accomplished chef, practically a chemist, not some lowlife thug dealing smack to junkies."

The Gonk laughed. "He should maybe think about taking a few chemistry classes."

"There's a rumor going around that you're enrolled in a class at the college. Art or painting or some shit. What, did you find out there were a few desperate coeds willing to pose in the buff for a perverted continuing-education student? With so much teenage trim around, you must be in your glory. Now you don't have to settle for your old lady's baby sister. Say, I bet you got a whole lot of pretty watercolors you're wanting to show me."

"Goddammit." He stopped, and with his eyebrows gathered together said, "I think maybe we should reschedule for another time. When your sugar daddy can make it."

"Oh, don't you worry. Xavier's a real go-getter. He'll haul away this contraption of yours. That is, if I give him the thumbs-up. Besides, he'd like to see how his old pal is getting on without me."

The Gonk snorted, but because he wanted to finish this business as quickly as possible, he decided to play along. As it happened, there were certain advantages to having things unfold this way. He guided Sadie through the kitchen and waved her down the dark and winding stairs. The cellar, though damp and clammy, was pleasant compared with the winter weather outside. It was also very quiet. The large sandstone blocks absorbed even the smallest sounds. He watched with amusement as his ex-wife walked through the sawdust where he'd constructed the pieces of the birch box. Sadie approached the still and rapped her knuckles against its copper pipes.

"No doubt about it," she said. "If you get caught with a monster this size, you'll be charged with intent to sell."

"Consider it a wedding gift," said the Gonk.

She ignored him and began counting the empty mason jars on the wooden shelves and the big sacks of cornmeal and sugar in the corner. "Jesus, how the hell are we supposed to get this out of here?"

"That isn't my concern. I just want it gone. One thing's for sure, it'll make Xavier the biggest distributor of shine in the county, maybe the whole damn state. Of course I'm not sure he has brains enough to handle a large-scale operation. Before long he'll be a wanted man. His face will be in all the papers. He'll do time, probably a lot of it. Two years in solitary is my guess. That's how these judges roll nowadays.

Zero tolerance. I tell you, Sadie, solitary changes a fella. Xavier won't ever be the same once he gets out. Who knows, he might even drop a few pounds."

"If you had any balls," she said, "you'd sell the shit yourself, make something of your life. Instead, you badmouth Xavier. Hell, yes, we'll buy your damn still."

Worried his nemesis might show up and take him by surprise, the Gonk started pacing the cellar. His trembling fingers grazed the weeping sandstone walls and scraped a yellow fungus from the cement mortar. Long ago, in his hell-raising days, he relished the thrill of violence, but about the art and science of cold-blooded murder he knew absolutely nothing; nevertheless, when the moment seemed right, he was able to steady his hands and retrieve the long length of braided rope coiled beside the boiler. Like a pathogenic virus, the ability to kill lay dormant within him, building suddenly and without warning in every cell of his body, and with one swift motion he wrapped the rope around his victim's lovely stretch of throat.

He enjoyed watching her eyes bulge, her legs thrash, but he was no sadist and had no intention of prolonging his ex-wife's suffering. For a few minutes she put up a fight and managed to scratch his face, but she was no match for a man who outweighed her by nearly one hundred pounds. When she finally went limp and slumped to the floor, limbs askew, mouth hanging open, she looked scarcely human at all, like a department-store mannequin whose polymer face had been melted from the heat of a blowtorch.

From the back pocket of her jeans, he took the crumpled pack of cigarettes, and for thirty minutes he sat on the steps, smoking one after another. It took all of his willpower not to chew the things, to grind them between his teeth and swallow them. He'd only meant to render her unconscious but had gotten a little carried away. He wouldn't make the same mistake with Xavier.

In the silence of the cellar, Sadie's shrill screams and strangled cries for help continued to ring in his ears like a furious raga that alternated between harmony and dissonance. Hoping to stop these unendurable sounds, the Gonk dipped the sleeve of his shirt in a jar of moonshine and dabbed the angry lacerations on his cheeks and neck. He relished the sharp sting, the comforting pain. When he finally mustered the courage to look at his ex, his jailor, his beloved, his obsession, he noticed how her lovely skin had turned a chalky blue and how her body seemed to yearn for burial. He was surprised and a little ashamed that he did not weep, but like a dutiful husband, he carried her carcass upstairs and over to the cemetery.

Under the distant winter sun, he loosened the rope from Sadie's throat, tied it around her waist, and gently lowered her into the oversized birch box, the "double wide," as he called it. He whistled a dirge for the dead and noticed while gazing at her wrecked body how her clothes seemed drab, wrinkled, ill fitting, altogether lacking in her usual sense of style. Her shoes were knockoffs, her ring cubic zirconia. Maybe Xavier had been unable to give her the life she'd always dreamed of after all.

The Gonk bit his lower lip and circled the hole. Something wasn't right. Then he remembered: though he was never entirely convinced of God's existence, he did believe in things equally tyrannical and grotesque, like the sanctity of marriage, and he bowed his head in prayer, hoping Sadie now soared on angels' wings through a gaudy gold digger's paradise. Since there were no flowers in this winter desolation, he made a hasty bouquet of holly branches and in a last, wild gesture of love tossed it on her shriveling corpse.

This perfunctory ritual complete, he returned to the house, where he gathered the necessary tools—kerosene lamp, shovel, hammer, box of nails—and then waited for his dear friend to arrive. Together they would sit on the porch and enjoy one final drink, a kind of valedictory toast. It would be like the old days when Sadie joined them on the patio of the Victorian house near the college, just the three of them, and they laughed and told stories and sometimes, if Xavier's poison was strong enough and the mood struck them, they undressed in the moonlight and slipped into the hot tub and, after much grappling and groaning, emerged bright pink and well lubricated from the steaming water and hurried to the bedroom. The Gonk should have suspected something was amiss when Xavier began holding out a little longer each time, continuing to pleasure his wife and pollute her barren womb even while he, exhausted and insensible with drink, drifted off to sleep beside them, the spinning room perfumed with chlorine, the bedsprings squeaking a rhythmic and unrelenting lullaby, their arms twisted in extraordinary configurations like a dancing god of death.

Of course, what the Gonk had in mind now wasn't anything at all like those nights when they found themselves luxuriating in the warmth and wetness of the anonymous dark, the comforts of drunken debauchery, their pitiful excuse, but he'd always suspected that the time would come when the wicked pleasures of the flesh would give way to the splendid pleasures of retribution and, with Nature's mercy, the gracious gift of total annihilation.

14

Prior to unlocking the front doors at eight o'clock for those overeager and obstinately punctual first guests, Xavier D'Avignon was charged with the formidable task of preparing the bistro for the highly anticipated party. Earlier that day, under Marianne Kingsley's supervision and with Morgan Fey's grudging assistance, he set up additional tables and chairs, inflated dozens of black and silver balloons, draped foil streamers from the wooden rafters, suspended pretty paper lanterns from the exposed heating ducts, and, since the other members of the staff were too busy getting drunk at parties of their own and had either called in sick or patently refused to work that night, saw to all of the preliminary custodial duties—scrubbing toilets, scouring sinks, mopping floors, scraping mildew from the white subway tiles. He also assembled, to the best of his limited abilities, the giant clay sculpture of the college's notorious founder, Nathaniel Wakefield.

Commissioned by the board of directors, the thing was an outrageous challenge to good taste. By far the largest exhibit on display, the sculpture, with its frightening discrepancies of scale, seemed to wobble back and forth as if pushed by invisible fingers of heat. Like some self-important plus-sized model striking a languid pose for the paparazzi, it leaned against the exposed-brick walls, its impressive girth preventing any fresh air from sweeping into the cavernous space and filtering out the nostril-puckering scent of poorly prepared French food. Brutal in its aspect, the sculpture in some strange way seemed to nag Xavier, begging him to lavish it with an attention he did not wish to bestow upon it.

Now, dozens of resolutely radiant faces, beaming with a kind of social legitimacy, surged back and forth through the bistro in a great, roaring sea of taffeta and silk ties, everyone much too busy admiring each other to stop and consider the paintings hanging on the walls or to ponder that bizarre sculpture blocking an unremarkable view of the crumbling slate rooftops and the badly battered church steeple on the square. The happy, chattering mob, decked out in bespoke suits and extravagant cocktail dresses, jostled for position beside friends and colleagues, pleased and maybe a bit relieved to be counted among those important and influential enough to have received an invitation in the mail, an exquisitely designed card with raised lettering and a shimmering vellum overlay.

Marianne Kingsley, standing at the threshold, looked like she should have been reading their fortunes with a deck of Tarot cards and forecasting some imminent disaster. A prim and painted proprietress in a fanciful frock of blue with a ruched bodice and sequins around the waistline, she greeted each guest with two wet kisses to the cheek. "A lovely affair, isn't it?" she said, unable to suppress a small smile of professional vanity. "I wanted to make the bistro a gathering place, a fashionable salon, the beating heart at the center of this moribund community. Martin? Oh, I'm afraid he couldn't join us tonight. Yes, I know, a pity. But do make sure you enjoy the Red Death. It's a cocktail he discovered over the summer."

The professors and their spouses, divulging departmental gossip and expropriating bits and pieces of each other's banal conversation, glided like trained dancers through the bistro while Xavier, watching these precisely choreographed rumbas and cha-chas, burned with envy. While on one level he may have despised those well-heeled urbanites for their airs and graces, on another level, somewhere above the malodorous smell wafting either from the kitchen or from the depths of his soul, he couldn't be sure which, he knew it was small-minded to begrudge them their achievements. Successful people were entitled to a bit of swagger, especially if they'd struggled against and triumphed over life's insurmountable odds, and if things went as planned tonight, he would soon surpass this impolite, parasitical bunch of bores, these local-culture creeps, and live a life of ease and privilege far from this incest and hookworm belt of the state.

Back in the smoky kitchen, unable to cope with the demands of the prattling partygoers, Xavier maneuvered tubbily between the gas burners and the big chopping block. Ever since the night Lorelei danced on the bar top, he'd cut back on his alcohol intake, but tonight the pressure proved too much for him, and in haste he prepared another batch of carrot juice, a recipe he'd finally perfected after years of practice. While he could, of course, make extravagant and delicate dishes that appealed to the most discriminating palate—baked custards, stewed pears, a sour-cherry compote, the decidedly fussy cheese soufflé, the notoriously temperamental *blanquette de veau*—he took the greatest pleasure in mastering those subtle and obscure culinary techniques that to the untrained eye must have seemed deceptively simple, particularly the preparation of his precious carrots. For him there was an ascending and descending order to the cutting of carrots that he often likened to a musical étude. The slicing was an exact exercise, like fingers gliding nimbly over the correct keys of a piano, octave after octave, shimmering glissandos, rolling arpeggios, a forward momentum, a driving rhythm, a skill that was unquestionably athletic as well as artistic and one capable of producing a trancelike state in its humble practitioner.

First, he had to choose a knife for its workmanship and durability, the feel of its handle, the smell of its wood, the glimmer of its blade when testing its sharpness against a thumbnail. Most chefs preferred the ever-reliable "master of cooking" knife, with its straight, deep blade designed to cut with surgical precision through tough meat and gristle, but several years ago he had the rare pleasure of watching a self-described "bushman from French Indochina" use a jungle hunting knife, a barbarous weapon with a thick, serrated top edge that might have been the obvious choice of indigenous warriors for the purposes of slaughtering sworn enemies and hacking the tough hides of water buffalo. Never taking his eyes from the cutting board, the reputed bushman shaved a dozen carrots and then arranged the paper-thin slices one by one on a platter until they resembled the swells of a tropical sea at sunset.

Tonight Xavier chose a similar knife because he didn't trust the Gonk, not for a single second, and he feared the man would be well equipped with a knife of his own, a gun, a chain, a length of rope. If this deal for the moonshine still was on the level, he would need to go upstairs and remove one small bundle of cash from the safe. He checked his watch again. He picked and clawed at his shoulders, rubbed his neck and elbows, scratched the side of his leg as if a double thread of red ants had crawled up his black slacks and now balanced like trapeze artists from his short hairs.

Morgan burst into the kitchen with a tray of dirty dishes and looked at him with grave concern. "Hey, are you all right?"

Xavier swirled the juice in his glass and said distractedly, "Never better, never better. Listen, I may have to leave the party in an hour."

"Very funny."

"Don't worry. I won't go until after I close the kitchen for the night. I'm supposed to meet the Gonk in the valley. Seems my old chum wants to unload a moonshine still. I don't need to tell you, *mon chéri*, that quality moonshine goes for *beaucoup* bucks around here."

"The Gonk?" She shook her head in astonishment. "He'll gut you like a fish."

"Oh, he would never harm me. I'm much too important, a prominent member of the business community." Insensibly drunk, rocking back and forth on his heels, Xavier set the *jazar* down on the counter and shoved a platter of frozen food into the microwave oven.

"I don't want to be involved in your crazy schemes," she said. "When someone plays a potentially lethal game, it's wise not to ask too many questions." She grabbed a bag of garbage from the corner, slung it over her shoulder, and made her way toward the back door. "I'm tossing this and then having a quick smoke."

"Yes, fine, fine. But let me tell you something, Morgan. Do you know why most people never escape from this god-awful town? Do you know why they never rise above their pitiful circumstances?" Xavier thrust his face toward her, and his enormous pupils seemed to gather all of the available light in the room. "It's because they're afraid. Afraid of risk. They refuse to gamble. But I believe this meeting tonight is a risk, a calculated risk, and one well worth taking."

Marveling now at the bleak and frozen landscape of Normandy Falls, Morgan Fey descended the icicle-sheathed steps, her fingers sliding clumsily along the banister. Through ankle-deep snow she trudged toward an overflowing dumpster near the river and took a moment to watch the steaming water as if waiting for a makeshift raft to come floating along and carry her away to a place of safety and comfort. Only three months ago the riverbank was green and lush with reeds and cattails, but now it was featureless except for the sad flotilla of cans and bottles bobbing through a narrow channel warmed by the power plant, the fatal gash of its twisting current a cramped and constricted eternity colored by a blue-black seepage that had risen from the muddy bottom. For too long the citizens of this cursed town, an obscure and irrelevant people, had desecrated these waters, and now the river demanded some kind of restitution. Only then could it be cleansed and purified of human sin.

For Morgan Fey, who resented the fact that she was at the party as hired help rather than as a guest, the whole gaudy affair, like much else in life, was another long exercise in shameful servitude, a festival of regret, a cruel lampoon of old hopes already crushed. She was never more aware of her dirty uniform, her clumsy black shoes, her twenty-dollar haircut, the dime-store dye job. With each sip of the Red Death the guests grew louder, their voices crackling with hilarity and scorching wit, and soon they circled the bar like a herd of stamping, snorting, fly-swaddled wildebeests protecting a coveted watering hole. As Xavier's sole assistant and confidante, Morgan was tasked with working the bar and ladling the wicked tincture into plastic cups from an enormous crystal punch bowl. She also had to dispose of the garbage, of which there was quite a lot.

As she continued to monitor Xavier through the kitchen window, she managed to ignite her cigarette, and for the first time in her life she was truly frightened, terrified by the thing she was about to do that night. With any luck she would never have to worry again about the river or the disinherited and vengeful people who lived along its polluted banks, but now there were serious considerations of safety as well as common sense. During the past few weeks, Morgan and Lorelei had exchanged a number of lingering and conspiring looks, and in recent days they'd begun to discuss openly and in detail the fantastic heist that would liberate them at long last from Normandy Falls. The bistro's safe, Morgan believed, contained close to fifty thousand dollars in cash, more than enough money for the two of them to make a fresh start in the world, in some other town, in some other country, a suitable refuge for Lorelei and her unborn child. Because the Gonk was the type of man who, if he found out about the pregnancy, would hunt for Lorelei and try to take the child from her.

Xavier's early departure from the party would make Morgan's objective all the easier to accomplish. When she was sure he wasn't observing her through the window, she reached behind the dumpster and checked again on the toolbox she'd placed there. Inside was everything she needed to bust into the safe—hammer, hacksaw, crowbar, drill. Keeping her head down, worried that a shadow of criminality lurked in her eyes, she made her way back to the bistro and waited for the right moment to climb the narrow staircase that led to Xavier's quarters.

Among much glitter and glare the great fête raged on most furiously, and as midnight drew near and the party reached its supreme madness, I parked my car on the street and watched as Professor Kingsley, clearly drunk on *jazar* juice, stumbled toward the bistro. Before going inside he covered his mouth against a gurgling belch and loudly smacked his lips with the vile sting of acid reflux. I was surprised to see him arriving so late and hoped his present condition wouldn't compromise my plans. I followed close behind him and managed to slip unnoticed through the double doors, the only guest wearing jeans, a houndstooth sport coat, and a hastily knotted knit tie, although I did dress things up with a boutonniere, a bright peacock feather that fixed its unblinking blue eye on everyone in the room, a poor substitute for a functioning eyeball perhaps, but all things peacock were supposed to be in this year, that's what the fashion magazines said, and if the feather failed to provoke discussion among the guests, it at least warned them away and made them keep their distance. No doubt they took me for another slightly loony and unlettered townie, a coarse-featured, conniving, sadly diminished man whose brain had been starved and looted of its creativity and whose pinched and predatory face had been scarred by bitterness and sorrow. Instead of the arrogant smirk of a college kid on a full scholarship, I wore the hangdog expression of a native. The look was unmistakable—a sickly pallor and a crooked smile stained from bottomless pots of black coffee.

As he jostled through the crowd, Kingsley scrupulously avoided making eye contact with his colleagues in the department, some of whom were deplorably sober and yet somehow excessively happy, and this made him want to avoid them all the more. How in the world could anyone possibly be happy without the assistance of drugs and alcohol? He was mystified. The provost in particular had a habit of abstaining from all stimulants and depressants, coffee and cigarettes included, and judging from the dour expression on his face he was in no mood for idle chitchat. At the moment he was embroiled in what appeared to be a serious labor dispute. No one had seen the men from the Department of Plant Operations in several weeks, and the assumption, at least on the part of the provost, was that the ticks had joined a union and were on strike. As I slid behind a support beam and watched this gleeful circus of rumor and innuendo, I wondered if I should tender my own resignation, leave town, start a new life in another college town, far from this awful place.

While I pondered the matter I noticed Marianne Kingsley storming up behind her husband. I have always enjoyed watching the full extravagance of domestic dramas, and it occurred to me that the impending confrontation was a small but crucial scene in an elaborate play that Mrs. Kingsley had scripted well in advance—she'd been anticipating and preparing for her husband's inevitable arrival, rehearsing her lines, doing vocal warm-ups, but she had not anticipated the presence of a stranger in this story, and now she was in serious danger of overplaying her part. As I followed her across the tawdry stage of the bistro, I wasn't entirely sure how to play my own role—charming, defiant, deranged, morally ambiguous?—and before she could reach her husband I managed to stop her.

Reaching a hand into the pocket of my sport coat, I said, "Forgive the intrusion, but I've come with an urgent message from Emily Ryan."

Without taking the time to relish the puzzled expression on her face, I presented her with the pieces of pink stationery and then vanished into the pitching and swaying crowd. For many minutes she stood immobilized against the wall, her eyes scanning the pages. She continued to smile prettily, but she'd never been especially skillful at disguising her feelings, and her face gave off an incarnadine glow. The note was less a revelation than a confirmation of what she'd long suspected, and with the calm and confidence of proprietorship she clasped her hands behind her back and approached her husband.

"Are you totally fucking mad?" she said to him. Her dark and dangerous eyes had turned into tiny tar pits, and anyone foolish enough to get too close would soon find that he was unable to extract himself from their steamy bitumen.

Kingsley blinked at the heat of her anger and answered with a stoic smile, "Oh, a bit imprudent maybe, but there's no need to be crude, is there?"

"You're supposed to be home watching the children," she said, her voice dripping with scorching acid. "I should have you arrested for child endangerment."

"Idle threats seldom foster a productive dialogue between partners." He wanted to sound confident and formidable, but the words felt heavy on his tongue. They tumbled from his lips like little lead weights and clattered on the floor at his feet, where his wife could have gathered them up and rammed them back into his mouth, shattering his professionally bleached and polished teeth. "Marianne, I came here to speak to you. Next week is our tenth wedding anniversary. Ten long years, a not insignificant milestone, and I've been busy searching the antique shops for mementos made of tin. In case you didn't know, tin has long been a symbol of the flexibility one needs to weather the storms of a long-term relationship and is given and received on the occasion of one's tenth anniversary. A charming if curious custom that, at least in this particular situation, makes perfect sense."

"How so?" she asked.

"Through the ages marriages have been multitudinous in form and configuration. They are strange and unpredictable and flawed, but for these same reasons they can also be pliable and endlessly adaptable."

She breathed deeply and once again became the aspiring and fastidious socialite. "Do you see those two men standing over there by the sculpture? They might be interested in this information."

"Why?"

"They're police detectives, that's why."

"They are? What makes you say that? They don't *look* like detectives."

"Because I had the pleasure of speaking to them on the night Emily Ryan died."

"Are you sure?"

"It isn't the sort of thing you're likely to forget, Martin. They wrote detailed notes, photographed everything. And I'm sure they'd be delighted to hear about your involvement with our neighbor."

"What are you talking about?"

"Martin, if you know my secrets then I certainly know yours."

Kingsley reflected on this for a moment, struggling with how best to proceed, and then backed slowly against the exposed-brick wall. "But I don't know your secrets, Marianne. I've *never* known them."

Now she positively radiated hostility, and her animated smile abruptly hardened into an expression of permanent displeasure. She straightened the hem of her sleek skirt, adjusted her silk scarf. "It's almost midnight and I need to deliver my speech. If you'll excuse me, please . . ."

There is no one in the world more lonely than an uninvited guest at a party, and with my hands buried deep in my pockets, I made my way around the room. To me the guests looked like mischievous children suffering from progeria, dozens of prematurely shriveled faces crammed into the confines of the converted warehouse, an image reinforced by the powerful presence of Colette Collins, the crazed and sainted guest of honor, an individual so reclusive and so seldom photographed that very few people knew what she looked like. A brazen woman deep into her senescence and the only person present tonight who could get away with violating the town's strict smoking ban (one of the few privileges of being both a genius and frightfully frail), Colette Collins finished the cigarette already burning close to her knuckles before flicking the butt to the floor and grinding it under the heel of an orthopedic shoe. Her hair was a tangle of white curls; the lines on her face hinted at self-loathing and self-confidence; her bright blue eyes, ringed by dark circles, glowed like gas jets and made her appear both weary and excited, clever and naive, intelligent and dull, creative and destructive, reasonable and deranged. Many of the guests were quick to point out how similar she was to one of her own creations—spectral, strange, infuriatingly enigmatic—and how her words were slightly cryptic, a secret message, an obscene overture, an expression of her splendid and sickening desires.

She looked like a reanimated corpse that through some evil hocus-pocus had risen from one of the cold, metal tables in the refrigerated holding room of the county morgue; the only thing missing from her ghoulish ensemble was a large candelabra to light her way through the bistro's semi-luminous shadows. She hobbled over to the ransacked buffet table ("*Banquet* table," Marianne Kingsley politely corrected her) as if her very bones were on the verge of disintegrating, and there she nibbled on a roasted radish drizzled with garlic-infused olive oil and several pieces of stale *bâtard* heaped with Swiss chard, crushed red peppers, and thinly sliced ribbons of carrot. With trepidation she sniffed a skewer loaded with chunks of wine-drenched turkey vulture.

"You mean to tell me this chef considers himself an *artist*?" she said with ecstatic disgust, her voice deepened by decades of nicotine abuse, her mouth becoming a raw, pink crevice of contempt. "Wild animals rendered down to mucilage!"

"Ms. Collins," said Marianne Kingsley, taking her by the hand, "come along with me. It's time I introduce you formally to our guests."

While I waited for Mrs. Kingsley to speak, I studied the strange sculpture in the corner. Superhuman in its enormity, a misshapen mound of kiln-fired mud baked hard as rock and cracked from limb to limb, the sculpture proved difficult to interpret. Its single eye was a large piece of banded black onyx that reflected the distorted faces of the revelers, its feet long protrusions of petrified earth, its toes curled and askew like concrete cucumbers scattered on the floor, its primitive ape-like knuckles tough and calloused as any schoolyard bully's, its glazed torso purple as an eggplant, its hollow limbs as deceptively sturdy as the wooden beams holding up the ceiling and walls, its gut as bloated and slovenly as a beer-guzzling laborer who might feel at ease in a saloon, a strip club, a bawdy house, and its prominent and irascible brow hinted at a simple masculine predilection for pillage and plunder. But the sagging breasts, the dimpled backside, and the general air of inaccessibility made the thing seem somehow feminine, an overbearing mother ready to pounce upon and severely reprimand its naughty progeny for the most minor of infractions.

Near the bar, gazing in mock adoration and secret scorn at the perplexing installation, the two detectives—if, in fact, they were detectives as Mrs. Kingsley claimed—made guesses at what the thing might be. The first man said: "It's a depiction of how time has devastated this once strong and beautiful town, now a defeated ogre, continually ravaged by the incurable pestilences of addiction and violence." The second said: "No, it's a representation of our sad society, a confused Colossus of Rhodes, a woebegone Mother of Exiles overwhelmed by so much wretched refuse."

Professor Kingsley cautiously approached the men and tried to think of something clever to say. For most academics, no matter their area of expertise, there were only two rather contradictory rules of art criticism: the first was to be as insightful as possible; failing that, the rule was to be humorous, snide, acerbic. After all, when confronted by a baffling work of modern art, the best way to disguise one's lack of erudition and stark incomprehension was to try to lighten the mood in any way possible. The problem, so far as I could tell, was that these men had no sense of humor whatsoever. Wishing to prove his innocence and profess his undying devotion to his beautiful bride, Kingsley impudently declared, "I say it's Marianne, the bare-breasted avatar of the revolutionary spirit, symbol of *liberté, égalité, fraternité*, trying to fight past the barricades of ignorance and folly that the people of this town have erected."

The men barely acknowledged his comment and clinked the ice cubes in their otherwise empty cups.

The first quipped, "These artists are like modern-day witches, concocting gobbledygook all night long from the fiery cauldrons of their minds."

The second said, "They are like the gods of old, fashioning primordial beings from clay and water."

Feeling increasingly ill at ease around these men, the professor offered a decidedly less perspicacious response. "They are expert forgers and frauds, endeavoring to stitch together from so many scraps stolen from the masters a work they can claim as their own. And judging from the smell of those so-called cigarettes Ms. Collins is smoking tonight, I'd say artists are, in all likelihood, a hopeless bunch of chemically dependent oddballs. Just like the rest of us, gents. Nothing very special."

The men sneered, and before the conversation took a precipitous plunge into the intellectual void of more congenial topics like the weather and work, Kingsley said, "We should replenish our empty cups, but first I'd like to ask you gents about a matter of great consequence." He came a little closer and said in confidential tones, "Of all the women here this evening, who would you say is the sexiest?"

Hoping this most taboo of questions might provide further evidence of his fidelity and bring to these invariably dull proceedings a much-needed spark of life, he took a step back as if he'd just pulled the pin on a grenade, but the men were far too diplomatic to answer honestly or engage in a heated discussion, maybe because they, like practically every guest at these painfully polite cocktail parties, adhered to the credo of political correctness and possessed a collective sense of guilt about any topic that struck them as even remotely sexist and discriminatory—could someone be sexier than someone else; wasn't sexiness a purely subjective and thus entirely relative assessment of a fellow human being; and didn't such a question fail to take into account the more important and complex notion of inner beauty?

Growing impatient with their evasive answers and awkward mumbling, Kingsley pointed to his wife, who now stood at the podium near the entrance, and unashamedly proclaimed her to be the most attractive woman *by far*. From the uncomfortable silence that followed and the nervous adjustment of coats and shirtsleeves, he knew at once that he'd crossed the elusive line demarcating bad taste and outright incivility. Disappointed with the results of this innocuous parlor game and somewhat embarrassed by his inability to strike up a conversation, he slunk away and wandered dejectedly through the bistro.

Cursed with the task of addressing the guests, Marianne Kingsley gripped the sides of the podium with both hands and said, "May I have your attention?" With a manicured finger she tapped the microphone three times. Above the confusion of cackles and the vacuous gabble of the sweaty mob, she shouted, "Ladies and gentleman, your attention, please! I would now like to say a few words about our honoree . . ." When the room finally came to order, Mrs. Kingsley regained her composure and spoke once again in the manner of a woman whose accomplishments seemed complete and unassailable. "Some of you can probably guess my two favorite words in the English language." She paused for effect before saying, "Captive audience."

Reluctantly, the men and women set their empty drinks aside and offered their polite, ceremonial applause, but many looked with longing at the shallow punch bowl, hoping to get one last cup of the Red Death before ringing in the New Year. The old woman, meanwhile, doddered quietly away from the hostess's side and made her way to the bar.

"Most people," said Mrs. Kingsley with a small smile cemented to her lips, "or at least those people who strike us as well adjusted to their current circumstances, are understandably reluctant to disclose those aspects of their personality that others might regard as not merely odd but positively wicked. We tend to treat our secret desires, our questionable impulses, our perverse proclivities as monsters. We lock them away, hopefully forever, in the dark dungeon of our soul and then throw away the key. But artists are different in that they keep the key close at hand. They become society's dungeon masters and make the treacherous descent to visit those fearsome creatures, to marvel at their strange, hideous beauty, to listen to the filthy secrets unspooling from their souls, their leaky brains, their ruptured hearts. Occasionally, despite all of the taboos against doing so, artists dare to release the monsters and let them stretch their legs in the confining prison yard of the canvas. Some of us, for a short while at least, like to gather around and gawk at them. Then the artist, like any responsible warder, returns the beasts to their proper place in the dungeon, confident they will go undisturbed until the next visit, or until such time as the key is misplaced and they can no longer gain access to those dark realms. A good thing, too. Because sooner or later the monsters always seem to turn on their keepers and destroy them."

By this time Mrs. Kingsley's voice had taken on the rhythms and cadences peculiar to this small town, and I noted the unsettling way her body language had changed. From a distance, because of that turquoise dress she wore, she looked like Emily Ryan, and as I listened with growing excitement to her bracingly weird words, I became convinced Emily was speaking directly to me, telling me what I must do and where I must go.

"The dark dungeon," I murmured. "The treacherous descent."

The people standing beside me inched away as they might from a lunatic on the street corner.

"And so what has Colette Collins dragged up into the daylight? What subterranean goodies will she show us now? Well past the age when most artists experience a decline in their creative output, Ms. Collins continues to labor intensely at her craft and has given us, I'm sure you'll agree, her most ambitious work thus far." Marianne gestured to the giant clay sculpture towering above the guests in the back of the bistro. "For this particular commission, she was obligated to name the sculpture after the dear founder of Normandy College, Nathaniel Wakefield, but under ordinary circumstances she doesn't call her sculptures anything. Rather, they call her. They create themselves, name themselves, force her to do their bidding. And if you listen closely you can hear the thing whisper its terrible truth."

Mrs. Kingsley looked down at the pieces of pink stationery, and as she read from them her voice took on notes of alternating intensity. "College is an intellectual garbage dump; students are free spirits, a term that best describes the dispirited, the enslaved, the unenlightened; enlightenment is a religious euphemism for death; death is a consistent and universal truth, the afterlife only a speculation; God is a mask used by weak individuals to disguise their own powerless egos; the ego is an hallucination with no clear foundation, no ultimate reality." Her scratchy voice had now reached manic levels, and she drummed the lectern with a tight fist. "And marriage? Why, marriage is a *long, brutal winter*!"

From the safety of the shadows, Martin Kingsley listened with growing alarm to his wife's wild imprecations and felt the heat and pressure of her serious stare as she leaned over the podium and glowered at him. He inched toward the bar, his throat clutched tight with terror. He loosened his tie and wiped a bead of cold sweat from his forehead. It was almost midnight, but something was wrong with these traitorous clocks. The seconds stretched out, surreal, displaced, misaligned, and he believed the New Year might never come. Most of the guests, unable to follow the thread of this strange speech, grew agitated and restless. There were whispers of confusion and disapproval, groans and sighs, a general stamping of feet against the floor. Hoping to get some badly needed laughs, Kingsley cupped his hands around his mouth and gave a loud boo.

"Where the hell is that bartender?" he said, topping off his cup with the dregs from the bottom of the punch bowl.

Colette Collins watched him with amusement. "Haven't you had enough?"

He bristled at her question. "I've had enough of my wife's sancti-monious rhetoric."

"You'll excuse my saying so, Professor, but you look like death."

"Do I? I certainly *feel* like death."

"It's a terrible thing for a man to die before he has a chance to become old." She spoke with the amiable harmlessness of a potential madwoman. "Well, maybe you *are* dead. Maybe we both are. At my age, each day is a reprieve from the grave. It could be that we've crossed over and are in hell right now. That would explain a great many things, wouldn't it? For instance, why are the walls slowly converging? And why are all of the faces melting?"

The levity vanished from Kingsley's eyes. He looked more intensely at the guests and began to tremble. "My God, I think you're right. Everything seems to be *dripping*." He touched his cheeks, his nose, his chin. He lowered his head and gasped. "I think I'm going to be sick. Yes, I'm definitely going to be sick."

Colette Collins clapped a hand on his wrist. "You'd better come with me!"

They made for an incongruous pair, an old woman leading a young man through this witches' sabbath where the monstrous crowd gam-boled and clamored and cavorted. Kingsley gasped and panted, and as he weaved his way toward the restroom, he saw his former pupil leaning against the clay sculpture, his arms crossed, a triumphant smile stretched across his swollen and infected face, a peacock feather dan-gling from the lapel of his sport coat.

"A magnificent work of art, isn't it, Professor?" I said with a smile of purest complicity.

Morgan Fey returned to the kitchen, her vision obscured by antic clouds of hot steam swirling massively from a big pot of boiling water.

Like poisonous vapors from a cauldron, the long tentacles caressed her skin and scattered the fluorescent light. Infuriated by Xavier's incompetence, she turned off the gas and swept her consternated gaze around the empty kitchen. If he didn't lay off the booze, or at least cut down from two gallons a day to one, he would burn the place to the ground.

"Hey, genius! You left the burners on again."

She wiped the condensation from the round window of the swinging door and scanned the dining room but didn't see the chef waddling around that buzzing hive of earnest faces. Maybe, she thought, he'd already left the bistro for the night to see about his latest business venture. Turning away from the window, she fixed her eyes on the stairway with its bare boards, its tacks, its splinters. A faint yellow light burned inside Xavier's quarters. She hesitated, knowing the second floor was strictly off-limits to her, to everyone.

"Xavier? Are you up there?"

For some reason the flat sound of her own voice made her tremble. No doubt the steam had created a slight alteration in the air. She desperately craved a tall glass of the Red Death to steel her sorry body and fortify her weak nerves. When no one answered her call, she climbed the staircase. Each creaking step sounded like a thunderclap, and on the landing the smell of slow corruption struck her with visceral force. The place needed to be fumigated. In the hallway outside his bedroom door, through a dirty pane of glass, she could see the black maw of night, the stars gleaming like fierce diamonds above a fringe of pine trees crusted with snow. She glimpsed the moon shining on the frozen river, its pale fire swallowed up by a passing cloud. Great whistling funnels of snow sprang up around the polluted embankment, and for a moment she believed the flakes had found their way into the hallway and were now blanketing her shoulders. On the street a truck thundered by, shaking the building's foundation and shattering the lethal icicles hanging like fangs from the eaves.

With all of the fear drained out of her, she approached his room and pushed open the door. Glossy brochures of a tropical island lay scattered on the floor, and on the opposite wall the Toulouse-Lautrec poster that had once concealed the safe now leaned against the unmade bed. Morgan didn't move, didn't take another step. She scratched violently at her arms, leaving angry red trails on her skin. She wondered if she would have enough time to retrieve her toolbox from behind the dumpster. It might take thirty minutes or more to break into the safe, and even then she couldn't carry away so much cash in her pockets. She turned her eyes to a wooden wine crate engraved with Gothic script: *Châteauneuf-du-Pape.* There was something almost eerie about it, the way it resembled a miniature sarcophagus, a pauper's pine box, a baby basin from a demented nursery.

She reached for the phone on the nightstand and dialed the number.

"It's me. Are you ready to go? Right, meet me at the bistro as soon as you can. And bring our bags."

She placed the phone back on the receiver. Lorelei and Morgan had been living together now for several weeks, but to stay the night in the row house would have been too risky, maybe even suicidal. After emptying the safe, they planned to swipe the keys to Sadie's new truck and then skip town as quickly as possible.

From downstairs in the dining room there came a horrific crash, wild screams. Terror crawled down the back of her neck and rested at the base of her skull.

"It must be midnight," she assured herself. "Only midnight."

15

The previous summer had been an exceptionally wet one, and all through the valley the frozen bogs were deep and dark and bottomed with an acidic black silt that reeked of corruption. Just above the tree-tops, hovering low in the bat-infested sky, an enormous moon drifted across the horizon cloaked in the sulfurous gases rising green and ghost-like from a narrow stream warmed by peat and decaying vegetation.

The Gonk turned off the headlights and brought Sadie's pickup to a stop at the edge of a small ridge overlooking the wetlands. He put the truck in neutral, got out, and walked to the back of the vehicle. A cold wind came in fierce blasts. Pulling the collar of his coat close to his neck, he felt like a conscript marching unwillingly to the eastern front in the middle of a Russian winter. Fallen branches snapped behind him. He stopped, reared his shaggy head back against the sky, and sniffed suspiciously. Dozens of flaming eyes stared at him from the safety of the sturdy, pitch-black pines. Impelled by some sort of fascination, yapping and dancing and sniffing out the madness wafting from his sweaty flesh, a pack of coyotes emerged from the woods and watched him.

The Gonk smiled in solidarity. With his hands pressed against the rear bumper, he gave the truck a forceful shove down the slope. Now the seasons would become his clock and calendar, and in the coming months, when spring arrived and the ice melted, he would derive enormous satisfaction as he watched first the cab and then the bed fill with water and disappear under long tendrils of carnivorous pink sundews. Last of all to go would be those truck nuts that were sure to float white and swollen on the surface before the powerful suction swallowed them whole.

Pleased with this vision, he crammed a wad of tobacco into his left cheek and hiked up his jeans. It was a fair distance to the cottage. Across hillocks of snow the coyotes followed the new caretaker in an unnatural procession to the cemetery, where a lavish midnight feast awaited them. Through a scattering of naked winter willows, the Gonk could already hear Xavier's needling voice calling to him.

"That you? Hey, what the hell? Been waiting ten minutes now. Don't you have electricity out here? I can't see a damn thing."

To conceal the scratches on his face, the Gonk wore his baseball cap so low that he could barely see above its bent and ragged brim. He lit the kerosene lamp and held it aloft to observe his nemesis, the proud and swaggering "stunt cock" who night after night climbed on top of his wife and emptied himself into her like rancid bouillabaisse from an overturned creamer.

Taken aback by the amount of weight Xavier'd put on since opening the bistro, the Gonk playfully tapped Xavier's stomach and said, "Must enjoy your own cooking, huh? Compensation for your sexual aberrations, maybe?"

"You're hysterical."

The Gonk lowered the lamp. "How'd you manage to get out here without a vehicle?"

"Left my car on the road," Xavier said. "Hoofed it up your driveway."

"Just in case you have to make a quick getaway."

Xavier made several small adjustments to the swampy pit between his legs. "Felt like a mile hike in the snow."

"Nothing wrong with a little exercise now and then."

Tufts of black hair sprouted from Xavier's nose, and he buried a finger deep inside one whistling nostril. "Okay, friend, where's Sadie?"

The Gonk shrugged. "The hell should I know? She waited here for you for more than an hour and then she split. Must have gotten your lines crossed. Didn't you call her?"

The question seemed to irritate Xavier, and from his thick lips there came a high-pitched wheeze that may have been contemptuous laughter or a fearful gasp. "You trying to be cute or something? There's no service in this valley. Besides, I left my phone in her truck."

"Well, you're more than welcome to use my landline. You should give Sadie a ring. Tell her you made it safe and sound to my place. I'm sure she's worried about you. It's getting late."

"I don't need to check in with Mommy."

"I insist. Phone is in the kitchen."

"Screw that. I'd like to hurry this along, okay?"

"Naturally. But first, let me treat you to a sample."

"This isn't a social call. I'm here to conduct business."

"Look, we're going to do this thing the right way or not at all." The Gonk mounted the porch steps and handed him a mason jar. "Shit'll knock you on your ass if you're not careful. Been known to blind some people, kill a few others. Of course it's a hell of an improvement over the junk you've been selling. That *jazar* juice is like heroin, isn't it? People don't do it socially. They don't try it on the weekends just for fun."

Xavier waved the jar under his nose and inhaled its overpowering bouquet. After puckering his lips and darting his yellow tongue around the rim, he took an experimental sip. He slurped and swished the oily liquid in his mouth. He sucked and gargled and spat.

"Well?" asked the Gonk.

"I'm not convinced it's a hundred proof. I'd say it's more like eighty. You told Sadie it was a hundred proof, didn't you?" He dropped the glass on the porch and watched it roll down the steps into the snow.

The Gonk shrugged. "You're the chemist. Take some home and test it."

Xavier looked hard at him. "That crazy old woman who lived here, Colette Collins, she just gave you the whole setup?"

"Yeah, she told me it came with the house. As a signing bonus. That and the cemetery over there."

"The what?"

"When the moon is high, like it is tonight, you can make out the headstones. Didn't you see it as you came up the driveway? That's where I keep the still. Come on. I'll show you."

Xavier hesitated. No doubt he sensed something very wrong with this scenario, but the *jazar* juice had dulled his instincts, which were never particularly sharp even when he was sober, and the prospect of owning a still to manufacture his own moonshine proved too tempting. He followed the Gonk down the porch steps and into the immense and unremitting darkness that waited for him beyond the circle of feeble light.

The Gonk raised the lamp higher. "I'm just relieved you agreed to take the still off my hands. The feds have been snooping around lately, checking things out. I don't feel comfortable anymore with all of this contraband in my possession. Besides, I don't drink much these days. Not since the divorce anyway. Sadie must have told you, right?"

Xavier sneered. "You never could hold your liquor, limp dick."

The Gonk roared with laughter. "Life can get pretty dull when you abstain from the bottle, I can attest to that. With so much time on my hands, I've started taking classes at the college. But mostly I've been doing a lot of reading. You might say I'm diseased with the reading bug."

"Reading what? Girly magazines?"

"Books on the moonshine trade. Do you know a smart distributor, if he doesn't get clipped, can clear six figures every year, all tax free? A good still is worth thousands."

"I'll be the judge of that, friend. It all depends on the output. For me this is just going to be a side operation. Something to supplement my income, understand? That ex-wife of yours has damn expensive tastes."

Step by fatal step they marched past the wrought-iron gates and into the cemetery. Beneath their feet the snow crunched and the dead leaves crackled like the shells of bugs.

"I've been reading about other things, too," said the Gonk. "Books on the history of religion. It amazes me how horrible some religious practices used to be."

"Religion, too? By God, you've finally cracked, haven't you?"

"Like I told you, it's awfully lonely out here in the woods. I have to find something to occupy my time. This valley is a funny place. A lot of folks have been known to turn into mystics. Anyway, at the college library I found a book of Indian lore."

"Redskin or towel head?"

"Hindu," the Gonk answered. "It was written a couple hundred years ago by a French Jesuit. The good father ran a mission near the city of Pondicherry, but while he was in the jungle, doing the Lord's work, he witnessed dozens of gruesome rituals."

"What the hell are you talking about?"

"Well, according to the priest there was a great swami in a remote village who died after a prolonged illness. The people held a feast to honor him, and during the funeral rites his widow appeared dressed in blue robes and presented herself for burial with her husband's corpse. At first the priest thought the woman had gone mad, that a legion of devils had taken possession of her, but the villagers insisted that this was the most natural thing in the world, a widow's way of showing devotion to her spouse. The people placed the woman inside the coffin and buried her alive. Later, after the celebration was over, the priest claimed he heard her scratching wildly at the lid, like maybe she realized she'd made a horrible mistake, but after a few hours the scratching grew fainter and fainter until it finally stopped. Suffocated probably."

Xavier's face twitched in an absurd and clownish manner. "That's fucked up."

"You won't get an argument out of me. But something has been bothering me about the story. During all those years he spent in India, the priest never saw a man come forward to be buried alive with his deceased wife. Or with his fiancée. Not one time." The Gonk stopped walking and turned to Xavier. "What's your view on these matters? Would you be willing to follow the woman you love to the grave? It's one way of assuring allegiances, isn't it?"

"You trying to be funny?"

The Gonk smiled, his face raddled and drawn. "Oh, yes, funny."

"What is this place, anyway?"

"I *told* you." The Gonk sighed and shook his head. "Okay, I confess. I've always been a bit superstitious, and at night I never come alone to the graveyard. That's why I keep the still here. Helps me fight the urge to fix myself a bottomless drink." He pointed to the hole, hoping the coyotes hadn't made a premature feast of Sadie's remains. "Here, take hold of this rope. Give me a hand pulling 'er up, would you?"

"You've gotta be kidding," said Xavier with growing apprehension.

"Yes, I'm kidding."

The Gonk waited, and when he saw the imbecile leaning over to inspect the hole more closely, he grabbed the shovel off the ground and let the blade drop on the crown of Xavier's head, not so hard as to render him unconscious, no, just hard enough to rattle his brains momentarily and make him see more stars than were actually there in that glorious patch of sky unobstructed by trees or dulled by the distant lights of town. He wanted Xavier to know exactly what was happening to him, wanted him to understand the seriousness of his offenses.

For one uncertain moment Xavier teetered back and forth like a man doing a drunken dance, and then with a high-pitched scream he toppled into the wormy hole, landing squarely inside the coffin. His body trembled, his jowls jiggled atrociously, and when he was able to breathe again, he let out a long, tortured groan. "Oh, that hurt," he croaked. "Oh, I think—yes—I think I'm seriously injured."

The Gonk didn't hesitate. When he heard those rhapsodic notes of pain, he gathered up the hammer and box of nails and jumped into the hole. Before slamming the lid on his friend's uncomprehending face, he tossed a flashlight in the box and said, "You'll find this useful. Consider yourself the first person in over one hundred years to participate in a most sacred and ancient ritual."

Time was of the essence. At any moment Xavier might come to his senses and begin to beat at the lid with his fists. Though the flickering light of the kerosene lamp made the work difficult, the Gonk managed to close the lid and seal the corners of the coffin. He then made his way around the perimeter, pounding in the nails two at a time until he was satisfied that there was no possibility of escape. Above him the great limbs of the white oaks groaned as though burdened with the weight of a hanged man, and the dim band of the Milky Way grew ever more brilliant as it arched across the sky and boiled through the black flume of icy space.

He began to heave dirt into the pit, and to his amazement he had the hole halfway filled before he perceived Xavier's feeble and impotent laughter.

"This has to be a joke. Tell me this is a joke."

Apparently, the poor fool hadn't switched on the flashlight.

"That's right," said the Gonk. "A joke."

There was a long and obstinate silence. The Gonk leaned over the hole, thrust the shovel deep into the loose clods of dirt, and rapped three times on the lid.

"Hey, did you run out of oxygen already? Hello?"

"Ha! Ha! Ha!—He! He!—an apology, of course, I should have known—He! He! That's all you want? I'm sorry, then. So terribly sorry. For everything. Now let me out. I'm begging you."

The Gonk resumed filling the hole. That's when the screams started in earnest, screams so sharp and clear, so powerful and unrelenting in their madness, that not even the earth could soften them, a howl of impossible sonorities, and the Gonk worried that his nemesis might scare off the coyotes waiting patiently beyond the gates to dig up his putrid flesh and scatter his bones.

After an hour he tapped the last shovelful of dirt on the unmarked grave. He turned down the kerosene lamp until the flame sputtered and vanished, and then he marveled at the apparitions hovering through the trembling blue mists of midnight. In the lurid glow he could see dozens of eyes, yellow and black ringed, their pupils small as pinpoints, and he could feel the warmth of the circling coyotes. The deranged moans and screams gradually subsided, and soon the Gonk heard only the constant whispers of the winter wind. He never imagined silence could be so terrible, so absolute.

"Xavier?" he whispered. "Xavier . . ."

His faith began to waiver. He pressed his ear against the earth and listened.

From within the coffin there came a high-pitched, tremulous wail that filled the blustery air, a shrill and lamentable voice that made him shudder.

"Oh, my darling. What has he done to you? What has he *done*?"

As in a dream the words seemed to metamorphose into the wedding toast delivered long ago by that inebriated jester now beating his fat fists against the wooden casket, a toast not simply to the Gonk's blushing bride but to her singular beauty, to her high cheekbones, to her full lips, to her generous and accommodating mouth, a toast so unabashedly vulgar it drowned out the gasps of the scandalized guests and the sheepish laughter of the groom.

The Gonk now set the shovel aside, unzipped his pants, and sent a wide parabola of urine onto the shallow grave, where it pooled and glittered in the moonlight. He heard the distant sounds of fireworks, car horns, church bells, but he was no longer in a celebratory mood. The euphoria he'd been anticipating was slow in coming. His lungs burned, his back ached, his head pounded with wretched sobriety. He thought of Colette Collins and wondered what she was doing tonight. Finally, he raised a jar and made his own lunatic toast to the happy couple, but his voice sounded so weak and false that he barely recognized it.

"For all eternity," he said, "may you each enjoy the other's foul evacuations and gruesome decomposition."

16

Martin Kingsley concentrated on keeping down the carrot juice, and he very nearly succeeded, but then made the terrible mistake of focusing on the long strands of black hair and the discarded bits of tissue paper on the restroom floor. "Don't puke, don't puke, don't puke . . ." He dropped to his knees, and all at once the *jazar* burst from his lips, splattering the toilet with superhuman force. He marveled at the bright orange streaks dripping down the sides of the bone-white bowl, believing that this was what a man must experience in the seconds after he has been decapitated, his broken body reaching blindly for his severed head floating in a shallow pool of foul water.

"Best to get it all out, eh?" Colette Collins produced a cigarette from her hip pocket and struck a match. "That juice you've been drinking is well laced with formaldehyde."

Kingsley gasped, "I have a weak constitution, that's all."

"Yes, I gathered that from the speech your wife delivered tonight."

Startled by the amount of strength it took, Kingsley lifted his head and through bleary eyes peered up at her. He hadn't realized the old woman had followed him into the restroom. He wiped his mouth on his French cuffs and said, "Marianne must have copied every word out of some trashy romance novel."

"Did you see the guests staring at her? Like cows in a meadow." She gave him an arch look. "I understand you're writing a book on *Madame Bovary*."

Even though he wanted to curl into a ball and remain on the floor for as long as possible, he struggled to his feet, his abdominal muscles cramping, his whole body shaking as with a fever. Using both hands he clutched the paper towel dispenser and then went to the sink to wash his hands. "I think it's time I abandon that project," he said and splashed cold water on his face. "You would make for a far more interesting subject."

Colette Collins took a long drag on her cigarette until the jets of smoke streaming from her flaring nostrils became the coiling twin serpents of a caduceus. "I'm afraid that after years of diligent research, you'd be quite disappointed by what you'd find. Oh, I suppose you could tell potential readers how I went through three husbands, one after another, a fact which is sure to raise an eyebrow or two, and you could tell them how much I smoked and drank each day, a fifth and a pack, respectively."

"If nothing else," said Kingsley, "people might enjoy reading about your theories of art."

"Oh, I'm not dogmatic. My ideas are in a constant state of flux. In a world that operates on one basic principle—the law of evolution, of incremental and ineluctable change—to believe in a single, permanent reality means to be content with self-delusion. Consistency reeks of ideology."

"Hmmm, yes, yes," said Kingsley, but he was no longer listening to her. After straightening his tie, he went to the door, only to find that it was locked.

"If readers insist on a manifesto of some sort, there is one important thing they need to know. It isn't complicated, and it certainly isn't a secret. I believe art serves one purpose: to wake people from the world of illusions. To startle them out of their silly daydreams, fantasies, phobias, demented fixations. But this turns out to be something of a paradox, don't you think, Professor, since art itself is also a kind of dream? We dream that we're awake, then art wakes us from our dreams, but then we discover that we're in a dream again, and so forth and so on, ad infinitum, until we arrive at the only logical conclusion: that we are all captives of a hallucination from which we can never truly escape."

"Goddamn lock," he muttered. A ferocious heat poured in from under the door, turning the cinder block cell into an oven. Unable to disguise his own scorching sarcasm, he said, "At least you have the consolation of knowing that your work will survive long after both of us are gone."

Now the old woman's face, blazing red as a torch, swung toward him. "Don't count on it, Professor. Much of my work is housed in this gigantic firetrap." She tapped more cigarette ashes on the floor and watched the warm draft scatter them around the white tiles. "But nature has a way of performing a stress test on itself, destroying its own dangerous surplus. Wildfires rage in part because the landscape has become burdened by trees that are old and vulnerable. But people focus far too much on the destructive rather than restorative power of the inferno, forgetting that new and beautiful things, remarkable and unanticipated things, always emerge from the flames."

The old woman jabbed her finger into his chest, and Kingsley felt she was threatening to do him bodily harm. His head started to spin all over again. He heard a countdown followed by whumping blasts, bloodcurdling screams, the persistent scratching of a frenzied animal after it has eaten a maddening weed. Deciding death would be preferable to remaining in this claustrophobic restroom and enduring the old woman's nauseating oration, Kingsley managed to turn the lock and twist the knob, and with many a gasp and twitch he prepared himself to face whatever unspeakable horrors awaited him on the other side of the door.

In the furnace heat of the bistro, red confetti and silver streamers spiraled through the air like little licks of fire, and a smothering blanket of black balloons fell like volcanic ash from the rafters. Martin Kingsley watched it all with horror, and right away the words "psychotic episode" popped into his head. Unsure if this arresting vision was real or the broad burlesque of a terrible delirium, he staggered from the restroom and pushed his way through the thrumming nest of bodies. Professors and their spouses, formerly isolated like enemy camps, having fled the social ignominy of being seen at a swanky party with their partners, now joined hands and sang in a spirit of camaraderie. They danced and whistled and wept with joy, and one of the musicians in the band put aside his steel drums and brought out a hurdy-gurdy. He began playing French folk songs, daft little ditties about love and heart-break, but the charming *chansons à boire* soon became bawdy *chansons paillarde*, the lyrics of which were so filthy they beggared description—all involved the most unnatural forms of love between merry milkmaids and braying donkeys.

The guests boldly joined in the chorus, and Kingsley, casting stro-bic glances around the bistro, listened to the mingled roar of words and laughter, the droll banter, the casual innuendo, the hilariously raun-chy conversation. In the smoke-laden lamplight, he spotted Marianne shamelessly flirting with his former pupil. They stood beside the giant clay sculpture, and between them there was much tittering, ear nib-bling, massaging, stroking, fondling. Kingsley burned with jealousy. He'd never known humiliation like this before, and he understood that he was about to do something awful, something he could never take back, something that would never be forgotten or forgiven—the irrevo-cable action. Like a rampaging animal, his head lowered, teeth barred, fists flying, he charged across the crowded room, but before he could land a single blow he stumbled on a discarded bottle of champagne.

His wife gave a hearty laugh and effortlessly put him in a head-lock. Dangerously close to the new sculpture, slapping and squealing like a pair of children, he and Marianne engaged in a clumsy wrestling match. With a gasp of collective shock, the guests scuttled away from the bedlam and watched in disbelief as the snarling couple struggled against the bar. Marianne knocked over a glass of the Red Death, and a bright borealis of wavering blue-green flames raced across the bar with a loud and sudden whoosh. The highly combustible punch bowl exploded with the force of a fifty-five-gallon drum of gasoline. The fire ignited the dry kindling of cocktail napkins and the blizzard of confetti. Within seconds the whole bistro was in the grip of disorder.

Kingsley stumbled through the fluted columns of smoke, gray and chambered in turbid hoops of orange firelight, and made his way to the nearest window. He smashed a pane of glass, and the fire sucked the cold night air like a gigantic vacuum. In an instant the bistro became an immense, sacrificial pyre, a brazier of people bursting into flames, their faces peeling like curled sheets of bark from beechwood trees after a powerful windstorm, and in mindless confusion they stampeded blindly through an impenetrable hell. Wearing halos of fire, men and women beat frantically at their hair and careened into one another at top speed, everyone, that is, except the elderly artist, who tore a blazing white wig from her head and hurled it to the floor, where it burned like a hairball coughed up by a hacking dragon.

Kingsley looked into the fire as if searching for portents. Rather than rescue his wife from this epic conflagration, he decided to save only himself. He ran across a fantastical hellscape of blackened bodies and charcoal ruins, but before he could dash to safety, he heard a loud crack. The floor was splintering, giving way, and the ceiling threatened to smash them all beneath the heavy timbers. The building burned bright and clean, as if the fire had been locked within its very walls like sparks within flint. Minutes later the entire structure was reduced to an unstable skeleton of steel beams that came crashing down one by one.

Through the rippling heat, Kingsley thought he saw the giant sculpture swinging its clay arms. From two perfectly symmetrical holes in its head, the thing emitted a low hiss, a mighty beast disturbed from a deep slumber, and then it all became perfectly clear to him: this wasn't a sculpture but an extraterrestrial that Colette Collins had found in the valley after the Perseids made their annual summer flyby, the scattered meteors damaging the church steeple. With grandmotherly kindness she had nursed the creature back to health for the sole purpose of bringing it here tonight and setting it loose on the people she most despised. It could move, it could speak, and in a spectacular basso profundo it demanded that Kingsley bow down and pay homage to its unique majesty.

His eyes widened. "The children!" he pleaded. "I must go home and check on the children!"

The sculpture teetered back and forth, vomiting liquid fire from the black portal of its mouth, and when he saw that it might topple over and crush him under its immense weight, Kingsley pressed his back against the brick wall and cringed. There was no time to scream, and he watched helplessly as the old woman's masterpiece came crashing down, trapping him inside its superheated shell like a bull of Phalaris, gorging itself on his roasted flesh and slowly digesting his incendiary soul.

17

Happy to be liberated from that oppressive, professorial gulag, Madeline and Sophie Ryan sang and danced at the stroke of midnight. After fifteen minutes of twirling and spinning and doing clumsy cartwheels, the girls became bored, but even with the heavy drapes pulled shut they knew it was much too risky to sit on the couch and watch the strange and violent images on TV. Someone might detect the distinctive blue glow of the screen and become suspicious. All of their hard work that night had made them hungry, and they searched the kitchen for something to eat. Unfortunately, before shipping out on the *Rogue*, their father had tossed every bottle, box, can, and gnawed gobbet of greasy meat from the cupboards and refrigerator, and the few crumbs that remained in the breadbox had been hauled off long ago as booty by an army of black ants.

When they grew tired they went to the crawl space under the basement stairs and hid behind a fortress of cardboard boxes. They struck matches and in the penumbra of orange light found themselves surrounded by dozens of tiny bugs scurrying blindly in and out of the cracks in the cinder block walls, their bodies plump and translucent. Using their father's discarded mason jars, screeching with revulsion and delight, the girls trapped the bugs and dared each other to eat them. As they were about to drift off to sleep, they thought they heard a persistent scratching coming from inside the walls. For a moment they wondered if the sounds might actually be the growling of their empty stomachs, and then they remembered the bats.

"Maybe we should leave," said Madeline. "When they come home the Kingsleys will look for us over here."

Sophie nodded. "Yes, they'll notice the key is missing."

The girls gathered up their coats, boots, and dolls and on tiptoe hurried to a door at the side of the house. Without looking back to see if the other neighbors had observed them, they sprinted through the nighttime streets and alleys. Suddenly they found civilization, with its glaring sodium lights, backfiring cars, and lonely train whistles, an alien and unwelcoming place, and as they swerved in and out of the shadows and sidestepped overturned garbage cans, they felt exposed and vulnerable like a pair of feral cats. Thinking what to do next, they recalled the abandoned barn in the valley, a secret place that over the years had served as a refuge for innumerable runaways and drifters.

"But we can't go there," said Madeline.

"Why not?" Sophie asked.

"Because Lorelei's a werewolf, remember?"

"No, she said she would never hurt us. She said if we ever felt sad or lonely, if we needed anything at all, we could always go to the barn."

Madeline seemed doubtful.

The moon, burning white and clear, had reached its apex, and snow spouted and whirled above the skeletal treetops. The girls bucked the wind and traversed a series of steep and narrow ledges. Deep in the forest they looked like a pair of wraiths, their hair long and tangled, their clothes hanging like rags from their thin and pale bodies. They made their way along a snow-covered trail beside the river, its frozen surface telling of skittish coyotes, their tracks veering into the buckthorn and knotweed. In the highest branches of the gray-haired pines, a murder of crows assailed them with a loud, mocking chorus. Such was the salutation of the night.

The twins battled ever onward. After crossing the desolate fields, they could see in the clearing the steepled outline of the roof. They raced inside and barred the door, pleased to find the barn largely unchanged since their last visit in the fall. One at a time they climbed the ladder, and in the loft they found stowed in their proper places all of Lorelei's prized possessions—the dog-eared paperbacks, the stuffed animals, the cooking utensils, a butane lighter, and, lined neatly against a far wall, a dozen mason jars filled with wild berries. Only the gun seemed to be missing. Lorelei had warned them that some of the berries might be unsafe to eat, but it had been hours since the girls had enjoyed a meal of any kind, and the Kingsleys, confident of their own sagacity, had taught them that it was only through trial and error that intelligent people learned the important things of this world. Unable to stave off their hunger any longer, the girls opened the lids and plunged their frostbitten fingers into the jars.

"Maybe she'll come back," Madeline said.

"Or maybe she's out hunting," countered Sophie.

Each argued her case, but minutes later the preserves started taking a terrible toll on their empty stomachs. Even though they felt nauseated, they did not vomit. Hunched over and moaning, struggling to keep warm, hoping Lorelei would soon return and nurse them back to health, the twins clutched their dolls and thrashed on the mattress. They cried in agony, and after much panting and writhing they both lay perfectly still and grew very quiet, their febrile eyes fixed on the blue stars that sparkled between the cracks in the warped and rotted planks of wood.

Gradually, the sickness subsided, but now a strange and terrible sensation came over them, an unfamiliar combination of desperation and hopelessness, two particularly communicable emotions that, once they had wormed their insidious way deep into the soul, often mutated into something dangerous and even fatal. The girls had witnessed how, in the final months of her life, their mother had fallen prey to these feelings, and for her the damage proved to be irreversible and incurable. Regrettably, she'd tried to treat herself with the wrong kinds of medicine.

Now they called upon their mother for help, but the falling snow seemed to deaden the sound of their fervent prayer. Their breathing became shallow, their vision grew blurry, but instead of fear they experienced a profound sense of tranquillity, so much so that they no longer seemed to be corporeal beings subject to the unremitting pains and pleasures of life. Like their dolls they felt immortal, indestructible, unbanishable, and soon they slept soundly, eternally, their faces blue and motionless in the sub-zero temperatures, their lusterless eyes staring with curious abstraction into the night, their tiny mouths twisted and puckered as if, before taking their final breath and being carried off into the huge darkness, they had tried to whisper to each other in a dream language unique to them alone, and though their hearts were no longer beating, they felt a satisfying warmth drape over their bodies.

Some people, when they pass away, leave behind fond memories and wonderful legacies of love, but many more leave long trails of misery and despair, and when the bereaved claim to sense a presence floating along dark hallways or glimpse hooded figures rising up in shattered mirrors or witness fantastic apparitions advancing and receding above bogs and fens and festering swimming pools, they likely are perceiving the enduring gravamen of the dearly departed, a disappointment so profound that it somehow transcends death. So who could say for sure if the spectral figures that emerged from the barn and floated above the streets of town were in fact ghosts or illusions conjured up by the drunk and disorderly revelers stumbling their way home on New Year's Eve? Madeline and Sophie wondered the same thing themselves: was this how ghosts were supposed to feel?

They made for the vast, inland desert of the frozen lake and like graceful skaters glided effortlessly across cracks and fissures until they found the mighty *Rogue* trapped in ice, all engines stopped, a wisp of pale smoke rising from its black funnel, its wheelhouse glowing in the dark and throwing sharp splinters of light across the ice. One thousand feet long and carrying sixty thousand metric tons of taconite iron ore, the *Rogue* had passed through dozens of canals that year and had seen the rough, quartering seas of two oceans and all five Great Lakes. The twins slid between the thin cracks of those weird, wind-sculpted formations of silt-laden water, what the sailors called "rotten ice," and entered the ship through the propeller shaft. From there they shimmied into the briny ballast tank, where they marveled at the bizarre creatures floating dormant in the hull, zebra mussels, round goby, sea lamprey, a hundred invasive species from across the globe that had hitched a ride

and awaited the return of warm weather so they could shiver themselves awake and wreak havoc on foreign ecosystems.

Passing through an open hatch, the girls slipped unnoticed into the
freighter's wheelhouse, a structure as wide and tall as a six-story apartment complex, and wandered in a maze of empty companionways until
they found near the stern a mean little cabin where a frightened sailor
stared into the dark. Earlier that day the captain had informed the crew
that the icebreaker *Prometheus* should reach the ship and free them by
dawn, and even though all engines had stopped, the walls of the cabin
vibrated from the shifting ice. In the early-morning gloom a foghorn
moaned, drowning out the low, steady hum of the bilge pumps and
generator.

Without making a sound, the girls approached their father's bunk.
There was a prophetic hush, and for a moment they listened to his panicked breathing and watched his eyes grow wide with alarm.

"Is someone there?" he said, stretching out a shaking hand. "Is that
you, Emily?"

Another powerful gust pelted the *Rogue*, and Charlie Ryan, unable
to sleep, continued to tranquilize himself by drinking another cup of
the Red Death. He had made a big batch before leaving home and
smuggled it aboard, stashing his jug of contraband beneath the bunk. In
two quick swallows he finished it, letting the last of the liquor drip onto
the tip of his tongue, and then he pressed the empty cup like a cold pack
against his burning forehead. Before embarking on his latest voyage,
he'd searched his bedroom closet for the .38 but couldn't find it. Not
that it mattered. There were certain mechanisms in the human heart
that prohibited most people from checking out early, and even if he'd
found the gun, he wasn't sure he'd be able to use it, but now, as the waning winter moon filled his cabin with inexplicable shapes and colors,
he contemplated a slow and painful death from the awful island recipe.

Two faint shadows hovered at the foot of his bed, and Charlie, who
harbored many superstitions, took them at their word when they said
they badly needed his help. The girls beckoned their father to follow
them, and he watched in wonder as they passed right through the cabin
wall. He pulled on his boots and lurched toward the door, not bother-

ing to grab his coat and hat. At this hour no one was stirring, and he hurried down the stairs to the main deck. Wearing only jeans and a flannel shirt, he was poorly equipped to face the wrathful winter night, but the girls assured him that his journey would not be a long one. The coast was only ten miles away, and if he moved at a steady pace, taking long strides, he was certain to reach the nearest town in two hours, three at most. He could endure the frigid temperatures for that long. The girls had confidence in him.

Charlie braced himself as he pushed open the hatchway. The wind whipped around the wheelhouse, screaming furiously, creating powerful updrafts that whistled along the deck. At first the shock of icy air invigorated him and helped focus his mind on higher matters, but soon the cold assaulted his lungs and froze the tears at the corners of his eyes. As the stinging snow found its way inside his shirt and down his back, Charlie lowered his head and crossed his arms. This wasn't cold so much as it was the complete absence of heat, what deep space must feel like, and after a few minutes his muscles tensed and his hands turned into useless claws. He considered going back to his cabin to get his gloves but decided to press on. Careful to avoid the patches of black ice, he made his way down the middle of the enormous deck, three times the length of a football field. Water from heavy seas had frozen inside the narrow gaps between the holds and around the bases of the giant crane towers that rose like round steel stanchions sixty feet above him.

Ten years a boatswain on the Great Lakes, he stood cargo watch most days and directed the crane operator who lowered freight into the holds. Sometimes during his shifts, he imagined the *Rogue* to be a voracious sea creature that prowled the deep and devoured enormous wooden crates destined for faraway lands. It must have been obvious to all hands that Charlie was not well, that he should never have come back to work, that he needed to take more time off, seek counseling, sedate his reeling brain with a strong prescription. Privately the crew, but especially the captain, believed he was a hopeless alcoholic and an unfit father, a man unsound of mind and body who was in danger of losing his children to the courts. Charlie knew what they thought. He couldn't stand most of them, especially the captain, the vessel's sober and unsmiling commissar, an insidious company man, a team player, a professional ass kisser who had a faintly executive air about him and who always stank of freshly brewed coffee and warm blueberry muffins.

Determined to prove he was an exceptionally dedicated father, Charlie hurried after the girls as they glided along the deck but was frightened away by a red-throated loon wrenching its way out of the sky. He worried he'd drawn near a nest of dead and frozen hatchlings, the distressed mother diving toward the rail near the ship's bow and trying to warn him away with a short, croaking bark. But it was the wrong time of year for loons. He stood absolutely still, hoping the captain, always at the helm, hadn't seen him.

"Be not afraid," said the girls as they drifted hand in hand into the night.

It never occurred to Charlie to question why the gangway had been lowered. He simply followed the twins down to the surface of the frozen lake, but when he rounded the stern he lost sight of them.

The lake and winter sky were nearly indistinguishable, the horizon nothing but a blur of deepest purple, its ethereal beauty nearly paralyzing. He coughed, exhaling a thin vapor into the inky darkness, and offered a quick salute to four or five rats, honorary passengers, gathered at the stern and crouched on their hind legs as if inspecting the ship's rudder. Worried now that his little girls were gone forever, Charlie started to jog across the ice but slipped and fell, badly banging his knees. He cursed, brushed snow from his pants, and through that immense solitude he limped determinedly southward.

An hour later the clouds started to roll in, piling deep and dark above the lake, and Charlie Ryan watched a light snow begin to fall and believed the universe was draping his body with cosmic ashes. At the edge of the sky, hundreds of light years away, entire solar systems were dying, extinguished in an instant, planets far older than Earth with civilizations far more advanced, their inhabitants consumed by supernovas and expelled as precious stardust into the vast, galactic waste, and Charlie hoped his substance would mix indiscriminately with the remains of those ancient worlds and rest here undisturbed for eons. He turned around to face the *Rogue*. From this distance the bulk carrier looked like an alien rocket ship that had crash-landed on an inhospitable planet, its crew marooned on a ball of ice spinning through the dumb immensity of space.

Above the shrieking wind, he thought he heard the voices of his girls telling him to navigate by the stars, and he knew they were mocking him. Struggling valiantly against a wall of blinding wind, his head covered in a crown of ice, he plodded doggedly onward, a task beyond endurance, but he knew that to stop now meant certain death.

A short time later the *Rogue* disappeared below the horizon, and Charlie could no longer tell if he was heading in the right direction. He paused, his body steaming ponderously in the bitter cold. He shielded his eyes with his hands, hoping to spot the gravel beaches and high shale cliffs of the coast and the orange glow of distant towns, but he saw only miles of indomitable tundra, treeless and absent of landmarks. It looked as though some cataclysmic, natural force had drawn back the blue waters to reveal the barren lake bottom, a vast quarry empty but for the detritus of a solitary man charged with the impossible task of surviving this wicked weather.

Cold and hungry he staggered across a sublime, superterranean lunar crust, the wind creating a vast moonscape of shallow holes and diamond-shaped parallel terraces on a jagged surface that, only a few moments earlier, had seemed as smooth and polished as a knife blade. His boots were frozen hard, his feet useless cement blocks, heavy and without feeling, and every step felt like an upward slog. The wind squeezed and smashed his body, and he started to shiver uncontrollably, but shivering required calories, and he hadn't eaten all day. The blood vessels in his fingers constricted and his hands had taken on the unnatural color of a yellowing corpse.

The singing wind became a sustained moan, and for a moment he thought hypothermia must have slowed his thinking because he heard the voices of a dozen deranged seamen. The sounds came from his left and then his right and then from directly behind him. A high gobbling laughter burst out of the darkness, rising and falling until it turned into a hectoring scream. Just ahead, no more than one hundred yards away, the mast of a sailboat protruded from a fissure in the violent jumble of keel ice, and upon reaching it Charlie decided it was time to stop the machine. His jeans and flannel shirt, damp with sweat, the cotton fibers soaked through, were becoming stiff and crackling with ice. He couldn't take another step, and with something like deep gratitude he collapsed to his knees and heaved a heavy sigh.

The mast loomed over him thirty feet high and pointed north like the needle of a compass. In the strong gusts the tangled forestays, still attached near the masthead, whipped around on the frozen lake like a pair of sparring snakes. Listening to the unevenness of his own breathing, Charlie rested his head against the clanging mast of the wrecked vessel, and in his darkening, dwindling stand against the cold he laughed at the absurdity of his situation.

He scraped away the snow and peered through a polished lens of ice, and in the murky depths he perceived twelve faces, bloated, grotesque, congealed together like a genetic mutation sealed within the world's largest mason jar. Their fleshy heads bobbed back and forth with knowing nods, and above the baleful wind they asked the stranger to release them from their prison. But Charlie was in no position to help anyone. He was an outcast, banished long ago from a broken home where he foolishly attempted to seek refuge.

Once again he gazed into the bleak and immeasurable expanse, an unforgiving wasteland endowed with supernatural powers, and glimpsed the girls floating toward him. His daughters, he was sure of it now, had led him to this place, but before he could ask them why, he heard the din and boom of shifting ice and felt a crevasse opening beneath him. A dozen pairs of hands shot out of the black chasm and clasped onto his arms and legs. He screamed, but even as the men pulled him under, he wondered if his boiling brain would sizzle and hiss in the water and if all the painful memories would rise like steam and vanish into thin air.

Madeline and Sophie seemed to know the answer. The heavy flakes that came sifting down from the sky settled in their haystacks of hair, transforming them into a pair of prematurely gray hags, two forlorn visitants from a world where night reigned supreme, a profound darkness, cellar darkness, and in the bracing winter wind they whispered a final farewell to their father before they pitched and swiveled and twisted through the antic clouds and dissolved forever into a roaring white funnel of snow.

"Goodbye, Daddy. Goodbye . . ."

18

At dawn on New Year's Day, with the sun little more than a spark buried under a kindling of dark clouds, grateful that my ordeal had come to an end and that the ghosts of Normandy Falls had returned to the cold comfort of the tomb, I marched across the deserted campus quad and toward the Department of Plant Services. Since I was the last surviving member of the Bloated Tick, I was now required to work on holidays and weekends, but the Gonk, poised in a state of constant anticipation, had been busy interviewing and handpicking a brand-new batch of ticks, twelve young men just like me, college dropouts one and all, unhappy, naive, adrift, always poking and prying into matters that did not concern them, eager to be schooled by the master and begin living more authentic lives. As I approached the garage, I wondered how their adventures would be similar to and different from my own, because no two stories are exactly alike, and I was curious to know in what gruesome manner they would obtain their nicknames.

Outside the building, leaning against a wall that glimmered with hoarfrost, his customary predawn cigarette burning bright in the corrosive, lead-colored light, the Gonk greeted me with a grin that, under normal circumstances, I would have confused for the cruel smile of a monomaniacal tyrant. Without having to ask the reason, he seemed to know why I was late for work that morning, and in a gesture of friendship and mutual respect he slapped my back and invited me inside for a strong cup of black coffee.

"Better hustle, Cyclops. These parking lots aren't gonna clear themselves."

During the next eight hours we shoveled sidewalks and scattered salt on slippery steps and plowed the streets of campus, and for the first time since taking that execrable job at the Bloated Tick, I felt like we were blood brothers, comrades in arms, and from a distance we probably looked like a father and his grown son. While I felt no remorse for the abominable deeds I'd carried out that night, I did lament my decision to leave the city of my birth to reside in this strange and sinister town where someone like the Gonk, possessed with a singular genius for finding the most astonishing solutions to life's most insoluble problems, was destined to become my mentor.

At the end of the day, after we finished clearing the last parking lot near the faculty lounge, the Gonk adjusted the greasy brim of his baseball cap and asked if I cared to join him for a drink. "To celebrate the New Year," he said, but it sounded less like an invitation and more like a command, and I noticed how his clothes were muddy and clotted with gore.

Back at his cottage I wandered through the cemetery, sidestepping the headstones peeping through the hard clumps of snow, and I watched a single snowflake slip along a marble monument and fall onto the bruised and muddy earth. Like a blind man reading braille, I traced the name that had been erased by the gray roar of the wind.

The Gonk searched his pockets for his keys. "Heard some interesting news this morning," he said. "Seems a professor disappeared last night after leaving the party at Belleforest. People said he got into a fight with his old lady. Just another fool, I suppose, who fell into the river, out of his gourd on *jazar* juice. Well, the police are sure to retrieve his body sooner or later. Probably find him hooked on the limb of a fallen tree, lassoed by the brambles and branches below the falls."

He unlocked the door and waved me inside. "Welcome to my castle."

I climbed the porch steps, but before passing over the threshold I paused to read the name painted in Gothic script on the mailbox flap. I looked at him. "Wakefield?"

The Gonk smiled and jerked a huge thumb at his chest. "That's me. Nathaniel Wakefield the Fifth." He showed me into the front room and scraped his muddy boot heels against the splintered hardwood floor. Part gallery, part armory, his living room was decorated with antique guns and sepia-tone photographs of revered ancestors. He beamed with pride at a portrait of the college's founder. "We're a strange breed, us Wakefields. At least we were at one time. I'm the last of their number. Our line has been called a race of visionaries. But over the years our blood has been watered down." Obsessed with the remote and unreachable past, he told me how he hoped one day to sire an heir of his own, and from his enthusiastic tone I gathered the Wakefield name had become for him a kind of irredentist death cult.

"Hey, Cyclops, I don't think you've had the pleasure of seeing the still, have you? While I search the kitchen cupboards for a fresh pack of smokes and a lighter, why don't you go to the cellar and fill a couple of jars with moonshine? I think you'll enjoy what you find down there. Oh, yes, you're in for a real treat."

Of Colette Collins the Gonk had told me much, and I couldn't help but admire and envy her independence and artistic integrity. Most sculptors, in order to express themselves with such confidence and bluster, required an adoring public and financial independence, but Colette Collins had neither legions of fans nor stockpiles of cash. She never sought that kind of worldly success. Maybe that's why so many academics and critics believed her to be so dangerous—because she never gave a damn about money or public opinion. "It's one of the many hypocrisies of conventional liberalism," she told the Gonk on the day she handed over the keys. "While they profess a genuine commitment to free expression, scholars and reviewers secretly demand that artists bow down to their authority."

While she may have escaped from one particular form of servility, she clearly remained a slave to her own imagination, and as I passed down the stone staircase, I felt a tingling in my spine, though I couldn't be sure if it was from excitement or fear. For a while I marveled at the indisputable masterpiece standing at the center of that dank and dripping cellar. Using my cracked and bitten fingernails, I scraped away the stubborn patina from the copper so I could see more clearly the strange story that this Podunk prophetess had etched there years ago with a claw hammer. Like parables carved into a church wall, the still told the story of a cloud-stained and lawless town and its deranged citizenry deprived of a shaping and sustaining purpose: there was a swimming pool and an abandoned barn and a frozen lake. There was a wild party and the figure of a woman carrying a wine crate, and near the back of the still, very close to the sweating limestone walls, there was an image of two men walking deep into a midnight forest.

As I fixed my intense and searching gaze on the still, I began to see Colette Collins not as an artist but as a misanthropic redactor of black books who'd chronicled persistent legends and sent back insanity reports from some faraway place that existed at the margins of civilization. With pleasure I poured the grain alcohol into an empty jar, and I thought how, since I had a peculiar talent for ekphrasis and hermeneutics, I should put pen to paper and describe in detail the meaning of those final images before someone else came along and interpreted them as just another awful farce.

I knew it was important to bury all of the people and places that had once injured me, but before climbing the slick steps and joining the Gonk beside the fire, I let my mind turn back to last night and recalled the details of my final encounter with Professor Martin Kingsley.

All over Normandy Falls the New Year's Eve festivities were coming to an end. On the desolate street corners and in the vacant lots of Normandy Falls, spinning columns of powder snow created a kind of dusty light that partially concealed the unlikely figures that emerged from the alley beside the bistro and came staggering down the street. It had turned tremendously cold by then, and the susurrating pulse of frigid air sounded like a child's cries of inexpressible grief, but from the speakers on my car radio a distant, jovial voice faded in and out. "Cabin fever can do some peculiar things to a person, but if the cold weather is beginning to mess with your heads, folks, I do have some hopeful news for you. The *Farmers' Almanac* is calling for an unusually balmy summer . . ."

I snapped off the radio. "A man shouldn't be alone at such times, Professor," I said. "Parties are meant to be communal."

Snow hurtled wet and heavy against the windshield, accumulating in tapering turrets on the worn wiper blades, and it took Kingsley, a man who once believed he was immune to misfortune, a moment to realize he was now slumped sideways in the passenger seat, his head resting against the door. The air inside the car was cold, hostile, uncomfortably quiet, and he sat up with a start, expecting to see Colette Collins flying away on a tired broom and the bistro roaring like an enormous kiln, people leaping from the blast furnace heat, their charred bodies piled around the shattered windows.

To his amazement the bistro appeared undamaged, and the departing guests, maximally drunk and chattering outside on the front steps, looked like the last surviving members of an economic apocalypse in a once productive and prosperous workers' paradise. They took the night air and stomped their feet to keep warm, and as they said their heartfelt farewells to dear friends, they peered into the gray and frozen taiga of the town. Many seemed hesitant to leave, as if they'd changed their minds and were debating whether to continue the party elsewhere. Pretending not to notice their pitiful colleague slouched in my car, they focused their attention first on the smashed cans of beer and broken bottles of booze twinkling in the street, and then on the two young women, one with a wine crate cradled in her arms, staggering from the alley and through the deep drifts of snow.

"I didn't mean to disturb you, Professor. 'Disturb,' now that's a funny word, isn't it? To varying degrees I suppose we're all disturbed."

"Your eye . . ." Kingsley gasped.

"Oh, it's nothing," I told him.

"I see," he muttered, not seeing at all.

I could smell the liquor on his breath, thick, heavy, noxious. It anchored his thoughts to the deepest depths of his brain, but somehow he willed the words into existence, pulled them up from the abyss by sheer strength. I'm sure he badly wanted a glass of water, a handful of snow to soothe his burning throat. He slouched so low in the seat that he could barely see above the dashboard. With a deep moan of shame, he wiped away a trail of blood from the corner of his mouth and in bewilderment looked at his trembling hands. Tomorrow would be a day of exquisite agonies.

"I saw things tonight," he muttered, and I noted with pleasure the slightly weepy cadence of his words. "Things too terrible to describe."

"You must tell me about these things. It might help if you talk about them."

"Did I attack my wife?"

"'Attack' is too strong a word. You tussled. You tangled. You made a scene."

Kingsley shrank against the door. "I've become a self-saboteur, no better than Charlie Ryan."

"Don't worry, Professor. People enjoy drama. It gives them something to talk about. And to be perfectly honest, the party was getting pretty boring anyway. Your wife asked me to take you home. As a student of yours, I thought—"

"*Former* student," Kingsley corrected me. He seemed to consider this for a moment and then said, "What are you doing here, Mr. Campion? This event is for faculty and staff only. My wife's budget doesn't allow for parasitical slackers."

Sheathing my impatience, I said, "Emily Ryan couldn't make it tonight, so she asked me to come in her place."

"Emily Ryan?" He removed a handkerchief from his pocket and wiped the veneer of academic detachment from his face. Suddenly he looked older, due no doubt to the ravages of drink and the aimless life he now led. "Did you know her?"

"Sometimes the dead will not sleep, Professor." The sound of fireworks came faintly over the river and a flash of blue illuminated the cracks in the windshield. "Emily confided in me, told me everything, and I think you should know, sir, that—oh, this is difficult—that she was deeply concerned about you. Concerned about your mental health."

He chuckled. "*My* mental health?"

"Yes, you see, at unexpected hours of the night, Emily would visit me to discuss *Madame Bovary*. She would go on and on about you and provided a number of interesting insights that helped a great deal with my thesis." I caressed my handwritten copy of Emily's note neatly folded in my pocket. "In time I became her amanuensis, guilty perhaps of inserting words into the mouth of a master poet but remaining ever faithful to the spirit of her ideas. By the way, I finally finished it. My thesis, I mean. I brought it with me. It's a bit late, I admit, but I thought maybe you'd like to take a look."

"Your thesis . . ."

"That's right, sir." I turned on the headlights and put the shuddering car in drive. "And now we start the 'treacherous descent,' if I may borrow a phrase from your wife's speech tonight."

I could see the anxiety in Kingsley's eyes. These days colleges and universities specialized in mass-producing emotionally disturbed basket cases, rolling them off the assembly line of higher education with ever-greater efficiency, overgrown children who, unable to control their tempers, focused their anger and frustration on their instructors and innocent classmates. The teaching profession had become a dangerous one, and Kingsley, lacking the proper training, didn't know how to de-escalate a potentially lethal confrontation.

"Where are you taking me?" he demanded.

"Time to return the beast to its proper place in the dark dungeon," I told him. "Try to stay calm. Your perception is off-kilter. Probably due to that poison you drank. Drugs can adversely affect a man's sense of right and wrong, guilt and innocence. But we must hurry. Emily Ryan has spoken, and it isn't right to keep the dead waiting."

The oncoming headlights of my car illuminated the faces of Morgan and Lorelei as they walked down the street. Where before there had been only resignation and defeat, a look of triumph now blazed in their eyes. Never turning back to see if anyone was following them, they set out on a journey through the blighted town, a long and relentless march past crooked lampposts, crumbling warehouses, and the lonesome white clapboard church, its soot-covered windows dark at this late hour, the pages of its hymnals hibernating in the long, winter evening.

At tomorrow's sunrise service the pastor would assure his congregation that all who sought God's forgiveness would go to heaven, but I had no use for heaven. I needed badly to believe in a place of everlasting punishment and torment. Some people meditated on Paradise; I meditated on the Inferno. Speeding along the icy boulevard, I found it hard to suppress my laughter and pressed my foot against the gas. I could have run them down like a couple of stray dogs, saving them the trouble of making the futile and dangerous journey to Delacroix Cay, but in recent days I had developed certain sane affections for them both, an inexplicable expansion of spirit.

In my apartment late at night, with my ear pressed against the register, I'd overheard their ill-conceived plan to steal the money from Xavier's safe, and now the wine crate in Morgan's arms looked like a madhouse bassinet. As if to assure themselves that the big bundles of glorious greenbacks hadn't melted away like snow, they stopped on the street corner and cracked open the lid. When they peered inside they could practically smell the salty sea air and taste those first daiquiris and margaritas. In rapt contentment they saw it all: in the mornings they would walk along a pale band of beach, dipping their toes in therapeutic water as bright and blue as Chagall's stained glass; in the afternoons they would snorkel along the barrier reef that teemed with sea turtles and parrot fish; and in the early evenings, as they gazed at the lavender mountains, they would nap in hammocks gently rocked by the warm trade winds.

At the last possible moment, moved by an unfamiliar sense of compassion, I swerved out of the way and continued driving into the night. A few guests leaving the party stopped to watch Morgan and Lorelei pass through the monochromatic backdrop of the square, and for days and weeks to come, for as long as their memories served them, the people of Normandy Falls would speak of the contents of that wooden box, the fabled "lost treasure," somehow thrilled by the telling of it, the bitter satisfaction of having indemonstrable proof, if more proof were ever needed, that this town was as impious and corrupt a place as anything dreamed up by the devil and forged by his own assured hand in a forgotten corner of hell's horrid foundry.

How my old beater, with its rusted underbelly and rumbling engine, made it as far as the valley I'll never know, but when it reached the two massive gates of Twisted Willows it finally stalled and died. As the headlights dimmed and went dark forever, I turned to my shivering passenger and, grinning with false amiability, said, "I'm afraid we walk from here, Professor. My apologies for the inconvenience."

From the glove compartment I removed a flashlight and the .38. I knew nothing at all about guns, had never even held one before retrieving the pistol from the hayloft on the night after I followed Lorelei to the valley, and I worried that I might badly botch this exquisite execution. In my unblinking, bloodshot eye Martin Kingsley must have seen something wholly irrational, unappeasable, final, and he must have understood that I was determined upon a certain course of action and that he was powerless against me, his former student possessed by secret, towering furies.

"The valley looks like a different place in the winter," I observed, enjoying how the snow muffled my voice and how it slowed our delicious advance through the woods. But now the time had come for the accused to speak.

"Listen to me, young man. You're making a serious mistake. You're obviously drunk. Or high. Quite possibly both."

I raised the gun and shook it at him. "A gift from Emily Ryan. It's almost as if she dug herself free from the grave and personally handed it to me."

Kingsley was quite stern. "I wish you would say something intelligent."

"No, really, I found this pretty pistol inside an abandoned barn. The barrel was glowing in a beam of moonlight next to an old mattress, if you can believe it. Positively radiating, all cleaned and oiled and ready to be discharged. When I climbed the ladder to the hayloft, I fully expected my brains to splatter against the floorboards. But no, Emily would never lead me back to the barn just to see me die. I wondered for whom the gun was intended, but your mistress soon whispered the answer."

"My mistress?" Now, instead of being merely frightened, Kingsley seemed deeply offended. "I'm dealing with a criminally insane clown. Things don't happen this way. This is some kind of demented fiction you've dreamed up, Mr. Campion. A sick fantasy. De Maupassant's influence, no doubt. I told you to study Flaubert, didn't I? I told you to focus on *naturalism*, not sensationalism?"

"But death is quite natural," I said. "And so is revenge. Murder, too. Old as Cain. A very natural inclination."

"You're mad."

"I like to think of myself as a writer, and writers are not mad; it's the logicians who are mad, the mathematicians, the chess players, the scholars who spend years tearing Flaubert into extravagant tatters."

"Help! Will someone please help?"

I pressed the gun into the small of his back. "Trust me, Professor, no one can hear you. Not way out here." We moved on, and I said, "This part of the valley remains a silent and secluded place, one that has gone virtually unchanged since the earliest times when the first hunters came in search of beasts that no human eye has seen for many thousands of years—mammoths, mastodons, giant ground sloths with peg-like teeth and great lethal claws. Now you and I are the only monsters roaming the valley."

I led him further into the woods, my useless keys jangling like silver coins in my coat pocket. We fought against a bracing wind, two lonely figures dwarfed by hardwood trees that hemmed us in on either side. Above us the limbs of the mighty oaks, frost stiffened and black, creaked and groaned and called down in sibilant whispers. Under our feet the dry snow crunched marvelously like a pile of skulls inside the catacombs of a medieval monastery, the cracked and brittle craniums of a thousand Capuchin monks reduced to dust.

"Life is full of marvelous serendipities," I said as we approached the crumbling foundation of the ancient farmstead. "Several weeks ago I wandered through these woods and happened upon this very path. I followed it to a clearing where coyotes had scratched away the dirt and scattered the fallen leaves, exposing a heavy iron door. It took all of my strength, but I managed to pry the thing open. The muscles in my hamstrings and lower back ached for days."

I pointed the beam of my flashlight past the cruel protrusion of jumbled sandstone blocks to a spot in the snow that looked glazed and dotted like an old painting.

"The door should be right there. Open it, would you please, Professor?"

I cocked the gun, and he complied without a word of protest. Using his bare hands, Kingsley scooped the snow until his fingers were pink and numb. When he could see the broad outlines of the door, he took hold of a steel ring large as a hoop and pulled hard. The earth released a fierce breath that reeked of fungus and decay. Under the domed cathedral of trees, the screeching hinges echoed like the angry cries of an owl that now circled slowly overhead. Kingsley, gasping with the effort of his task, wanted to clamp a hand over his nose and turned his face away.

"Steady," I cautioned him. "If you drop the door you might lose a few toes."

After lowering it gently into the snow, Kingsley fell to his knees and peered into that improbable abyss. The flashlight revealed a winding staircase that vanished into a cavern shimmering with a lurid green light.

"From up here it looks rather like a subterranean grotto," I observed. "Or a swimming pool. Care to take a midnight dip, Professor?"

Kingsley rose to his feet and backed away. The raw wind ripped open his sport coat, exposing him to ice and snow. Except for the blood pounding in my head, everything was still and quiet. Maybe, he thought with waning hope, it wasn't too late. Maybe I would laugh and tell him that I'd taken this joke far enough. But I didn't laugh, and I didn't move the barrel of the gun from his heart or the beam of my flashlight from the pit.

"Another explosion of homicidal rage in small-town America," he said miserably.

"On the contrary," I told him in a very businesslike manner, "you'll be safe down there, I promise. It's warm as the womb. See the steam drifting up?"

Massaging his stiff fingers and struggling mightily to escape the insuperable effects of drugs and alcohol, Kingsley tried to muster the sobriety to beg for mercy, but he could only whine and whimper and gave a loud sob of dread. He followed the steps into that chthonic chamber, and with outstretched hands he groped the deteriorating masonry of the slick walls until his feet touched the floor and sank into the treacherous slime. He almost fell but managed to regain his balance.

"Ah, yes, I understand now," he said, peering into the algae-skinned passages of that subterranean storehouse. "I'm still hallucinating. The Red Death is to blame."

I regarded him with a cold, steady eye and answered with almost total indifference: "Yes, Professor, you're hallucinating."

How else to explain the grotesquerie before him? Hundreds of glass jars, sealed tight with zinc canning lids, lined the shelves from floor to ceiling, and floating inside like the mutant aftermath of some long-ago atomic blast, hundreds of creatures, their stunted arms wading through a thick fluid that glowed faintly with phosphoric light. Kingsley saw reflected in those jars his own haggard face distorted by the darting death-fire of my flashlight. Maybe he felt a certain kinship with those lonely creatures floating forever in that ominous vault. He gibbered and laughed and tried to assure himself that they weren't real, but until these visions came to their inevitable, cataclysmic finish, whether through annihilation, rescue, or magic, his mind continued to populate the dark depths with the dumb lumbering beasts of his imagination.

"A fairy tale," he breathed.

"That's right," I said, "a fairy tale."

It seemed senseless to argue with him, to convince him that this was all very real.

In my hand I waved a copy of Emily Ryan's letter, and one by one I dropped the sheets into the hole and watched them land in a puddle of acidic groundwater at his feet. "I'll leave you with a final story then, this one penned by the long-suffering wife of a merchant marine. Of course the words 'long-suffering' and 'wife' are a tad redundant, don't you think? Better perhaps to describe it as the supersavage poetry of a vindictive lover, a snarling woman under terminal stress."

I raised the black eye patch and directed my left eye at him. Now covered in a cloudy film of pale blue, the eye seemed to lack an iris and pupil and moved independently of the right, more slowly and often in a different direction. I had trusted Emily to cure me of this affliction, but I had received instead a compensatory gift, for in that blind orb I could now see things others could not—dreams and visions and premonitions—and through its rotten lens Kingsley looked alarmingly like Father Montague, my former headmaster at the Jesuit school, his moon-blanched face old and weathered and bearing the handwriting of no common fate, one that made me shudder. Kingsley's mind, I believed, had been violently and permanently altered, his synapses wrested from their normal pathways and hastily rerouted in unknown and lunatic directions, and his incredulity, I was now certain, would remain intact and wholly undiminished up until the end.

But then Kingsley lifted his face, and between his inconsolable keening and his mad, murderous laughter, he spoke with perfect lucidity: "My family, my *family* . . ."

An inexplicable fear washed over me and shut out the sound of his voice. Desperate to extract myself from this inept nightmare, I used the limb of a fallen tree to lift the iron door, but before I could slam it shut and seal him forever within that impregnable dungeon, I felt as though I were burying two stillborn versions of myself, and the echo of Kingsley's low and foolish screams became the antiphony of their distinctive voices—one belonging to a man entering middle age, the other to a man entering the last stage of all, second childishness and mere oblivion, his voice all pipes and whistles.

For the first time since coming to Normandy Falls, I was satisfied that some mysterious cosmic circle was nearly complete, that justice had finally prevailed, and so it was only fitting that without pretense or ceremony, without giving Kingsley time to curse his preposterous fate, I bowed to the darkness and uttered these parting words: "There should be a law. A law of nature as well as a law of man."

Acknowledgments

First, I thank my agent, David Patterson, a consummate professional, who in a wonderful flash of insight trimmed the original title. David has guided me in the right direction from the very start. He made certain I had this incredible opportunity to complete my second novel and see it in print with a major house.

I was privileged to work with Timothy O'Connell, my editor at Pantheon. Tim showed an enormous amount of patience as I submitted draft after draft of this novel, and he endured my sometimes obsessive rewrites. He pushed me hard to do my very best work, and his insights helped enormously in shaping the structure of this novel. I consider Tim a fantastic collaborator as well as a talented and committed editor.

I am also indebted to Jordan Rodman, my publicist at Pantheon, for her enthusiasm and hard work, as well as Tom Pold at Pantheon, who provided valuable insight along the way.

I must express my enormous gratitude to the Cuyahoga County Community Partnership for Arts and Culture for awarding me with a 2014 Creative Workforce Fellowship. The fellowship, and therefore my fellow citizens of Cuyahoga County, provided me with the financial resources to weather a particularly wicked polar vortex.

There are also many friends and acquaintances who continue to support my work, including Matthew Nocella and Ann Marie Latiak, tried-and-true pals who read portions of this book when it was in its infancy; Barry Goodrich, a longtime contributor to *Cleveland Magazine*, who checks in from time to time to make sure I'm still an interesting person; author Michael Garriga, who is always around to talk shop and encourage me with his wild and scarcely believable monologues on the writing life; and Karl Taro Greenfeld, who plucked me from obscurity.

Thank you to my brothers, my parents, my wife, and my daughter, all of them secretly conspiring to keep me grounded in reality. While this book is officially dedicated to Katie and Rose, I also dedicate it to the Keatings, the Milligans, the Edwards, the Christies, and the Scanlons.

Finally, I must offer thanks to a number of my literary gurus whom I paraphrase and allude to throughout this novel, including Homer, especially *The Odyssey*, in both the Robert Fagels and Robert Fitzgerald translations; Ovid, particularly the *Metamorphoses* as translated by Ted Hughes; three masters of twentieth-century American horror—Stephen King, Peter Straub, and H. P. Lovecraft; two masters of nineteenth-century "weird tales"—Nathaniel Hawthorne and Edgar Allan Poe; the crime writer Dashiell Hammett, and his postmodernist successor Paul Auster; the screenplays of Robert Bolt, especially *Ryan's Daughter*. I also owe a debt of gratitude to those two greatest of contemporary prose stylists, Martin Amis and Christopher Hitchens. And is any novel complete without some kind of nod to the bard? Attentive readers may recognize a line or two from both *The Tempest* and *As You Like It*, specifically the Seven Ages of Man speech.

After working as a boilermaker in the steel mills in Ohio, Kevin P. Keating became a professor of English and began teaching at Baldwin Wallace University, Cleveland State University, and Lorain County Community College. His essays and stories have appeared in more than fifty literary journals. He lives in Cleveland.

A NOTE ON THE TYPE

This book was set in Janson, a typeface long thought to have been made by the Dutchman Anton Janson, who was a practicing type-founder in Leipzig during the years 1668–1687. However, it has been conclusively demonstrated that these types are actually the work of Nicholas Kis (1650–1702), a Hungarian, who most probably learned his trade from the master Dutch typefounder Dirk Voskens. The type is an excellent example of the influential and sturdy Dutch types that prevailed in England up to the time William Caslon (1692–1766) developed his own incomparable designs from them.

Typeset by Scribe,
Philadelphia, Pennsylvania
Printed and bound by Berryville Graphics,
Berryville, Virginia
Designed by Soonyoung Kwon